PRAISE FOR
THE TRIALS OF LILA DALTON

"I found this book to be unputdownable from the first page. As the mystery deepens, readers will be on the edge of their seats, desperate to know what happens next."

—Sophie Hannah, *New York Times* bestselling author

"A wonderfully ambitious book that never runs out of ideas or surprises."

—Stuart Turton, bestselling author of *The Last Murder at the End of the World* and *The 7½ Deaths of Evelyn Hardcastle*

"A mind-blowing, audaciously inventive thriller."

—Chris Whitaker, *New York Times* bestselling author of *We Begin at the End*

"Stuart Turton meets Agatha Christie—a locked-room puzzle with hints of the supernatural, brilliantly told through the lens of the judicial system. A truly intriguing and intelligent mystery, which had me gripped from the start. Totally recommend."

—Sarah Moorhead, author of *The Treatment*

"L. J. Shepherd is one of the most exciting new voices in crime fiction. In *The Trials of Lila Dalton*, she crafts a psychological tour de force reminiscent of Dennis Lehane. Grand, ambitious, and achingly atmospheric, it may just be the cleverest novel I've read all year."

—Kia Abdullah, author of *Take It Back*

THE TRIALS OF LILA DALTON

L. J. SHEPHERD

Poisoned Pen
PRESS

Published by Poisoned Pen Press, an imprint of Sourcebooks
P.O. Box 4410, Naperville, Illinois 60567-4410
(630) 961-3900
sourcebooks.com

Cataloging-in-Publication Data is on file with the Library of Congress.

Printed and bound in the United States of America.
MA 10 9 8 7 6 5 4 3 2 1

To Mum and Dad

A NOTE FROM THE AUTHOR

On November 30, 2020, I had an idea for a novel. I imagined a barrister standing in court, addressing a jury, with no idea who she was or how she came to be there. At that time, we were still in some version or another of lockdown in the UK, and as a consequence, I was spending an inordinate amount of time on the internet. I was troubled by the rise of the far-right political movement and the proliferation of their ideas on social media platforms. What worried me most was how they seemed able to shift political discourse from the center toward the extreme.

Regrettably, since then, the far-right have shocked the western world with electoral performances that are astonishing because, mere years before, these politicians would have been dismissed for their fringe views. So, when I sat down to write the first draft of this novel in January 2021, I had to decide on what sort of criminal my fictional barrister would have to defend. Given the context, perhaps it is unsurprising that I decided to write about a terrorist attack by a far-right extremist. Rather than draw on contemporary examples, I went back to the 1990s, where this new strand of extremism we now call the alt-right was in its nascency. The terrorist act committed by the accused in my novel is loosely based on two far-right terrorist attacks that took place in the U.S.

and UK in the 1990s. These particular attacks are still used today by far-right extremists as propaganda to suggest that there was some false flag operation and that what the world describes as a terrorist attack was actually government misfeasance.

As a result of exploring these topics, the book contains instances of racism, discrimination, violence, misogyny, and trauma. The reason my novel contains these themes is because I thought that shying away from the horror and pain caused by these extremist ideologies would be an insult to those who have been killed or injured in attacks by far-right extremists.

Above all, I want the novel to be an entertaining read. People might wonder why I've chosen to draw on such serious subject matter for the purposes of entertainment. The best answer I can give is this: for me, I'm sometimes entertained by what scares me the most. Experiencing the thing I'm most afraid of through a fast-paced and entertaining plot is the spoonful of sugar that helps me to process it. I hope the same goes for you.

I've done my best to handle these issues sensitively and have asked people with different backgrounds to read the novel. I have taken their feedback on board during the editorial process. Any mistakes or misrepresentations are my own and are wholly unintentional.

In spite of the dark themes, I hope you enjoy *The Trials of Lila Dalton*. See you on the other side!

L. J. Shepherd

January 2024

CHAPTER ONE

I LOOK UP TO find twelve strangers staring back at me: six in the front row, six in the back. They seem expectant, like an audience waiting for a comedian to deliver the punch line.

I realize I'm the one they're waiting for. Now would be a good time to tell a joke, just to ease the tension, or fill the silence at the very least, but I can't think of anything to say. My mind has gone blank.

I don't know where I am, or how I got here. I'm not even sure where "here" is.

It's an old-fashioned place. The twelve strangers are sitting in a wooden box— like pews in a church, except the back row is higher than the front, so more like seats in a theater. Sort of. Everything from the skirting board to eye level is oak-paneled.

"Miss Dalton?"

I look around for who spoke and, at the front of the room, staring down at me from an elevated bench, is a man robed in scarlet and black. A judge. His eyebrows rise to meet his wig. I quickly decide that it's a good thing I didn't deliver any funny lines. It doesn't look like he'd appreciate them.

The presence of a judge tells me this must be a courtroom. That's why everything looks so strange, why the walls are made of wood. Wait, am I on trial? What have I been accused of?

"Miss Dalton?" says the judge again.

I guess that's me. *Dalton... Dalton...* The name means nothing to me.

"I think the jury was hoping you might tell them which witnesses you'll be calling for the defense."

I repeat the phrase several times, but quietly so that only I can hear. With each repetition, my head pounds and brings with it a wave of tinnitus. *Witnesses...jury...defense.*

It doesn't matter how many times the words slosh around my pitching ship of a brain; I can't think of anything to say. I feel sick with dread. Everyone is expecting me to know the answer, but I couldn't even tell them what day it is. There's been some sort of mistake. A horrible mistake.

Needing to feel my skin, just to check that there's some fleshy casing for my broken mind, I raise a hand to my temple, and my fingers brush horsehair curls. I'm also wearing a wig. At least that explains why everyone is looking at me.

I cast a look around for more clues, even though the list of potential explanations is dwindling by the second. And those seconds are as long as minutes. Each one drags out into eternity while everyone waits for me to speak and I stay silent, though my mind is full of noise.

I turn to see what's behind me. No longer looking for clues, I'm looking for an exit. In the middle of the courtroom sits a man encased in a glass box. Next to him is a uniformed officer with a pair of handcuffs chained to his belt.

Witnesses for the defense. This must be the defendant. I feel a rush of adrenaline that curdles with the realization that I'm supposed to be defending him.

I cast my mind back. How did I get to court? Did I take the train? I don't even know what the case is about. Everything that came before is just... Nothing came before. This sends a fresh jolt of panic through me.

"My lord, may I trespass on the court's time for a few more moments and request a short break?"

I have no idea where I learned to speak like that.

The judge's nostrils flare and he turns to face the twelve strangers. "Right.

Members of the jury, I do apologize, but I'm afraid I must ask you to return to your room. I'm sorry about all this back-and-forth. As soon as we get into the trial proper, there'll be no more games of musical chairs."

There's a titter that masks a grumble of impatience. As I sit down, my heart rams into my rib cage.

The judge watches the jury leave one by one. When the door closes, his eyes whip to me. I stand up—not entirely sure why—but I suspect it's the right thing to do.

"Ten minutes." He gets up to leave.

"Court, please rise," comes a voice from somewhere at the back.

Everyone does as they're told.

I've got to get out of here, find someone who'll help me. It looks like I'm a barrister, someone who has responsibilities and knowledge and—God help me—*legal* qualifications. That person, whoever she is, feels as much of a stranger to me as the judge or jury. Who knows what I'm supposed to be doing today, where I'm supposed to be? A word swims out at me from the depths of my nonexistent memory. *Clerks.*

I find that I'm in the very pit of the court, sandwiched between rows of oak pews. The jury box, the judge's bench, and the public gallery all rise around me like an amphitheater. I go to leave when—

"Miss Dalton?"

It takes me a moment to remember that's my name. I turn to see a man wearing a black robe so tattered and worn he looks like a wraith. His wig is the color of earwax.

"You're making the right decision," he says. "Don't call your client. It'll only let his form in."

The only thing worse than not knowing how to respond is knowing exactly what he's talking about. He means that calling the defendant to give evidence will cause his previous convictions to go before the jury. How can I possibly know that? I don't even know my name, my birthday, anything. I can't picture my own face.

"Take as much time as you need," he says, his voice mellifluous. Instinct warns me not to trust him.

I've got to get out of here.

He continues muttering behind me, as though my turned back has rendered me deaf. He says something about why I've asked for a break. From the tone of his voice, I recognize that *he's* telling a joke. Well, good for him. I can't catch all of it because I'm heading away now and don't want him to know I'm eavesdropping.

"Her hemline will get higher with every day of this trial… His lordship will be…pleased."

I look down at my skirt. It's straight and black and hits my calf just below my knee. What does he mean, "His lordship will be pleased"? My cheeks flush. What sort of person is renowned for the length of their skirt? Perhaps I use my body, my "feminine wiles," to get my own way in the courtroom. But that doesn't seem like me. I *know* that's not me.

I almost laugh; how should I know what I'm like? I'm the last person to be an authority on that subject.

But the shame brought on by his comment lingers, a weight that hangs around my neck. I don't need to remember my past to know I've been spoken to like that or looked down on every day of my life.

I get away from the row of benches as fast as I can, glancing up at the poor sap in the dock. It looks like I'm his only hope. God help him.

There's barely anyone in the public gallery. A couple of hacks sit on the press benches. I head for a pair of double doors at the back of the court with dusky-pink curtains shielding the windows.

After climbing a flight of stairs, I find myself staring at a long, low-ceilinged corridor. There are rooms all along the right-hand side like bunkers, and on the left is a windowless wall of glossy brown bricks.

"Are you OK?"

I nearly jump out of this stranger's skin. There's a man standing next to me. Where the hell did he come from?

"I'm Malcolm," he says.

Malcolm is a middle-aged man wearing the black robes and government-issue lanyard of an usher. The only hint of individuality is found in his glasses, which are round and golden. Something about his calm demeanor comforts me.

"I need to speak to my clerks." How I know this is a mystery to me. But that clerks look after barristers is a piece of knowledge I've retained, so I clutch at it.

Malcolm smiles politely, ignoring my abruptness. "Follow me."

Rather than going down the long, straight corridor, we turn right and go up another flight of stairs and through another pair of double doors that open out into a hall the size of a small church.

My heels clatter on the black-and-white stone floor. It's like a chessboard except, rather than squares, hidden beneath tables and chairs are triangles, diamonds, and circles. Above me, there are three plaster ceiling roses held up by Doric columns.

Just as I've finished taking in the spectacle of the main hall, the clacking of my heels is muffled by red carpet. We're navigating a maze of rooms and windowless corridors. Or Malcolm is.

Eventually we end up at a door that says LISTING on a brass plaque below a leaded-glass window.

Malcolm knocks before poking his head around the frame. "Miss Dalton wants to ring her chambers."

He waves me inside to where a woman is already dialing the numbers into a desktop rotary. She holds out the handset and I take it.

I don't have enough time to wonder who will answer because after the first ring—

"Two, Lawn Buildings, Tony speaking." Tony's voice has a distinctive South Walean lilt.

"Hi, Tony."

"Lila! How's you?"

Lila... Lila... Still nothing. I feel the two Ls on my tongue but there's... nothing. "What case am I doing today?"

There's a wooden desk calendar next to the phone so I check the date. I realize that I don't even know what year I'm in. "18 November 1996" it says in red letters.

"Very good." Tony laughs nervously. "It's ten forty. Shouldn't you be in court?"

"Seriously, what case am I doing today?"

"You are joking? This isn't the time for... This is the biggest case of your career. You're doing Eades."

Eades?

"Eades," I repeat back to him.

"The mass murderer? Bombed the Home Office building?"

Shit. I'm trying a murder? A mass murder?

"But..."

"We had this conversation on Friday... Do you know how many juniors dream of their QCs being in a car crash the week before a trial?"

"Jesus."

"All of that hard graft and there you are, doing it all on your own." Tony sounds like a proud father. It makes it harder to disappoint him.

"But...I can't."

"You *can*. Don't doubt yourself now. Pat wouldn't have chosen you as junior if you weren't up to it."

"When are they coming back? My silk?"

"Seriously, Lila. What's wrong with you? Are you having another one of your...?"

Is this something I've done before? Am I unbalanced? Does Tony keep tabs on me, making sure I don't take on too much work in case I burn out?

"There was a car accident on Friday. Pat's still in a coma. You know all this."

"Oh my god. I'm so sorry... I'll go now, Tony."

"Go get 'em!"

I hang up, thanking the woman who dialed the number, and leave to find the main hall. Thinking over the conversation, I realize three things. First, as with *clerks*, I know what the words *silk* and *QC* mean. QCs—Queen's Counsel—are senior barristers who wear silk gowns and take on only the most difficult cases. Second, I realize that Pat is *my* QC. Third, I realize he's not here, so I have to do the case in his stead.

Just reciting these facts makes me feel calmer. But what I still can't reconcile is my detailed knowledge of the legal world on the one hand and my total lack of knowledge of my own life on the other.

This must be what's happened: I was so stressed about doing the case without a silk that I spent the weekend working into the small hours. Maybe I mixed caffeine and alcohol. Do I take drugs? Maybe I took drugs. This must be just sleep deprivation or something. That's why I can't remember how I got to court. It'll come back. I just need to take a few deep breaths, clear my head.

I'm not losing my mind. That's one thing I know for sure.

I mean, as I look at this logically, there's nothing wrong with my cognitive functioning. Well, if you discount the fact I don't know who or where I am, or what the last…however many years of my life have involved. Yes, ignoring that, I'm eloquent and methodical and seem to know stuff about the law. It sounds pretty temporary. It could just be stress, which would make sense given this is the biggest case of my career. I can't give up just yet. What if in a couple of weeks I'm fine, and I've just thrown away the opportunity of a lifetime? What will the future hold for me then—sitting out my days representing petty shoplifters until retirement?

If I tell people what's happening, they'll think I've lost the plot, they'll want to shove me in an institution, and that seems a bit drastic given… Given I'm basically fine. See, perfect example. Just then, when I thought about being sectioned, an image came to me. Not a memory as such, not something I've actually experienced, but word association. A sterile corridor, long and white. It looms larger in my mind's eye.

This thought jolts me back to where I am, where I'm supposed to be going. I've been walking along the same corridor for what feels like an age. I turn in the direction of what I'm sure is the main hall only to find that I'm back outside the listing office again.

"Lost?" It's Malcolm. Christ, that man knows how to appear out of thin air.

"I want to go to the robing room."

CHAPTER TWO

I'M NOT SURE WHERE my urge to find the robing room came from. It was an emotional pull: *find sanctuary.*

Except the robing room I find is nothing like that. It's all stale cigarette smoke and male body odor. The smell of smoke stirs something in me, a tug at the curtain in the far reaches of my mind. I think it's a memory fighting to get out. I stop and try to reach for it, but it fades away, leaving me frustrated. Still, the fact that a memory tried to knock at the door gives me hope.

I look around to get my bearings. Everything in this room is either cherry red or cherrywood. The carpet, the wing-backed armchairs, the leather top of the vast oval table that dominates the middle of the room, and the velvet lining of the dozen or so chairs that surround it.

Hanging from the domed ceiling is a dusty, cobwebbed chandelier with frosted orbs casting a yellowy glow.

I head for a wall lined by wooden cubbyholes. Wig tins and Bible-size books poke out from the odd open door.

One of the wooden boxes houses a mirror. Tabs hang limply from the compartment below.

When I look at my reflection, a stranger's eyes stare back at me. They belong to a woman who looks to be in her thirties. I lift a hand to my face and am surprised when the hand in the mirror follows suit.

I remove the wig and run my fingers through my black hair and wince when my nails snag the knots. In this moment, I'm struck by how real I am, how corporeal. This is *my* body. I touch my stomach, all too aware of its softness, and find it odd to think that there is a whole machine of internal organs inside, working to keep me alive.

I look back at the woman in the mirror; it's still too strange to think of that person as me. Dark-brown eyes stare back at me, framed by thick, well-groomed eyebrows.

That feeling I had earlier—tinnitus—it's coming back, but it's stronger now. I bare my teeth against the pain of it.

Constricting my neck is a collarette—a sort of bib with tabs jutting out of the front. I rip it off so I can breathe, and the Velcro snags the hair at the nape of my neck. I wrestle out of the gown, throwing it at one of the chairs. There are too many trappings. I just need to be rid of them all.

A childish thought takes hold: What if I can stay in here and never leave? Hole up among the coat pegs and make a den? The idea is so tempting, I've almost made my way over to the rows of pegs when something catches my eye—

A purple trench coat stands out from the tan-colored raincoats and charcoal duffel coats.

Was it there before?

I look around and realize that I am not alone. In my panic, I failed to realize that sitting with her feet on the table is the only other person in the room. Her wig has been discarded, but her tabs are still in situ. She's not wearing a collarette. Instead, she wears the tunic shirt and tabs that male barristers wear.

"Good morning," I say, politeness filling the large hole in my mind where intelligent thoughts should be.

"Are you feeling all right? You seemed a bit rattled." She gestures toward my discarded wig and gown.

I look back at them, embarrassed. "I'm just feeling a bit…nervous." I join her at the oval table.

She surveys me, waggling her crossed feet, which are shod not in heels but in patent brogues.

She catches me looking at them. "I never wear heels. Torture devices."

"No, I wasn't… I'm jealous, actually." I rub the back of my ankle. Already my heels have made red dents in the skin.

We sit in silence. She looks at me like I'm an interesting exhibit while I search for a conversation starter.

"So, my opponent is a bit of an arsehole," I say.

She laughs. The sound is rich and gravelly, earned by Scotch, cigarettes, and age. God, how I long to sound like that. "They haven't tried to old soldier you, have they? Don't fucking let them."

"Well, aside from a sexist remark about my skirt…"

"How original. You know, I think misogynists would be a lot easier to stomach if they showed a bit of imagination."

I laugh. It feels good, almost human. "Then he told me I shouldn't call the defendant to give evidence because it'll let his previous in."

She frowns while thinking over my predicament. Something on her arm is clearly irritating her as she reaches into her gown to scratch at the inside of her wrist. I see a flicker of faded ink before her gown falls back over her wrist.

She says, "Clients do have a habit of convicting themselves the moment they get in the box… But it's poor form to rely on pre cons. I always think of it as cheating."

"Maybe he won't want to give evidence. He doesn't look very chatty."

"My fucker won't shut up. Can't wait to be rid of the old perv."

"What's he accused of?"

"Just being a perv. Serial perv. It's all I do these days."

The way she talks: the battle weariness, the warmth, the humor. The way she peppers every sentence with *fuck* and *perv*. It's such a welcome oasis in this strange world of wigs and gowns and glass boxes.

"What did he do?"

"Woman walks into a bar for a drink with her colleague. Next thing she remembers is waking up in his bed with a sticky substance between her legs. Repeat ad infinitum."

Something about her story stirs something in me. I can picture the bar so clearly. The moody lighting—tinted blue. The sticky floor, the too-high stools. Even the smell of alcohol. I can picture it all. How? How do I have a frame of reference for that, what, with my puddle of memories gathered over the course of ten minutes?

"Are you OK, dear? Thousand-yard stare there."

"Oh, yes. Sorry. I've just had a bit of déjà vu."

She smiles warmly. The kindliness of her face stands in stark contrast to her severely cropped gray hair and square, thick-rimmed glasses.

"And what terrible crime brought you to this underworld of never-ending torment?" she asks.

"I'm a mass murderer. My silk's been in a car accident. I'm all on my own."

"There you are; you've probably just got a bit of impostor syndrome, doing a murder all on your own."

"Yes, that's it!" I say, so happy to finally have a name for it. Impostor syndrome is exactly what I'm experiencing.

"Let me show you a trick I use whenever I feel a bit disorientated." She swings her feet off the table to stand up before walking over to the rows of wooden boxes. "Surname?"

A beat while I search for the information. What was it the judge called me?... *Miss—*

"Er, Dalton."

Her features betray a glimpse of recognition for a millisecond before she remembers herself. She searches the boxes, each one bearing a brass card holder, and finds one with *Dalton* written in blue calligraphy. She opens the drawer and pulls out a copy of *Archbold*, the book barristers use as a reference text.

As she's flicking through the pages, she says, "You know, déjà vu is completely natural."

"How so?"

"Time is an illusion created by human memories. Everything that has ever been and ever will be is happening right now, in this moment."

My mouth is open. This was not where I was expecting the conversation to go.

"It's true; look it up."

"I wouldn't know where to begin," I say.

"I don't know—a book?" She frowns as she flicks through the pages of *Archbold.* "Not this one, obviously. Dry as a bone, this unwieldy thing. You'd want one on quantum mechanics or something."

I think over what she said. *Time is an illusion created by human memories.* "And…what if you have no memories?"

She smirks. "You'll have to ask someone much cleverer than I. Ah!"

Having stopped looking through the pages, she lays the book open on the red leather inlay of the oval table.

"Draw a mark here," she says. "If you have been here before, you'll know because there'll be a mark in the book. It's my little trick for dealing with the totally normal and natural phenomenon we call déjà vu."

I hesitate before getting up, feeling a little silly. Her smile is too encouraging to rebuke the offer of help, so I walk over, take the pen she holds out for me, and make a little fountain-pen scratch in the top right-hand corner of the page, not really believing this will work.

She pulls the red ribbon from the binding and uses it to mark the page before handing it to me.

"And impostor syndrome?" I ask.

"No cure, I'm afraid. Get stuck into the case and you'll be too distracted to worry about whether you're up to it."

The purple coat catches my eye as I cast around for a way to say thank you. Instead, I say, "I love your coat."

She turns to look at it and smiles fondly. Scratching again at the patch of skin on the underside of her wrist, she says, "Anyway, best be off. My client's probably in the cells now, dying to tell me how *she* came on to *him*... Revolting." She shivers before ramming her wig unceremoniously onto her head. She goes to leave before turning back to say, "Oh, and if the prosecution is trying to rely on some tatty old pre cons from when your client stole chalk at school, they're clutching at straws, my dear. Don't let them get away with it!"

And with that, she's gone.

I stand for a while, mulling over what she said.

"Miss Dalton, the court is waiting for you."

———————

"No."

I'm in among the coat pegs. The musty whiff of the rain-flecked trenches I'm wedged between confirms it.

"His lordship is waiting."

"It's not that I don't want to. It's just that I really can't." I stare up at Malcolm, my eyes wide and pleading, trying to communicate that this isn't a joke and I really need help, just not of the medical variety. "Please."

"He'll put you in contempt of court. He put a barrister in the cells last week when his conference overran by five minutes."

"But..."

"You've got ten seconds, or you'll be late." He starts counting.

I close my eyes and picture a set of scales. Placing weights on the one side, the side representing getting the hell out of here, I consider that I don't know who I am or what I'm doing. There's no way I should be defending an alleged mass murderer. But if I run away now that wouldn't give me much of a head start, even if I managed to get past security. I take some weights off the scale before considering the alternative in which I play along and wait for the opportune moment. The scales drop to one side, and I resolve to at least get through the morning. Once it's the lunch hour, I'll make a break for it.

"OK," I say, following him.

Before leaving, I stand in the doorway and take one last look at the robing room over my shoulder.

The purple coat is no longer there.

———————

Though I've only just met Malcolm, what I like about him is that he lets me think in peace. Doesn't try to strike up small talk. And boy, do I have some stuff to think about.

I decide to consider the evidence, put my critical thinking skills to the test. All of the empirical evidence suggests that I am indeed a qualified barrister. I seem to have some grasp of the law, and I'm certainly wearing the right outfit.

However, the evidence of my eyes and ears doesn't seem trustworthy, not when I can't remember anything. That's another puzzle: how do I know anything, speak English, let alone understand legal principles? If I have no memories, shouldn't I be like a baby? When a child touches a flame, it burns their skin and they learn not to do it again. Knowledge and memories are intertwined, yet mine seem to have become…untangled.

Perhaps I should test myself, feel out the edges of my knowledge. What would a doctor ask if they were trying to ascertain whether someone was sane? They'd probably ask who the prime minister is. The desktop calendar in the listing office said that today is the 18th of November 1996. Assuming that's correct, the prime minister must be… I stretch for the piece of information, and my brain creaks with the effort of it, an old, infirm person trying to reach their toes.

John Major.

I did it! A rush of happiness and I beam.

"Are you all right?" asks Malcolm.

"Yes, thank you."

"I saw a smile for a second there."

"I just had a thought about the case, a new line of attack, you know? It's nice when you get a bolt of inspiration."

Malcolm nods and retreats into silence as we walk along the red-carpeted corridor that connects the robing room and the main hall.

I turn back to my predicament. If my general knowledge is fairly intact but my personal knowledge isn't, then it seems as though I'll recover from whatever is the matter with me. If this memory loss is temporary, and I have to hope that it is, there's a Lila Dalton in here whose career is resting on this case, on me getting it right. Maybe Lila's memories will come back, and so will Lila, with all of her quirks and foibles. And her experience, for Christ's sake. That's what I need right now.

The alternative is that it's permanent and I will never regain my memories. Either way, I need to get out of here. It would be wrong, unethical even, to represent someone when I'm psychologically compromised. But then if my memories do come back and I've withdrawn partway through a trial... Cross that bridge when I come to it, I suppose. I notice signs overhead with arrows pointing to different courtrooms, to the washrooms, to the cells, and take note of where the exit is for when the opportunity to escape presents itself.

We're in the main hall again. The clattering of my heels echoes in the empty space. It feels like a metaphor for my head.

This strikes me as odd. If I'm defending a mass murderer, why aren't there more people here? Why isn't the public gallery filled to the rafters? I only spotted two hacks on the press bench. Surely there would be national media?

Instead, it's eerily quiet.

"It's quiet today," I say to Malcolm.

"Yes, yours is the only case in the building," he replies.

"What? But there are"—I check the nearest sign—"nine courtrooms?"

"Ten," corrects Malcolm. "It's only your case for the whole week."

"But... why?" I look around at this vast, stony space.

"This court building is only used to try terrorists and foreign criminals now."

"But I just met a woman in the robing room. She said that she's representing a per—" I catch myself before saying *pervert*—"She's doing a sex case."

Concern ripples Malcolm's forehead. "There are no other cases this week. You couldn't have seen that woman."

"But I did. I definitely did. She wore brogues. Her hair was gray. She was posh and funny. You'd recognize her if you saw her."

Malcolm refuses to meet my eyes. "I'm sorry, Miss Dalton, but you're mistaken. There are no other cases being heard in the court building this week."

I was so sure she was real.

I despair. It seemed as though I was doing OK, that my mind was mostly intact, and now it turns out that I'm seeing things. My copy of *Archbold* is tucked under my arm. Its weight is comforting. Later, when I get the chance, I will see if the fountain-pen mark is still there. If it is, I'll know I wasn't seeing things.

I don't push the subject with Malcolm. Right now, I need to work out how to represent an alleged mass murderer with no knowledge of his case. Or at least do a good impression of it. I feel a strange sense of grief for the intelligent, professional woman I used to be. I also mourn the end of my legal career, for it surely can't survive me absenting myself halfway through the first day of a murder trial.

We're outside the courtroom again. I recognize the tacky pink curtains.

"Watch out, Miss Dalton."

"What?"

Why am I always so rude to Malcolm?

"Look around. Water, water, everywhere and not a drop to drink."

"What the hell are you…?"

It's too late. We're in the courtroom again. Everyone is looking at me, waiting for my next move.

"Malcolm?"

He's vanished.

CHAPTER THREE

I STRIDE UP TO the front row and take my seat next to the prosecution QC.

"What are you doing?"

"Well, my silk isn't here so I thought…"

"You thought wrong. This row is for silks and you're not a silk."

Humiliated, I move back a row, taking my copy of *Archbold* with me. Once I'm back where I'm supposed to be, I get my bearings. I'm on the defense side—closest to the jury, farthest away from the witness box.

The prosecution QC is still muttering, "In my day there used to be respect for tradition."

The recipient of this diatribe is a barrister who is of a similar age to me. I can see red hair peeking out from beneath his wig. We sit at the same bench although he is a few paces to my left. Behind him is a team of four: a mix of CPS lawyers and investigating police officers.

I have only one person sitting behind me. This must be my instructing solicitor, another person whose role I understand instinctively. The solicitor is the bridge between barrister and client. They do the background work preparing the case and representing the client in the police station. They also choose which barrister to instruct.

My instructing solicitor wears Buddy Holly glasses and smells overpoweringly of cigarettes. I smile at him. He smiles back, but it's more of a grimace because he has a habit of wrinkling his nose to keep his plastic frames from sliding off.

"Miss Dalton?" asks the QC.

I tug at my skirt self-consciously.

The QC smirks. "Have you decided whether your client will give evidence yet?"

I glance back at my solicitor. He returns my gaze, his eyes magnified to three times their normal size by the thick-rimmed specs.

"I'm not deciding now," I say, each word delivered slowly in case my solicitor signals midsentence that I'm saying something wrong.

The QC searches for something on the writing bench in front of him. "Just so you know, this is what we'll be relying on to say your client's pre cons are related to the bombing." He brandishes an amateur publication. Emblazoned on the cover is a black symbol; it looks like a diamond that's grown legs.

"Interesting…" I say.

"It's an Odal rune," he replies.

"And?" I go for disdainful.

"It's a neo-Nazi symbol."

I thought that this would be a game of make-believe, of trying to imagine what a barrister would do in this situation and imitate it. Anything to get me through to lunchtime and then I can get away—away from the threat of institutionalization and, more importantly, away from the responsibilities of the person I'm inhabiting.

But it's not like that at all. If anything, this is the most natural I've felt all morning, glaring back at the QC with steely determination, not rushing to fill the silence he's left. It's a buzz and, in spite of myself, I find that I'm enjoying this pantomime. I must have been good at this once. Perhaps I might be in the future, and suddenly the pressure of representing the man in the dock settles on my shoulders, accompanying the weight of the woolen gown.

"Your client has two previous convictions for criminal damage. One for smashing a parking meter and the other for vandalizing a letter box."

I think about the woman from the robing room, her give-a-shit persona. It gives me a boost of confidence that dims when I remember she might not exist. I set this worry to one side and try to channel her when I respond.

"That strikes me as scraping the barrel," I say.

The corner of the QC's mouth twists. "When you look at these…*magazines* that were seized from his address…" He shakes the pamphlet as though he's expecting winning scratch cards to come loose.

"Being on the distribution list of a magazine proves nothing," I say.

He turns to a page. He does it as though at random, but it's too practiced. I suspect he's kept a thumb in place the whole time he was waving it around.

"Here, they champion *leaderless resistance*. In other words, he didn't need to be a member of the group. They suggest that people who want to be part of the movement partake in any acts of destabilization of the state that they can."

"That should be in the dictionary definition of 'tenuous.'"

I can see that I've gone too far this time. The QC's sallow complexion sprouts angry red patches.

"If you want to be like that." He turns his back on me.

The negotiation is over. We'll have to fight it out in front of the judge. I say as much to his junior before turning to my solicitor.

"Are we calling any other witnesses apart from the defendant?"

His magnified eyes blink. The worried look I get tells me I shouldn't have had to ask. "No."

"Just double-checking."

I look down at the five box files of evidence in front of me. I flick through until I find the neo-Nazi zines. Pulling one from a sheet protector, I approach the dock.

All around the glass box are vertical slits. I get close to one of them and whisper, "Are these yours?"

Eades doesn't look at me, doesn't register my existence. I look to my solicitor for a bit of backup, but he only gives me a one-shouldered shrug.

"Court, please rise."

I hurry back to counsel's row and remain standing until the judge takes his seat.

"Are we ready to have the jury back in?"

"My lord, I've clarified the position regarding defense witnesses. There won't be any save perhaps for the accused. I'll review the position as the evidence progresses."

The judge nods at this. I sit down.

If I'm carrying on with my tactic of doing whatever the woman from the robing room would do, she wouldn't have stood for what just happened, wouldn't have allowed herself to be "old soldiered" like that.

Emboldened, I get to my feet again. "However, there is one matter I wanted to raise, and that is my learned friend's intention to introduce these highly prejudicial documents *and* my client's previous convictions in his opening." I wave the rune-bearing zine.

The judge turns to prosecution counsel. "Mr. Paxton?"

"My lord, it has always been a main plank of the prosecution case that Mr. Eades's murderous spree was motivated by his far-right views..."

"What about his previous convictions?"

I interrupt. "Two appearances for criminal damage, my lord."

Judicial scrutiny lands on Paxton like a searchlight. "What did he get for those? A bind-over and two slaps on the wrist? Really, Mr. Paxton, you'll need better similar fact evidence than that."

"My lord, it's really about the operation of these far-right cells."

"Miss Dalton?"

The searchlight swings around. "My lord, there is one man in the dock and one man alone. If the prosecution's case is that he was part of a cell, I'm surprised we don't see them sitting alongside Mr. Eades."

God, that was good. I'm good. I must be good to have that up my sleeve. The judge turns again to Paxton.

"My lord." His voice is so quiet, it's almost patronizing. Only a slight vibration betrays his annoyance. "These groups operate without a chain of command. The prosecution says that he was motivated by the principles of this abhorrent group but acted alone."

The judge considers the point. "Here's my determination: You won't refer to it in your opening to the jury, but I will hear further argument after you've opened the case." He turns to look at me, and the shadow of a wink plays across his face.

"Very well, my lord." With a shake of his head, Paxton sits down.

A fire of pleasure glows in my chest. I get it now. I understand why I do this…did this. It's a rush. The back-and-forth, thrust and parry. And I won. I won the point. Not only that, but I'm hopeful. I seem to have retained my abilities. That means I must have memories and they will come back. I just have to be patient.

I turn to share a grin with my solicitor, and he returns his half grimace, half smile. It's endearing. Then I look up at my client. He should be smiling too, sharing this moment, congratulating me on my performance. He doesn't meet my eye. His expression is unflinching. He stares straight ahead.

———————

The jurors return to their seats, and I make a concerted effort not to look at them. My end of the bench is closest to the jury box, meaning they're only a few feet away, and I don't want to unnerve them by eyeballing them.

"Miss Dalton, I understand there are no names or defense witnesses you wish to make the jury aware of?"

"That's correct, my lord."

"Very well. Let's put this jury in charge."

The clerk who sits at the desk below the judge's bench gets to her feet. "Will the defendant please stand."

I look behind me. Eades takes his time but does as he's told. His face doesn't move. I'm not even sure I've seen him blink.

The clerk reads from a piece of paper in her hand. "Jonathan Eades, you are charged on this indictment as follows: Count 1, Murder. The Particulars of the Offense are that you, Jonathan Eades, on the 23rd day of May 1995, murdered Sally Carpenter."

There are twenty-seven counts of murder. I count every one of them. Each one representing a victim, a whole life ripped away.

There's also one count of causing an explosion likely to endanger life or property.

Pleas would have been entered months ago. My client needn't say a word. He just has to stand and listen.

The jurors take the oath, all but one swearing on the Bible. The outlier makes a nonreligious affirmation. I take the opportunity to scan the jury. The nonreligious member of the jury is female and looks to be the youngest. I count five women and seven men, and I'd guess at an average age of forty-five. If my client is indeed a right-wing terrorist, white middle-aged males are probably my best hope for an acquittal. Ideally, they'd be too young to have fought in the Second World War, but old enough to hate immigration and liberalism.

His lordship gives directions, telling the jury they can't discuss the case with anyone outside of their number. His words fade to white noise as I scan the box files in front of me and notice a blue notepad covered in barely legible scribbles. Is this my handwriting? Maybe one of the good things that could come of losing all my memories is the chance to turn over a new leaf and start afresh. I could make new habits. Maybe I could become one of those people with neat handwriting who trim their cuticles when they need trimming and wash everything up as soon as it's dirty rather than letting it all pile up at the side of the sink until there's nothing left to eat off. Something tells me I'm not that sort of person.

As the judge is concluding his directions, my ears prick. "Now, members of the jury, I'm going to hand you over to Mr. Alasdair Paxton QC, who is going to open the prosecution case."

Paxton gets to his feet. A little slowly. Perhaps he does that for effect, keeping everyone guessing. There's a palpable tension in the room now. The jurors are sitting forward. With all the delays and musical chairs they're eager to know what this case is all about.

"Members of the jury." A pause. He knows how to speak, Paxton. His decrepit gown, yellowed wig, and doddery posture are at odds with his voice, which is smooth and rich, oozing private-school confidence. "The prosecution's case is that the defendant, Jonathan Eades, who goes by 'John,' entered a Home Office building on the 23rd of May last year, where he detonated four bombs before leaving the scene. He injured one hundred and twelve people and murdered twenty-seven."

Another pause. Let that sink in, he seems to suggest. Twenty-seven. *This was a terrible thing, ladies and gentlemen.*

It rankles me. The jury isn't here to decide on the severity of the crime; they're here to determine whether my client did it.

So just get on with it.

In spite of myself, I find I'm getting drawn into the drama of the case when I should be focused on my escape plan, keeping my eye on the lunch-break prize. The reality is I'm as curious as the jury to learn what allegations my client faces.

"It's at this stage when I give you a brief explanation as to what the case is about so that you can understand the evidence as it unfolds."

That's right, you sly bastard. Stick to the facts. No supposition, no comment. No wondering about the motive. Definitely nothing about my client's passion for the far-right…

"You must remember that what I say isn't evidence. Evidence comes from the witnesses who come into court, videos that might be played to you, and any documents that may be put in front of you."

The jury sits up at the mention of videos.

"So, what is this case about? What do we have to prove to you?"

CHAPTER FOUR

"LET'S START WITH THE scene of the crime, shall we?"

With an almost imperceptible movement of his hand, Paxton motions to the barrister sitting behind him. Like clockwork, his junior pulls out a small bundle of laminated photographs that are handed to Malcolm without a word. Malcolm places a copy before me before distributing the rest to the judge and jury.

I look down at the photo, bracing myself for the horrors of a crime scene: blood splatter, broken glass, little numbered cards. The picture I'm confronted with is nothing like that.

A gray, uninspiring building stares back at me. A municipal eyesore sticking out of a nondescript city center like a malignant growth. All four sides are perforated with hundreds of rounded rectangles, like a dystopian seed pod.

"Abbott House," says Paxton. "A Home Office building in the middle of Birmingham." His eyes scan the jury. With a twitch of his mouth that doesn't qualify as a smile, he adds, "Not an attractive building, by any means. Well, that's sixties architecture for you, isn't it?"

There's a smattering of polite laughter from the jury.

"Twelve stories dedicated to everything from asylum interviews and processing passport and visa applications to immigration control and Criminal Records Bureau checks. The first three stories were public-facing. The rest were reserved for administration. In other words, this was a building that kept the country turning. It wasn't glamorous or exciting. This was a building filled with good, honest people doing those workaday tasks that no one gets congratulated for but everyone would complain about if they weren't done."

I've got to hand it to him; Paxton can tell a story. And in a trial, that matters.

"May the 23rd was a day like any other. Twenty-seven people arrived at this dull, gray building expecting to have a dull, gray day. Perhaps they'd been on stuffy commuter trains. Maybe some of them were late getting in to work. Maybe they had the windows open and the fans turned on to try to coax some lukewarm breeze into a sweaty office on a muggy May afternoon. We'll never know, will we? Because we'll never be able to ask them."

With another wave of his hand, Paxton sets in motion the well-oiled machine that distributes another photograph to the jury. This time, the picture is of the waiting area on the ground floor of Abbott House. There's a reception desk in front of revolving doors and rows of plastic seats bolted onto rails, the sort of thing you'd have to sit on in an airport and then spend the next three days regaining feeling in your buttocks.

"It was half past three in the afternoon. Dick Wilson sat at the reception desk, waiting to serve people coming in through the revolving doors." As Paxton says this, he peers at another photograph. He goes misty-eyed, as though looking at a long-lost relative.

Malcolm waits patiently at the side of counsel's row for Paxton to hand him the photo. Paxton jumps and looks surprised to see Malcolm standing there. I look over at the jury, willing them to see through his act.

They're hanging on Paxton's every word.

Eventually, he pretends to summon up the courage to part with the photo. "Dick Wilson is Count 4 on the indictment. He was killed in the blast, instantly."

Dick's photo lands on the wooden bench in front of me, and I peer into the eyes of a man who looks not a day over twenty-three. I have no idea why they started with this victim. I was expecting Paxton to choose the most beautiful woman. But then I take a closer look at the picture. Dick's face is marked, the ghost of acne leaving its shadow. He is—was—a bit scrawny, like adolescence came a bit too late and left without having completed the job. He looks like a son. And not the sort you'd be happy to send off into the world. The sort you'd fret about. Maybe he'd never find a girlfriend, maybe he'd get mugged walking from work to the train station…

Now I understand why they chose Dick Wilson first.

"Dick was one of the lucky ones," continues Paxton, "if you can call them that. He didn't have to wait under rubble, pressed in by the dead bodies of colleagues you resent getting half as close to you at the Christmas party, didn't have to have any limbs amputated without anesthetic. No, some might disagree, but Dick was one of the lucky ones. You can't say the same for his family, who heard about his death while listening to Radio 1."

There's a sharp intake of breath. Paxton pauses. I find myself imagining what it must be like: hearing about a disaster like that on the radio, hearing that it happened at your son's place of work. Knowing there were fatalities. Hoping, praying that it's not your loved one who's on the list of dead bodies. Imagine hoping that they're *just* in the emergency room. Imagine ringing up every hospital within a ten-mile radius and panicking when your son *isn't* on the list.

It must be the worst way to lose someone: not knowing, allowing yourself to hope, and then being sideswiped by the brutal truth when a police officer knocks on your door.

"Dick Wilson's job was to greet everyone who came through the door and provide them with helpful information. Where to sit, where to wait, when their appointment would be. From his prime position, Dick would have seen a man walk through the revolving doors weighed down by an enormous sports bag that was slung over one shoulder. He would have been walking lopsided with an unnatural gait.

"Of course, John Eades walked into the Home Office building without anyone checking his bag. There were no security guards. People just walked in. We haven't yet descended to the level of barbarism that requires every-one to be searched as though they're a criminal." Paxton removes his glasses and polishes them. "Eades didn't ask Dick for instructions. He strode past the waiting civilians—many of them immigrants—and headed straight for the public restrooms."

Paxton stops again. Replaces the glasses.

"What would he have been thinking, ladies and gentlemen? Looking around at all of those faces, of all colors and creeds…?"

I try to catch the judge's eye, try to get him to stop Paxton, but before the judge notices that I'm trying to attract his attention, Paxton has already moved onto the next part of the story.

"No one questioned the bag. Until *someone* questioned the bag. Just as Eades was about to duck into the gents, out came Kwame Adebayo carrying his mop and bucket. Mr. Adebayo was a cleaner employed by the Home Office. His patch was the ground floor of Abbott House, the public-facing part. When Mr. Adebayo came across John Eades carrying this enormous sports bag, he asked him what was inside. Eades, in what I'm sure we can all agree was a moment of questionable wisdom, imitated an Eastern European accent and said, 'I homeless.'"

Paxton stops to stare around at the jurors, as though he's sharing a joke with them, knowing the court's audio recording equipment won't capture his facial expression.

"Mr. Adebayo simply said 'OK' and asked no further questions. What Eades didn't know at that time was that Kwame Adebayo had gone to let the security guards know that someone was in the building behaving suspiciously."

Another photo is distributed, this time of a two-cubicle, three-urinal washroom.

"Once inside, Eades put the sports bag down on the just-mopped floor. His movements were more urgent now—what if he had been spotted? He pulled out two brown-paper bags from a fast-food outlet and put them on the floor, then extracted a rucksack that he slung over his back. Each of these bags con-tained a homemade bomb."

The plosives of that final word echo in this cavernous room, the perfect acoustics for Paxton's dramatic delivery.

He continues, "Eades lugged the sports bag in his grip, only a fraction lighter for having removed the three smaller bags. Think, members of the jury, of the effort required here. A heavy sports bag he's already had to carry through reception. Imagine his back slick with the effort of carrying it that short distance.

"After removing the first three bags, he went into one of the cubicles and used his boot to knock the lid down. He climbed onto the toilet seat and moved one of the ceiling tiles. Teetering on the U-bend, he bent down and hefted the sports bag to waist height. Then he raised the bag above his head and eased it through the ceiling space. He had to be careful. Inside that sports bag was fifteen pounds of ammonium nitrate and fuel oil, lined with blasting caps. The largest of the three homemade bombs."

Another pause. By this point, I'm worried. The story is watertight. A lot of supposition in there, but the judge isn't interrupting Paxton and it's too early for me to start jumping up and down. Too many interruptions and the jury might think I'm trying to hide something. If the prosecution can prove that Eades walked in carrying the bomb, what possible defense could he have?

"Next, he pulled himself up through the hole made by the missing ceiling tile. He set to work. Connected to the bomb was a clockwork timer. He set it for ten minutes—he needed time to plant the other three bombs and get out. He checked his watch and memorized the time down to the second. There was a noise down below. Someone opened the door. That was OK, wasn't it? All they'd see were two brown-paper bags. They wouldn't look inside, would they?

"But, ladies and gentlemen, they did. Mr. Adebayo, back from speaking to security, opened the door a crack and saw the two brown-paper bags on the toilet floor. Thinking it strange that two of them would be left unaccompanied in a toilet, he decided to take them. What would Eades have seen at that point? Perhaps he lowered his head and shoulders through the ceiling, just in time to see his two paper-bag bombs being taken away by a hand. We know that he finished setting the timer and lowered himself through the ceiling tile, leaving his deadly weapon in place. Next, he needed to get hold of those two brown-paper bags. With a rucksack's worth of explosives on his back, he left the toilet in search of the bombs.

"Eades began looking in the bins. But he couldn't see the paper bags. Things were getting serious now. He was running out of time. Having set the timer on the largest of the four bombs, time was literally ticking away. So, he turned and headed back to the toilet. While in there, he returned to the same cubicle and began setting the timer on the rucksack bomb. His fingers were shaking. Maybe with excitement, maybe with nerves.

"That was when he made the error. He set the timer for three minutes, not eight. We assume they were all supposed to detonate together. It would make sense, wouldn't it? But now he had a five-minute gap, and he didn't know how to reset the timer. We don't know how or why this mistake was made, but it's clear that his plan was unraveling apace.

"There was only one thing for it. He took the rucksack out into the main waiting area. He ditched it in a bin and took out matches from his pocket. If he couldn't get the paper-bag bombs to detonate with the timer, he'd have to do it manually. We can only guess at why the defendant did what he did next. However, the prosecution surmises that Eades assumed Mr. Adebayo would not have realized that the two brown-paper bags were bombs. We suspect that he thought Mr. Adebayo would have merely performed his duties as a cleaner by putting them in a bin.

"As you will hear later in this case, Mr. Adebayo was much more dialed in than the defendant gave him credit for and had alerted security as soon as he found the two unattended bags. It appears that, suspecting that the bombs were now in the bin, Eades threw lit matches into all of the bins in the reception area. Perhaps he thought that looking in bins or rummaging around would raise the alarm.

"He checked his watch. One minute until the rucksack bomb would go. There were still two bins to light, but people had noticed the first one smoking. People were looking at him. His plan—to draw as little attention as possible—had failed.

"So, he lost his nerve. He ran from the building, getting caught in the revolving door—he kept kicking it—until finally it budged. He was free. Then he disappeared."

Paxton takes a deep breath, lifts a cup of water from the bench to his lips, and takes a noisy sip. His speech had been getting faster and faster until he reached the part of the story when Eades left the scene.

I start looking for the cracks in the evidence, trying to spot weaknesses. There's only one thing that bothers me. The sophistication of the timing mechanism on the bombs is at odds with the shoddiness of the plan's execution.

How could someone be so callous, so evil, and yet...so incompetent?

It's a scary thought. I think it's the fact that someone, anyone, could kill so many people without seeming to know what they were doing. All it takes is enough hatred.

I look over at the jury, a quick glance. A woman in the front row is openly staring at me. I look her way, and she turns her head to avoid meeting my eye.

"Eades didn't disappear entirely. The police found out how he left the scene. He ran to Snow Hill Station and got on a train to Solihull. He didn't pay for a ticket.

"Meanwhile, on the other side of the city center, at the Birmingham Children's Hospital, was Zhu Zhang. She heard the first blast as she was leaving after finishing her shift. It didn't matter that she'd spent the last twelve hours without so much as a toilet break. Dehydrated with an unpleasant cramping in her stomach, she was probably looking forward to a bath and a pizza. Wouldn't we all? But when she heard the first blast, her first instinct was to run toward Abbott House. As soon as the first bomb went off—killing most of the people in the waiting area—the building was evacuating. With that many floors and so many people, it was a crush. Then the second bomb went off."

Another picture is distributed. A dead body, barely recognizable. A set of scrubs can just about be made out beneath the dust.

"The second bomb went off just as Zhu was coming in through the revolving doors. She's Count 20 on the indictment."

Another picture, this time of a kind-faced Chinese woman, is handed out. She's wearing her nurse's uniform and holding a certificate. It seems this picture was taken on the day she qualified as a nurse. I fight to keep the lump in my throat suppressed.

"One hundred and twelve people were injured in the second blast," says Paxton, his voice barely above a whisper. "Meanwhile, speeding toward the leafy suburbs on the West Midland Railway was John Eades. He was buzzing, overjoyed. Other passengers thought he was 'weird' and didn't mind telling him so. Eades was oblivious. He had done it, done what he came to do.

"Then someone asked to see his ticket."

CHAPTER FIVE

PAXTON CONCLUDES HIS OPENING by playing the CCTV to the jury. A television set is wheeled out from the corner of the room and pushed in front of the jury box while another is placed in front of counsel's row so that we can all watch it at the same time.

Paxton hands two VHS tapes to Malcolm, who feeds the first into a slot below the monitor. We wait while the film crackles to life. The footage appears to be taken from the inside of Abbott House, with the camera facing outward, focusing on the revolving door in the foreground, with the busy street in the background. It's in Technicolor, but there are so few frames per second that people seem to walk and move in a very strange and jerky manner, frozen and then moving at great speed. Eades jerks into shot before walking through the revolving doors into Abbott House, weighed down by an enormous sports bag.

It has to be him. The man in the video is as thin and short as Eades. In the video, Eades has a "boy band" haircut—gelled until he looks like a hedgehog and complete with frosted tips. He's been on remand awaiting his trial for more than a year, and his lank hair now hangs below his ears. Eades's face is fairly unremarkable, but it's definitely his profile. Once through the revolving doors, he goes off-screen.

The clip lasts twenty seconds at most, but it couldn't be more incriminating.

As I turn to look at Eades, the fold-down bench I'm perched on creaks. His face remains as expressionless as ever. Did he even watch the footage? Does he care what it shows?

The screen goes black, and a horizontal white line cuts it in half. Malcolm ejects the tape, replaces it with the second, presses some buttons on the remote control, and we see Abbott House from a different perspective. This CCTV is in black and white and from a building on the opposite side of the street. Abbott House can be seen in the background, recognizable for its ugly architecture. The quality of this tape is much better, and the greater number of frames per second compensates for the lack of color. We see the first blast, the blown-out windows, the billowing smoke. The camera shakes from the force of it. And just before devastation rips through the building, we see Eades running through the revolving doors—kicking them when they don't turn fast enough—no longer burdened by the bag.

He pauses for a moment after leaving the building and then runs toward Snow Hill.

The screen goes black again.

I chance a glance at the jury, trying to see what they've made of all this. I'm surprised by how well they've managed to keep their composure. They're doing their best at playing judge by not predetermining anything or betraying precon-ceived ideas. But even through the stoic masks, I can see that they're appalled. The eyes don't lie, and several pairs flick toward the man in the dock as a few more pass over me. I know what they're thinking. *How could you defend him?*

After Paxton's opening, the judge announces a break for lunch and the jury leaves. Paxton's junior—the man with the red hair—slides a handwritten note across the bench toward me. It's torn from his blue notebook. I smile and nod my thanks.

Scrawled at the top of the page are the words *Batting Order*, and below is a list of names numbered from one to eight. Topping the list is Dr. Brian Sheridan. It's an unwritten rule of etiquette to let defense counsel know the bat-ting order of the witnesses in advance.

I turn to show my solicitor the note.

"They're calling the expert first, then," he says.

"Mmm," I reply, not sure what his area of expertise is.

"Cells?" he asks.

I hesitate. This is my moment, my chance to get out of here. The last thing I want is to go down to the place where they keep people locked up. But my plan was to slip away when no one would notice, to be well away from here by the time anyone comes looking for me, so I must keep playing along for now.

Getting up, I notice that my instructing solicitor stands at no more than five feet. His gray pin-striped suit is much too large—so much so that the hem of the jacket skims his knees.

As I follow him out of the well of the court, my ears prick with heat. I'm being watched. It's not the same as when the jury looked at me, a cursory glance as though at the front page of a tabloid; this feels different. I scan the courtroom and notice that one of the suits who sit behind the prosecution is staring at me. She sports a blond shag haircut and a gray pin-striped suit. Her mouth twists into a smirk. I can still feel her eyes on me as I walk toward the exit. She must be one of the police officers working on the case, as anyone sitting in that row would be involved in the investigation.

Once we're out of the courtroom, I let the solicitor go first in the hope he'll show me the way. We take the same route that Malcolm and I took only a couple of hours ago.

After walking across the main hall, we take a right-hand turn and go down a winding stairway. I lose count of the number of flights, but a chill descends the lower we get. The stairs stop at a gray security door. I buzz the intercom and wait for a response.

"Cells."

"I'd like to speak to Eades, please. I'm his counsel."

The guard on the other side of the intercom half laughs, half growls. The buzzing stops.

I turn to look at my solicitor.

"Did you bring any cigarettes?" he asks.

What? I pat down my suit and am surprised to find a bulge in my pocket. I fish out a packet of Bensons. He grunts his approval.

I look down at the golden packaging.

With a slice of pain splitting my head in two, a memory returns. The throbbing prevents me from appreciating that this is my first one. I see the packet of cigarettes not in my hand but in the hand of someone sitting across from me. I watch their fingers slide a tobacco rod from the box.

The memory goes as soon as it came. Straining to re-remember only worsens my headache. And the more I try to recall the details, the more they swim out of focus and distort. The golden cigarette packet becomes too shiny where before it was dull and worn. The fingers become slender and unblemished, but I was sure they belonged to someone older. Or so I think, because the memory is like a pebble dropped in murky water. All I can see are the ripples it left on the surface.

I look around, surprised to find myself facing a gray security door. Behind me are the stairs I came down a few moments ago. My solicitor is looking at me with concern, but he's saved the bother of having to check if I'm all right, because from the other side of the door, keys jangle on a ring, and then we hear the scrape of the lock.

The security guard who opens the door is reassuringly massive. Not that Eades is a violent man, not unless he's armed with several pounds of explosives. Still, the size is comforting.

"Wait here."

My solicitor and I do as we're told. We look around at the blank walls as though looking for a conversation starter, but it's difficult to imagine a room more void of character.

The officer comes back and leads us from the anteroom into a long corridor paved with grimy off-white tiles. All along the corridor are open doors that lead into conference rooms. I look into them as we pass. Like cells but larger, each conference room holds a table sandwiched between benches. They're bolted to the floor.

As we pass each door, I can't help but look inside, even though I know it'll be identical to the last, not to mention empty.

Except one of them isn't. I do a double take at first. I look again. Inside is an old man with white hair sprouting from the sides of his otherwise bald head in tufts. There's something so familiar about him, but also so wrong.

We're past the door before I can take a better look.

"I thought we were the only case this week."

"You are," says the officer.

My stomach tightens. Averting the guard's eyes, I decide not to push the subject, not to say out loud that I've seen something no one else seems to. When it's the second time in as many hours, it's not too much of a stretch to say the problem is with me, with my brain, and this isn't some temporary memory loss that will fade away but a much more serious problem.

I think back to the man in the cells. There was something transient about him, anyway. Like seeing an old picture of your grandparents. They're not quite tangible unless you're looking at them with their wrinkles and liver-spotted hands.

I shake my head, which turns out to be a mistake. The headache returns and I'm wincing against the throb.

The officer stops and indicates that we should take a left into the next conference room. I follow the solicitor inside. Legal representatives sit nearest the door while clients sit facing it. Except Eades isn't. He has his back to us, facing the wall.

"John, your barrister's here to see you," says my solicitor.

Nothing.

I take out the pack of cigarettes and place them down with a satisfying slap that echoes around the cell. He remains with his back to us.

"John, come on. Don't play games," says my solicitor. "We've only got an hour and I would like to eat at some point."

Still nothing. I retrieve the cigarette packet from the table and stuff it into my jacket pocket. Eades continues to act as though unaware of our presence.

I don't have time for this, so I butt in. "Mr. Eades," I say. "Mr. Eades, I need your instructions." I look at my solicitor. He gives me the one-shouldered shrug again.

If I could just force Eades to acknowledge me. I go to stand up, but the guard rests a hand on my shoulder.

"You sit there," he says.

"But—"

"No ifs, no buts. You need to be closest to the door at all times."

I slump back onto the bench, dejected.

"Lila, look," says my solicitor, his fingers twisting. He's focusing on them, rather than on me. "Maybe it's best if I speak to John and then report back to you."

I nod, my face burning with the humiliation of it, and follow the officer out into the corridor. While we're waiting outside, I can still hear every word of the conference.

"Trev, I'm not talking to her. Where's Pat?" Eades's words echo in the tiled corridor.

The officer glances at me. I look down at my patent court shoes. It stings, even though it's him that's saying it, even though it should mean nothing. In the end, I'm just a girl in a wig.

"There's been an accident, John. Pat can't be here and Lila's the junior, so she's taking over your case from now on."

"She doesn't know what the hell she's doing."

He's not wrong there.

"She's friendly with the judge. It's good to have her on your case."

So, that's the reason I'm here, doing this enormous case. It has nothing to do with my skill or intelligence. In my previous life, I knew the judge. A life I can only remember useless glimpses of.

I run a finger around the inside of my collarette. It's time to enact my original plan of getting the fuck out of here, so I turn on my heel and head for the exit.

"Wait, you won't be able to get out." The officer looks torn: watch my solicitor (Trevor, apparently), or let me out so I'm no longer his concern?

The latter wins.

And I'm running now, away from the cells, running up those flights of stairs. No matter how much it stings when my toes pinch together, no matter how much sweat is gathering under my wig, I've got to get out of here. There's been a mistake. I can't do this. I've been set up to fail. A client who won't talk to me, a solicitor who doesn't believe in me, opponents who are out to get me. That's it. I'm leaving, and then I'll disappear. I don't want to be a barrister. Fuck the money. I'll stack shelves in the supermarket if it means I never have to come back here again and be sneered at and picked over by these utter, utter pricks. My ears are on fire with the fury and shame of it all.

Once I'm back in the main hall, I head down the imperial staircase. I open the door to leave. Wind hits me—an icy blast—as soon as I'm out of the building.

I'm at the top of a set of stone steps. I was expecting to come straight out into a busy thoroughfare—perhaps see a red bus fly past or hear the traffic and noise of a major city. Then I would have melted into the crush of humanity and allowed myself to get caught up in the tide. That won't be possible here.

Now that I come to think of it, I didn't hear any ambulances or fire engines whirl by when I was inside. There was only an amniotic silence, which makes sense now that I can taste the salty tang on the air.

When I think back, the only sound I heard from inside the courtroom was the odd squawk of a seagull.

Now I know why. The court is perched atop a hill that looks over a sedate town—more like a fishing village—and stretching out for miles and miles is a vast expanse of choppy water. The light from the overcast sky glints on the waves so that the water takes on the submetallic luster of anthracite.

This isn't what I expected.

"Welcome to Assumption Island."

I turn to see the officer who stared at me as I left the courtroom.

"Pardon?"

"You were looking puzzled." She drops her cigarette on the Portland stone and rubs it out with her foot.

"I'm used to being landlocked," I say, trying to hide the fact that this new piece of information hit me like a truck.

I'm on an island, a bloody *island*. So that's my Plan A out the window. I need to find somewhere I can get my bearings, develop a Plan B. Where on earth is Assumption Island? I make to go back into the court, but she puts a hand on my arm.

"When you're ready, I've got some questions for you."

"For me?"

"Come now, Miss Dalton. The innocent act won't work with me. We all know how lawyers like to twist the truth."

From her handbag she pulls a blue star-shaped bottle of perfume and spritzes the lapels of her gray pin-striped suit. Being downwind of her, I get a whiff of the cloying sweetness.

"What's that supposed to mean?"

She shrugs and rakes her fingers through her blond hair. Her highlights are grown out, revealing mousy-colored roots, and there are bags under her eyes, hastily but unsuccessfully concealed by powder. She trains her steely-gray eyes on me.

"Don't know how you sleep at night. Representing filth like that." She jerks her head back toward the court building.

"Good to know that the concept of being innocent until proven guilty isn't lost on the police."

"You're actually trying to prove that he's innocent? I thought this would be a joke trial because no one pleads guilty to murder, do they? No matter how damning the evidence. But you're actually going to run a defense?" The corner of her mouth curls into a smirk. "Good luck convincing the jury of *that*."

"Thank you so much for the chat. This was lovely," I say, turning to go back into the court building.

"You're as bad as he is if you're willing to stand up in court and defend him."

"Haven't you ever heard of the cab-rank rule?" I ask.

Her face draws a blank, but my mind starts working. I realize that I've discovered another piece of retained knowledge: cab-rank rule. I instinctively know what it means: a barrister must accept all instructions—regardless of personal opinions or prejudices—except in a few limited circumstances.

"No?" I say, taking advantage of her momentary silence. "Well, it's quite important. Look it up."

And with that—and a theatrical swish of my gown—I stomp back into the court building.

My breathing is ragged as I walk through the main hall. I replay the conversation, turning it over until it loses its form. Why on earth does that woman want to question me?

I need to find somewhere I can catch my breath, work on another escape plan, hopefully something a bit more sophisticated than "run away" this time.

I'm struck by an idea, my parting comment to the police officer.

Look it up.

Maybe cab-rank rule is my way out of here. I need to get my hands on a very specific book. As I'm making for the robing room, Malcolm emerges from a side door, and I raise my hand toward him.

He tilts his head to one side, which makes me lower my hand in embarrassment. What was I thinking, trying to wave him down as though he's a bus? I'm always so rude to Malcolm.

"Miss Dalton?" he asks.

"Can you show me where the library is?"

The library is immense—at least three times as big as the robing room—with shelves of books lining the walls from floor to ceiling.

I cast a glimpse around, looking for a section on professional ethics. After a couple of fruitless minutes scanning the shelves, I start looking at the tables. It makes more sense for it to be ready to hand, discarded after another desperate barrister in an ethical quandary turned to it for guidance. Sure enough, I find it on the middle table.

I thumb through the handbook until I find the section on the cab-rank rule. One of the limited circumstances that allow barristers to withdraw from a case is the death of a family member. Only close family members will do.

While I've got the book in my hands, I check whether illness allows a barrister to withdraw, but it looks like it has to be pretty bad to meet the threshold. That sounds too complicated to fake and could go very badly if I accidentally poisoned myself. Being honest about my memory loss is also out of the question, as that will take far too long to investigate, by which time they'll have worked out how to section me.

No, I'll have to go with my first idea.

If I had a family—or remembered who they were—I might have felt guilty about what I was about to do. But I don't. They're strangers to me.

Five minutes later and I'm outside the judge's chambers, which are his private rooms.

When the judge leaves through the side door, it's tempting to think he steps into an abyss, into an unknown realm. Really, he steps into this corridor. It's wide and long, more luxurious than the public-facing parts of the court, which are tired despite the efforts of the hard-wearing paint.

Courts are like theaters, full of secret passages and drawn curtains. Mirroring the public half of the building is the secret half where they keep the judges and jurors. Only the ushers are allowed in both halves; everyone else is confined to their side, only ever meeting in the courtroom.

Here I am, backstage, waiting outside the star's dressing room. I pace back and forth, praying that my idea will work. This conceit of pretending to be a barrister, of pretending to know what I'm doing, feels like it's falling apart at the seams, and all the while I'm pushing the stuffing back in, hoping that no one will see. I feel exhausted with the effort of it and know I can't maintain this charade for much longer.

Malcolm knocks on the judge's door and leans around the corner. "Judge, Miss Dalton for you."

I remove my wig as I step inside. The judge sits at a mahogany desk with his back to the window. He's also taken off his wig. Then I get a horrible shock. The man—the mirage—the person I thought I saw in the cells. It was the judge. I didn't recognize him at first because he wasn't wearing his wig or robes. What was he doing down there? I shake my head, trying to dispel the image of him sitting in a cell. It must be my mind playing elaborate tricks on me again. Perhaps I really am going mad. This only serves to underline the importance of getting out of this case and off this island.

Composing myself, I take a seat opposite, forcing myself to focus. "Thank you for agreeing to see me." I allow my voice to catch. I've been so close to tears today it's not difficult to fake.

"Lila, what can I do for you?"

"Judge, I'm afraid I can't do the case anymore. I'm going to have to withdraw."

"Oh dear. What's happened?" He steps out from around the desk and comes to my side. His stomach brushes my arm. While every inch of me is on fire with repulsion, I stay stock-still.

"It's my mother. She's dead."

The judge bends lower and wipes a tear from my cheek. His hand lingers. "But Lila, it's been years since your mother died."

My mouth opens to speak, but the drawbridge between my tongue and brain has been raised, leaving my jaw to hang lamely.

I know it sounds crazy, I know it makes no sense that I should mourn a woman whose face I can't remember, whose smell I can't imagine, but I can't stop thinking about how I'll never hug her again. And any memories I might have of feeling her embrace have been ripped away from me so all I'm left with is a fragment of a feeling.

"But how do you…?"

"As your head of chambers, it was my duty to have an intimate knowl-edge of members' personal matters. Didn't you think I'd know? When I got appointed, I always made sure to be gentle with you." He squeezes my shoulder.

I'm aware that he's no longer by my side. He's moved around so that he's perched on the desk in front of me, legs splayed. Then he reaches forward and caresses my leg.

I'm so shocked that I don't respond at first.

"Let's see what we can do for you." His hand goes further up my thigh.

Once again, I'm transported away from the present and into my murky past. This time, I get the merest snatch of a memory.

All I can remember is a man whispering in my ear, "No one will believe you," as blue smoke curls from his lips. I choke on it, his breath filling my mouth.

I stand up, no safer in the present than I was in the past.

"What's the matter?" The judge looks angry.

He's angry? Why should *he* be angry? I find that my ears are burning again. It's the indignation of it, how he knows there'll be no consequences, and how he knows I'll just submit because it's easier than making a fuss.

"You're right, my lord." Calling him that leaves a bitter taste on my tongue. "I should just get on with the trial. I don't know what's come over me. It's… I'll go back. Thank you for your kind words."

It takes all of my self-restraint not to run for the door. I take one last look at him before turning the handle. I can see the sheen of his bald pate. It's burning bright red.

CHAPTER SIX

HIS LORDSHIP BREEZES BACK in to resume the afternoon session, all traces of his earlier anger dissipated. Etiquette demands that I bow to him before he takes his seat at the bench. This small show of deference is enough to cause a part of me to shrivel and wilt.

I feel trapped. The machinery of the trial is in motion, and I can't escape its teeth. My feeble attempt at running away seems laughable now, like I'm the butt of the joke the world is sniggering at.

Paxton addresses the judge before I've had a chance to consider what might happen next, never mind what I might say.

"My lord, I understand that you wanted to hear legal argument before I call the prosecution expert?"

"Well." The judge turns to me. "Miss Dalton, you're the one who seems to have a problem with this evidence. It falls to you to tell me why." He laces his fingers and sits back. His tone couldn't be more different from that of the man who heard submissions before lunch, who seemed to be on my side.

Yeah, he thought he could get into your knickers then.

My cheeks are aflame with the injustice of the situation. Paxton's smugness, the judge's scorn. I know I'm smarter than this, better than this, and I'm determined to show them up. So, I rise to my feet, albeit a little tentatively. On the wooden bench before me—varnish all but worn by years of use—is my copy of *Archbold*, a large, red leather-bound book.

"My lord, if I might refer you to the relevant section of *Archbold*."

"Paragraph?"

"Er…" I flick to the index. My fingers fumble on the Bible paper.

I look up and see that the judge is peering down at me. The room is silent. Every eye is on me, and I'm still struggling to find the page. My face burns under the collective glare of everyone's judgment.

I run a finger down the index. "Evidence." This is what I need. "Evidence, abuse of process." No, that's not it. "Evidence, accomplices." No, wrong again. "Evidence, admissibility. See Evidence, admissibility of."

My finger glides down the page. It's going so fast I can barely read the words. What if I've gone past it? Go slower, get it right the first time. "Evidence, admissibility of… exclusion of evidence [204.56]."

"My lord, it's paragraph 204.56."

"Page?" His impatience is palpable.

I flick through the pages, some of them sticking to my sweat-pricked fingers. Then, my nail nudges the place-holding ribbon. I wedge my finger in the gap and lever the pages. The book falls open at paragraph 204.56. I see a blue ink mark in the top right-hand corner, the one I made earlier, when the woman from the robing room showed me her trick for curing déjà vu.

She's real.

"Page 2558, my lord," I say, faltering.

I was right. Our meeting in the robing room definitely happened. Is it a coincidence that the mark I made is exactly where I need it to be? We discussed excluding the previous convictions, so maybe she was giving me a helping hand by putting the bookmark in just the right page.

"And?" says the judge, and I realize I've been silent an unusually long time.

"As you will see from this chapter, you have wide discretion to exclude any evidence that is prejudicial."

"Where does it say that?"

I look down, and the words swim on the page. I start reading, but they're just a bunch of letters, more ciphers than sentences. I blink and stare harder, all the while conscious that my palms are slick, leaving marks on the translucent paper.

"Case law?"

"My lord, the discretion is statutory. Section 78 of PACE."

I didn't read that. It came from nowhere. It scares me, makes me feel like I'm an automaton. What other things might my unconscious brain be capable of?

"Right. And?"

I've found it now. I've found the part that deals with exclusion of evidence.

"Subsection 1 states that 'In any proceedings the court may refuse to allow evidence on which the prosecution proposes to rely to be given if it appears to the court that, having regard to all the circumstances…the admission of the evidence would have such an adverse effect on the fairness of any proceedings'—"

"I know what the statute says. You don't need to read it out to me."

A droplet of sweat makes steady progress down my back. *Why ask for the reference, then?*

"My lord, it would be unfair for the prosecution to call evidence to prove that my client holds these views. It's an attempt to sully the good name of the accused—"

He interrupts me again. "Good name? Doesn't he have previous convictions?"

"Yes, my lord, but they don't go to the issues—"

"Mr. Paxton says otherwise."

"The factual nexus is too weak. The zines found in the defendant's house—"

"The what?"

"Sorry, my lord?"

"What is a 'zine'?"

"An amateur magazine."

"Right, and he's signed up to it, is he?"

"Some material was found in his room, but that only means he holds certain political views. Being right wing does not make someone a mass murderer—"

The judge holds up the zine. "It's got a swastika on it."

I go to correct him. "It's an…Odal rune," I say, before backpedaling on seeing the judge's expression. "Yes, well, I'm not saying those views are mainstream, but that makes it even more prejudicial that the jury should be told about them when there's no causal link."

"Miss Dalton." The judge takes on the silky-smooth voice he used when he touched my leg. It repulses me. "The Odal rune is a neo-Nazi symbol, is it not?"

"Some groups may have appropriated it."

"And I assume you've learned about the Holocaust?"

I hold his gaze. I might not remember the lesson, or the teacher, or the configuration of the classroom I was in, but that word is synonymous with evil. "Of course, my lord."

"How many people died?"

I have to reach again. This knowledge is in there, I know it, but it's a strain to recollect, so I simply say, "Er…lots."

"Lots indeed. I think the accused's political views—if you choose to call them that—are highly relevant."

I sit down, beaten, aware of the collective gaze of the courtroom on me.

Out of a masochistic need to meet that glare, I look around. Paxton and his junior have their eyes fixed on the judge. The blond police officer is smiling at the other officers and conversing in whispers. Last, I turn to the press bench. As has been the case since this morning, there are only two reporters. One of them is a middle-aged man who is several stone overweight and wears scruffy clothes, and the other is a woman dressed in bohemian fashion with wavy auburn hair. The shabby-looking man seems disappointed in me. This irks me because no one has a right to be disappointed in me but Trevor, Eades, and me.

I'm aware of Paxton getting to his feet.

"Do you need to hear from me, my lord?" asks Paxton.

The judge speaks to him like an old friend. *Thank goodness; someone sensible is here.* I rage in silence.

"I needn't trouble you, Mr. Paxton. This application is totally without merit. You can call the expert in the morning. I've told the jury to go home for the day. We'll begin again at ten."

He leaves the courtroom.

I sit in a puddle of self-pity, seething that I can be spoken to in that way simply because I rebuked an old man's advances.

I'm staring down at the open pages of *Archbold* when a shadow falls across them.

"You know you can trust me in the future?" It's Paxton, his voice full of mirth. "I've been doing this a while, you know."

With that he ambles off, his junior and the four suited people who sit on the back row trailing after him, including the blond woman I met on the steps. She turns to look at me, her lopsided smile baring her lipstick-smeared teeth.

I look around for my "team." Trevor is at the dock, speaking to the client, who bends down so that I can only see the top of his ungelled head. The greasy roots have all but suffocated the frosted tips we saw on the CCTV.

I don't want to speak to either of them, so I leave counsel's row without saying goodbye.

As I'm making for the double doors with the dust-pink curtains, I can't help but glance over at the press bench again. The scruffy reporter is still watching me. Not with the open hostility of the police officer but with the hardened eyes of a disappointed teacher.

————————

Back in the robing room, I feel exposed. I want to go somewhere private where I can lick my wounds and be somber. Here, with the prosecution watching, I have to keep a brave face when all I want to do is cry. I'm a failure, an embarrassment. Eades's words fill my mind like smoke.

She doesn't know what the hell she's doing.

And that's even with the help of the mysterious owner of the purple raincoat.

I shrug off my robes and drop my head forward until my wig falls into my cupped hands. It's the first time I've paid any attention to it. On the inside, at the nape of the neck, is a piece of fabric sewn into the wefts. A name tag. Written on it are what look like three slanted Ls. I say my name to myself again. There are three Ls in total in my name, but it seems a strange way to mark one's belongings, especially when I think of what would happen if my wig was handed in as lost property. Who has time to go around counting Ls?

I pop open my wig tin, where my actual name is printed across the top in golden copperplate, and inside, lying at the bottom, is a piece of paper. I take a cursory glance around. No one is here. As I unfold the paper, blood pulses in my ears.

Where's the Eighth?
Follow the Sevens.

CHAPTER SEVEN

IT'S APPROACHING THREE O'CLOCK by the time I leave court, but it feels more like five o'clock and the light is fading fast. I have a box of files resting on my hip and my handbag slung over my arm. At least I assume it's my handbag; it was in the cubbyhole with my name on it.

Since I found the note in my wig tin, I'm no nearer to figuring out its meaning. Where's the eighth? The eighth what? The eighth juror? The eighth courtroom?

At the top of the court steps, I look out at the vast sea surrounding Assumption Island. The main town is nestled in a sheltered cove, but the rest of the shoreline is jagged, with sheer cliffs of volcanic rock. Broken black rocks litter the bottom of the headlands. Away from the town, the island is bleak—rolling green hills with no vegetation. Only sheep appear able to survive. The mist obscures my view of the other side of the bay, and I wonder if it is the only part accessible by sea.

A gust of wind moves through me like a ghost, lacing my lungs with seawater.

It's only now that I question where my hotel is, where my possessions might be.

At the foot of the steps is a small turning circle for cars, set off from the street. There's a patch of grass in the middle of the road that doesn't know whether it's a feature or a mistake. Across from the court is a run-down hotel that doesn't look as though it's been updated in twenty years. The letters on the Castle Hotel's sign are dotted with cabaret lights, of which at least one-quarter are broken.

Given its proximity to the court, it looks as good a bet as any, so I head over.

There's a half-asleep woman in her late thirties staffing the reception. She's looking at a well-worn paperback.

"Hi there," I say.

She looks at me. In a manner of speaking.

"I'm checked in at this hotel, but I can't remember my room number."

"Name?"

"Dalton. Lila Dalton."

"You're in 224." She turns to a mounted wooden box and retrieves a key.

I look around.

"The lift is that way." Her gaze wanders back to the pages of her book as she raises an arm, pointing to a darkened corridor. Its strip light flickers.

The dingy hall is so intermittently dark that I struggle to see where the button for the lift is. I wait for the next flash, jab the up arrow, and stand by while the lift cranks into life.

When I reach the second floor, the doors open to reveal a pistachio corridor with cream dado rails and doorframes. Only they're not truly cream anymore; they're the color of gone-off milk. Even the paint takes on the same texture—fat separating from water.

My room is at the far end of the corridor.

The room is just as gaudy and old-fashioned as the rest of the hotel. Above the tufted viscose headboard is a fake canopy, an impression of a four-poster created by stapling leftover fabric to the wall.

I kick my shoes off while staggering over to the bed and collapse on it, staring up at the ceiling.

I'm Lila Dalton. I'm on Assumption Island. I'm a barrister.

It's a vain hope that repeating these facts will revive my memories.

My name is Lila Dalton. I'm on Assumption Island. I'm defending a mass murderer. An alleged *mass murderer.*

Who am I fooling? Eades was caught red-handed on CCTV and isn't saying a word, I assume because he doesn't have an explanation.

More important is what I'm going to do, how I'm going to escape.

I sit up too quickly and regret it. The tinnitus returns with the pounding in my head. I reach for the drawer and am pleased when I discover a half-empty packet of aspirin sequestered next to a Gideon Bible. There's a pharmaceutical brand printed across the foil: the earth held in cupped hands.

The bathroom light sends black spots dancing across my eyes. I move tenderly toward the sink. I turn the cold tap, but nothing happens. No gush of cool water. I twist it harder, willing it to work, but to no avail. Admitting defeat, I take the plastic cup from the shelf under the mirror and fill it from the hot tap before draining the cup of lukewarm water and washing down the aspirin with it.

When I return to the bedroom, I sit at the desk so I'm not tempted to lie down. Something happens in the moments between me sitting down at the desk and coming around in a dark room, the light outside dramatically different, as though I am in the midst of a solar eclipse. What happened there? What time is it? My watch tells me that I've lost nearly three-quarters of an hour. Perhaps it's not so surprising that I dozed off; it's been a long day.

I reach across to the Anglepoise lamp and pull the cord, illuminating the desk. My hands pass over its surface. As well as a lamp, there's a telephone. I wonder if there are any guidebooks in the room, something to tell me about the history of the island, its geography. I open desk drawers at random. They're all empty.

I wonder when I arrived on the island and how long I've been inhabiting this room. Long enough to leave a mark? Long enough to leave clues about who I used to be? I doubt it. Not if the room is to be ready for the next guest with a quick vacuum and change of sheets.

THE TRIALS OF LILA DALTON

I open the wardrobe only to find a funeral procession of black suits and white shirts. The suitcase below is, again, unassuming. No discernible clues as to who Lila Dalton is or was.

I lug the suitcase out of the wardrobe and open it up to find the clothes rumpled and creased. No effort has been made to fold them neatly. I add to the chaos by rummaging around, looking for some form of ID. A passport, driving license, library card, anything that confirms I am who everyone says I am.

There's nothing in my suitcase. I start opening drawers again. I look under the bed, in my handbag and wallet. Nothing but a few twenty-pound notes and some coins that jangle while I'm searching for my ID.

Perhaps the hotel keeps my passport behind reception.

By the time I've finished the search, I'm standing in the middle of a pile of clothes.

I take off my jacket, feeling the bulge in my pocket from the cigarette packet. I pull it out and throw it on the bed. The throbbing pain returns in waves, cleaving my head in two. I see the nimble fingers once more, sliding a cigarette from the golden box. This time there's more. I see a pair of blue eyes, closing as the smoker takes their first puff, and I remember that feeling of the smoke in my chest as they whisper in my ear that no one will believe me.

The memory fades as quickly as the last time, already distorted by my attempts to recall it with greater clarity, as though taking it from its drawer and holding it up to the light only serves to bleach it like a photograph left in the sun.

The throbbing in my head still beating a drum against my skull, I reach for the aspirin. The packet seems to zoom in and out of focus. I pop another pill before remembering that you're not supposed to take these on an empty stomach. As though it heard me thinking about it, my stomach cramps to remind me I haven't eaten for as long as I can remember, which would sound dramatic if my memory spanned more than a few hours. I should find some food, but first, I need to get out of this suit.

When I wriggle out of my tights, I find a band of red around my waist from where the material has cut into my skin. I select a pair of jeans and a jumper from the pile of crumpled clothes. I'm beating the creases out of the jeans when I hear a noise.

I stop moving.

There's someone in the corridor outside.

I stand frozen, listening.

My suspicion is confirmed—footsteps.

Why am I panicking? I can't be the only person in the hotel. But my room is the last in the corridor, and now it sounds as though they're directly outside my door. I'm in my knickers and a white shirt, feeling exposed. Then I remember that I don't need to panic; people don't tend to enter hotel rooms unless the occupant lets them in.

I watch the door, just in case. The white edge of an envelope slides under the door. I stay still, watching until the whole appears on the carpet.

Only then do I grab it and run back toward the bed, tearing it open. Inside there's a piece of printer paper with a symbol stenciled onto it. It's the Odal rune.

I rush to open the door and see a woman with short gray hair running away from me, wearing a purple coat that flaps behind her as she runs. She disappears down the stairwell, but I can't chase after her because I'm still in my underwear.

"Hey, hey!" I call after her, but she ignores me.

The coat is familiar. I'd recognize that color purple anywhere. It belongs to the barrister from the robing room. Why is she sending messages bearing neo-Nazi emblems?

I look back down at the piece of paper, hoping clues will be printed there in plain English. The rune is accompanied by stenciled words.

Get him off or you'll never see her again.

You'll never see *her* again? I mull this over, wondering who they could be referring to. I fold up the piece of paper and throw it onto the bed in frustration. "What's all this supposed to mean?"

On my desk there's a phone with a laminated list of numbers. I punch a 0 into the dial pad and listen to the ringing tone.

"Reception. How can I help?" There's something strange about the quality of her voice, like she's underwater.

"Hello?" I say. "It sounds like you're down a well. Is there something wrong with the connection?"

An unpleasant crackling sound comes down the line. "How can I help?"

"Er, OK." Maybe she didn't hear me properly. Maybe her end is disturbed by the same incessant crackling. "Did you see a woman in a purple coat come in and out of the hotel?"

"A what, sorry?"

"A purple coat. Vivid, like the chocolate bar…" I squeeze my brain, hoping to wring the brand name from it. I can see it in my mind's eye, but the name is just out of reach.

"You mean Dairy Milk?"

"That's it! Exactly, the color of Dairy Milk. Can't miss it."

"Oh, no, haven't seen anyone like that."

"So, there's no one who's been in or out of reception for the last five minutes?"

"You're the last person I saw in reception."

"OK, thanks." I put down the phone.

That must mean the barrister who delivered the note is a guest in the hotel, staying here while her trial is ongoing, just like me.

I look down, realize that I'm still only half-dressed, and go back to what I was doing before. I pick up the pair of jeans from the bed, uncovering the cigarette pack lying beneath. After pulling on the jeans, I stuff the cigarettes in my back pocket, the only memento of my empty life.

I wander over to the window, look out at the sedate little town on the bay. The houses are nestled together as though huddling together for heat. The roofs are pitched to weather any storm. It's the sea that whispers menace.

Even in a place as provincial as this one, there will be a police station. And the note I've just received could be perceived as a threat. More than a threat, an attempt to pervert the course of justice. This might even be my way out of the case.

I rush back over to the desk and dial the number for emergency services. The ringing tone resumes, along with the underlying crackle. Maybe the island has this effect on landlines. Come to think of it, I'm surprised it has electricity.

"Police. What's your emergency?"

"I've received a threat."

The phone line cuts out. Dead. I put the phone down and dial 999 again, but I just get a long beeping sound.

Someone is trying to stop me from calling the police.

CHAPTER EIGHT

THERE'S SOMEONE ELSE AT the reception desk when I get down there. This time it's a young man in his early twenties. He's so thin I doubt he'll ever fill the uniform they've given him.

"Hi there. Could I have my passport, please?"

"Sorry?"

"My passport. Do you keep it behind reception?"

"Room number?"

"Er...224."

"Your checkout date isn't scheduled until next week."

"Can't I check out early? I'll settle the bill now, thanks." I reach for my wallet and pull out a wad of twenties.

"Sorry—I need to see another form of ID before I can give you back your passport."

"But my passport's my ID. Look at the picture."

The man behind reception gives a sad smile as though he genuinely regrets what he's about to say. "I haven't been trained in facial recognition, so I'll need another form of ID."

"The passport *is* my ID. Compare the picture with my face and you'll see it's me. I think that's the conventional way of doing it."

"I'm sorry. Hotel policy. You need to show me another form of ID."

I bite back another response. We're going round in circles. I could ask to speak to the manager, but I'm sure I'll get the same bland smile, the same courteous coercion.

An angry rumble from my stomach reminds me I haven't eaten, and there are several hundred milligrams of aspirin eating into the lining of my stomach.

"Do you do room service?"

At this, his face brightens as though he's back on familiar territory. "We don't have a restaurant, but there are a range of eateries on the island that might take your fancy." He fans a selection of leaflets on the desk.

Eateries?

"Er, thanks." I collect them off the desk and go to leave the reception area.

"If you're looking for the town center, take a left when you leave the hotel. Walk down the hill toward the harbor and you'll find the high street."

"Thanks. I mean, it doesn't look like there are enough streets to get lost."

"Oh, you'd be surprised."

Unnerving and intriguing in equal measure, this stops me in my tracks. "Wait, you don't happen to have any guidebooks, do you? Or anything about the history of the island?"

He smiles placidly. "I'll look into that for you."

"Thanks. Does that mean you don't have any behind the desk?"

"Don't worry; I'll look into that for you."

"Is there anything stopping you from looking into that now?"

"I'm busy right now. Feel free to come back later."

After that last infuriating comment, I leave the hotel in search of food. It's bitingly cold outside, and I mourn my decision not to grab a coat. In a town this small, the "eateries" can't be too far away.

I walk toward the high street, forcing myself to breathe, to get control of the situation. I pass a red telephone box and consider using it to ring the police, but there's someone inside. I get the uncanny feeling that they've just turned away to stop me from seeing their face.

I decide not to wait for them to finish. First, I need food. My stomach is already cramping again and I'm feeling light-headed. I flick through the leaflets I was given in reception. The first is for a fish-and-chip shop, which leaves me feeling pessimistic about the rest of the recommendations. There's a mini map on the back, so I follow the route and find a paved high street. It's not long before I come across a pub, the Golden Cross, which looks as though it might do food.

When I step inside, the first thing I notice is the hostile turn of every head in the pub. The wave of sweaty, beer-tainted heat is the second.

The barman eyes me as I approach, but everyone else appears to have registered me for long enough that they can return to their pints. Assumption Island is clearly not a tourist destination. Everyone is noticeably pale, or else ruddy from the wind.

"Newcomer, I see," says the barman as I climb onto a stool.

"That's right."

"And what brings you here?"

"I'm working up in the court."

"Ah, working up in the court, are you?"

"Yes."

"Right."

I sit and wait. This isn't exactly what I'd call hospitable.

"Do you do food?"

"Aye. S'long as you want nothing fancy."

"What are the options?"

"Fish and chips, steak and chips, gammon and chips, and pie and chips."

"What's in the pie?"

"Chicken."

"I'll go for that."

The barman shouts through the hatch. "One pie and chips!"

A figure in a raincoat enters the pub. His presence is met with nods of the head and grunts of recognition. I can feel his eyes on me as he approaches, but I busy myself with reading the noticeboard behind the bar. The man who just entered takes the stool next to mine while I keep my attention determinedly on the notices pinned to the board. There are pictures of men in front of boats, some of them holding enormous fish. There are newspaper articles covering the island's news: obituaries, the man who lived until he was 106, the woman who claimed to have had a virgin birth. ("Five witnesses attest otherwise, and her fiancé has called off the wedding, not being one of the five.") There are other helpful notices: the number for emergency services, what to do if you see an escaped prisoner—

"Will you be wanting a drink with that?"

The barman's question pulls me away from the noticeboard. I realize that the man in the raincoat is no longer sitting next to me.

"Er—"

There's a laugh from down the bar, like a pneumatic drill. In unison, the barman and I look for the source. Sitting a few seats down from me is a woman in her forties wearing a leopard-print miniskirt. I make one hundred judgmental assumptions, and I can see the same calculations being performed on the barman's face. The woman paws at the chest of the man she's talking to and whose joke I assume she found so hilarious.

The barman turns to me. "I'll guess you're having what she's having?" He laughs at his own joke, making it clear he expects me to reciprocate.

I attempt a laugh, but it comes out more like a "Hmm."

"Are there many escaped prisoners on the island?" I point to the noticeboard. One of the notices is a large poster bearing an artist's impression of a white man in his sixties with the question "Have you seen this person?" printed in red capitals across the top.

"Too many if you ask me. Bloody foreigners. Why did they have to stick them on our island?"

"Is he foreign?" I gesture toward the poster.

"German, or supposed to be."

"What came first? The prison or the town?"

The barman crosses his arms. "What are you after?"

I look around me. "Food and a drink… Have you ever seen one?"

"What?"

I shrug. "An escaped prisoner."

"No, and it's lucky I don't. I don't believe in the prison system. It's a drain on the state. Much simpler to ship 'em off the island in a cardboard box if you ask me."

"I'd like a Coke, please."

"Pardon?" asks the barman.

"You asked me earlier if I wanted a drink with my pie. I'd like a Coke, please."

"One coming up. Take a seat."

The eyes of the locals follow me to my chosen booth in the corner. There's a man in the corner playing a slot machine and a friend standing by, watching his progress.

While I'm waiting for the food, I think over the day, each thought punctuated by the sound of the slot machine.

Something isn't right about this island. I get the sense that everything anyone has said to me since I came around in the courtroom is a lie.

There are too many inconsistencies for me to ignore, and I know, just as I know about the rules of evidence, that the best way of unearthing lies in any narrative is to interrogate the parts where the stories diverge. Pull at those loose threads and the lies will unravel.

There's a *ka-ching* sound from the slot machine and the gambler's friend shouts, "Lucky sevens!" Three sevens show on the machine, and there's a shower of change as the machine ejects the man's winnings.

I wish they'd be quiet and let me think in peace.

The unpleasant sensation of being watched turns my ears pink. I look around. The man in the raincoat isn't looking in my direction, but I have the strangest feeling that he turned his head the second I looked up.

When the waitress places a pie and chips in front of me, the fragrant steam reminds me of how much I need the food.

"Can I ask a question?" I say to her.

"Suppose so."

"When's the next ferry out of here?"

"Boats don't run November to February because of the weather."

"When's the next plane?"

"Not until Friday at the earliest."

"And today's Monday?"

The waitress shrugs.

"So, if people want to get back to the UK—"

The waitress laughs. "Only people here for the court cases come and go. And they have to wait for the next supply plane like the rest of us."

"How far is it to the mainland?"

She looks at me like I've lost the plot. Not the first person to look at me like that today. "We're in the middle of the North Atlantic. You're talking over five hundred miles."

This sobers me. Over five hundred miles. I feel the urge to drink wine but wonder if it's a good idea to drink alcohol on a school night. Stuff it. If ever there was a time where alcohol was needed, now seems it.

"Could I get some wine?"

"We don't do wine. Beer or spirits."

"Whiskey."

"Coming up."

She returns to the area behind the bar, shaking her head as if to say *newcomers*. As I watch her go, out of the corner of my eye I see the man in the raincoat duck out the door.

The day seems to have wound my stomach tighter, squeezing out any possibility of hunger, but now the food is here, I'm ravenous. The piping contents of the pastry burn my tongue, so I make a start on the chips, stuffing them into my mouth.

The warm meal does little to calm my racing mind. I start examining the inconsistencies, hoping to find truth in the lies.

Malcolm and the prison guard pretended that my trial is the only one in that building, but how does that explain the woman I spoke to? She seemed so real to me, more real than anyone else I've met so far. It felt as though I could have reached out and touched her. And I was right. She must be real, or how else do you explain the mark in the book? What's more, I've seen her just now, putting the note under my door. But why she delivered a note bearing a hate symbol I can't say. I know we only spoke for a few minutes, but to me she seemed warm and friendly, not the sort of person who'd be on speaking terms with white supremacists.

Then there was the receptionist who wouldn't give me my passport or give me any information about the history of the island. And then there's the interference on any phone calls I make. Someone must be listening in, which would explain why the call cut out as soon as I tried to ring for help.

The tinnitus returns and my head pounds. I slake my dry throat with the Coke. It doesn't make me feel better. Now my brain fizzes as well.

With the throbbing comes a memory. I'm no longer in the Golden Cross but in a low-lit bar, where lazy jazz music winds between conversation and laughter. I take a sip of my drink and look at the man sitting across from me. All I can see of him are his blue eyes, eyes that rake over me so that I feel naked. I cross my legs a little tighter, and he pulls a cigarette out of his pack.

And then the memory disappears.

The dregs left at the bottom of the cup are emotions rather than memories. Shame.

I pull the pack of cigarettes from my back pocket, squashed now I've sat on them. They were his cigarettes. The person in the memory. Who is he?

I start going over every piece of information I've gathered so far. It's surprisingly easy, almost as though an empty mind makes for a tidier one. The answer is in one of my first memories. Of speaking to Tony on the phone, when he told me my silk was in a car accident. It's got to be him. He must have lent his pack of cigarettes to help me build rapport with the client.

Only it didn't work, did it, Pat?

If only he were here, doing the case, and I were five hundred miles away.

A drill-like laugh cuts through the low-level noise in the pub. It's the woman in the leopard-print skirt again.

I see the barman look to the person now occupying my stool and say, "I guess you'll have what she's having then?"

The customer laughs raucously, playing ball in a way I wasn't willing to. I shake my head, frustrated to find myself on a small island with small-minded people. Even more, I hate that my first reaction was to judge another woman because of what she's wearing. Where did that come from? If I don't have any autobiographical memories, how have these preconceived ideas found a way to pollute my brain?

Too agitated to stay and finish the meal, I put down my fork. I pull out my wallet and look around for some change. As I'm doing so, I notice something I missed when I was searching for an ID in the hotel room. Behind the plastic film that should house my driving license (if I have one) is a piece of paper with a crayon picture of a pink and lilac unicorn, or that's what I think it is, because it was obviously drawn by a child. For example, it's impossible to say whether that's a horn sticking out of the unicorn's head or a leg sticking out of the unicorn's body. Smiling, I turn it over and see a childish scrawl on the back. The card is small, and it's clear that it was a struggle for the child to fit their message onto it. It simply says:

Mummy good luck on trip x.

Below the message is a heart.

My eyes fill against my will.

Then I realize what was meant by the note: it was a threat.

Get him off or you'll never see her again.

I have a daughter. Who's looking after her? Do I have a partner? I'm not wearing any rings. Perhaps I'm rich enough to afford childcare for the duration of the trial.

Without me knowing it, I've been performing, not just for my client's liberty but for my daughter's right to see her mother again.

My tears clear as panic takes over. I start nibbling at the hangnails on my fingers.

After downing the last of the Coke in one go, I ruck some cash beneath a place mat and leave the booth, half of the chicken pie still steaming in the dish, the whiskey yet to arrive, and walk out into the brisk night.

I try to picture my child's face but there's nothing, nothing at all that comes to me. An involuntary choking noise escapes my lips. What sort of mother am I? I can remember the Turnbull Guidelines for identification evidence, can quote statute at random, and understand the principles of hearsay evidence (which are unnecessarily complicated), but I can't picture my own child's face. What sort of woman, after losing her memories, can retain legal expertise and some fragments about a man smoking a cigarette but no recollections of her child?

Well, if I was a bad mother before, then I'm determined that I won't be in the future. The old Lila Dalton is dead, and I care as much for her as I do for my client. It's down to me to choose what I become from now on.

———————

The high street creates a wind tunnel for the breeze coming off the sea. I cross my arms and hug myself tight, as though trying to stop the heat from escaping.

The street is deserted. It seems the nightlife on the island is limited to trips to the pub. Posted at various intervals along the street are the pictures of the escaped prisoner.

Something moves at the edge of my vision. I turn to look but there's nothing there. Perhaps it was just a piece of litter blowing in the wind.

I turn and walk toward the harbor.

Once I'm in the darkness between streetlamps, I get the feeling that someone is behind me.

Footsteps. Heavy feet hitting the damp, stone-clad street.

Perhaps it's someone going in the same direction as me, a drunk from the pub. I don't want to look over my shoulder in case it's nothing. Or worse, someone following me who doesn't think I've noticed.

I quicken my pace.

The footsteps quicken in time.

I cross over the road and the footsteps follow.

Moving to my right, I twist my torso to see if I can catch anything in my peripheral vision. There's no one behind me. I come to a halt and look around. The footsteps have stopped and there's no one in sight. Perhaps it's just an echo, my own footsteps rebounding around the empty street.

My heart is ramming into my sternum and my ears are on fire.

I spot the red telephone box I saw earlier and run toward it. There's even a poster on the side of it.

Once inside, I close the door and turn to look out of the glazed window, my breath throwing circles of steam onto the glass. Sure there's no one out there, I rest my back against the door, forcing myself to calm down. The telephone booth has a list of important numbers, a list of pager codes, and a price list. The telephone handset is inches from my nose. Now that I'm in here, I may as well try to call the police again.

I dial 999. The dial tone is crystal clear. I wait.

"Police. What's your emergency?"

I'm on an island I can't leave, with no memories of how I got here, and now I'm imagining things.

I decide against saying that and instead go for "Hi. I'd like speak to someone about a threat I've received."

"I'm a police officer, so… tell me."

"Oh. I thought this would be the operator."

The officer laughs. "You think they give us enough staff for operators?"

I'm struck once again by how cut off the island is from civilization. "I guess not. OK, so, it's a couple of things, really. First, I received a threatening note under my hotel room door. I'm working in a trial—defending a man accused of murder—and the note I received communicates an intention to pervert the course of justice."

The line goes quiet now.

"Hmm. Where is this note?"

"I left it in my hotel room."

"OK, what's the second thing?"

"There's a lot of interference on my telephone in the hotel—"

"Have you complained to the hotel?"

"Yes," I lie.

"They should complain to the network provider."

"But I think it's more than that. Someone has interfered with the line. I think they're listening in on my calls."

He sounds bored, like he just wants this conversation to be over. "Anything else?"

I clutch the phone to my chest and look around. There's no one outside. "I think someone's following me," I whisper, almost in tears.

"Can you see them now?"

I look around again.

"No, I think they've gone."

"Where are you?"

"Near the high street."

"OK, well, stay in well-lit areas and make sure to knock on someone's door and ask for help if anyone follows you."

"Right…" I say, looking around at this unfriendly town, clutching its secrets in the dark.

"Look, I can't come over right now. I'm the only one in the station tonight—the other officers only work part-time—but I'll drop by tomorrow."

"Really?"

"Sure."

"You're going to help?"

"It's in my job description. Is there anything else?"

"No, that's the measure of it."

"See you tomorrow—"

"Wait, don't you need to know where—"

"There's only one hotel on the island."

I breathe a sigh of relief.

"I will need your name though."

"Lila Dalton."

A beat. "See you tomorrow, Miss Dalton." He hangs up, leaving me with the infinite buzzing sound of a disconnected call. The noise is interrupted by crackling. I press the handset closer.

"Hello?" My armpits prick with sweat. "Officer, is that you?"

I hear heavy breathing. Someone is there.

"Officer?"

The voice that greets me is nothing like the friendly professionalism of the policeman. It's deep and gravelly. "They're watching you."

I slam the handset back on the hook.

CHAPTER NINE

I'M RUNNING NOW, DOWN toward the sea. It's a cruel fiction, but I feel as though every step is taking me closer to my daughter and away from whoever was following me.

I'll find my way back to you, sweetheart.

Is that the term of endearment I use for her, "sweetheart"? I decide against giving her a name, or assigning a face to her, because I don't want to grow attached to an imaginary child only to get home and find that my own daughter is more of a stranger to me than my invention.

It doesn't take me long to find the harbor. The island's main town is the size of a village, so it's only a matter of minutes before I'm at the marina.

When I find the timetable, it's been taped over with a sign saying No Trips until the Spring. The passenger boat really is out of the question. That, at least, wasn't a lie.

A pinpoint of white flashes in the distance. I walk closer to the harbor to get a better look. From here, the island shore curves around banana-like, and whatever is emitting the white light stands out on the peninsula.

I look around at the ghostly hulls in the harbor, swaying gently as though breathing. The ocean looks tame. There are merely surface waves, and a cold breeze stings my skin.

Panic seizes my chest. My daughter is out there, waiting for her mother to come home. What is she doing now? Who's looking after her? Is she safe?

The world I came into this morning is so hostile, so abrasive, it seems impossible that something as defenseless as a child would be able to survive in it. And I can't help thinking about how far away she is, and how powerless I am to protect her.

My need to return to her is too powerful to ignore. So, I leave the shore and walk along the wooden jetty. It's silent and dark. I walk among the boats, weighing each for the purpose I have in mind. Considering it unlikely I have expert sailing knowledge, I look for something that's both manageable and large enough to keep me safe.

Some of the boats are little dinghies only capable of going a mile out, while others are seafaring yachts. There's nothing enormous here. Nothing that would befit a villain in a movie. Nothing large enough to land a helicopter on. But then, I wouldn't pick something like that anyway. Not if I'm to sail it single-handed.

I decide to leave the sailboats alone and look for something fully motorized, like a cabin cruiser or motor yacht. Even a fishing trawler would do.

A few spaces down I find a fishing boat. Once aboard, I duck under the standing shelter and look for the ignition. When I find it, I press it, hunching my shoulders against the sound that's about to rip through the silence. None comes.

I think I just heard a noise. Is someone on the jetty? I hold my breath. It's scary to realize how far along the road toward criminality I've come in the space of five minutes.

Because that's what I've done. I've attempted to commit a criminal act. All five elements of theft are made out. I've appropriated (check) property (check) belonging to another (check) with the intention of permanently depriving another of it (well, I've no plans to sail the boat back, so, check), and I've done it dishonestly, by cover of night without asking for permission or telling anyone what I'm doing (check). That's enough to get me struck off.

Perversely, the thought lifts me. If it means never having to deal with judges bullying me, opponents muttering behind my back, or clients being rude to me, maybe it's for the best. There's a happier, simpler life waiting for me in the UK with my daughter, and in a few hours, maybe a few days, I'll be there, reunited with her.

Once I'm sure that the noise was a false alarm, I make my way back to the jetty. I try the next boat, this time a small powerboat. There's a pull cord, a bit like you'd find on a lawn mower. I tug it as hard as I can, but there's no sound. It's as though the boat has no engine.

I get out and try three other boats. None of them will start.

A harbor full of boats and not one with a working engine.

I turn and run away from the jetty, unsure what's worse: being caught stealing, or being caught trying to steal something that can't be stolen.

The further away from the harbor I get, the darker it becomes. The streetlamps are sparser, and any light from the buildings is shrouded by curtains or shutters. The telephone box stands out, positioned directly beneath a streetlamp, bathed in orange light.

Inside is a homeless man, sheltering in the telephone box. Outside is a shopping cart full of his worldly possessions.

A shadow falls across the ground in front of me.

Emerging from the darkness is a figure. The sheen of the raincoat is picked out by the sodium-vapor streetlamp. It's the man who was watching me in the pub.

From his pocket he pulls out a warrant card. Before I have time to check that police ID, he moves forward and slaps a hand on my shoulder.

"Where have you been, Miss Dalton?"

"What do you mean? I've been here."

"You disappeared on Friday. We haven't been able to find you since."

"Who's 'we'? I'm the one who's been trying to contact the police."

He swings my arm behind my back, putting me in an armlock.

I know better than to resist arrest; that only leads to being charged with more offenses. I wait to hear what I'm being arrested for, probably some obscure maritime offense of commandeering a craft or something else equally tongue-twisting—

"I'm arresting you on suspicion of murder..."

My mouth gapes, and the urge to say something, to deny it, to shout, "No, it's not me, you've got the wrong person," is overwhelming. I feel a small prick of sympathy for criminals who don't know they're better off keeping their mouths shut until they speak to a solicitor. Maybe they do know to stay quiet, but they just can't help themselves.

As I'm being dragged unceremoniously toward a car, I look around, thinking I spotted something in my peripheral vision. Whatever it was, whoever it was, they're not there now.

CHAPTER TEN

THE BACK OF A police officer's car is not an illustrious setting. This one is made even less so by the presence of my riding mate, the homeless man from the phone box. I know it's not his fault, but the smell is eye-watering.

"You too?" I ask in a friendly attempt at conversation.

He eyes me sideways, mistrusting.

I turn to the headrest in front of me, cursing my foolishness for trying.

"You too?" he repeats back at me. "Are you enlightened?"

"Erm… I'm not sure. What are you in for, then?" I ask, trying to steer the conversation away from religion.

The man jerks his head toward the telephone box.

"What?" I ask.

"It's the sign. The sign of the enlightened."

"Right…" I look closer, finally seeing what he's talking about. Graffitied onto the side of the telephone box is the Odal rune. In fact, it's been graffitied onto the poster, distorting the face of the wanted man.

"Fucking hell," I say. "Did you do that?"

"The earth is hollow," he says. "You'll see it everywhere once you start looking. Trust no one, question everything. Always think for yourself."

I'm glad when the conversation is interrupted by the return of the police officer.

"Right then, Stan," he says to my riding mate. "Ready?"

Stan nods enthusiastically.

The officer looks at me through the rearview mirror. "We'll go to the police station in a minute; just need to drop Stan off first." He grants Stan the dignity of turning his head to look at him as he says, "No more graffiti, please."

"Question everything," Stan whispers once the officer returns to facing the steering wheel.

After two minutes of driving, the car pulls up outside a shabby but cozy-looking terraced house. Stan jumps out and waves a thanks at the officer for dropping him off.

Whose trolley was that, then? I wonder, realizing I have made a lot of unhelpful assumptions about Stan.

"Next stop, AI Police Station," says the officer when he climbs back into the driver's seat.

I remain silent on the short journey to the police station, which takes all of two minutes because the station is next door to the court.

Once inside, I'm led to a room where I'm supposed to hand over anything on my person. I do as instructed, emptying my pockets of all my possessions, including the note from my daughter, the only thing I have in this rotten world that confirms she exists.

"Can I get that back?" I point at my wallet.

"We'll see," says the officer as he dons a pair of latex gloves and seals the contents of my pockets in evidence bags.

After having been stripped of my possessions, I'm taken to a cell where I'm left to stew. Despite the smell of disinfectant, nothing feels clean. Perhaps it's the gray, mottled tiles or the sticky blue plastic mat topping the bunk. The lights are harsh, clouding my vision with black spots.

Murder was the word he'd used. *I'm arresting you on suspicion of murder.* There's no point wondering whose murder, because try as I might, I can't seem to squeeze from my mind any details or memories from before this morning.

The strain of trying is enough to bring on a dull thud at the base of my skull, the return of my headache.

The only data at hand is that which I've gathered today. I can see everything with crystal-clear clarity—all of the memories of the last ten hours mapped out—but I can't make sense of it, can't see any patterns. It's just evidence unwilling to coalesce into a conclusion.

I'm unsure how long I've been here when the door opens and a different police officer opens the door. He looks older and more browbeaten than the officer who arrested me.

"Can I have my phone call, please?" I ask him.

"Who do you want to call?"

"I want to speak to Trevor; he's a solicitor."

"Do you have his number?"

"No, but—" I stop. It's his voice, the one from the telephone box.

"It's you," I say. "I'm Lila Dalton. We spoke about an hour ago. I rang the police station, and I'm sure you were the one who answered."

The officer remains tight-lipped as he leads me toward the front desk area for my phone call.

"Whoever I spoke to said they were the only person on duty tonight. That must be you."

He stays silent. Meanwhile, my mind is active, replaying the conversation I had in the phone box.

"And the man I spoke to said he was the only officer in the station, but the one who arrested me..."

"He was off-duty."

I think about what happened when the call cut out, when the voice at the other end of the line said, "They're watching you." Was it this officer or someone intercepting the call?

"Was it you?" I ask. "Were you the one who—"

He cuts me off. "Trevor, did you say?" The look he gives me is firm, a warning.

"Er, yes. He's only here temporarily. He's like me, working on the court case…"

"I'll find his number."

After a few minutes, the officer returns with a Post-it note, which he uses to dial Trevor's number into the telephone on the wall.

"Was it you, the one I spoke to, then?" I ask.

The officer fixes his eyes on a point in the corner of the room. I follow his gaze to see a camera, the red light confirming it's switched on. The officer scratches his nose but as he does so gestures at me to be quiet by placing a fleeting finger over his lips. It seems that I'm not safe to talk openly in a police station. Perhaps he *was* the one who warned me that I'm being watched.

After the first ring he hands the handset to me.

"Trevor?"

He sounds croaky and disgruntled. "Lila? What's wrong?"

"I'm…sorry. I know it's late." There's something wrong with the connection. It's not just that Trevor sounds tired and annoyed. The familiar crackle is there on the police station phone. I look to the officer and point at the mouthpiece to indicate that something is wrong. He shakes his head, his expression shuttered.

I speak back into the handset. "I need some help."

"You what?"

"I'm in trouble… I'm at the police—"

The connection cuts dead, replaced by a long, monotonous beep.

I look to the officer. "It's…stopped working. Just like it did in my hotel room, like I told you. Cut dead… What's going on?"

He shrugs. "The connection is never great on the island. The wind doesn't help."

I stare at him, hoping to communicate something. His eyes return an unspoken warning; we both know there's something wrong, but he can't tell me what it is, and I'm not supposed to ask.

I'm taken back to my cell, through the small rabbit warren of corridors and rooms. Everything is gray and lit with economy bulbs.

Door locked behind me, I pace back and forth across the cell: three steps one way, three steps back. The monotony of it should help me to think, but until they show me some evidence, there's nothing to jog my memory. These spartan surroundings feel like sensory deprivation or imaginative deprivation. All I'm left with is the white noise, a mind with no memories. A mother without her daughter. Severed.

A noise outside heralds the return of the older on-duty police officer.

He leads me to an interview room that is only two doors along the corridor. Already sitting at the table is Trevor. The officer leaves us alone.

"Hello, Lila," he says, apparently unperturbed to see me rather than Eades.

In this moment I'm struck by how fragile, how meaningless the monikers of *barrister* and *defendant* really are. I came around this morning a person of status and expertise. And now I'm here being accused of a murder I can't remember committing.

"Thank you so much for coming," I say.

"I'm the only duty solicitor on the island. It's my job."

"Well, thank you all the same... Can you tell me more about the accusation?"

He looks down at his twisting fingers, just like he did a few hours ago when we were in the cells with Eades. It feels like I've stepped out of the universe where I sat on one side of the conference table, and by dint of being on the other, I've found myself in a parallel dimension.

"It's serious, Lila."

"I guessed that," I say, my voice breaking. I swallow, trying to moisten my dry throat. "They did say 'murder.'"

"They think you killed Pat."

"But...but..." My mind churns over this new information. "But it was just a car accident, wasn't it? And I thought...just a coma or something..."

I go back to that first conversation on the phone, when I spoke with my clerk.

Do you know how many juniors dream of their QCs being in a car crash the week before a trial?

Trevor shakes his head. "It happened a few hours ago. This is now a murder investigation."

"And they think it was me?"

I don't know why I'm so incredulous about this. It could have been, for all I know. It might even explain why I have no memories, as though my brain won't let me remember what I did.

"What evidence have they got?" I ask, businesslike. This feels natural, throwing my brain at a problem.

"They haven't said. They're keeping their cards close to their chests."

"Which means if this goes to trial, they won't be able to draw an adverse inference from my silence in interview."

Trevor nods. "That was going to be my advice. Let's give a 'no comment' interview and see where we go from there."

There's a knock at the door. I take my seat next to Trevor as the officer walks in.

"Had enough time?"

Trevor and I share a glance and nod our assent.

"Apologies for keeping you waiting, I hope it wasn't too uncomfortable."

His pretense at politesse only serves to remind me of the long time spent in the cell, on the sticky blue mat. The antiseptic mingled with the smell of urine still lingers at the back of my throat.

The officer feeds a tape into the recorder and waits for the reels to start turning.

"This is Detective Sergeant Grant here with the detained person, Lila Dalton, and her legal representative, Trevor Moretti. The time is 20:23 on 18th November 1996, and I am about to commence the interview. Lila Dalton, you have been arrested on suspicion of the murder..."

I zone out on hearing the words of the caution. Without even knowing how, I know them by heart.

"Anything you do say may be given in evidence. Now, where were you on Friday the 15th of November?" he asks.

I glance at Trevor. "No comment."

"You were a passenger in this car." He places a picture of a silver Ford Mondeo on the table.

I was in the car? That explains it. Maybe I hit my head or something. The headaches...

"No comment."

"Really? We have a witness who says they saw you by the cliffs immediately after the accident."

There's no question, so I don't answer.

"The cliffs where we found the vehicle."

I stay quiet, waiting for the next question, but the whole time my mind is whirring, trying to use the picture of the Mondeo, my recollections of the island's jagged cliffs, anything to piece together what happened. No memories come flooding back, so I do my best to keep my face impassive.

"Can you explain why the driver's side seat belt wasn't working?"

"No comment."

"Was it you who tampered with it?"

"No comment."

"This," says DS Grant, pointing to the picture of the car, "is the vehicle before the accident. We got this from the car-hire brochure. Both of your names were on the documentation. Who was driving?"

"No comment."

"Was it Pat?"

"No comment."

"This," says DS Grant, pulling out another picture, "is the vehicle after the accident."

The image shows the car at the bottom of the cliffs, mangled almost beyond recognition. Surely no one could have survived that.

"Yes, nasty, isn't it?" Next, he pulls out a close-up image of the Mondeo. "Can you see that?"

The silver paintwork of the Mondeo is scuffed.

"There appears to be some paint transfer from a red vehicle." He points at a close-up of the scratch marks. "Can you tell us anything about that?"

"No comment."

"How did you get back to the main town after the accident?"

"No comment."

"Did you see anyone driving a red vehicle?"

"No comment."

"Did the red vehicle force the Mondeo off the road?"

"No comment."

"Do you know how many road traffic accidents there are in Assumption Island?"

"No comment."

"I've dealt with one. One. Mrs. Morris had mild whiplash but was right as rain after a couple of weeks. We don't have accidents here because the roads are so empty." After having built up a head of steam, DS Grant pauses.

"Where have you been, Miss Dalton? Why did you disappear after the accident?"

I wish I knew. Wandering in the wilderness as far as I can make out, mind gone, lost.

"No comment."

He reaches below the table and pulls out an evidence bag.

"We found this in the car." He holds up the clear plastic bag so I can see what he's referring to.

It's a pearl earring. Dark bloodstains spatter the stem. I feel my earlobes. There are hard lumps at the center where holes for earrings used to be but have since closed up. This earring can't belong to me. I marvel at this for a moment. Here's the very physicality of my body telling a story, a road map to my past. At one time, I had my ears pierced. At some unknown point in time thereafter, I stopped wearing jewelry. What does that say about me? That I'm not vain, or that I don't have either the time or the inclination to take care of my appearance? All of this makes the real Lila, the old me, feel more distant.

An unknowable stranger with whom I'm trying to have a conversation in semaphore.

"We only found one. You wouldn't happen to know where the other one is, would you?"

I'm tempted to tell him that this earring can't be mine because my ears have closed up, but I resist. I stick to the plan.

"No comment."

This piece of information is important. An earring that can't belong to me was found in the car. That must mean that there was someone else, a woman, involved in the crash.

DS Grant frowns. When he speaks, it's with a mollifying frankness. "Miss Dalton, there's evidence linking you to this crime. In fact, you brought it to the station this evening." DS Grant pulls out a second evidence bag from under the desk and places it on the interview table. Inside is the pack of Benson & Hedges.

"Partial to B&H, are you?" asks DS Grant with a hint of provocation.

"No comment."

"The information we have is that your colleague *was* partial to this particular brand of cigarettes. What do you have to say about that?"

"Wait a second," says Trevor, holding up his hand to stop me from answering. "You haven't disclosed this to us. You need to give us everything you have so that I can have a proper conference with my client before the interview starts."

DS Grant goes to respond when there's a frantic knock at the door of the interview room. Through the small wired-glass window, I see the familiar and unwelcome face of the blond police officer who was rude to me on the court steps.

DS Grant huffs before answering her knock.

"Can I have a chat?" I hear her say before the closing of the door muffles the rest of their conversation. I strain to hear what they're arguing about.

"Just give me a minute with her..."

"This is an active investigation...*my* island."

"You don't want to get in the way of Special Branch."

"These threats don't bother me. The Met has no jurisdiction here."

"The Met does have jurisdiction over terrorist activity—"

"Keep your voice down."

They bicker more quietly in fraught whispers. It appears that the female officer wins because she opens the door and steps into the conference room. Her face is a mask of disgust, not too dissimilar to the one she wore when rebuking me for defending Eades. She pulls out that blue bottle of perfume, spritzes herself, and takes a seat in DS Grant's vacated chair.

"Detective Constable Parks, Special Branch," she says. "Although you already know that, given I'm the investigating officer in your boy's case."

"And what's your jurisdiction here?" asks Trevor.

"I just wanted a chat with Miss Dalton."

"This is harassment," replies Trevor. "You're trying to intimidate defense counsel."

DC Parks ignores Trevor and turns to me, fixing me with her dead-eyed stare. "Where's the eighth?"

There it is again. *Where's the Eighth? Follow the Sevens.*

"Pardon?" I ask.

"Lila, we agreed no comment. In fact, don't answer any of her questions. Let's get out of here. They haven't got any evidence to hold you."

"Where's the eighth?" she asks again, this time with an exaggerated upward inflection to indicate the reasonableness of her inquiry. Her eyes are hypnotic, steel gray, demanding my attention.

I'm vaguely aware of Trevor leaving my side to go toward the door. "Don't say a word," he tells me.

"Where's the eighth?" she asks, this third time more of a bark.

"You know I'm not under caution? Nothing I say can be relied upon in court."

She smiles at me. Each word is slow and measured when she asks, "Where is the eighth?"

I want to ask *her* questions, ask what she means by the eighth. What is it, who is it? Why on earth do I have to tell her where the eighth is, and did she have anything to do with the notes I've been receiving?

Our little chat is cut short when DS Grant returns, looking furious.

"Let's go," says Trevor, who has come back in behind him. "They're not charging you; they haven't got anything."

DS Grant and DC Parks are both standing now, squaring up to each other.

Not caring to hear their arguments about rank and jurisdiction, I follow Trevor's advice and leave.

We walk together through the gray, dingy corridors, past the custody desk and out into the cold night air. Trevor hands me back my wallet. I open it up without saying thank you. I turn to the clear plastic section that is clearly meant to hold a driver's license. The drawing of the pink and purple horse is still there. I clutch the wallet to my chest, not caring how strange it looks. Perhaps later, I will treat myself by reading the message on the back of the picture. Is that a treat, or is it torture?

Trevor lights a cigarette, then turns to me, looking a little repulsed.

"Tell me about the earring."

"What?"

He still fixes me with his intense, magnified stare. The pockmarks on his skin are lunar craters in the half light.

"You can't be serious. I had nothing to do with the accident." I sound more confident than I feel.

He takes a long drag before shaking his head.

"I thought you were on my side," I say.

He chuckles darkly. "That's what all clients think, isn't it? That we defend them because we're on their side, because we believe them. We both know it's not our job to believe them; it's our job to represent them."

"You don't believe me?"

"How many of the fuckers we represent do you actually think are innocent?"

"But, Trevor—"

"Save it," he says, making a sudden gesture of disgust with his fingers as he taps the ash off the cigarette.

The problem is that Trevor has heard it all before. How many times has he been dragged out of bed in the middle of the night to hear denial upon denial only to find out later that the client's DNA found its way into the victim's body?

He looks at me now with disdain, and it's a look I recognize because it's how I feel when I look at Eades.

"I'll see you tomorrow." He walks away, leaving me standing in the cold night air, more alone than ever.

CHAPTER ELEVEN

THAT SOMETHING IS DIFFERENT in my room is apparent as soon my heel presses into the envelope that lies waiting for me on the other side of the door. I crouch down to pick it up, brushing away the dirt left by my trainer.

It's not just the letter that's alien. I would be fooling myself in thinking otherwise. The air isn't as stale as it was before. This isn't a room that's been shut up.

Across the room, the curtain ripples.

The window's open, just a sliver. If it weren't for the wind that whips the island, I probably wouldn't have noticed.

Was it open before?

I can't lie to myself. I know it was shut. But it wasn't just the rippling curtain that alerted me to a foreign presence in my room. It's the smell, cloying and sickly sweet. I've smelled it recently. Having a limited range of memories to choose from, I land on the correct one quickly. DC Parks's perfume. The one in the star-shaped bottle.

I came back here to this place of false security, hoping it would make me feel tethered. But the discovery of this trespass, of this horrible smell mixed with the accumulated sweat of a day in court, has left me feeling cut loose. There's nowhere on this island I can hide.

I turn my attention to the envelope in my sweaty clutch. As I run my nail beneath the seal, dread settles at the bottom of my stomach. I pull out a photograph. I turn it over. A whimper cuts through the silence of the bedroom, and I realize after an indeterminate amount of time that it escaped from my lips.

The photograph lands on the bed. It shows a little girl sitting on a swing. Her eyes are the same as mine. They sit a little close together just like mine. Her lips are stretched into a toothy smile of even baby teeth. She's wearing a lilac gingham dress with a big flower sitting on her sternum. Her arms— bare and bathed in afternoon sun—have the slightly pudgy appearance of a child only just emerging from her toddler years. I'd put her at four years old at most.

I turn over the photograph. A stenciled message reads:

GET HIM OFF OR YOU'LL NEVER SEE HER AGAIN.

The note bears the Odal rune, the same as the last one.

I stare at the picture of my daughter. It seems laughable now that I spent any time worrying about growing more attached to an imaginary child than to the real thing. She is so much more beautiful than anything my wretched imagination could conjure.

I want to carry on staring at it, as though looking at her will bring us closer together, but I know there's only one way I can help her.

If the note is to be believed, the only way I can ensure both my and Eades's freedom is to secure his acquittal. Even if the threat is empty, I can't take that risk. Not when my daughter's life is at stake. After one last look at her smile, I turn the picture over, placing it face down on the desk, my eyes closing in a silent apology as I do so.

I lug the cardboard box of box files onto the desk and empty them onto it, separating them out. A loose piece of paper rests at the bottom of the box: the batting order I was given earlier.

Does it make me an even worse mother that pushing all thoughts of that photo to one side and focusing on the cool logic of the case makes me feel calmer? Shouldn't it be the other way around? But taking the mass of information and ordering it into neat little compartments is therapeutic, a bit like taking a messy house and tidying it from top to bottom. Thinking about my daughter makes me feel disconnected.

I touch my stomach, wondering how it must have felt to carry her. I'm struck again by my body's existence. It's just there, functioning away, a suit of armor being driven by a damaged brain.

After pulling the cord on the Anglepoise lamp perched on the desk, I scan the batting order and cross-reference the names of the witnesses to the statements in the box files, which are organized into different sections: the indictment, the witness statements, the exhibits, the defense statement, previous convictions, and unused material.

I turn up the defense case statement first, a document that would have been drafted by Trevor on Eades's instructions. It forms his case. The defense statement is one line long: *I did not murder anyone.*

I frown at this. What am I supposed to put to the witnesses? Where is the case theory—the story I'm going to tell the jury? The only way to win is to find an attractive alternative version of events and suggest that maybe, just maybe, that's what happened.

That's a lie, actually. That might be what the law says, that the standard of proof in the criminal justice system is "beyond reasonable doubt" that Eades needn't put up a defense to be acquitted, that it's for the prosecution to prove his guilt, but anyone with an ounce of common sense knows that isn't the case. It might be so for something low level—a fight in a pub, theft from a shop, even a burglary—but for anything emotional like child abuse, an assault resulting in long-lasting facial disfigurement, and definitely the mass murder of innocent people, the jury will acquit only if they're satisfied of the defendant's innocence. That's just the way it is.

All of this I know instinctively, much like everything else that's to do with the case. I don't even have to stretch to find the knowledge; it's at my fingertips.

Looking down the batting order, I check the witness list against the statements and write down each person's role in the case next to their name as I go along. For example, PC James Sharpe is the arresting officer, so I put "AO." The officer in the case is DC Stephanie Parks, the pleasure of whose company I have only just recovered from. I write "OIC" next to her name. There's one other name on the list that draws my attention instantly.

A.N. Other.

The mystery that surrounds their identity is at once enticing and infuriating. They are last on the list.

Something else strikes me. There's no report from a forensic explosives engineer. I flick through the countless witness statements in the bundle to see if the defense has "agreed" that evidence, but there's nothing there. This strikes me as odd.

I need to get started on the expert witness statement—Dr. Sheridan's—if I'm to cross-examine him at 10:00 a.m. tomorrow morning.

Attacking his evidence is my only priority now. I'll forgo digging deeper into the other witness statements and concentrate all of my efforts on the first witness, taking each one of them at a time.

I turn over the page. His report is titled:

Report of Dr. BL Sheridan: in the Case of R v Eades
Date: 30th July 1996
Subject Matter: The Order of Eights and Sevens

More eights and sevens. So, this is it, the numbers I'm supposed to follow? The answer was here all along, in my brief? Was that what all of this has been about, trying to get me to do my job?

I read on, intrigued now that I know the answer to getting off this island and getting back to my daughter lies in the case.

My Qualifications, Relevant Experience, and Accreditation

I, Dr. BL Sheridan of Bridewater University, have been an academic since 1972. I was until 1994 a senior lecturer in history and religious studies at University of Wales Institute, Cardiff, before going on to lecturing in my current role where my particular focus is occultism and its influence on the far right. I did my PhD in 1977 and my thesis was titled "Helena Blavatsky and the Third Reich." My CV is attached as Appendix 1.

Instructions

I have been instructed by the Crown Prosecution Service to prepare a report with specific expert opinion regarding:

a. Whether Jonathan Eades was a member of the Order of Eights and Sevens;

b. The organizational structure of the Order of Eights and Sevens; and

c. Whether the bombing attack on Abbott House was inspired by the philosophies and ideologies of the Order of Eights and Sevens.

At the beginning of his report, Dr. Sheridan sets out the facts and documents provided to him that are material to the opinion he expresses. He then goes on to set out his duty to the court and responsibilities of an expert witness.

I should set out at this stage that I do not have access to all of the literature I would like because some seminal texts, such as *The Aryan Guide to the Destruction of Society*, are now banned books in the United Kingdom. I still have high hopes that I shall have it in my possession one day, but sadly I was unable to acquire a copy in time for completing this report. Nevertheless, I am the owner of a considerable library of far-right literature. My collection is probably the vastest of any academic on the topic.

The reverence with which Sheridan treats his topic is remarkable. He speaks of these hate manuals as though they're rare butterflies, artifacts of beauty to be caught and preserved. I try to envision him. What sort of man spends his life researching the most despicable aspects of humanity?

What is the Order of Eights and Sevens?

The Order of Eights and Sevens is a secret religious movement that originated in the UK in the 1970s. It combines elements of occultism and satanism with white supremacism.

Since the late 1980s, it has been associated with neo-Nazi violence.

What are the Origins of O87?

In the 1970s, Simon Cox—a pseudonym—formed the Order of Eights and Sevens by taking Hellenic hermeticism (as popularized by Aleister Crowley in the first half of the century) and combining it with neo-Nazi white supremacism. Simon Cox is considered by many in the field to be the Grand Master of the Order. For reasons I will develop later on, I do not agree with this analysis.

The O87's development involved the publication of its foundational texts in the 1970s. The bulk of the O87's philosophy was developed by "Cox" in his writings. Cox's identity remains a mystery, but from his writings we know that he was highly intelligent, being well versed in ancient languages, as well as the occult and the paranormal. He was almost certainly a classicist.

I stop reading for a moment. Dr. Sheridan's choice of words is interesting. He seems to view his study of the order as deserving of the same intellectual

rigor that might be applied to a study of the ancients. He calls the order's theology "labyrinthine," a draw for some and a system of self-selection to deter
others. It seems so enticing to Sheridan that he's lost in the maze. If his CV is
anything to go by, he's spent the entirety of his career looking for the Minotaur,
his ball of string long forgotten.

Trying to discover Cox's true identity appears to have been the single great-
est pleasure of Sheridan's life. So much so that I wonder how he would feel if he
ever unmasked him. I carry on reading, now somewhat wary of Dr. Sheridan's
distasteful admiration of his subject.

What does the O87 believe?

The O87's blending of satanism, white supremacism, national social-
ism, and elements of pagan mythology is unique. The O87 follows the
left-hand path, which embraces magical techniques viewed as taboo,
using sex magic and embracing satanic imagery. As anyone who was
left-handed at school can attest, the left-hand path is associated with
devil worship, black magic, and evil.

The "Eights" in the order's name could refer to 88, which corresponds
to HH in the alphabet (Heil Hitler), while the "Sevens" could refer to
the seven celestial bodies. Seven is a particularly important number in
neo-Nazi circles. Please see Appendix 3—Glossary of Terms.

The O87's theology is contained in long, rambling pamphlets authored by
Cox. One of their weirder beliefs—and that really is saying something—is in
mind control.

I pause to imagine Eades with a bunch of oddball white guys with poor
personal hygiene practicing mind control.

Sheridan opines that the order isn't even a group per se, but an idea. An
idea that festers, permeating other far-right groups. Cox wanted to create a

monster. Something that the legal system could never catch up with or cut off the head of the Hydra before it multiplied. In fact, outlawing those methods of communication would only make them more attractive.

As well as pseudo-religious texts, the literature of O87 includes works of fiction that act as instruction manuals to followers, in which the protagonists carry out terrorist acts, mass murders, and rape. These crimes are glorified. Even minor acts of vandalism are encouraged, anything to disrupt the foundations of society. Not even parking meters are safe.

Members of O87 dedicate themselves to the task of ensuring white people become the "master race." This is achieved via a process called *extraction*. They remove members of society deemed to be weak or suboptimal, paving the way for total domination.

Cox advocates that by extracting the undesirable members of society, they can lay the ground for the new world order.

I lean back in my chair, feeling my eyes droop under the weight of the day.

Reading about O87 has made me feel sick. I have the urge to disinfect my eyeballs, rid them of this material. I go into the bathroom and try turning the cold tap, but it still won't work so I settle for splashing my face with warm water.

I return to my desk and slump down on the chair. My eyes are yearning to close, to cede to this wave of tiredness. A sense of intoxication settles over me until I'm staring into two cavernous eyes, beetle black. I've seen these eyes before. Blank, dismissive, uninterested in the world around them.

I'm looking at my client. He's in the dock smiling at me, baring his teeth.

CHAPTER TWELVE

OUTSIDE OF HIS LIVING room window, the street was quiet. He sat with his backpack wedged between his twitching knees.

"Sweetheart, are you sure it's a good idea to be going out in this weather?"

Anger flared in Fenriz's chest. How dare his mother call him *sweetheart*? It was bad enough when people at work used his old name and he had to answer to it. He didn't need his mother treating him like a baby.

"It's a Territorial Army exercise, Mother. I don't get a say in when we go on them."

"Do you have to call me that?"

His mother looked hurt. She stood in the door that connected the living room and hall, her forehead creased in that stupid, simpering way.

"What am I supposed to call you?"

"You used to call me Mam. Am I not your mam anymore?"

He didn't answer, just went back to looking out of the window. The houses on his street were stacked on top of one another so that the roofs made a flight of steps from the bottom to the top of the steep hill. Everything in his world was made of pennant measures. It was as though the stone beneath them mirrored the slate-gray skies that pressed in from above.

"Don't you need me or your father to take you to the base, love?"

"No, Mother. A friend is picking me up. Like I told you."

"And when is this friend bringing you back?"

"Monday, like I said. It's a long weekend."

"Right you are, love. Your dad and I are just worried about you is all. It's cold out."

"It's the army. They're teaching me how to survive."

Then what he'd been waiting for all morning happened. Coyote's car trundled up the steep hill and stopped outside his house.

"Bye, Mother."

His mother didn't even try to kiss him as he pushed past her to get to the front door.

"See you Monday," she said meekly.

Coyote didn't get out of the car. Didn't smile to say hello. That wasn't his way. Fenriz popped open the boot and shoved his bag inside, squishing it in between the tent and Coyote's bag of supplies.

The car jerked up the hill. Fenriz knew that his mother would be waving goodbye from the front porch, but he didn't look back and wave. A little part of him wanted to. He'd never admit it to himself, but deep down, he'd miss her. There was something like sadness in his chest as the car pulled away, struggling to gain traction as it chugged up the steep incline.

Coyote said, "I hope you're ready for this."

"I am," said Fenriz. He didn't want Coyote to think he was scared. He even lowered his voice an octave to prove it. The problem was that he was scraping the bottom of his vocal cords and they wobbled with the effort of it.

"When I was at your stage, I started with six months in the wilderness, rather than four days."

"I could do six months."

Coyote laughed and shook his head. "Know your limits. You'll have to build up to it."

"Why? I'm ready. Let's just stay out there once we get to the mountains."

"Can't. You've already told Mummy you'll be back by Monday."

"She doesn't matter."

"Of course it matters. She'll be ringing the police as soon as you're not back, and she knows my license plate number."

Fenriz went quiet. Coyote was right. He'd have to think of a new story that would allow him to be gone for six months. He'd never ascend otherwise.

"What's the stage after being a super, again?" asked Fenriz.

"For fuck's sake, have you not been reading the materials I sent you?"

"I have, of course I have."

"Then you would know that it's ascension."

That was it. Ascension.

"So where do we ascend to?"

"We ascend to different levels of humanity. At the moment you're just a mortal. Even worse, you're a weak mortal. You need to be stronger so that you can ascend to the next level of being: a super. After you're a super you can ascend to immortality. That's what I'm working on at the moment. Once there are enough of us immortals, we can go beneath the earth's crust to find our Aryan descendants."

"Inside the earth?"

"I thought you'd read the materials? We're going to the mountains so we can touch the sky. In the future, we'll go beneath the earth's crust to revive our ancestors. They will be gods among men."

"Because they're giants?"

"Exactly."

"And this will happen in my lifetime?"

"If you ascend to immortality, then yes, obviously." Coyote shook his head.

"Sorry."

"Don't apologize. Only females and weak males say sorry. And you're not one of them anymore."

Fenriz nodded. He was about to say sorry for saying sorry but just went quiet instead.

The hatchback drove up to the Heads of the Valleys Road, past vast aqueducts bridging the mountains, past rocky summits and green slopes, until they reached the Brecon Beacons.

Coyote pulled up by the side of the road. It was a three-mile trek carrying their equipment until they reached the spot where they would set up camp.

He led Fenriz to a sheltered nook between two peaks, where a mountain lake pooled in the hollow. On a day like today, it was difficult to see the full vista. Fog shrouded the ridge that ran along the top of the largest mountain. The cliff face had horizontal grooves, each shelf a different chapter in the rock's history.

"Shouldn't we go further away from the lake? Won't we get eaten alive by insects?"

Coyote grinned, revealing his sharpened teeth. "The lake is important," he said.

"You know I can't swim, right?"

"You'll learn. You can't be a super without such basic skills as swimming."

Fenriz felt his heart start thumping faster. He was scared now, but he tried to hide it from Coyote. Unfortunately, his companion had a knack for knowing what he was thinking. It was unnerving.

"Don't fear. Fear is for weak mortals. This weekend will stamp some of that weakness out of you, but you need to work harder from here on. This is what will make us rulers of the world. We must be the master race."

Fenriz nodded enthusiastically. "And I will, I promise."

Coyote laughed again, like his namesake, and began setting up the tent. It was so cold, Fenriz could feel the heat leaving his feet, being sapped away, even through the thick soles of his army boots.

The pegs sank into the saturated turf like needles in butter.

Although the sky was overcast, the thin layer of grass settled over the landscape was an almost radioactive shade of green.

While Fenriz was unpacking Coyote's supplies in the tent, he opened a bag and caught a glimpse of what was inside. He expected to see the candles and rune charts but was surprised to see the sort of armbands that children wear for swimming.

"Don't look in there," said Coyote. He made up the distance between the two of them astonishingly quickly. He was a super, after all.

"Are these armbands for me, because you knew I couldn't swim?"

Coyote relaxed and smiled. "That's right. Knew you didn't like the water, but it's important. I'm going to teach you."

Fenriz felt a little safer. Coyote really did just want to train him up to become a perfect specimen of man's power and strength.

"Thanks. I wouldn't have thought of that."

"Well, you've ruined the surprise now, haven't you? Dickhead. Give that bag here and don't go looking in it again."

Coyote's tone was jovial, and he gave Fenriz a hearty shove on the shoulder. Fenriz had to really focus on holding his core and keeping his feet planted to stop himself from going flying. Coyote probably behaved like that with the other supers who would see a push like that as a gentle tap. Maybe a normal person's friendly push wouldn't register—like a fly landing on your shoulder.

Fenriz watched as Coyote stuffed the bag in the corner of the tent.

What was the surprise? If he wasn't mistaken, the other objects were used to perform spells. Fenriz was so new to all of this that he wasn't yet learned in the ways of magic. He was desperate to learn more, though he understood that pushing himself to his limits had to come first. Only when his mind and body had been taken to the brink and won against nature would he be able to study the darker arts.

He'd also seen what looked like a couple of guns in there. He hoped they were going to do some hunting this weekend. They were given guns in the TA and were allowed to practice, but it wasn't the same as hunting real, living things. Man against nature.

CHAPTER THIRTEEN

SOMETHING WAKES ME. AT first, I'm not sure what it is, but then I hear—

Beep-beep.

It feels as though I've barely dipped my toe in sleep, and I'm as tired as I was last night, if not more so.

Beep-beep.

I have no idea where the beeping is coming from.

Beep-beep.

The room is so dark that there's no discernible difference when I open my eyes. Perhaps I am sleeping, and I've woken from a dream within a dream.

Beep-beep.

I look down. I'm still in my jeans and jumper, having drifted off to sleep at my desk fully clothed. There's a pain in my neck from where my head lolled to one side.

I scrabble around for the lamp and find the cord. The assault on my retinas is painful. I screw up my eyes and keep them shut for a few more seconds, waiting for them to become accustomed to the light.

The digital clock by the side of the bed reads 07:05.

Perhaps this hotel's previous occupant set an alarm and forgot to turn it off.

I slam the alarm, hoping to silence it, but the sound continues. I press all of the buttons, experimenting with how long to hold them down and in which order, but the time on the clock stays the same. My wristwatch is on the bedside table and reads 03:37, so the alarm clock must be broken. No matter what I do to it, the beeping doesn't stop.

Beep-beep.

Where the fuck is that coming from?

Beep-beep.

It's nearby.

I pull open the drawer of the bedside table. The Gideon Bible is no longer there. In its place lies a child's toy: a pink horse with a long purple mane and matching tail. The beeping is coming from inside.

At first, I shake it. There's something inside the horse. Then, I try to twist the head off. It doesn't work. Only brute force will do the trick. Finally, after yanking the head off the horse, I tip out the contents. A black pager falls onto the bedsheets.

Flashing across the liquid-crystal display is a code: 187.

I press a button and the noise stops.

The silence left in the wake of the beeping is restless, humming.

Now that I'm awake, I feel alert. Connections are firing off in my brain. I hold the decapitated horse up, turning it around before replacing the head, a little lopsided. It reminds me of something. Something I've seen recently. I quickly land on what it is. My daughter's drawing: the horse that might be a unicorn, sketched in crayon. My wallet is still in my jean pocket. Carefully pulling the paper from behind the plastic film like an archaeologist touching papyrus, I look at the crayon sketch and then back at the semi-decapitated horse toy on my bed. This must belong to her.

Someone is sending me a message. They have one of my daughter's toys, which means they have access to her. Does that mean they've broken into my house back home? Or did they meet my daughter on the way to school and ask if they could borrow her toy? If so, how long have they been planning this? How did they get the toy to the island?

Unless…unless my daughter is being held on the island, and that's how they have access to her toys.

I pick up the two notes bearing the Odal rune.

```
Get him off or you'll never see her again.
```

When I first read this, I assumed they were threatening to keep me on the island, prevent me from leaving. But what if the truth is something much worse? What if they're holding her here?

I look down at the pink horse. I clutch it to my chest, praying that it will trigger a memory. Nothing comes. A sinkhole forms in my chest, and any residue of hope falls through it.

All of last night's reading about the O87 confirmed that they glory in violence. They believe in weaponizing rape, they deny the Holocaust but advocate for genocide, they are men who believe the true path to satanism lies in inflicting pain and misery.

I fight the urge to go looking for her. Before I do that, I need to think. I look again at the pager code.

187

Follow the sevens, where's the eighth? That again?

On my bed, I spread out all of the messages I've received, like the finds from a dig or exhibits in a murder investigation, laid out in a re-creation of the crime scene.

First, there was the message left in my wig tin. I pick up the scrap of notepaper and examine it. It looks like it has been torn from a counsel's notebook, a blue book full of foolscap paper commonly used by barristers to take notes during trials. The script is an elegant fountain-pen scrawl, which surely indicates that they weren't worried about their handwriting being an identifying piece of evidence.

Whoever left me this note must have had access to the robing room. The only people on that list would be the prosecution barristers, Malcolm, and the woman in the purple coat. But that note was more like a clue than a threat, albeit a cryptic one at best.

Why do I have to *follow* the Sevens but work out *where* the Eighth is? None of this makes sense.

Second, there was the note slipped under my door, apparently left by the woman in the purple coat. I still can't see her as a neo-Nazi, yet the note bore the Odal rune. Maybe she didn't know what was in it; perhaps she'd been asked to deliver it by someone else. But that doesn't explain why she ran away when I was calling after her. It doesn't seem like the sort of thing she'd do.

Third, there was another note, apparently also slipped under my door, the one containing the photograph of my daughter.

Who is behind those notes? Are they the same people who have taken my daughter's favorite toy from her, broken into my room, and left this pager? DC Parks's perfume betrayed her presence in my hotel room, poorly disguised by opening the window. Does that mean she has something to do with all of this?

But that makes even less sense than the woman in the purple coat having anything to do with it.

I look again at the Odal runes.

If the Odal rune is to be taken at face value, the person responsible for sending me these threats must be O87, which means there must be someone on the island who is O87.

Next I consider the pager. The number 187 continues to flash silently.

"What does any of this mean?" I ask the empty room.

There must be some sort of manual or guide or…something. A memory rises to the surface, like a fish wanting to be caught. The telephone booth had a list of pager codes.

I hold on to my daughter's toy, hoping that touching it will stir something.

How can looking at a stupid pack of cigarettes prompt memories but not one of my daughter's toys?

I walk over to the window and look out at the sea. Moonlight dances on the jagged waves. In fact, it flashes, regular as a beeping pager. I look up and stare into the darkness of the night. The moon is hidden behind clouds. I wonder where the flashing light is coming from, as there's not a single celestial object in the sky. Only then does it occur to me that the light is artificial. I can't see its source, only the reflection on the rippled surface. I wonder, not for the first time, what lies on the other side of the island.

"Are you out there?"

If there's even a chance she is out there right now, scared, alone, wondering where her mummy is, then I am going to find her, no matter how futile the task.

The only clean clothes in my wardrobe are my court suits, so I don one of those and decide to make do. I push my wallet into the jacket pocket. It's a silly thought, but I feel closer to her when I've got her crayon sketch on my person. If only it could glow or start beeping when I get near to her.

Outside, the night is not as complete as I thought it would be. No longer a mass of pure navy, the sky is turning sulfur yellow, streaked with coal-black clouds that look like vapor trails. My breath curls in front of my face. It's so cold out here, made even more unbearable by the wind. It's incessant, bashing the island with gusts. I blow into my hands, hug my elbows, and carry on.

My first stop is the red telephone box. The poster of the wanted man shivers in the wind. On closer inspection, I read that his name is Charles Smyth. He's wanted for crimes of treason, but he escaped from prison before he could receive his death sentence. According to this poster, he's highly dangerous, and providing information about his whereabouts attracts a large award that is not quantified in monetary terms. Stan's graffiti obscures his face. My finger traces the rune, the same as on the notes I've received saying I'll never see her again. Are these the people who have my daughter? It doesn't bear thinking about. I need to find her. First, I decide to work out what the 187 message means, in case it's a clue.

Inside the booth, I locate the list of pager codes and read from the list.

153: I hate you

178: I'll call you back later

180: Yesterday

183: I'm busy

My finger runs down the page, looking for the right code.

187: You're dead

CHAPTER FOURTEEN

WERE I NOT WANTED for Pat's murder, now would definitely be a good time to call the police. But they won't help me, and even if I called them, I'll only get that same interference, as though someone is listening in on the call.

I'm on my own.

I leave the telephone box and look out at the island, barely visible in the half light, with whatever isn't obscured by darkness masked by thick tendrils of mist.

The fog pools in the cove, but I know some basic geography of the town from last evening's wanderings. The road down to the bay is the main artery, connecting the harbor with the huddle of municipal buildings that sit atop the hill, including the court and police station.

The high street, on the other hand, branches off at a right angle, running parallel to the coast. Other streets fork off, some forming neat rows, others more haphazard. I will have to wait for it to get lighter or for the fog to clear before I can begin to explore the more remote parts of the island.

I walk over and inspect one of the local government buildings, which has a sign next to it. It's hard to read the words in this strange mustard-tinged darkness. I can just about make out Assumption Island British Overseas Territory, followed by some indecipherable coordinates.

I look out at the main town falling away in front of me, as though it's about to slide into the sea.

There can't be more than four or five hundred people living on this island, maybe even fewer. I wonder what brought them here to this weird outpost of British life in the middle of the North Atlantic. What reasons do people have for living in a British Overseas Territory other than for work on some government program, which, for reasons of national security or geographic necessity, needs to be offshore? And what is this island's purpose, if any? Are all of these people civil servants here temporarily for work, or have previous generations settled and made a way of life in this isolated corner of the world?

I push these thoughts to one side and focus on my task: finding my daughter. As I set off, looking for the sort of place where she might be held, the futility of the situation is already creeping up on me.

To begin with, I start walking down toward the harbor. Though it's unlikely I'll find her there, the best I can do right now is gather information. The more data I have about this island, the better placed I'll be to work out where she might be.

I spend what feels like two hours wandering the streets with no other purpose than to be out here doing something, no matter how silly, how unlikely it is I'll achieve anything. As long as I'm doing something, the panicky feelings about my daughter can be kept at bay. I inspect every street, look down side passages, all the while drawing a map in my head. The houses are mostly terraced, with steep gables and wooden siding of various colors: green, black, terra-cotta. Union Jacks fly from some of the homes and businesses, never still, always sailing in the wind. There are shops for fishing, two grocers, and one handyman store, all on the high street. A recurring motif is the poster of Charles Smyth, some of them disfigured by Odal runes, others all the more menacing for showing his face. The further out I go, the sparser the homes become. I'm no longer walking down streets but dirt tracks toward farms. After this long period of walking around in some sort of trance, I stop to look up.

The sky darkens. The nicotine stain has been replaced by a deep, uniform turquoise. The fog has lifted. I've walked almost every residential street of this infernal place.

Two things strike me. First, there are no playgrounds. Second, there is no school on the island. What do the children do? The civil servants who live here must have somewhere to send their children during the day.

It's only in stopping that I realize how cold I am. Though I've been walking around, I've been leaking body heat, my temperature dropping. The tips of my fingers are a nasty shade of purple, and I can't feel my nose. My feet are clumsy with cold.

But I can't give up yet. I need to know more, need to know where she is.

The sky brightens just as quickly as it went dark, the deep turquoise draining from the sky like water through cupped hands.

I can see more of the island now. Gray sheep and black-paneled cottages with white crosses for windows pepper the bleak hills. Apart from the harbor, everywhere seems hemmed in by steep cliffs. I wonder where Pat's car went off the edge, where he fell to his death.

Nestled in a valley about a mile away is a large concrete facility. It's a blight on the otherwise bucolic—albeit bare—landscape. Is that the prison? The one Charles Smyth escaped from? How big a prison does an island this small need? There are probably more cells in that prison than there are people on the island. This is another mystery I decide to shelve for the time being. I'm sure I'll find it more fascinating once I know that my daughter is safe.

Now that dawn is on the verge of breaking, I can see my surroundings more clearly, including the sea. Miles and miles of uniform steel-gray water dominate the panorama.

I'm drawn toward it again, as though it calls to me. It's both my prison and my means of escape. When I get down into the sheltered cove, I get some relief from the wind. I find a path that leads up the side of the headland, away from the court and toward the far end of the island, which seems more remote. The path is steep and muddy, dotted with stones. I begin to climb. It's a strange feeling to be so out of breath while my fingers are still ice-bitten. The cold burns my windpipe while I gulp the freezing air. The numbness in my feet doesn't help with my dexterity, and I trip a couple of times, my hands reaching out for the rocks to save my suit.

When I get to the top, I realize that on the other side of the headland is another small bay. The inlet that leads into the harbor is a deep V shape, while the one in front of me is just a pebble beach with a gentler C-shaped curve. The tide is out, and I suspect this beach would be underwater at full tide.

I hear a strange chanting sound carried across the wind.

I look behind me at the town. I can't see the steeples of any churches, and anyway now would be a very strange time of day for a Christian ceremony to be taking place. The chanting is coming from below. I move closer to the beach. There are several paths in different directions, one of them going down and another going right out toward the tip of the headland. I follow that one, hoping it will give me the best view.

Once I'm out as far as I can safely go, I crouch in the middle of some rocks, one side providing shelter from the wind, the other hiding me from the view of whoever is making the chanting noise.

In the middle of the beach, there is a cave. Firelight dances on the inside wall. I look closer at the beach, just visible in these moments before the sun breaks over the horizon. Drawn in the sand is a large Odal rune. There are other things. Red swastika-bearing flags are held down by pebbles, and candles have been placed in circular patterns. The chanting appears to be coming from inside the cave. It seems I got here just in time to watch two candle-bearing cloaked figures disappear into its mouth, toward the fire.

"What the fuck?" I mutter to myself.

Are these the same people who've been sending me messages bearing runes? Do they have my daughter?

Horrible images arrive in my mind uninvited. Ritual sacrifice, satanic abuse...

I shake my head. This is too surreal, too bizarre for words.

But something is going on. I need to find out what it is. I go to stand up when I catch something in my peripheral vision. Someone is coming.

Walking toward me, his face a storm, is DS Grant.

Close enough to whisper, he says, "What the hell do you think you're doing?"

I point at the beach. "There's something going on," I say, "down there."

"I've had complaints. People have rung in with reports of some woman walking the streets in the middle of the night, looking in everyone's houses, in their windows. Why? What are you doing?"

I scour his face. Can I trust him? I want to tell someone about my daughter, that she might be down there with those awful, dangerous people, but with everything that's happened, what with my arrest, I don't know whether I can trust the police.

"Couldn't sleep," I say, my eyes returning to the beach. "Anyway, aren't you going to do something about this?" I point to the Odal rune scoured into the sand.

"I can't."

"Why not? Isn't it your job to police the island?"

"It's…more complicated than that—" He stops himself. He was going to say something, going to divulge more. "Look, we can't talk here, but I need to speak to you, urgently."

"No, I need to go down there," I say and make as though to leave.

He grabs my arm. "Don't." He releases his grip. "Don't make me do this, but if you try to go down there, I will have to arrest you, and I'll put you in a cell for the rest of the day."

"You can't do that. I won't be able to represent my client."

He shrugs.

"You'll be perverting the course of justice."

"Please, come with me." His face looks sincere, but it's still hard to trust him.

I look down at the cave. She's probably not down there—that was just my imagination running away with me—and I want to know what DS Grant has to say. There's an abandoned sheep croft not far from the headland. I gesture toward it. "What about over there?"

DS Grant checks over both shoulders and his eyes scan our surrounds. The message he gave me on the phone still rings in my ears.

They're watching you.

Who? Who is watching us?

DS Grant makes me go first, alone.

Inside the croft, the roof has collapsed and only the walls remain. I perch on a piece of rubble, careful to find a place not covered in sheep poo.

DS Grant arrives a short while later. "What on earth do you think you're doing, wandering around on your own in the middle of the night?"

"I told you; I couldn't sleep."

"Don't you think it's a bit stupid, when your silk is killed the week before the trial, for you to go wandering around in the dark on your own?"

"What are you saying? Am I in danger?"

DS Grant doesn't say anything, just paces back and forth.

"Do you think Pat was killed because of Eades? Because of the trial? Why did you arrest me if you know someone else is responsible?"

"I never said I knew."

"But you think—"

"What I think is irrelevant. The truth is, Miss Dalton, that there are other people who are very interested in you."

"Like your Rottweiler."

"Who?"

"DC Parks."

DS Grant takes a measured breath. "Not. My. Rottweiler."

"Whose is she, then?"

"She's Special Branch."

"Why is she interested in me?"

"You tell me, Miss Dalton; you tell me."

Only his eyes seem to move. They bore deeper into me. For one insane moment I wish he'd find whatever he's looking for. Perhaps then he could share his findings with me, and I'd know once and for all who I am.

"Who's watching me?" I ask, my voice rising. "I know it was you on the phone last night. I know you're the one who warned me. I recognize your voice—"

"Quiet," he says in an angry whisper. "You never know who is listening on this island."

"What does that mean?"

He rakes his fingers through his hair. "It's hard to explain, but this island... It's... I mean, you must know, working up in the court."

"Let's pretend," I say, choosing my words carefully. "Let's pretend I know nothing about this island, don't know why there's a prison on it, or why there's a court. Tell me about it as though I'm an alien who was beamed down or someone who was born yesterday."

"Why?"

"Just go with me on this," I say. His eyes widen with surprise, but there's a trace of recognition, as though he's come across this before.

"OK," he says. "A few years ago, the government decided to solve the problem of having foreign criminals tried and imprisoned in British courts and incarcerated in British prisons. Their solution was to offshore foreign criminals, sending them to an overseas territory to be tried for their crimes. Not just foreign criminals, but domestic terrorists. They're shipped over here to wait on remand; then they're tried here, and if they're convicted, they're imprisoned here."

"The locals aren't happy about it," I say, remembering the barman at the Golden Cross.

"So long as the prisoners don't get loose, I'm sure they're glad of a boost to the economy. There's a reason there's only one hotel on the island."

"But, why have prisoners *here*?"

"Don't you know? It was all over the papers..."

"Humor me. Why would a government want to offshore foreign criminals, and—what was it?"

"Domestic terrorists."

"Yes. Why? Isn't it more expensive to do it over here?"

"It is, but it's worth it for the optics. The public hates the idea of people from abroad coming to Britain, benefiting from our NHS, our welfare system, and then betraying that trust by committing crimes, no matter how petty, no matter the mitigating circumstances. Prison, in those circumstances, isn't enough for some people. So, the government decided to offshore them as an extra punishment."

The UK has an island dedicated to imprisoning foreign nationals? Something about this strikes me as odd. My experience of the world is of an unsympathetic place where differences are rooted out and punished, but for the UK to treat foreign criminals as the same as terrorists seems particularly warped.

"Why domestic terrorists as well?"

"So they could include the IRA in the scheme."

"Christ."

"I know."

"What a way to foster Anglo-Irish relations."

"It's not helped."

"What, so John Major's government did this?"

DS Grant looks confused. More than that, he looks worried. "No."

"John Major isn't prime minister?"

"No… Don't you get out much?"

"Sorry, my head's just a bit… Jet lag."

I can tell he's not convinced. He's looking at me harder now.

I'm too busy turning this new piece of information over. It was the first question I asked myself to test my sanity: who is the prime minister? It looks like I can't even get that right. Perhaps my general knowledge isn't as intact as I thought it was.

"So, this policy, was it ever intended to cover people like Eades?"

"Not really. He'll be the first non-Irish white terrorist to be imprisoned here, if he gets convicted."

"That backfired."

"Sort of."

"What do you mean?"

"There are people high up who would be very happy to see Eades convicted."

"That's odd. It sounds like they'd get on."

Wind whistles through the holes in the croft's masonry.

I look back toward the beach. The chanting has died away now. "Why aren't you doing anything about that?"

"It's not within my jurisdiction."

"It's happening on your island."

"O87 activity is DC Parks's domain, not mine."

"Is that why she's here?"

"That and the trial. She came a few months ago. We had an escaped prisoner."

"Charles Smyth?"

"Yes."

"I bet she wasn't happy about him getting out."

"You can say that again. It's not good for Special Branch's image for there to be a Nazi running loose on an island stuffed with government secrets."

"Well, let's call her. She could go down there now and break up their little ritual. Maybe Smyth's down there right now."

"They're not real O87."

"They've got swastikas."

"Those guys are O87 light. They just enjoy the ritualistic bullshit and saying horrible stuff about immigrants."

"I can't believe you're apologizing for—"

"I'm not. I'm just stating facts. Those guys down there are not the real danger... Look, I need to go. I just came here to warn you. It's not safe to be wandering around at night. Especially until we know who killed Pat."

"Why did you let them arrest me if you don't think I'm guilty?"

"Because you went missing. We couldn't find you all weekend. Where did you go?"

If only I knew. "I don't know. I'm sorry."

"Is there anything going on that you're not telling me?"

"No." My answer is too quick, and DS Grant picks up on it. He regards me with something between pity and frustration. "I wish you'd tell me the truth. I know there's more you're not telling me."

"You're one to talk."

"It's complicated."

"I thought you were on my side."

"I am. You're making me reconsider." He turns to leave. "Watch how you go, Miss Dalton," he says kindly. It doesn't make it any less threatening.

———

I return to the tip of the headland to look down at the cave. The tide has crept in, covering most of the beach. The flags have disappeared, and flames are no longer licking the mouth of the cave.

I make my way back toward the hotel. The sun has risen fully now, and I can already tell that today is going to be clearer. As I'm walking along the high street, I notice a woman opening the shutters on her shop. I see something that makes me stop and stare.

A purple trench coat. So brightly purple, it stands out against the drabness of the high street. It sits in the bay window of a secondhand shop.

I approach the woman.

"Hi," I say.

"Good morning," she says, looking annoyed that I've disturbed her. She retreats into the shop, a slight limp slowing her progress.

I follow her inside, and the bell chimes. She turns to see that I've come in and frowns at me. It's strange, almost as though she doesn't want me to buy anything.

"Good morning," I say. "This coat, the one in the window. Could I ask you about it?"

A look of annoyance passes over the shop owner's face. "Go on."

"Can I ask whose it was? Do you have a record of the sale?"

"Who are you, the police?"

"No, I'm just a friend of the previous owner, and I know that she regrets selling it. I thought I'd buy it back for her as a present, but I wanted to make sure it was this exact one."

If she buys my story, it will be a miracle. I don't think she does, but she's sniffed the opportunity to make money so goes into the back room before coming out with a ledger.

"Delia Lewis," says the shop owner.

"Could I just ask when she sold it?"

"Don't you know—"

"I do, but I just want to make sure."

The woman eyes me suspiciously, so I pull out a ten-pound note to prove I'm serious about buying the coat.

Her quick eyes dart to my wallet and then back at the ledger. "1st April 1993."

"Gosh," I say. "Three years ago. Has it been that long?"

No longer willing to put up with my bullshit, the shop owner holds out her hand and I part with the note.

"Thank you," I say, but the shop owner returns no niceties.

"Can I ask one more thing?"

She folds her arms as though to say "*Make it quick.*"

I pull out the pink horse with the purple mane from my pocket. "Do you recognize this? I'm wondering if it was sold here."

She picks it up and looks at it. "We don't sell stuff like that here."

"What do you mean?"

"This isn't a good place for children."

"What?"

She starts moving toward me, ushering me out of the shop.

I leave, feeling harassed. Once outside I stop and think. What did she mean, "This isn't a good place for children"? But then I remember that there are no parks, no toys, no schools. This isn't a place for children at all.

How did someone get hold of a child's toy to send it to me? If there are no children on the island, this horse must belong to my daughter. If they have this toy, she must be here.

I need to find her, but the message they delivered to me echoes in my mind. *Get him off or you'll never see her again.*

For now, until I have more clues as to where they might be keeping her, the best I can do is ensure Eades's acquittal.

I need to continue preparing my cross-examination.

I pull on the coat as I walk away from the secondhand shop. The lining is made of silk, and I settle into it like a second skin. I love it in spite of myself. The wind on the island is so constant and seems to go through my every bone, so I'm grateful for the extra layer.

I thrust my hands into the pockets, and my right hand brushes a piece of paper. When I pull it out, I see that it's written on notepaper. The same notepaper as the *Where's the Eighth? Follow the Sevens* message. The handwriting is the same. This coat must have belonged to the woman from the robing room, or Delia Lewis, if the shop owner's ledger is to be believed. And she must have been the one to leave the note in my wig tin.

Written on this piece of paper are the words

I am not a number.

I turn it over to see if there's anything else.

Yes, you are.

Why doesn't she ever leave me a proper clue, not something so cryptic? *But she did.*

A little voice tells me. Yesterday, she left the book open to the exact page I needed. And she's delivered at least one of the Odal rune notes.

As I walk along the high street, I see another poster bearing Charles Smyth's

face pasted onto the brick wall between two shops. I think I can see some graffiti beneath the poster.

When I pull at the corner of the poster, it comes away and is carried off by
the wind. The Odal rune is visible beneath remnants of paper.

CHAPTER FIFTEEN

I APPROACH THE COURT building having picked up my files from the hotel. The weak morning sunlight is barely able to warm the expanse of tarmac between me and the court steps.

The courthouse itself is an impressive Edwardian building made of white stone, which glows flaxen in the sun. The entrance door is propped up by Greek-style columns, and rising above the main building are two stone turrets with domed tops.

It's a building that intimates power. I wonder at the lengths taken to make it so intimidating. No one who comes here to be tried for their crimes will enter through the front door.

Adjacent is the police station. It reminds me of last night's events and the accusation that hangs over my head. The proximity of the two places draws together the twin pressures resting on my shoulders: ensure Eades's acquittal, and somehow, in the time available to me, work out how to prove my own innocence.

I look up at the wooden front door, ornate and dark. Is it my fate to be tried in this building and never leave, never return a toy horse to a girl who misses it dearly? I shudder and tears bubble at the back of my throat. The brisk sea breeze continues to whip my hair and cheeks as I climb the steps.

As I open the door, I almost collide with a large man. My main impression is of a malodorous rugby player gone to seed. I step back and realize my almost-collision was with the scruffy male reporter who occupies the press bench. He grunts and pushes past me, cigarette in hand, clearly desperate to feed his nicotine habit.

"Charming," I say to his back.

"You're welcome," he answers with unfaltering sarcasm. His bonhomie disappears as quickly as it arrived as he says, "Some of us are taking this seriously."

I'm about to say "What do you mean?" but the door closes, putting an end to the conversation.

It's barely warmer inside the building than out. I head for the library. Gray light is just starting to pour through the sash windows.

I find a seat closest to a dusty cast-iron radiator, sure to burn anyone who would touch it but failing to heat anyone outside a three-foot radius.

I lug the cardboard box of box files over to the table and empty them onto it, separating them out. I turn up Dr. Sheridan's report.

Appendix 2

Theosophy and the Order of Eights and Sevens

Theosophy derives from the Greek term θεοσοφία (theosophia), meaning "divine wisdom." The theosophical movement experienced a renaissance in the nineteenth century, courtesy of Helena Blavatsky and others. They founded the Theosophical Society, which triggered the occultist movement in the late Victorian era. Many prominent occultists were influenced by Blavatsky's writings, perhaps most famously the members of the Hermetic Order of the Golden Dawn, whose members included Bram Stoker, author of *Dracula*; Irish poet W. B. Yeats, whose poem "The Second Coming" is packed with occultist imagery; and, most famously—or infamously—Aleister Crowley, "the wickedest man in the world," who established the Abbey of Thelema.

One of the key tenets of theosophical belief surrounds memories and how they are stored. According to Madame Blavatsky, memories are stored in "Akashic records," sometimes described as "the memory of nature": the subtle matter composing different planes of the cosmos, recording impressions of everything that happens on the terrestrial plane. She wrote:

"The records of past events, of every minutest action, and of passing thoughts, in fact, are really impressed on the imperishable waves of the astral light around us and everywhere, not in the brain alone; and these mental pictures, images, and sounds pass from these waves via the consciousness of the personal Ego or Mind (the lower Manas) whose grosser essence is *astral*, into the 'cerebral reflectors,' so to say, of our brain, whence they are delivered by the psychic to the sensuous consciousness. This at every moment of the day, and even during sleep."

The report goes into greater detail about how the occult movement came to influence the far right, or rather was used by fascists to prop up their hateful ideologies. I continue reading it until I come across a name I recognize in Appendix 3: The History of the Far Right in Britain.

In the postwar years, after Oswald Mosley fell out of favor and failed in his election campaigns to gain any traction for the British Union of Fascists (later the British Union), a strand of this belief was passed down, eventually headed by Colin Jordan, who also led the National Socialist Movement, an organization responsible for flying Nazi flags in Trafalgar Square, harassing, assaulting, and intimidating the Jewish community, and burning their synagogues. Another strand was headed by John Tyndall, who led the Nationalist movement. These groups both had strong Nazi undercurrents. Colin Jordan and John Tyndall fell out over a woman, namely Françoise Dior, who came to

England with the express wish to marry a top British Nazi. Perhaps more effective than any government campaign to break up these fascist movements, she played the two men against each other, causing a rift before eventually marrying Colin Jordan.

A third, more left-of-field strand was headed by an actual Nazi, Carl Schmidt, who, in an attempt to be accepted by British Nazis, renamed himself Charles Smyth. He was responsible for incorporating theosophical elements into the far-right movement, enticing people with its mystical overtones. Following his incarceration in 1973 for plotting to overthrow the queen, a new voice emerged on the scene. That of Simon Cox, whose writings went on to be the foundation of the Order of Eights and Sevens.

It is worth noting that electorally the far right have signally failed to gain traction. However, where they are most influential is in the underground, the grassroots of white supremacist thought, quashing debate about colonialism, sowing false tales about politically correct religious festivals, and challenging those not willing to bear the Union Jack for lack of patriotism.

I rub my eyes. Only having had three hours' sleep is starting to catch up with me, and the warmth of the radiator washes over me. My eyes droop. The words in front of me swim, and I try to battle it, keep reading. This is important.

CHAPTER SIXTEEN

ONCE THE TENT WAS up, Fenriz and Coyote made a fire. It was getting dark now. It was only half past three, but the winter days were being slowly stifled by the bitter nights.

They stalked through a nearby coppice, collecting sticks for the fire. Nearly all of them were wet.

Coyote's knife glinted in the moonlight as he sawed at the twigs and the sticks on the trees, away from the mulch of the woodland floor. Fenriz kept an eye on the knife. But Coyote always seemed to be aware of his gaze, because every time Fenriz shot a sideways glance at the blade, Coyote would turn and smile at him. And his smile was not something that warmed Fenriz's cockles. Coyote had filed down his incisors so that they were much shorter than his canines, and filed his canines into points, so that his mouth took the same shape as his namesake when he smiled.

When they'd collected enough twigs, they returned to the tent and stripped away the bark and wet wood from what they'd collected, then started a small fire with the wet offcuts. The smoke billowed and the smell was acrid.

"Won't people see the fire?" asked Fenriz.

"Only those who want to see will see," answered Coyote, who was still stripping firewood with his knife, even though the work had been done.

Then Coyote used the small fire to light the drier kindling, which blazed and warmed, the crackling sound comforting. The flickering flame highlighted Coyote's blade, which was whittling his piece of wood into a stake. Fenriz daren't ask what it was for.

"Tomorrow, we'll learn how to swim," said Coyote.

Fenriz shivered at the thought of dipping into the ice-cold water. Even if he could float, surely the cold alone would kill him. He looked again at the stake Coyote was whittling.

Fenriz struggled to sleep that night, despite it being deathly quiet. All he could hear were the sounds of Coyote breathing and the dying embers of the fire crackling.

Ascension was all about overcoming struggle, pushing his body to its limit. Perhaps surviving on less sleep would help him achieve that goal, make this long weekend more intense than it otherwise might be.

It was impossible to sleep. Fenriz had to check something. He couldn't stop thinking about what Coyote had in mind for the stake, why he was so cagey about Fenriz looking in the bag. So Fenriz let out a loud cough, pretended to hack away as though he'd woken up with a dry throat.

Coyote's breathing didn't falter. Fenriz looked at his face. His eyelids were flickering.

Fenriz pushed himself up onto his elbows and then to his feet. Being careful with where he was putting them, he lifted one leg over the sleeping bag that cocooned Coyote and felt around for the bag. There were lots of bags in the tent, some of them containing rations; others were empty, ready for the tent and remaining supplies to be packed back into them. But then he felt a bag that was still full.

His balance was faltering now. It was like he was playing that game he played as a child—the one with the plastic mats and the different-colored dots. Twister, that was it. He was right foot red, left foot yellow, right hand feeling around somewhere in the region of green.

The bag was zipped shut. He fumbled for the slider body and pulled on the tab. With each click of a tooth, Fenriz watched Coyote's eyes. They were still flickering.

When the zip was open, he rummaged around inside until his hands felt the PVC nylon mix of the armbands. But something was wrong with them. They didn't feel puffy and full of air. There was something dense inside.

He looked back at Coyote. His eyes were shut.

Fenriz went back to feeling the armbands. They were full of foam, and every now and then he felt something hard, like a rock.

Wait, there was something he'd missed. Something important.

Eyes shut.

He looked back down at Coyote's face. His eyes flicked open. The whites glinted, even though it was dark. The thing about the pitch-black is that your eyes are remarkably good at adjusting, and something as white as a coyote's eyes will stand out.

"Do you want the surprise sooner?" asked Coyote.

There was a hand on Fenriz's throat, and then there was another on his arm, and before he knew it, he was face down in the tent.

Searing pain split his skull in two. Everything went black.

CHAPTER SEVENTEEN

"MISS DALTON, THE COURT is waiting for you."

There's a knocking sound. Incessant.

My eyes are heavy. I open them—just for a peek. Over the top of my pillowed arms, I see the world tilted at ninety degrees. Through one half-shut lid, I see Malcolm on the other side of the room. His outline is blurred. I feel insolent, like a teenager being woken by a parent. *The court is always fucking waiting for me. Give me a break.*

I close my eyes again, ceding to the nectar of slumber. There's a twang in my neck from where I've twisted my head, and my cheek feels uncomfortable after resting on the leather.

"Miss Dalton, the trial is about to begin."

He walks toward me. I come around slowly, groggily.

What does he mean, "trial"? Then I remember. I'm a barrister. I'm in the middle of a trial. I'm defending an alleged terrorist. My daughter is in danger. My client must be acquitted if I'm to see her again.

It's yesterday's learning curve all over again but experienced in half a second.

I gather together my notes and files, my half-prepared cross-examination of Dr. Sheridan, and go as though to leave.

"Robes?"

I look down. I'm still in my suit, having drifted off to sleep before I could don my wig and gown.

"Shit."

Malcolm's got them. I didn't see him holding them before. But he must have been, because now he proffers a navy-blue bag that has my initials embroidered on it. I pull open the top of the drawstring and empty the contents onto the floor, scrabbling around for the tin. I pop it open and grab my collarette and wig.

I'm still shoving my right arm into the gown as I'm leaving the library, files wedged under one arm, my notebook tucked under my chin, and my pockets filled with anything I couldn't fit anywhere else.

Beep-beep.

"What's that?" asks Malcolm.

It's the bloody pager again.

"Er..." I try to think of a story less elaborate and far-fetched than the truth. "I set an alarm, but I don't know how to switch it off."

"Even a stopped clock tells the right time twice a day," he says.

What's he going on about? "Yeah, thanks for that," I say, searching for the pager. "Wait a sec." I drop everything on the floor and search through my belongings until I find the pager. I'm careful to look at it with my back to Malcolm, shielding the pager from his view. It flashes with the same number as before: 187. Next to it is my daughter's toy horse. My fingers brush the nylon mane.

"What time is it?" I ask him.

"Ten past."

"Shit," I say.

As Malcolm leads me along the corridor, I prepare myself for the task ahead. *Get him off or you'll never see her again.*

She's depending on me. I must get this right.

If I can pummel Dr. Sheridan in cross-examination, the path ahead will clear.

I look across at Malcolm, who is comfortably mute and seems to be happy to let me think in silence. A rush of gratitude swells in my chest, chased by a wave of guilt. I haven't thanked him for waking me yet. What could have happened if I'd slept longer doesn't bear thinking about. I'm always so rude to Malcolm.

He's an odd fish, though, with his funny little phrases.

As we're crossing the main hall, I decide to ask him something. "What did you mean by what you said to me yesterday?"

"What was that?" His feigned innocence does nothing to convince me. He shoulders open the double doors.

"You said something about water, water, everywhere."

"From 'The Rime of the Ancient Mariner.' It's just a silly little saying."

"What made you think of it yesterday?"

Malcolm averts his gaze. "It's an old adage that us islanders use to describe our predicament."

We stop at the bottom of the staircase that leads down to the courtroom.

"Thank you," I say to Malcolm. "Waking me up was beyond the call of duty and I'm really grateful."

Malcolm smiles without acknowledging the thanks. He disappears into a secret passage. Perhaps his silence is his way of getting back at me for my bad manners.

———————

When I finally step into the courtroom, everyone turns to look at me. I pat my hair self-consciously, thanking God for wigs.

The judge is at the bench, waiting for me.

"My lord, I must apologize."

He raises a hand to silence me. "I don't want to waste any more time." He turns to Malcolm. "Bring the jury in."

As I walk into the well of the court, I feel a pair of eyes on me. Instinctively, I know they belong to DC Parks. Her expression is difficult to decipher.

I ignore her and position myself in counsel's row. My cheeks redden as the prosecution barristers turn to me, smug at their own punctuality, disapproving my lack of it. The empty seat in front of me seems to solidify, as though Pat left a black hole, all the denser for his absence.

The press bench still only has two people sitting in it: the redheaded woman and the rude man I nearly collided with earlier this morning.

The prosecution junior barrister leans across to speak to me. I run my tongue over my furry teeth, hoping he doesn't get close enough to smell my morning breath.

"Look, change of plan. We're changing the batting order."

"What?"

"Yeah, we were going to tell you but…" He tilts his palms to the ceiling.

I could kick the bench, but I suppress the frustration with a measured breath.

"We're calling the arresting officer first," he says.

I turn to look at Trevor. He doesn't scrunch up his face to smile at me this morning.

"I'm so sorry—" I say.

Trevor's already holding out a piece of paper: PC 6745 James Sharpe's statement. It's only one page long.

"Thank you," I say, already skimming it for what I'm looking for.

In witness statements (or MG11s in police talk), they put spoken words in all caps. I'm grateful for this, because the only interesting part of an arresting officer's statement is the reply made by the defendant after caution.

The caution is the bit that everyone knows—"You do not have to say anything…" That bit. The same words DS Grant said to me last night. Once the police have cautioned the suspect, what they say after that is fair game.

I search the page and look for the lines written in capital letters.

I DID IT. IT WAS ME. I ACTED ALONE.

I stand up. "My lord, before the jury comes in, I have a point of law to raise."

"Bit late now, isn't it?"

"I've only just been told that the batting order has changed."

The judge's face crumples, and he turns to Malcolm and mutters, "Take the jurors back to their room."

Malcolm nods and disappears into a corridor.

The judge, resembling a grumpy, wrinkled baby, looks to Paxton. "Is this right?"

"Yes, my lord, we're calling the arresting officer rather than the expert witness."

"What's your problem with the arrest?" asks the judge. The heat is back on me.

"There's an inadmissible confession in the arresting officer's statement that I want to exclude under section 72 of PACE." It all comes out in one breath, before someone interrupts me. Paxton never speaks like that. He luxuriates in the pauses. It's never occurred to him he might be interrupted.

"You tried to exclude evidence yesterday, Miss Dalton. Are you going to do this for every witness?"

"If every witness's statement contains inadmissible evidence, I'm duty-bound to, my lord."

The judge drags a hand down over his face, a corpse closing his own eyes. "Very well. How do you expect me to deal with this?"

The answer comes from nowhere. I don't really know what it means, but it trips off my tongue before I've had a chance to second-guess myself. "I propose a voir dire."

The judge turns to Paxton. "Best get your officer in the box, shall we?"

"Very well, my lord."

I give myself a mental pat on the back before reading the witness statement. Eades confessed before he was cautioned. There's little chance of words given voluntarily before the caution being excluded, but I have to try. If that confession gets anywhere near the jury, we're finished.

My daughter's smile tugs at the edges of my vision, and I have to physically shake my head to clear my mind. Focus and discipline are my best weapons now. Sentimentality has no place in justice's oak-paneled coffin.

I leave counsel's row to approach the dock. As usual, Eades pretends I'm not there.

I hold the witness statement up to him. "Did you say this?"

He stares ahead unblinking, his hollow black eyes as lifeless as ever.

"Did you say 'I did it. It was me. I acted alone'?"

Nothing.

"I need your instructions on this." He carries on ignoring me. I want to reach through the Perspex and throttle him. Sick bastard. He probably did say it. I give it one last go. "Look, if you don't give me instructions, I'll abandon the application to exclude this evidence and allow the confession to go before the jury."

Eades turns his head toward me slowly, as though his neck is powered by hydraulics. His eyes are still hollow and unseeing. But his lips, his pale, chapped lips, part into a dead-behind-the-eyes smile, revealing his yellow teeth.

I stifle the urge to cry out. His canines have been filed to sharp points, like vampire fangs.

I nod and leave the dock.

Once I'm sitting down on the uncomfortable fold-down bench topped only with a lumpy velvet cushion, I read the witness statement over, closely this time.

Before I'm at the bottom, PC Sharpe is taking his place in the witness box, and his oath is being taken. Paxton is on his feet.

"Please can you give your full name and collar number?"

"PC 6745 James Sharpe." Sharpe is upright in his dress uniform. He looks young but capable, like he came into the force to do good. There's still something slightly green about him. He's not yet been corrupted by the job. He's just a young man who wants to catch the bad guys.

"And you're based at Ystrad Mynach Police Station, is that correct?"

"That's right."

"Were you on duty on the 25th of May last year?"

"I was."

"Did you make any arrests on that day?"

"Just one." Sharpe's eyes flick to the dock.

"Who did you arrest?"

"The defendant."

"Name?"

"Jonathan Eades."

"Why did you arrest him?"

"He was suspected as being the man responsible for bombing Abbott House in Birmingham."

"Where did you arrest him?"

"At his home address. In Blackwood."

Paxton nods, pauses. "What time was that?"

"Seven minutes past nine. In the morning."

Paxton enjoys the next pause even more. "What happened when you attended at his address?"

"His mother opened the door first." Sharpe is speaking so quickly, he's tripping over the last word to get to the next, as though if he doesn't get this out of his system, it will eat him from inside like poison. "I said that I needed to speak to John—"

"More slowly please, Officer," chides Paxton, whose voice is loud and ringing.

"Sorry. I said that I needed to speak to John." He slows down, but it's forced, as though he could lose the reins at any time and his words will gallop off. "She said, 'He's not in any trouble, I hope?' I reiterated that I needed to speak to John. She goes off to get John. He comes down the stairs. I ask his mother to leave. I says to him, 'John—' No, sorry, I don't say that to him, because before I get the chance, before I can say anything to him, he says, 'I did it. It was me. I acted alone.'"

Paxton lets that hang in the air. It does. Like incense. It wafts around, and I see the judge's nostrils flicker.

"And what did you take that to mean?"

"Well, I took it to mean that he was responsible for blowing up the building."

"Why? Did he make any specific reference to the building?"

"No, but you've got to understand, it was all over the news. It was all anyone was talking about. That added to the fact we had a positive ID for him… What else could it be?"

"And what happened next?"

"I had backup waiting in the police vehicle around the corner. I asked them to come and assist me. Then I cautioned Eades, placed him in a Home Office–approved position while I cuffed him to the rear and arrested him. I then took him over to the police vehicle, where he was conveyed to Ystrad Mynach custody suite."

Again, I'm reminded of being shown the inside of a cell by DS Grant, how my possessions were detained, and I was interviewed and picked over and analyzed.

"Thank you, Officer. If you wait there, there may be some more questions for you."

When I take to my feet, I wobble. It's like my center of gravity has been shifted. I place both hands on the bench to keep steady. I like this position: hunched over, like an old crone, peering at the witness from beneath the hoods of my eyes.

Everyone is looking at me. But the pause doesn't feel as impressive as when Paxton does it. People shift in their seats. Perhaps they're thinking I'm having another moment. Yesterday, the observers were nameless, faceless people, but in twenty-four hours I've amassed enough enemies that half the courtroom is hanging on every question, hoping I'll fail. My ears burn, and I know that DC Parks's eyes are boring into the back of my skull, wishing she could pry it open and watch my secrets pour out for all to see.

"Officer," I say. My voice is wobbly. I try to take a surreptitious breath to calm my nerves. "Do you have a copy of your statement there?"

The officer casts around. Malcolm walks forward and hands it to him.

"Let's have a look at this statement. You say here that Eades said, 'I did it. It was me. I acted alone.'"

"That's right." PC Sharpe repositions himself, as though he's expecting an attack.

"Did he really say that?"

"Yes."

I leave another pause. People fidget. I can sense that Paxton's lip has curled into a snarl dripping with schadenfreude.

"You're sure about that?"

"Yes, I'm sure."

"OK," I say before pivoting. "There's nothing in your statement about what Mr. Eades looks like, is there?"

"No, but I can tell you, looking at him now, that is the man I arrested."

"I think you misunderstand me, PC Sharpe. Please try to just answer the question rather than anticipate what I'm getting at."

"Sorry."

"No physical description," I repeat. "Why's that?"

"Didn't think it was relevant." He shuffles from side to side. He's wary of me. Thinks I'm lulling him into a false sense of security with these crappy questions.

"Is that because you didn't think his appearance unique or striking enough to warrant a physical description?"

"I just didn't think it was relevant."

"But would you mention, for example, if the person you arrested had a swastika tattooed to their forehead?"

"Maybe."

"Why's that?"

"Because it would be something odd. Something that would stick."

"Something that would stick," I repeat. I glance up at the judge, who gives me a warning look. Repeating a witness's answer back to them is a courtroom faux pas. "So, we're agreed that if someone has something unique or striking about their physical appearance, you'd probably make a note of it in your statement?"

"Yeah, I suppose."

"So, dyed hair, body modifications, tattoos, piercings?"

"Maybe."

"When Mr. Eades said 'I did it. It was me. I acted alone,' did he open his mouth to say that?"

"He must have done."

"He wasn't a ventriloquist, throwing his voice without opening his lips?"

"No."

"And you saw nothing striking about his appearance?"

Sharpe looks uncertain. *Was there?* he thinks. We can see the question broadcast on his face. He knows I've got him on something. I wouldn't have led him down this garden path for no reason. "Er, no, I don't think so."

"And we're agreed if there was something unusual, you'd have said so."

"Maybe, maybe not."

"Hang on a second. You said earlier that you would. Why has that changed?"

"I've thought about it now, and maybe I wouldn't have thought it was relevant."

"What if the body modification was dangerous, like a large spiky piercing? Wouldn't you note it so the custody sergeant was aware of it?"

A pause and then a reluctant "Yes."

"And at the time you wrote your statement, you wouldn't have interviewed the suspect, would you?"

"No."

"So, you wouldn't know whether identification was an issue?"

"No, but…"

"And it's good practice, is it not, to record a description on the off-chance ID is disputed?"

"Er… It wasn't necessary in this case because he said it was him, that he did it…"

"PC Sharpe, if I could ask that you look over at the dock." I turn around and glare at Eades, imploring him to smile.

There's a sharp intake of breath.

"Did you notice, PC Sharpe, that Mr. Eades's teeth were sharpened when you arrested him?"

"They can't have been. Must have had it done since."

"In custody?"

"People do that sort of thing in prison," says PC Sharpe, shrugging.

"Well, let's have a look, shall we." I'm really gambling now. It could all fall down here. This is reckless, stupid, but I have to trust my client. He wouldn't have showed me his teeth if he didn't think this would take me somewhere.

"My lord, I'm just going to find a copy of the custody record to hand up to the officer."

I riffle through the piles of unused material—material generated in the course of an investigation that is not relied upon by the prosecution. There's so much of it with an investigation this size that I'm struggling to find the document.

There's a tap on my back. I turn to see that Trevor is holding a copy of the custody record out to me.

"*Thank you*," I mouth, feeling awkward.

He scrunches his nose, and I think he's pleased with me.

I look for Malcolm, and he hands up the custody record to PC Sharpe.

"Where in the custody record would we find information to assist with health and safety?"

The officer flicks to the second page. "Here."

"Read out what it says in that section, please."

"Warning: weapons. The DP has filed down his teeth, so they are sharp." His voice trails away toward the end of the sentence.

"Thank you, Officer. What does DP mean?"

"Detained person."

"So, you can confirm that when Mr. Eades was taken into custody, he had filed teeth, as we see today?"

"Yes."

"Why isn't it in your statement, then?"

"I don't know."

"It's because you're not telling the truth, isn't it? This confession is made up. At no point did Mr. Eades say 'It was me. I did it. I acted alone.'"

"I'm sure he said that."

"Well, Officer, you were sure that there were no striking physical features on Mr. Eades's face, isn't that right?"

"Yes."

"And we agree he opened his mouth to give this confession?"

"Yes."

"Thank you, Officer. No further questions."

CHAPTER EIGHTEEN

SO, A VOIR DIRE, as it turns out, is a trial within a trial. The judge hears evidence on a discreet point and decides whether the evidence should go before the jury.

Paxton objected to my application to exclude the confession, but he didn't throw his weight behind it. That didn't stop the judge from giving him a hard time, questioning how anyone who had heard that appalling evidence could expect a jury to hear it. There was no option but to exclude it.

The judge is so unhappy about it that we take an extended midmorning break, meaning we don't have to return to court for another half an hour. I can barely believe my luck as I stride out of court, buoyed by adrenaline and feeling lighter than I have in twenty-four hours.

There's a bottleneck as everyone leaves the courtroom.

A hand on my shoulder. That cloying vanilla scent.

"Your luck will run out," murmurs a voice in my ear. DC Parks nudges me with her shoulder as she barges past.

Trevor comes to my side but doesn't make any reference to what just happened. We walk through the corridors together in companionable silence. There's no fawning over my performance or showering of congratulations. I get the feeling that no matter what happens in this trial, Trevor will take it in stride. It's as though he's been eroded by the constant tide of change: the witnesses who don't turn up, the defendants who admit their guilt partway through their evidence, the miscarriages of justice… It's all reduced Trevor to a pebble of a man, incapable of getting too excited about one good performance. He knows it's not over yet.

He's the first to break the silence. "Who's the next witness?"

I pull the batting order out of my pocket. "If they carry on as if Sheridan gave evidence first, the friend from the Territorial Army."

Trevor nods. "Aye."

We stop at the top of the flight of stairs that has us looking down the long, tunnel-like corridor. Trevor turns to me. "I'll go down and see him, then."

"OK."

There's no point insisting otherwise, and frankly, I'm not put out about it.

In the corner of my eye, I see something moving. At the end of the corridor, a figure runs away before disappearing down the steps at the other end.

I glimpse the rippling of a purple coat. It's her.

She's gone as quickly as I see her, and I wonder if it's my mind playing tricks on me.

"Lila?"

"Mmm?"

"What are you looking at?"

"Did you see…? Nothing. It's nothing." I smile at him, and he nods, taking it in his stride, as Trevor always does.

But it wasn't nothing. Déjà vu, I think to myself. I pull out my copy of *Archbold* and make a blue ink mark in the top left-hand corner of the pastedown before tucking it back under my arm.

When we get to the main hall, he goes one way to the cells, and I go the other. As I'm walking toward the robing room, Malcolm approaches me.

I go to say "Thanks again for this morning," when he passes me a scrap of foolscap.

"Thanks—oh. What's this?"

Rather than answer my question, Malcolm gives me his enigmatic smile. "Did you sort that problem out with the beeper?"

"Er, yeah," I say, regarding him more closely now. He's uncanny, Malcolm, but I can't put my finger on what it is about him. "Technology, eh?"

I hope that will suffice as both a suitable conversation ender and a good imitation of small talk.

But Malcolm doesn't leave. He says, "I rather think scientists should be on *tap*, not on top, don't you?"

"Yeah... What?"

"Winston Churchill."

I use my trick of reaching, searching for the piece of information, but I know it will take too long to be able to continue the natural flow of conversation, so I smile and look down at the folded notepaper.

"From the jury?" I ask, but when I look up, I see that I've asked the question of an empty corridor. Malcolm's vanishing act is disconcerting, but then, he knows the side passages and has access to them all.

Aha! I remember who Winston Churchill is. I know when he was prime minister, and that he gave famous speeches. Smirking, as a child would for retaining such a tiny piece of knowledge, I retreat into an alcove and open up the note. Scribbled in fountain pen—smudged by the folded paper—are the words *Courtroom 9. I've got food.*

Courtroom 9 is just around the corner from 8.

This note is different from the others I've received; the lined paper is different, and the handwriting is almost illegible. I wonder who it is—DS Grant perhaps? With more information for me?

When I get there, there's candy-cane tape across the entrance and signs saying DANGER: DO NOT ENTER.

I think back to the note that's stuffed in my jacket pocket. The mention of food seems vaguely sinister now, and a phrase resurfaces from the depths of a childhood lived long ago.

Drink Me.

Choosing my poison, I decide to go in anyway.

"Who's there?"

The courtroom has been abandoned. There are traces of scaffolding and half-finished repair jobs. It smells of damp and decay.

I move aside a dust sheet and see a man sitting in the middle of the courtroom.

"Hello?" I say.

The man is bent over one of the benches that barristers and solicitors sit at. He twists around, mouth stuffed with food, and waves for me to come over. It's the rude reporter from earlier.

"No way. I'm not talking to you," I say. I go to turn away, but then I hear a strangled noise.

The reporter tries to call me, but his mouth is full. I wait for him to finish, and he swallows with difficulty.

"No, I don't want you to go on record," he says.

"I'm not speaking to the press—"

"I've got some stuff you might be interested in."

"I take instructions from my client, thanks."

"How's that going for you?"

I hesitate.

"Come on, I haven't got all day." He says this as though *I* asked *him* to meet. Perhaps that's what intrigues me.

I approach the row of benches and sit down.

He holds up a white paper parcel with smudges of grease staining the underside. "Say 'please,'" he says, deadpan.

"Er, please?"

He throws the packet at me, so I have to scrabble to catch it. I open it up to find a bacon sandwich. I look at him.

"I guessed you hadn't had breakfast, given your...appearance."

I run my fingers through my hair, a poor attempt at taming it.

He swallows a quarter of the sandwich whole and begins chewing eagerly, so I follow suit.

It's the strangest feeling to sit here with a total stranger, tucking into greasy food with nothing but the sounds of our munching to fill the space. It's the most comfortable I've felt in anyone's presence since my memories began (or restarted).

The sandwich is glorious. I don't know whether it's because I can't remember the last time I had a proper meal, or whether I'm tired, or whether I'm scared, but I feel as though I'm eating the fluffiest white bread ever made by human hands and the crispiest bacon.

My stomach has shrunk from hunger, and the waistband of my skirt strains uncomfortably.

When I've finished, the reporter passes me a filter coffee full of milk and sugar.

He watches me through one eye like a seagull, his head slightly tilted.

"I'm Dev, by the way. Devin Hanlon." He goes to shake my hand, then seems to think better of it. Instead, he wipes the grease on his trouser leg, not bothering to proffer it again.

"I'm Lila."

"Yeah, I gathered," he says.

"Why did you want to meet in here?"

"Because no one else will come in. It's closed." He waves at the door, as if I missed the Do Not Enter signs, then shrugs. "Asbestos or something."

"We shouldn't be in here!"

"Every house built in the last fifty years has had asbestos in it. It's not done me any harm." He gestures to his less-than-peak physical condition before balling his fist in front of his mouth to stifle a burp.

"Yeah, but that's the problem with asbestosis. You don't tend to know about it until it's too late." I cover my mouth and nose, as though this can protect me from the deadly dust.

"I'm sure they've risk-assessed it. Health and safety gone mad and all that."

"There are Do Not Enter signs on the door."

"So, you *can* read. Good; that will make things easier."

"Sorry, who the hell are you?"

Dev cracks a yellow-toothed smile and throws a magazine at me. And I mean that. He literally throws it at me.

"Editor of *Beacon*, Britain's leading anti-fascist magazine," I say, reading aloud.

"As I said before, I'm very impressed that you can read, but most adults your age have progressed to doing it in their head."

"You're an anti-fascist journalist," I say. "So, you *are* here to berate me for defending a neo-Nazi."

"I'm only after the truth." Dev reaches into the khaki messenger bag beside him and pulls out a tabloid newspaper. He spins it around on the bench with the tips of his fingers and then jabs at the headline. "That is who the press initially said was responsible for the Abbott House bombing."

The headline reads *Birmingham Bombing Thought to Be the Work of Radical Muslims*, and the article below quotes the percentages of Muslim migration to Birmingham over the last fifty years. I look at the name under the byline, Agatha Price.

"Who's Agatha Price?"

"The other journalist reporting on this trial." He mimes wavy hair in an impression of the redheaded woman who sits next to him on the press bench.

"And she jumped to that conclusion?"

"Agatha's the print version of a shock jock. Anything for a reaction." He looks into the middle distance for effect. "Of all the trials in all the shitty islands in all the world, she walks into mine."

"Do you live on this island, then?"

"No, I'm only here for this trial." He heaves a big sigh. "One of the biggest mass murders in the UK's history and there are only two hacks. I guess that was part of the thinking behind shipping this grubby little corner of justice over to Assumption. Less accountability if news outlets can't afford to keep paying for flights."

"But you can?"

"I run my own magazine, and this is important."

I look down at Agatha Price's article. It feels dirty. "As if she can just play up to people's fears like that."

"Sells papers, doesn't it? Plus, she had an angle."

"What was that?"

"There was someone else there on the day of the bombing who is supposed to have been the drop-car driver. They looked Middle Eastern."

"Is that why she didn't jump to the Irish conclusion?" I ask.

"Maybe. Or she could just be a good old-fashioned racist. I prefer those. Know where you stand, don't you?" He looks at me expectantly, waiting for me to agree.

"What does the editor of an anti-fascist magazine want to say to the barrister defending a neo-Nazi terrorist?"

"Christ, I thought you were supposed to be defending the poor sod."

"I just got his confession excluded!"

"Ah, yes, 'the confession.'" Dev makes air quotes with his fingers.

"What's with the…?" I mime the quotation marks.

"Don't you have to be clever to be a lawyer?" A beat. "Clearly not. Who just comes out with that when the police come knocking? No, he'd had that lined up for hours, would have been waiting for it. As soon as the police came, he'd been told to take sole responsibility."

"By who?"

"It's 'whom,' but you are finally asking the right questions. That, I think, is the key to all of this." Dev waves at the abandoned courtroom.

"That's not the key to any of it. If he did it, whether or not motivated or assisted by anyone else, he's guilty."

"Remind me never to call you if ever I get into trouble."

The word *trouble* triggers that familiar knot I get in my stomach whenever I remember that I'm a suspect in a murder case.

"I'm doing my best with what I've got, but anyone can see he's banged to rights. He's on the CCTV, for Christ's sake."

"We'll come back to the CCTV." Dev raises a squat finger before raking it through his spare hair, which is white but looks yellow in contrast with his bacon complexion.

"Can you remind me why we're having this conversation? Why would an anti-fascist journalist want to help exculpate a man who kisses his Hitler poster before bed?"

"Are you trying to get him convicted? Is the prosecution paying you?"

I'm about to say "No!" but I stop myself in time, realizing he's taking the piss.

Dev fiddles with something in his pocket. He pulls out a cigarette and rolls it around in his fingers, considering me.

"Don't smoke that. There are enough health hazards what with the *asbestos*…"

He rolls his eyes and stuffs his cigarette into a random pocket. "I think there's a bigger story here. Much bigger than a lone nutter who hates foreigners."

I still don't see how this will provide Eades with a defense, but I'll let him finish this line of thought.

"Plus, I don't trust DC Parks. You know, the one with the Princess Di haircut?" Dev gestures toward his balding head.

My eyebrows rise against my will. "You know DC Parks?"

"Oh, yes. We go way back."

"How so?"

Dev swats my question away with a flat palm. "Never you mind. She plays dirty, and this looks like a case where someone has ripped up the rule book to get your boy potted. None of it makes sense. First, how did someone like Eades learn how to make bombs that could blow up a building?"

"They've got someone from the mining company he worked for coming to give evidence about how the bomb he used is made from the same material they use to blow up bits of the mountain."

"Yeah, but he wasn't on the demolition team. No, someone taught him how to do this."

I bite back my response; the fact that someone else is also guilty of a crime doesn't mean my client is innocent. Two wrongs and all that…

"It's too sophisticated. This was a timed bomb. So that's point number one." Dev holds up a finger to illustrate this. "Point number two is, where's the explosives expert? Where's yours, for that matter?"

"I don't know. My solicitor said there aren't any defense witnesses."

"We'll see what we can do about that—"

"When did this become a 'we' situa—"

"Point number three is our mystery chap," interrupts Dev. "Some say Middle Eastern, some say olive-skinned and Mediterranean. Point is, there are plenty of witnesses who say they saw another guy on that day. Where are those people?"

"All of that is great, but none of it really helps."

"It all helps."

"Not legally."

"Do I have to do everything for you? Think!" He jabs his temple with his stubby index finger. "The prosecution is hiding evidence—"

"We don't know that."

"That brings me on to the CCTV. Do you have a copy of the color tape?"

"No, I just brought a notepad and paper." I hold up my blue book.

"Do I have to do everything around here?" From his messenger bag, he pulls out a VHS.

"Where did you get that?"

Dev taps his nose. "Journalists' code of honor." He pushes down on the writing bench to heave his bulk onto his short legs.

I watch him go to the cobwebbed television stand in the corner of the room.

"If you think I'm coming over there..." calls Dev.

I go over to the TV, where Dev is crawling around on the floor, feeling for a plug socket.

"Don't mind me," he says. "I'll find it."

"I really don't think you should—"

There's a loud click as Dev sticks the plug in the wall, but no bang. He gets up and wipes his hands on his trousers before blowing at the screen, sending clouds of dust into the already musty air.

After he presses a few buttons on the tape recorder, the CCTV bursts into life.

Once we've finished watching it, Dev turns to me.

"What about that, then?"

I'm still staring at where the screen has gone blank. I've taken notes in my pad. I can't believe what I've just seen, and how I missed it when it was played in court.

"Right, so what are you going to do about it?" asks Dev.

"I could…" I think hard, turning my back on him so I can pace around better. It comes to me. "Make an abuse-of-process application?"

"That was exhausting. I'm going out for that ciggie, now."

"Wait! But none of this helps me with the next witness, the one from the TA, or Eades's old boss from the quarry."

"That's where I'm going now—to find the explosives expert you haven't bothered to get for yourselves." He shakes his head. "This is all about the bigger picture. Now that I've opened your mind, you should be able to find your own way through the rest." He stops to consider. "Actually, on the back of the conversation we've just had, I'd say you need a bit more help. Let's meet tonight."

I'm too offended to thank him.

The door swings shut, and Dev is gone, leaving behind thoughts and theories that swirl around like snow, clouding my vision, making it harder to see the "bigger picture" or whatever he called it.

I look at the pendulum clock housed in a wooden box on the wall, but it's long since been out of action.

Should I trust him? Dev seems like a mad conspiracy theorist more than anything.

Still on the writing bench are the papers he threw at me. The tabloid, his magazine, and a couple of other pamphlets. I pick up *Beacon* and riffle through it. Articles include "How Astrology Has Been Infiltrated by the Far Right: Why You Can No Longer Trust Mystic Meg, John Major, and the Secret State," and "Mind Disturbance, Dodgy Dealings in Surrey, and the National Front."

That settles it, then. Mad conspiracy theorist. He takes one grain of truth and runs wild with it. One article catches my eye, though, and I can't help but take a closer look.

VICTIM OF PHONE INTERFERENCE TARGETED IN PSY-OP.

I turn to the story and read the lede.

When Ken Duffy started hearing a crackling noise on his phone, he had no idea he was being targeted by a "psy-ops" operation courtesy of Special Branch, in which the government seeks to alter the victim's reality, leading to an irreversible decline in their mental health.

Utter nonsense, complete baloney. And then... And then there was the interference on my hotel-room phone. There was the unlawful arrest. The person who followed me, and the voice at the other end of the phone line: *They're watching you.*

I read on.

Since 1991, there has been a wealth of evidence that Ken Duffy (pictured)...

I pause to look at the picture of Ken Duffy. He stands in front of a village police station wearing a checked shirt, his arms crossed.

Has been monitored by Special Branch, that shady underbelly of the police who spy on trade unionists and acted as agent provocateurs during many of the strikes of the 1980s. More than that, this monitoring has been an attempt to bring him to a state where he doubts his own perception of reality.

Every landline and mobile device he uses has been intercepted. They want him to know that the interference is happening. That's the whole point. I think we can all agree that if the police wanted to hack your phone without you knowing, they would. The interception of his phone was used to harass him, particularly by ending calls whenever the person on the other end of the line seemed just about to get to "the point" of the call. When Ken tried to ring back, their phone would not be connected, meaning that the simplest of tasks such as changing energy providers became an arduous task involving multiple calls. He recounted to me the ordeal of canceling his TV subscription, something that took nearly a week. By the end, the hold music became like a hypnotic melody. Ken likened it to Chinese water torture. Enough to drive a person of reasonable firmness to suspect that they were going mad.

Then, things got worse. Ken was charged with murder and eventually convicted of manslaughter on spurious evidence. Officers lied in court.

"They beat and kicked my cell mate to death, not me. I am being persecuted for their..."

I stop reading, only skimming the remaining column. Dev goes on to expand on this factual account by using the evidence of Ken Duffy's harassment to mount a case that the Met was testing its psychological torture program, known colloquially as "the UK's MK Ultra," also known as "psy-ops."

I struggle to reconcile competing impulses, the first being the urge to scoff and write all of this off as conspiracy theorist bullshit, the second being fear. Pure, cold terror running through my veins and making my heart race. Perhaps the parallels between my experience and that of Ken Duffy are coincidental. Perhaps I'm seeing connections where there are none, but I leave the empty courtroom feeling unsettled.

CHAPTER NINETEEN

BY THE TIME I'M back in the courtroom, I find that I only have five minutes before the trial is due to recommence. No time to prepare my cross-examination and no instructions to guide my questions. I chastise myself for wasting time listening to Dev's conspiracy theories.

Ethically, I'm in a bind. Barristers can only act on instructions, and my only instructions are "I didn't do it."

Screw Dev for saying I'm being defeatist. This is just called being realistic.

Realism won't return me to my daughter, though, so I buckle up and try to harbor some of Dev's can-do attitude. My only move is to try to delay the next witness until Dev can speak to his forensic explosives engineer.

I approach Malcolm, who sits at a desk at the side of the courtroom.

"Have you got any copies of the CCTV?"

Again, no preamble, no "Hi, Malcolm. How are you?" I'm always so rude to Malcolm.

"Yes."

"Please could I play one of them on the TV?"

"Of course."

"Thanks."

I turn away from him and see Trevor in solicitor's row.

"Any instructions?" I ask when Trevor gets close enough for me to whisper.

"Said something about how he doesn't have to defend himself."

I stare at Trevor, at a loss. "But he does. Did you say that to him? He *does*. That's the whole…" I wave at the courtroom. I could scream. My future relationship with my daughter partly rests on the decisions of a psychopath.

"He doesn't think he's done anything wrong."

I'm still staring at him in disbelief. This isn't how it works. He can't just think something will be OK and it'll happen by magic.

Maybe Eades sees me as part of his game. But that's being a barrister, I suppose. You're not a mouthpiece as such, but you're still the conduit through which the client puts their case. And when you're representing murderers and abusers, you're bound to have some unpleasant stuff passing through.

How much of it gets left behind, I wonder?

Paxton's junior walks into the room, and I go over to speak to him.

"Hi. There was something I wanted to discuss with you and Alasdair if that's OK?"

"Go ahead."

"There's something wrong with the color CCTV."

He returns a quizzical look bordering on aloof.

"You know, the first one you played. There are parts missing."

"We've edited both tapes down to what we need, but the rest of it has been disclosed to you."

"No, it hasn't, I'm sorry. There's something missing from the footage."

God, I hope that's right. I didn't stop to check if there was any additional footage in the unused material. I just assumed we were looking at everything the prosecution had, because it would be strange to have a chunk missing from the middle without alerting the jury to this. It would be misleading by omission.

He rubs his temple with his fingers. "Leave it with me."

"Thanks."

I turn to Trevor and explain what I saw when I watched the footage over the midmorning break. I make it sound as though I watched it alone and remove any reference to Dev. I look over at the press bench. He's nowhere to be seen.

"Miss Dalton," says the prosecution junior. "Can you show us what you mean?"

"Of course."

I catch Malcolm's attention and explain that I want to look at the footage with the prosecution and ask him to request five more minutes from his lordship. He nods and disappears into the judge's chambers before returning and rolling the television set over to us.

"It's the first clip I want us to look at."

Malcolm feeds the VHS into the tape recorder. All over again, we see Eades approach the revolving doors and walk through.

I let everyone watch it one time uninterrupted. It looks as though he walks straight in.

Paxton looks bored. "And?"

I get out of counsel's row and stand next to the television set. "OK, watch again, but this time, watch the time in the top left-hand corner."

The time stamp is small, red, and heavily pixelated.

1995-05-23 15:25:12

It flickers and flashes as the tape starts playing, but I keep pointing at it. We watch the seconds go up. 12, 13, 14...and then, when we get to 15:25:19, the time jumps to 15:25:49.

"Thirty seconds," I say, as though Paxton is incapable of counting.

I look at him closely. He looks nonchalant, as though this is of no consequence. But it's forced. I can see that, which means that Dev was right. This footage has been tampered with, and the defense hasn't been sent the missing thirty seconds.

I look to Paxton's junior. "Am I going to find these thirty seconds in the unused material?"

He shrugs. "You tell me." Again, too indifferent.

"It's your duty to disclose any material that assists the defense case or undermines the prosecution case. What's in that missing thirty seconds and is it disclosable?"

Paxton's face turns a dangerous shade of puce. "What are you trying to say?"

"I'm not saying anything about either of you. It wasn't until I paid attention to the time stamp that I saw it was missing. The footage is so jerky anyway, it makes sense that you wouldn't notice it."

"Something wrong with the camera," sniffs Paxton.

"Can I have that as a formal admission?" I allow an edge to creep into my voice, a challenge.

Paxton taps on the desk with his fingers and looks away from me.

"If you can't give me an admission explaining why those thirty seconds are missing, then you need to disclose the missing thirty seconds."

"How dare you make these insinuations," says Paxton.

"I'm sure you made the same innocent mistake as me. We're only human after all."

The judge walks back in while I'm still out of counsel's row, next to the television. I hurry back to my position and bow as he lowers into his seat.

"Couldn't this have been discussed during the adjournment?" he asks. "You were given a great deal more time than is normal."

Paxton stands up quickly, confirming my earlier suspicion that his languor is all an act. "My lord, I must confess that my learned friend's last-minute ambushes are getting somewhat tiresome. We were only informed of her latest concern seconds before your lordship came in." He sits down, dramatic as ever, behaving as though he's been personally inconvenienced by all of this.

"My lord, I apologize for inconveniencing the court. However, given this is something both the prosecution and defense missed, I would ask for some clemency," I say.

A nerve in the judge's cheek twitches. "What's your concern now?"

I look to Malcolm, and we go through the process of showing the tape.

"And? What do you want me to do about this?"

"I'm seeking an adjournment for the prosecution to find the missing thirty seconds and disclose it to us."

He looks at the empty jury box. "The jury still hasn't heard any evidence yet."

"My lord, I'm sure there's a simple explanation for this," says Paxton while the wind is blowing in his direction.

"Then I'm sure my learned friend can provide me with that explanation in lieu of the footage," I say.

The judge looks between us, torn between the fear of handing me an easy point on appeal and the fear of inefficient use of court time.

"Miss Dalton, why wasn't this picked up before?"

"With respect"—everyone winces—"this should have been picked up by the police who investigated it, by the Crown Prosecution Service's reviewing lawyer, and lastly by my learned friend before it was served on the defense and presented to the jury in this incomplete state. There are several levels of failure on the prosecution side, and the only remedy for that is an adjournment so that disclosure can take place."

"Miss Dalton," says the judge, his voice barely audible, "I would tread more carefully where allegations levied against your opposing—and much more experienced—counsel are concerned." The judge looks over at Paxton, who returns a smug nod.

So that's it, then? This really is an old boys' club. I'm not allowed to say anything that might hurt Paxton's feelings because…he's more experienced?

"Miss Dalton, is there anything else you wanted to raise before Mr. Paxton QC calls the next witness?"

"I've voiced my concern, my lord." I can hear the tightness in my voice.

"Indeed, you have."

I turn to look at Eades as he's brought up from the cells. As usual, any attempt at catching his eye is deflected. I give Trevor a look and he approaches the dock but comes back empty-handed.

The jury trickles in. The next witness is in the box, waiting.

What the hell am I going to ask him? Desperation threatens to drown my thoughts. I mentally place the image of my daughter face down and focus on the task at hand.

There are only three techniques in cross-examination. All others are simply variations on the theme.

First and foremost is your tone. The way you ask a question. If you pitch it right, you can make almost any case sound reasonable. It works with uncontroversial facts as well. You can sound as though you're revealing some secret the witness has been keeping from the jury, when really, it's been in their statement all along. That's not available to me here. Mainly because I need a case in order to put it to the witness.

The second technique is building up little facts until they reach one undeniable conclusion. Again, not available to me. As with the first technique, that requires a case.

The last (and rarest) of the techniques is to find inconsistencies or logical fallacies in the witness's account. You can't prepare for this one. You have to wait for it, see what hand you've been dealt. It's every barrister's favorite tool, but it makes you a victim to chance.

So, I pull out the witness's statement from the box files, Daniel Hewitt.

"Repeat after me…" says the court clerk.

I have the time it takes for him to say the words of the oath and to give his evidence in chief to formulate a plan.

Hewitt swears on the Bible to tell the truth, the whole truth, and nothing but the truth. There's a flash of white and I see that his teeth look strange, Hollywood-like. He's had dentures fitted. Vain, then. Perhaps that will come in useful if I ever develop a strategy to cross-examine him.

This is the first witness the jury will hear. It has to go well. It has to stick in their minds and color the way they view the rest of the evidence.

But I can't think of a strategy. There's nothing. The pressure to think of something brilliant is still clogging up my mind, stopping any intelligent thoughts I might be capable of from coming to the surface. I look behind me at Eades, to see if he's going to give me another clue, but he's looking at the witness, unblinking.

I check to see if the jury is looking in Eades's direction. It wouldn't endear them to his case if they saw him looking at a witness like that, as though he was daring them to speak.

But they're not; they're looking at Hewitt, waiting with the same expression as yesterday, polite curiosity: *What are you here to tell us?*

I scan the witness statement, desperate to find something, anything that is illogical, that I can prove didn't happen. I can't find anything. I try to commit the statement to memory. That way, when Hewitt gives his evidence in chief, I'll be able to listen for any discrepancies.

Hewitt's statement details how he was in the TA at the same time as Eades, who refused to work with female, nonwhite, and non-British recruits. When the Gulf War began, and the opportunity to kill Middle Eastern soldiers came about, Eades frothed at the mouth to get out there and start shooting. Hewitt can't speak to much of this directly, and a lot of it is gossip.

I have to do something about this, so I lean forward and tap Paxton on the shoulder. I half stand and put my lips to his ear. "I hope you'll be avoiding the hearsay," I breathe.

He turns and frowns at me. "Bit late now," he hisses back.

"See you in the court of appeal."

And he turns to the front, feathers noticeably ruffled.

I breathe a sigh of relief; he knows I'm right.

Paxton has reverted to standing up with the grace and speed of an antique lift. "Can you give your full name for the court, please."

"Daniel Martin Hewitt." His voice reaches barely above a whisper.

I look up from the paperwork in front of me. The man in the witness box's eyes dart around the room, looking at anything but my client.

"Can you keep your voice raised? And remember to address your answers to the jury, even though this might seem strange, as I'm the one asking the questions." Paxton maintains his schoolmaster approach.

Hewitt nods.

"And remember that the judge is keeping a note of everything you're saying, so watch his pen and wait for him to stop writing before you continue speaking." Paxton picks up a piece of paper, whether for effect or for actual need, I'll never be sure. "You're here to give evidence today about Jonathan Eades, is that right?"

Hewitt nods.

"You need to answer the question," interrupts the judge, exasperatedly, pointing toward the digital clock on the clerk's desk indicating that the tape is running.

"You were in the TA when you first met the accused, is that right?"

Hewitt doesn't even nod this time.

"You knew Mr. Eades in the TA?" repeats Paxton, more loudly.

Hewitt looks petrified, a rabbit in the headlights. He's doing everything he can to avoid Eades's gaze.

I turn to look behind me. Eades's glare is fixed on Hewitt. Until now, I'd only ever seen him with a glazed, unfocused expression, as though nothing in this world is worth his attention. His head's probably full of the left-hand path and mythical races living under the earth.

Now, he's watching Hewitt with barely concealed hatred.

I check again to make sure the jury's attention is fixed safely on Hewitt, who remains silent.

CHAPTER TWENTY

WHEN FENRIZ CAME ROUND on the floor of the tent, he was lying on his back. It was morning. Sunlight was streaming through the tent, blinding him. He tried to raise a hand to cover his eyes, but he couldn't. It was strapped down. He looked down to see that his skin was tinged green by the subaqueous quality of the morning light.

A shadow moved above him, silhouetted against the brightness.

Then Fenriz felt the worst pain he'd ever felt in his life. Someone was filing his teeth. When the file hit one of his nerves, everything went black again.

———

Passing out from the pain had been a kindness, but a temporary one. When he came round, his gums were still bleeding. It felt as though every nerve was exposed to freezing-cold air, each breath the stroke of a bow across a violin.

And there, still sharpening his stake in the corner of the tent, was Coyote.

"Are you ready for your swimming lesson?"

Fenriz tried to moan, but that hurt too.

"Don't worry. I know you're not ready for that yet. It'll take a few hours."

For the rest of the day, Fenriz curled in a ball and sobbed without a sound. His chest shook, and he shivered against the pain and horror. Coyote left for hours at a time. When he came back, the fire started again and Fenriz could smell meat cooking.

He touched his fingers to his lips. He didn't think he'd ever be able to eat again. His stomach clenched in pain until the agony went and was replaced by nausea and headaches. All he could do was wait it out. Finally, Coyote came inside and zipped up the tent, falling asleep for the night, safe in the knowledge that Fenriz wouldn't wake again and wouldn't look for what was in the bag.

The next day—it had to be Sunday now—Coyote left the tent before Fenriz woke. His sleep was fitful, not nearly deep enough to be restful, but he went in and out of consciousness. He thought about what his mother might be doing now. Going to church, most likely. If it was Sunday. She wouldn't be worrying about him, that's for sure, wouldn't be ringing the police and telling them where he was in the Beacons, where there was a psychopath in a tent holding a stake.

After what seemed like an age, the night came. There was no smell of meat this time. Coyote pulled the bag of supplies that Fenriz had tried to open two nights before out of his corner of the tent.

He shuffled about outside. Fenriz edged over to the opening of the tent and peered out. Coyote was creating a summoning circle with rocks. More stones and pebbles kept a Nazi flag in place, and then he set about lighting multitudes of red candles.

Fenriz's mouth went dry. It was already dry, as he'd not had anything to drink since the morning (the second most painful experience of his life), but now he felt the back of his neck prick with sweat and turn cold.

Outside the tent, Coyote was chanting. Fenriz sat, watching and shivering. His disfigured teeth chattered.

The chanting went on for a long time. He prayed that it would never end, that something would go wrong with the ritual, that the demons or angels Coyote was summoning would come down and dispose of him instead. He'd never wished anything more in his life.

But it did end. And when it did, Coyote came to the mouth of the tent.

"It's time."

He grabbed Fenriz's arm and pulled him out. Fenriz was too weak, much too weak, to protest. He'd not eaten in three days, was dehydrated, sleep-deprived, and had spent every last joule of energy on staying conscious, not giving in to the oblivion that lingered at the dark corners of his mind, waiting for him. So, he allowed himself to be dragged along. Before long, he was looking down at the wet grass shining in the waxy light of the moon, his head lolling along as Coyote carried him over his shoulder. With each bounce, a new wave of pain flooded Fenriz, and he vomited down Coyote's back.

The next thing he remembered was lying by the side of the lake, glassy as a black mirror.

"No need for the armbands. Not now you know what's going to happen to you."

He hadn't got this far, hadn't survived everything to die now.

"Besides, you can't swim and your clothes will drag you down." Coyote smiled. "I want to make it easier to fish you out once you've drowned, so I'll be using this, if that's OK?" He held up a coil of rope.

Fenriz flailed and struggled, but it was no good. Coyote held down his feet and wound his ankles together and pulled on the knot. Next, he tied his wrists together. Then, his body was lifted, the same way Superman would hold Lois Lane after saving her. The classic hero's pose. And Coyote launched him.

The icy water turned solid as his back slapped the surface before plunging under.

But as Coyote launched him into the lake, Fenriz had the presence of mind to take one last gulp of air. Once submerged, he pretended to thrash about, flailing.

He'd lied about not being able to swim. In fact, he'd been practicing holding his breath underwater for ages. Getting in the bath at home and dipping his head underwater. He felt like Crowley, who once prepared for six months for his stay at Boleskine House, where he performed a ritual to summon an angel.

Fenriz dug deep, forcing himself to survive on no breath. Mind over matter, that's all it was.

After thirty seconds of flapping, he went still. Then he rolled onto his front so that his back crested the surface, floating. From Coyote's perspective, dead. While he floated, Fenriz untied his wrists, another thing he'd been practicing.

As promised, Coyote started pulling on the rope, and Fenriz felt himself being dragged through the water like a boat being brought to shore by the painter.

Fenriz forced himself to go limp as Coyote dumped him unceremoniously on the ground.

Then, he struck.

Pulling the stake from his sleeve, the stake he'd been hiding since he stole it that afternoon when Coyote was out, he stabbed Coyote with it several times.

Coyote choked on the blood, tried to fight back, but it was too late. No one expects a dead body to fight back.

Killing Coyote, his would-be murderer, was all part of his training to ascend. Coyote was no super. He was a fraud. Being big and muscular doesn't make you a super. Just because he was small didn't mean John couldn't be a part of the master race. Dammit, he already was part of the master race. He was born a white male, destined to rule.

"Are you ready for the ascension?" asked Fenriz of Coyote's dead body.

It took a lot of effort to lug the deadweight back over to the summoning circle. He used the rope, tied it around his waist, and pulled the body like a horse would pull a cart.

John knew all of the incantations and knew exactly what Coyote had been saying as he chanted earlier. Despite what he had let Coyote believe, John had been studying at home alone for ages, preparing for this moment, preparing for his ascension. Coyote was the perfect sacrifice.

He laid the body next to the circle and began to chant, saluting his leader, thanking him for his service to the true master race.

His teeth still hurt; of course they did. But this is what he was made for.

This is why he would ascend. He'd been training his pain threshold for months now, and the adrenaline of killing Coyote had all but driven the pain from his mind. He ran his tongue tentatively over his new teeth. He'd have had to do it at some point. Better to have had someone else do it for him. Coyote had had his uses.

God only knew what his mother would say when she saw them. That bitch would have to keep her mouth shut, wouldn't she?

After the long weekend, John drove back home to his house. It wouldn't be his last trip to the wilderness.

When, in a couple of weeks, he returned to the base, people looked at him differently. They'd always known he was different, superior to them, but now they were properly fearful, because Coyote, or James, as he was more commonly known, had told a few of them that he was going on a trip with John, and no one believed the story about a mountaineering accident.

But they couldn't prove otherwise, and no one tried.

Shortly after, John was asked to leave the TA. He didn't mind. Life had bigger plans for him now, and he was eager to see them through.

CHAPTER TWENTY-ONE

HEWITT HAS YET TO say a word, but Paxton's headmasterly demeanor is showing no signs of wavering.

"My lord, may I treat this witness as hostile?"

"No, Mr. Paxton, he's not a hostile witness; he's a mute one." The judge turns to Hewitt. "Look, you've come all this way to give evidence. Now just get on with it, please."

Paxton tries again. "You're here to give evidence today about Jonathan Eades, is that right?"

Hewitt remains frozen.

"Right, jury out," says the judge.

Malcolm leads the jury out through the side door. Once it is safely closed behind them, Paxton and I rise to address the judge.

"Mr. Paxton, I appreciate this isn't your fault, but we need to do something about this."

"Yes, my lord."

There's a hoarse whisper. The judge turns to the left. Hewitt is trying to say something to him.

"Can't look. I can't…" His eyes are bulging, and red blotches creep up his neck.

"What?"

The clerk sitting in front of the judge's bench turns around and whispers to the judge.

"Ah," he says. "I think Mr. Hewitt is saying that he doesn't want Mr. Eades to look at him while he's giving his evidence."

"My lord, perhaps we could close the curtains on the witness box or provide some screens?" says Paxton.

Instinctively, I know this would be disastrous for my client. If the jury think that witnesses need to be screened off while giving their evidence, they might start to see Eades as dangerous and scary. This is the last thing I want.

"Mmm," says the judge. "What do you have to say to that, Miss Dalton?"

"My lord, I would be opposed to the use of a screen."

"On what basis? It's a matter for my discretion, isn't it?"

"Yes, my lord. However, drawing the curtains is prejudicial to the accused, and adult witnesses should only be afforded the use of screens in the most exceptional circumstances."

"These are exceptional circumstances, Miss Dalton. We have a mute witness. How else is justice to be done?"

"My lord, I would appreciate at the very least the opportunity to cross-examine Mr. Hewitt in the absence of the jury and, if necessary, in the absence of the accused to establish why he feels the need for screens."

"Very well," says the judge. "Send Mr. Eades back down to the cells."

I turn to Mr. Hewitt, who is visibly shaking. I don't know how anyone can enjoy cross-examining a man in such abject fear. I certainly won't, but I must do it.

I use my calmest voice to speak to him. "Mr. Hewitt, why can't Mr. Eades look at you while you're giving your evidence?"

His eyes pinball around the court like a trapped animal.

"I'm scared."

"Scared of what?" My cadence is slow and inviting.

"He can…" He goes quiet again.

"He can what?"

Hewitt looks down at the floor. "I can't look him in the eye."

I pause, take my voice to an even softer register, and then ask, "Is that because you're not telling the truth?"

He shakes his head vigorously. "No."

"Then what is it about him looking at you?"

"He can…" Hewitt doesn't finish his sentence.

"He can what?"

"Do things."

"With his eyes?" I ask.

Hewitt nods. "By looking at you."

I think back to what I read about the O87 last night, about how the order believes in mind control. It seems like the exact sort of thing a pariah like Eades would do, go around telling people he can control them with his mind. It strikes me that these people are vile racists, but they're also total losers.

I ask the next question flippantly, as if I don't believe the words coming out of my mouth. "What, like mind control?"

"Yes." Hewitt's voice is barely more than a hoarse grunt.

"Again, please," bellows the judge impatiently.

"Yes," says Hewitt, refusing to look anyone in the eye.

"Thank you." I sit down.

The judge's eyebrows meet his wig as he looks at Paxton. "I'll grant the screens, but I'm going to break for lunch now, Mr. Paxton. Perhaps you can have a think about whether you'll be calling this witness given his…frailty."

"Court, please rise."

I enter the robing room and the first thing that hits me is the stench of Paxton's cigar. He's at the oval table in the middle of the room, happily puffing away as he removes his tunic shirt. I'm accosted by the sight of his shriveled upper torso, but it's the cigar smoke that makes me gag. I go over to the row of bay windows and pop open a casement, letting in a rush of freezing-cold air. The wind is incessant, like the background hum of a generator.

"What do you think you're doing?" Paxton's words are muffled by the cigar hanging out of the corner of his mouth. "I'm bloody freezing." He's holding a fresh oxford shirt. The tunic shirt with ungainly sweat circles is discarded on the table in the middle of the room.

"And I can't breathe with that filthy thing in here. You can't expect us to put up with it with no ventilation."

Paxton looks like he might burst. "Who do you think you are, making demands like that? You're lucky we even let you in these rooms." He shakes his head.

I scoff and walk over to the wall of boxes, ripping off my collarette as I go. I slam the lid down on one of the cubbyholes, still seething. Paxton, though small and thin, has taken up the entire room with the stench of his cigar and his discarded items of clothing. He's even managed to take up the real estate of where I can look, not caring that I might not want to be confronted by his bare nipples over the lunch adjournment.

Next to me, also packing his wig and gown into a box, is Paxton's junior.

He glances over his shoulder before turning to me and muttering, "Sore loser," so that only I can hear.

Taken aback, I look him in the eye, wondering if this is a prank. He smiles at me.

"Thanks, er…?"

"Andrew." He slides a hand toward me, keeping it close to his body as though to shield it from Paxton's view.

"Thanks, Andrew."

"Are you coming into the dining room for lunch?"

I look behind me. Paxton is shuffling around noisily. I imagine what it will be like, sharing a room with him while he masticates his roast beef. It's not the environment I need right now. I've been wound up so tight, I just need some space where I can clear my head, focus on the case.

"No, I've really got to look at the next witness."

"Your call," says Andrew before leaving the robing room after the newly dressed Paxton.

I tip my head forward and let my wig fall into my hands, seeing the three slanted Ls. I cock my head to one side and then flip the wig over. These aren't Ls. They're sevens.

Follow the sevens...

Is this another message left by the owner of the purple coat, Delia Lewis? I run my fingers through my hair, massaging my scalp. I feel like I'm on a hamster wheel of never-ending problems.

I sit down for a second, working out what to do with my lunch break. I know I should be focusing on the case, but I still can't keep thoughts of what happened in the early hours of this morning from my mind. When I saw those people in the cave. I need to go and investigate. I grab my handbag and head for the door.

CHAPTER TWENTY-TWO

WHEN I GET TO the cliff, the tide is in, as I should have realized. I'm here at the worst possible time, slap-bang in the middle of the two low tides. I'll have to wait until the end of the court day before I can come out here again.

Now the sun is fully up, and the day is much clearer so I can see more of the island. It's the shape of an exaggerated teardrop, with the court and main town resting in the curved bottom, a wooded area in the skinny middle before the land tapers to a pointed tip. Almost all of the island is hemmed in by steep black cliffs, any one of which could have been the place where Pat's car went off the edge. There's no way I can walk the perimeter of the island in the lunch break afforded to me, looking for the scene of the accident, hoping it triggers a memory. It would take hours. Anyway, finding my daughter is more important than that.

Where could she be? I've searched the main town, although that was never likely to yield any results. I suppose I hoped that if she was in one of those houses I couldn't enter, just by presenting myself in the vicinity, I'd increase the chances of her seeing me, and maybe she'd call out, "Mummy!" and I'd turn and she'd be there, safe and unharmed, and we'd be reunited.

That plan didn't work. But I can't walk out to the remoter parts of the island, investigating every little cottage, either. What can I do? What's the next step?

I close my eyes, replaying everything that's happened. The one clue I have about my daughter is that someone who is connected with O87 is sending me threatening notes about her. They use the Odal rune as their calling card. I go over the last twenty-four hours' events, trying to find the connection. There's one avenue of investigation buried in there that I've yet to explore: Stan. The Odal-rune-drawing graffiti artist I briefly shared a car with last night. The officer who arrested me dropped him *at his house*. Unfortunately, it was dark, and I was quite busy with my own predicament, so I can't be sure which house. But it's a lead, someone who I can ask questions.

I return to the telephone box—the place we were both arrested— then retrace the journey we took to Stan's house. Thankfully, the houses on Assumption Island are not uniform. Each of them is a different color, a slightly different shape, although they share similar traits: the square windows with white crosses in the middle, the two or more stories, some with the dormer windows, the wooden siding, and the pointed roofs. This diversity allows me to recognize Stan's house, a small, squat terrace with white siding and a green roof. I approach the door and knock.

There's no answer. I wait for over a minute. Then, impatient, I move to the downstairs window and press my face to the glass. I knock on the window. "Hello? Stan?"

The front door opens.

"Who are you and what are you doing here?"

The voice is female. I turn to see a somber-looking woman in a gray dressing gown, eyeing me mistrustfully.

"I came to speak to Stan."

Her eyes scan my black suit and white shirt. She presses her lips together. "What's he done this time?"

I realize that she's mistaken me for a police officer. Perhaps DC Parks has visited the house before and so Stan's wife (assuming this is his wife) suspects all women in suits of being police. It's tempting to consider adopting the identity, if only to benefit from the authority that opens doors to people's homes and gets their tongues moving. But are the words summoned by the flash of a badge worth all that much? Most people are too afraid to speak freely in front of the police, even if they haven't done anything wrong.

"I'm not with the police."

The woman sinks an inch or two from relief.

"Is he in?" I ask.

"Wait there."

She retreats into the house, and I hear her shout "STAN!" at the top of her voice. After a few loud bellows, she returns to the front door.

"Come in."

She shows me inside, into the small lounge stuffed with comfy chairs and settees. The fire is out, but the air is still thick with soot. I hear footsteps on the staircase and a fraught conversation outside.

"There's a woman here to see you."

"Who?"

"Don't know."

"You can't just let people into the house without asking me first. It's my bloody house…"

"Just shut up and go and say hello to her, will you? Before she nicks anything?"

I look around at the lounge, which is sparse. What does she think I'll be stealing? The brass poker by the fire?

I arrange my face into a neutral expression to pretend I didn't overhear their conversation. The door opens and I stand up, somewhat lamely, to shake Stan's hand.

He looks shocked to see me and, very quickly, angry. He moves toward me in a few brisk paces. My mind starts working through the possibilities. What is he going to do? Why is he moving toward me? I step backward. In my eagerness to put distance between us, I don't look where I'm going, and my heel catches on something behind me. The hearth.

I see the gleam in his eyes before a hand is at my throat.

"Who are you?" he asks in a gruff voice.

He pushes me so that my back juts into the lintel. A fresh swell of pain blossoms at the base of my skull as it hits the brick. The hand at my throat is covered in fingerless gloves that seem to have picked up every smell they've come into contact with. Black spots dance around my eyes and I recognize the signs; a headache is coming on, the sort that normally precedes a memory. After a swell of tinnitus blocking out all thought of who or where I am, I find myself in a different place altogether.

I'm somewhere luxurious, but I'm not safe. There's a hand at my throat, this time ungloved. I look to my left and see a golden packet of Benson & Hedges on a palatial bed. Returning to the man who has his hand at my throat, I can't picture his face clearly, only his eyes. Bright blue eyes encased in an otherwise unmemorable face.

He's angry with me. I push him away and knee him between the legs before throwing him onto the bed along with his cigarettes.

"Who are you?" asks Stan, not the man from my memories. I look to his eyes to make sure. They're brown, not blue, and I know that I'm back in Stan's home.

"Let me go!" I say.

He relinquishes his grip and I step away from the fireplace.

It still takes me a while before I'm ready to confront the present. Mentally, I'm scrambling, as though searching for coins lost down the side of the settee. I assaulted someone. An old man, kneeing him in the private parts before shoving him onto a bed... Why was the bed there? Oh, God, did we...?

The very real man in his living room is looking at me now, expecting me to answer his question.

"Who are you?" he says for the third time.

"Don't you remember me? From last night. We were both...er"—I search for a euphemism—"picked up at the same time."

He squints harder. "Oh, yeah," he says. "Sorry about that." He gestures toward the fireplace before sitting down on one of the squashy chenille sofas.

I follow suit.

"Can't be too careful," he says.

"Why's that?"

"When you tell the truth, reveal secrets the world is trying to hide…"

"What secrets?"

"We live inside," he says. "The signs are everywhere. You've just got to know where to look. I—we—have been trying to tell people, to show the world. They don't like it. They've put targets on our backs."

"Who's they?"

"Silly question. Who do you think? *Them.*"

"I'm not one of them, Stan. I just wanted to ask you about a couple of things, if that's OK?"

He nods.

"Great." I pull out my blue counsel's notebook and a pen and begin drawing an Odal rune. I hold it up to him. "What does this symbol mean to you?"

"The hollow earth," he says.

"Ri-ight. But how does it show that?"

He points to the diamond part of the rune and says, "This is the world."

"But it's not round."

"Yeah, but they couldn't do circles back then. This is a rune, see."

"I get that, but you *can* do circles now, so why keep the rune? I've looked it up and some people think that's a racist symbol."

Stan grabs my forearm. "It's not racist!" he says, his face is inches from mine, and I worry he's going to get violent again.

"OK, so going back to this rune. The thing is, Stan, that this rune means 'heritage' and it was used by the Nazis—"

Stan jabs a finger into my shoulder. "Why have you come here to lie?"

Fighting to keep my voice level, I say, "Go on, then." I show him my palms. "No questions; you just tell me about what the symbol means to you."

He picks up the notebook and pen. "This bit is the earth and these bits at the bottom are hands." Stan holds his own hands up in a V shape and says, "The cradle."

"The cradle?"

"Yes. The earth is a cradle, holding us and the sea and the sky in it. We live *inside*."

I blink and wonder for a second how that could work.

"And everyone knows it too, but *they* want to hide the truth. There is no religion higher than truth."

That stops me in my tracks. I've read that somewhere, and then I remember. It's on the Theosophical Society seal—one of the pictures appended to Dr. Sheridan's report.

"OK," I say. "But who are 'they'?"

Stan pulls a leaflet out from his jacket pocket and hands it to me. It's a chart of brand names and logos that in some way resemble either the Odal rune or the symbol of a world held in hands. I recognize one of the latter immediately, as it's the brand logo of the aspirin I took last night.

"See," he says.

I thank him before pocketing the leaflet, saying how helpful it is. "And Stan," I say, thinking about how he knew the words from the Theosophical Society's seal, "who taught you about all of this?"

Stan goes quiet and looks at the floor.

"Can't you tell me?"

"You must never tell."

"I won't. I promise."

"His name is Smyth."

"And who is he?"

"He is a speaker of truths. He's teaching us. The things *they* don't want us to know about."

"Right, I see. So, does that make you O87?"

Stan grimaces. "You must understand," he says. "We're not like them, the violent ones. We only care about the truth."

"What truth?"

He sighs, frustrated, jabbing at the Odal rune.

"I've just got one more question for you, Stan."

His expression clouds over, his patience running out.

"Down at the cave, do you perform…rituals?"

"There is no religion higher than the truth."

"Sure." Breaking my implied promise to ask only one more question, I pull the picture of my daughter from my handbag and hold it up. "Have you seen this girl anywhere?"

Stan's eyes flit between the picture of my daughter and me. His forehead wrinkles with confusion. "No."

"Are you sure?" I ask. "Please, look closer."

"I said no!"

Stan is on his feet again.

"Get out," he says. "Please."

I stuff the picture of my daughter back in my handbag and promptly head for the front door.

————————

I leave Stan's cold, dark house feeling oddly deflated. The walk from his street to the court building is short. I'm running out of lunch break, and I've got nothing to show for it. If I can't find my daughter, then my only hope is to comply with the messages and ensure Eades's acquittal. Instead, I've just spent a lunch break speaking to someone who believes the solar system sits inside the earth's crust. I mean, what am I supposed to do with that? How has that helped me to make progress with the prosecution witnesses?

The sky is covered with a thin gauze of clouds now, sunshine filtered as though through a tent canvas. My mood is somber, remonstrative. How could I have dropped the ball so badly, not paid more attention to the case when the people who have my daughter have told me quite explicitly that winning the case is my only chance of getting her back?

I follow the streets back to the court building, my eyes fixed upon the ground, only stopping to look up when I get to a junction, a road, anywhere that requires my attention.

Then I see her.

My first thought is that she must be cold. How could they have allowed her to be out in just that gingham dress, the one with the big white daisy on the front?

"Sweetheart!" I call, still so frustrated I don't know my daughter's name.

She walks away from me. She's holding on to an adult's hand. They're pulling her away. It's the woman in the purple coat, the woman from the robing room. Why does she have my daughter?

"Hey!" I start to run toward them. I'm desperate for my daughter to turn around, for me to see her face.

If she looks into my face, surely she'll recognize me, she'll know I'm her mother.

"STOP!" I shout, running.

They disappear around a corner.

"No, come back."

She's so close. If I can just get around the corner, she'll be there and I can take her hand, take her back into my care.

I turn the corner to find DC Parks standing in front of me.

"Why were you shouting?" she asks.

I look over her shoulder, go as though to push past her. I can't see them anymore. My daughter and her abductor have gone. How? It's impossible. They were just there.

"Did you see them?" I ask DC Parks, impatient.

"Who?"

"The little girl and the woman who was with her."

"What are you talking about?"

That girl was my daughter. I know it. She was the first child or even sign of a child I've seen on the island. She must belong to me.

"There was a girl," I say. My eyes are scanning the space in the middle of the government buildings, the alleyways down the side of each. "She was just here; I just saw her."

"I've just come from the police station. I've had eyes on this area for at least thirty seconds, and I'm telling you I haven't seen any children."

"That's impossible," I say. "This was seconds ago."

My knees feel weak. My grip on reality is slipping through my fingers. This is the third time now that I've seen something no one else claims to.

"Why are you lying?" I say to her.

DC Parks steps closer, her nose inches from mine. I can smell her perfume, feel her warm breath on my face. "Tell me the truth."

I step back, but she continues to invade my personal space.

"Where. Is. The. Eighth?" she asks.

"I have no idea what you're going on about," I say, sounding calmer than I am. "Now, please let me go past because I'm due in court in the next few minutes."

She backs off and holds her arm out as though to usher me along.

"You'll tell me soon," she says to my retreating back.

CHAPTER TWENTY-THREE

I RETURN TO THE robing room to find Paxton and Andrew already robed.

There's a knock at the door, shortly followed by Malcolm's bespectacled head. "His lordship is ready for you now," he says.

Paxton flaps an impatient arm at him. "Yes, thank you. We know."

The door closes.

I bristle at Paxton's behavior toward Malcolm. It was so unnecessarily aggressive.

"Are you relying on Hewitt's evidence?" I ask.

"Of course," says Paxton, as though my suggestion is ludicrous.

"And you'll steer clear of the hearsay?"

"You don't have to remind me about the rules of inadmissibility; I've been doing this rather a long time, you know." He strides out, Andrew in tow.

I robe up and return to the courtroom, still nervous about what I'm going to ask Hewitt, having done no preparation.

When I arrive, Hewitt is already in situ behind the dust-pink curtains that shield the witness from the defendant's view but allow the jury to see them.

I look over at the press bench. Agatha Price is there, glaring at me, but it appears Dev still hasn't returned from his errand.

"Mr. Hewitt," begins Paxton. "Did you know the accused?"

Hewitt closes his eyes and takes a deep breath. "Yes, I knew Jonathan Eades."

"Sorry, can't hear you." The judge cups his hand around his ear and bellows at Hewitt, as though his problem is deafness rather than dumbness.

"Yes, I knew Jonathan Eades."

"Right. Now keep your voice up."

And he does, just about. Paxton takes him through his evidence, expertly avoiding the hearsay like potholes, confining the evidence to the parts Hewitt personally heard and witnessed. Unfortunately, what Hewitt personally heard and witnessed was Eades's Holocaust denial, racism, denigration of women, and homophobia.

I look at the jury. They're still playing judge, not letting anything show on their faces. A man in the front row notices me looking at him, so I turn away quickly. It's a sign of weakness to keep looking at them to see what they make of the evidence.

Paxton concludes examining Hewitt in chief by saying, "I don't have any more questions for you, but if you wait there, my learned friend might."

I get to my feet, leaning on the bench in front of me for support, trying to forget about my daughter. Her toothy smile. A smile I'll never see again if this fails.

The jury's eyes are on me. I can feel them on my skin. With a sense of déjà vu that stops me in my tracks, I look up and find twelve strangers staring back at me.

I open my mouth to speak, only to find that my breath catches in my throat. It's such an illogical thought, one that has no place interrupting my cross-examination, but I worry that this is the moment I'll lose my memories again. Perhaps that's all it ever was—nerves.

I tear my eyes away from the jury. I make a fountain-pen mark, the third stroke in the tally chart at the back of *Archbold*. It calms me, anchoring me in the here and now.

"Mr. Hewitt, it won't have escaped the notice of the jury that you're giving evidence from behind a screen—"

"Miss Dalton, I will direct the jury that they shan't hold it against the accused; it's simply a measure in place to help witnesses give their best evidence."

"Thank you, my lord, but if I may be permitted to follow this line of questioning?"

"If you must."

"Why, Mr. Hewitt, can't Mr. Eades look you in the eye?"

Hewitt shifts uncomfortably. It's clear he'd rather be anywhere than here, and I feel a pang of sympathy for him. I hope he will let me get this over with as quickly and painlessly as possible.

"He can do things."

"What things?"

"If he looks at you."

"Like what?"

"He can… This is going to sound stupid, but I can one hundred percent tell you it's true." Hewitt turns to the jurors, wide-eyed, imploring them to believe him. "He can do mind control."

Whether because they want to stop themselves from laughing or because they can't believe what they've just heard, the jurors take a sharp breath. Hewitt's evidence has lost all credibility, which is the best I can hope for.

"Thank you, my lord. No further questions."

"Any re-examination, Mr. Paxton?"

"None, my lord."

"No, I should think not." His lordship raises his eyebrows at Paxton as though to say, "Well, I did warn you."

I return to my seat. The velvet cushion is so worn that the stuffing has taken on the same texture as the wooden bench. There's a feeling on the back of my neck, a burning sensation, and I know that someone is watching me. I turn and see DC Parks glaring at me with the same open hostility as Eades showed for Hewitt. Then, she smiles. She knows something I don't.

Paxton addresses the judge. "The next witness is Geraint Williams, my lord."

My victory is over before it had time to gain steam. I haven't read the next witness statement. I'm as taken aback by the change in pace as anyone. All I was focused on was the next witness, but now there's a whole afternoon stretching out in front of us, and I haven't had the chance to prepare. How stupid of me to go off chasing runes and numbers when I should have been here, prepping for these witnesses to the nth degree.

It takes a little longer for Williams to be brought in, and I use every second to scan his witness statement. There's an easy line of questioning that opens up and I feel a sense of relief. Whatever happens, I can damage this witness's credibility. A rush of nervous excitement flushes my cheeks as Williams clambers into the witness box, looking affronted to have been asked to come all this way to give some poxy account of Eades's time working for his company.

"I want to take you back to the 30th of April last year," says Paxton. "What happened on that morning when you opened up your yard?"

"I noticed there'd been a break-in," says Williams, his voice carrying to every corner of the room.

"What made you think that?"

"Someone had cut the barbed wire. Then when I went into the shed, I noticed that quite a lot of ammonium nitrate and fuel oil—we call it 'ANFO'—had been taken from the store."

Paxton leaves a long pause for everyone to put two and two together. It takes all of my self-control to keep my face neutral just in case the jury is watching me for a reaction.

"And why do you have ANFO stored in your yard?"

"I run a quarrying business. That's how you do it. You have to blow up bits of the mountain as well as drilling to loosen the material."

"Who did you employ at that time?"

"About twenty lads, including the defendant." Williams's eyes shift in the direction of the dock.

"How much was stolen?"

Williams's eyes roll toward the ceiling, as though he's performing calculations in his head. "About twenty gallons."

"What was John Eades's job while in your employ?"

"He drove the JCB to scoop up the material to then take it back down the mountain."

"How long had he worked with you?"

"Five years."

"And how much would he have known about demolitions using ANFO?"

"He'd have been right up close to it, because it's a tight-knit thing, lots of moving parts." Williams moves his hands in demonstration.

"Thank you; no further questions from me. Wait there because there may be some more for you."

The judge looks to me and I get up, my notebook quivering in my hand. I put it down on the bench and fix my hands on either side.

"Mr. Williams, this statement is dated the 6th of June 1995; that's right, isn't it?"

There's a minuscule change in his posture; he plants his feet a little further apart and broadens his shoulders. "Yes."

"So, you gave a statement *after* the bombing of Abbott House?"

He shrugs and says, "I don't know."

"Were you not aware of the bombing when you gave your statement?"

"I was, but I'm not too hot on dates." He does that thing with his posture again.

"When you were taken back to the 30th of April by Mr. Paxton, you were able to remember what happened on that date."

"That was in my statement, which I read this morning." He bites back instantly. Happy to get one over on me.

I ignore it and refuse to get drawn into a confrontation. My voice stays light, as though I'm only making a polite inquiry. "And you know the reason you're here today, don't you?"

"To say about the theft."

"But you know that this trial isn't about theft, don't you? You know the trial is about the bombing of Abbott House?"

"Er... Yeah."

"The explosive was discovered missing on the 30th of April, but this statement isn't given until the 6th of June." I hold it up for effect. "Why's that?"

"Well, that was when the police came to ask me questions." He's developed an unfortunate habit of flicking his head when he answers questions, as though he's flicking bangs out of his face, except he's got a buzz cut.

"They were there to ask questions about John Eades, weren't they?"

"This is over a year ago, now, mind." He flicks his head again. It started off as a shoulder shrug, maybe a dismissive shake of the head, but it's developed into a full-blown tell.

I keep my voice slow and measured so that the jury can hear each word clearly. "And you knew, when they were asking you these questions, that Abbott House had recently been bombed?"

"I heard about it on the news."

"And you must have known that John Eades, your employee, had been arrested?"

"I suppose so."

"When I asked earlier whether you gave your statement *after* the bombing, you said you didn't know. But you must have known, because you knew one of your men had been arrested for it."

"When you put it that way but..."

I wait for him to complete his sentence, but he doesn't. I let that "but" hang in the air. Because he doesn't have an answer.

"Was the 6th of June, when you gave this statement, the first time you spoke to the police about the theft?"

"Er... Let me think..."

I cross my arms and lean back, giving him all the time he needs.

He furrows his brow in a poor imitation of deep thought. "I think so, yeah."

"So, you didn't report the theft when it happened?"

"Er... I suppose not, no."

"Why not?"

"I…didn't know who was responsible for it then."

"But you did know that a crime of some description had been committed, so why not report it to the police?"

There's a long, uncomfortable pause.

"Did you get compensation for your stolen materials?"

"Yes."

"And did you make that claim before or after the bombing?"

"Af—"

"Right, jury out!" bellows the judge, but his expression is fixed on me. His eyes are blazing with hatred or anger, I can't tell which. I don't know what mistake I've made, but I must have done something. My heart pounds against my rib cage while I wait to see what caused this outrage.

The judge watches as the last juror slips through the side door before turning to me.

"Have you got an application to make, Miss Dalton?"

My mind has gone blank. What does he mean? This is normally the moment where my brain kicks in and the muscle memory of the job steps in to fill the void.

"Asking a witness if he's committed insurance fraud!" shouts the judge. "The jury has heard it now. Where is this in your defense statement?"

"I–I…" I stammer. "I didn't know that he was going to—"

"You knew *exactly* where those questions were leading. I only assume that Mr. Paxton QC didn't get up to interrupt you because he didn't think you would actually make such an accusation without making an application before the court!" Spittle flies from his mouth.

"My lord, if you give us some time…" says Paxton.

The judge slams his palms on the bench. "You better sort this out between you." His eyes narrow when he looks at me. He points. "And you, standing up to object at every little piece of prosecution evidence and now you've gone and said *that*. Decide between you whether this jury can remain in charge."

My cheeks are burning, and I can feel a lump in my throat the size of an orange. It's the bad character evidence rule. I can't levy allegations of wrong-doing against prosecution witnesses without asking for permission first, just as Paxton can't refer to Eades's previous convictions.

How could I have been so stupid? I was so happy when that line of questioning opened up, and now I might have ruined everything. The jury saw the way the judge bellowed at me. They'll think I'm an idiot, someone they can't trust. Will they even listen to my closing speech?

In an act of pure masochism, I look at DC Parks. Her gaze strips me bare, takes me back to being a child who has done a stupid thing and now all of the adults and children are staring at me. My ears become impossibly hot under her glare, and I glance away, too humiliated to hold her gaze.

I follow Paxton and Andrew out of the court in a dour procession. We walk up to the corridor with the underground bunkers for conference rooms. We all step inside one of them and Paxton slams the door.

"What the *hell* do you think you're playing at?"

I have no answer. "I'm so sorry," I say, my voice wobbling. Shock is the only thing stopping the tears from flowing.

"'I'll see you in the court of appeal' indeed. How you can have the *nerve*." He paces around and I look to Andrew, who avoids my eye, though he looks more disappointed than angry.

"The jury has fucking heard it now," says Paxton. "Are you going to make an application?"

"I'll have to."

"And if he doesn't allow you to follow that line of questioning?"

"I–I… I don't know."

"This is fixable, Alasdair," says Andrew, his voice quiet and calm. "If Lila just apologizes to the witness and rephrases her question, we can avoid having to throw the trial."

"But the jury has *heard* her now," hisses Paxton.

Andrew moves close to him, his lips nearly touching Paxton's ear. In such a small room I can still hear what he's saying. "We don't want a retrial, Alasdair. We'll never get *him* to come back."

So that's why he's being nice to me. One of their witnesses is flaky. I think over the batting order, which I've memorized. It's got to be A.N. Other, the witness who wants anonymity.

Paxton holds his hands up. "All right." Then he turns to me. "There's no need for us to discharge the jury and start over. But you better fix this. Either make your application—which will be opposed—or you correct yourself."

"Can you give me five minutes?" When I hear myself speak, my voice sounds totally unlike me. It's strained with the pressure of keeping tears at bay.

"We'll let the court know," says Andrew. He smiles at me kindly.

They leave the room and I lean against the wall. I feel so embarrassed, so stupid. There was me, thinking I was so clever, doing this amazing job. I thought that, in spite of some pretty astonishing mitigating circumstances, I hadn't lost my touch. Why didn't I just give up yesterday? Hold my hands up and say I'd lost my memories?

The toothy smile in the picture of my daughter haunts me again. I want to apologize to her, to say sorry for messing it up. More than anything, I want to promise her that I'll get through this, return home, and hold her close.

The door swings open and Dev strolls in, looking like an ambling pile of dirty laundry.

"Where've you been?" I ask.

"Speaking to your witness."

"What?"

"It's polite to say 'pardon.'" Dev sniffs and drags a finger under his nostrils.

"I didn't realize we were in a Regency drama," I snap back at him.

"Sarcasm is equally ungracious."

"Yeah, and you're a paragon of manners."

As if to underline the point, Dev scratches his crotch. "How did it go, then?" He mimes boxing—jab, jab, hook.

"It...went."

"Ah."

"I've just been given a dressing-down by the judge after asking the boss—"

"Whoa, whoa. You're on the boss already?"

"Yes!"

"What happened with the bloke in the TA?"

"Not a lot. I damaged his credibility by getting him to admit he believes in mind control."

Dev grimaces and scratches his scalp. "Nothing else? So now the jury thinks that Eades is some sort of mind-fucking psycho as well as a Nazi? Fucking hell, are you even qualified?"

"There was nothing *to* say. All he did was accuse Eades of being a racist, sexist homophobe. And the jury thought the mind-control thing was stupid."

"And you couldn't think of a single additional question?"

"Look around. We're on a whitewashed island still living in the 1870s, never mind the 1970s. Who is going to want someone like me lecturing an army volunteer on the niceties of race relations?"

Dev considers this for a while, which he communicates by furrowing his brow and scratching his armpit. "You know, and really don't get used to this, because I think you are genuinely the worst barrister ever to have existed, but you might have a point there. Play up to the bigots. Good plan."

This is the moment the dam of tears I've been holding back breaks. My daughter has been banking on me, and I've only enlarged the gulf between us with my ineptitude.

Dev shuffles uncomfortably. "Shit, I'm sorry. I didn't mean *literally* the worst…"

"It doesn't matter; it's true. I shouldn't be here, doing this. I'm… Something's happened to me—"

"Here, have a Werther's." He holds out a packet of caramel sweets that looks like it was opened ten years ago and has been left at the bottom of Dev's messenger bag to collect grit.

I'm glad he stopped me from speaking. It wasn't a good idea to tell him. No one should know about my memory loss.

"No thanks. Not good for public speaking."

"Here." He hands me a wad of typewritten notes, most of them covered in greasy fingerprints and coffee stains. Dev looks at the stains and says, "Yeah, sorry about that."

"What is it?" I reach out to grab the papers, but he jerks his hand away so that they're just out of reach.

"Say please."

I roll my eyes, tired of playing his stupid games. "Please."

"Some information from a contact."

"Why are you giving it to me?"

"This is painful." Dev shakes his head, ruffling his hair. "Right. What is your job?"

"I'm a barrister."

"Which means you have to?"

"I don't have time for this."

He continues to hold the bundle of documents at arm's length.

"Oh, for God's sake. I represent clients, put their case, challenge the prosecution—"

"Bingo! This will help you."

He hands me the pile and I look down at it. "But how?"

"There's some stuff in there about explosivey-type things. You'll have to work the rest out for yourself. I'm not the one being paid."

"Er, thanks," I say, flicking through the papers.

"I wanted to get it to you before they called the boss, but I banked on you at least asking a few more questions. You asked about *mind control*?"

Ignoring him, I riffle through the papers in search of something that can help me cross-examine Williams without having to resort to unverified accusations of insurance fraud. "What does all of this mean?"

"Buggered if I know. That's expert stuff."

"Right."

"My lord, I have an application to make." Five minutes later, and the judge's color has receded somewhat.

"That will be opposed, my lord," says Paxton.

"I want to put to the witness that he wouldn't have personally owned the explosive material, because the demolition team tend to be subcontracted. Of course, this will mean that I will be accusing the witness of, among other things, insurance fraud."

"Why isn't any of this in your defense statement?"

I keep my eyes on the judge. Then they can't involuntarily flit toward Dev.

"Evidence has come to light since that defense statement was filed," I reply and pull two slender reports from the wedge of papers Dev handed to me minutes before.

"My lord," interrupts Paxton. "The evidence referred to by my learned friend is news to the prosecution."

"Miss Dalton?"

"Nevertheless, my lord, this information is now in my possession, and I feel that, in the interests of justice, I should be allowed to put it to the witness to establish that there was no theft from his stores."

"My lord, this is sending the jury down a blind alley. What does denigrating this witness's credibility have to do with anything?"

I get to my feet. "Perhaps if we take a break to get these documents photocopied; then the prosecution can have the time to peruse them?"

The judge raises his eyebrows at Paxton. "You can't object to that, surely?"

"Very well, but I'm conscious of the fact that the witness is waiting…"

"We've got all afternoon," says the judge.

Paxton gives a resigned shrug. I hand the paperwork to Malcolm to photocopy; about twenty pages of material in the first report, and forty pages in the second. It takes Paxton and Andrew approximately half an hour to read it.

"What relevance is this?" asks Paxton.

"You heard what I said when I addressed the judge," I reply. "It's about establishing (a) whether the witness has knowledge of the explosive, as he says the defendant would, and (b) whether anything was stolen from the yard—the only piece of evidence you have to establish the link between my client and the explosives."

He shakes his head, irritated, as though I'm being purposefully disruptive rather than acting in my client's best interests. He turns to the clerk. "We're ready for his lordship."

When the judge returns, he looks to Paxton. "Yes?"

"Well, we've read the documents—"

"Are you happy with their validity?"

"It's more a question of relevance—"

"I know that. I heard what you said earlier, but I've had time to think about this." His lordship's voice is low, as though he's resigned to his decision. "I will allow Miss Dalton to continue her questioning of Mr. Williams, seeing as it is reasonable for her to try to establish that these explosives were not stolen by her client. But I would like it to be known that I am not impressed by the manner in which Miss Dalton has conducted this trial thus far."

My cheeks flush, but I'm more relieved than anything. I turn to Trevor and mouth "*sorry*," but he waves my apology away. Next, I glance over at Dev. It's dangerous and I shouldn't, but I'm so grateful to be out of this hole. As the jury trickles in one by one, I have flashbacks to the judge's bulging eyes, spittle flying from his mouth, and feel the humiliation all over again. I screw up my eyes, cringing. There's not enough time to dwell on it, because Williams has returned and the jury is watching, looking eagerly now because the last thing they saw was the judge shouting at me.

"Mr. Williams, would John Eades have the wherewithal to build a bomb?" I ask.

"I should think so."

"Do you know how to build a bomb?"

"I know the basics."

For a moment I consider forcing him to explain how. I could hand him paper and pens and make him demonstrate building a bomb so the jury can understand how complicated it is. But never asking a question you don't know the answer to is the first rule of cross-examination, so I stick to chartered waters.

"Earlier you said that he stole the ANFO. What did you mean by that?"

"Well, there are barrels of ammonium nitrate and fuel oil on-site, and he nicked some."

"Barrels of them, are there?"

"Yes."

"Are you sure about that?"

"Yes." The shrug-cum-head-flick returns.

I hand a piece of paper to Malcolm, who in turn hands it to Williams.

"This is a paper from the Royal Institute of Demolitions Experts. Please turn to page five. There you'll see that ammonium nitrate—sometimes known as fertilizer—is to be stored in separate barrels. It's not ANFO until it's mixed, is it?"

He flicks his head. His worst yet. "I'm not sure."

"You said you knew the basics. It's pretty basic, isn't it, that ammonium nitrate is one component and fuel oil is the other? They're not stored as ANFO."

Williams blinks and stares hard at the piece of paper I've handed him, no doubt hoping to find answers.

"Why did you say he stole barrels of ANFO?" I ask.

"He stole them both."

"So, it wasn't kept in a mixed form on-site?"

"Er... No."

"It wasn't kept on-site at all, was it, Mr. Williams?"

"It was."

"That brings me to this document, from your company's brand-spanking-new website."

Malcolm takes the pages from me and hands them to Williams.

"Your company doesn't carry out the demolitions, do they?"

"How do you think we blow up the mountain?"

"Let's have a look at page twenty-three of forty-two." I wait for him to turn to the page. "You use subcontractors."

There's a long silence during which I can imagine the wheels spinning in Williams's brain.

"Look, it's all part of the team." He makes a circle with his hands.

"They're not part of your company though, are they?"

"May as well be."

"When you told the police that ANFO had been stolen, that was a bare-faced lie, wasn't it?"

"Er…"

"Because you don't own the ammonium nitrate or the fuel oil; the subcontractors do."

"Well, it was still from my site."

"And the compensation claim? Was that for your company or the subcontractors?"

"It…was for my company."

"But it wasn't your explosive?"

"Look, I'm not the one on trial here!"

"Thank you, Mr. Williams. You've been most helpful."

CHAPTER TWENTY-FOUR

I'M LEAVING THE COURT building, walking across the road between the court and the hotel, when Dev comes up beside me.

"What happened to 'meet tonight'?" he says.

"You didn't say where or when."

Dev waves at the open space. "On the square?"

I look around. I suppose it is a square, in the British sense of the word. A bit of land where random roads meet, or where the town planner had a bit of space left over and no one knew what do with it, so they bestowed the title of "square" upon it as though that makes it legitimate.

"You didn't say that."

"Well, it was implied, and you're supposed to be good at inferences and implications."

We arrive outside the Castle Hotel, and I stop walking, feeling awkward. I don't want to invite a strange man up to my room, but I also don't want to suggest that he's creepy, because I really owe him one.

"What's the plan?" I say instead.

"I was thinking: get pissed, trash the hotel room, order some prossies, and snort some coke?"

I stare back at him blankly.

"I'll sort out the skirt and powder, and you can make a start on the criminal damage."

"Are you taking the piss?"

"You know that lobotomy you've had? Did you get it done privately, because they've done a really good job. I'd like to get my lips done, you see." Dev pouts to demonstrate his under-plumped lips.

I roll my eyes. "Are you coming up, then?"

"Steady on. I was planning on an exchange of information, not bodily fluids. I like to keep mine to myself, thanks."

"I was just suggesting that perhaps it's not prudent for us to be standing around outside chatting." I look around. "We could be seen."

"Good thinking, except this is my hotel too, so I'd rather not do two laps of the block before getting into my comfies."

I look at Dev's khaki slacks and checked-shirt combination, which is so crumpled already that I'm struggling to imagine how much comfier he can get.

Dev clicks his fingers in front of my face. "Eyes up, pervert."

"Excuse me, Miss Dalton. Is this man bothering you?" I start and turn, surprised to see Andrew, looking disarming with his disheveled appearance and wig-hair.

I look back at Dev. "Yes, he is, actually. But I can handle it."

Dev raises his hands in surrender before retreating into the hotel lobby.

I nod toward the Castle Hotel. "Are you staying here, as well?"

"Oh, no, Alasdair and I have a nice little B and B down by the harbor. I was just going to ask how far along you are with preparing the case dinner?"

"The case dinner?" I repeat, feeling stupid.

"Yes, well, we thought you'd be organizing it, given that you're…" He stops short of saying "a woman" and instead says, "We trust your judgment. I hear there's a nice Italian on the high street. Perhaps we should check it out tomorrow, see if it's up to scratch?"

"Er, sure," I say, not knowing what I'm signing up for, not sure if I care either. Andrew looks rather handsome with his ruffled red hair and square glasses.

"Great, well, have a nice evening and see you tomorrow." He smiles and leaves.

Behind the reception desk is the woman holding the book she's not reading, or perhaps a more accurate description would be that she's developed a unique method for doing so.

I scan the chintz settees and armchairs that scatter the bar area, which is desolate but for a couple at the bar, a man playing solitaire, and Dev, who is "hiding" behind a newspaper. I slump into the chair opposite him.

Dev lowers the paper with a flick of his wrists. "How's lover boy?"

"Were you listening in on my conversation?"

"Journalist. Old habits and all that... Old dogs an' all." With another deft flick, the paper shields his face once more. "Woof woof."

"So, what's the plan? Who's the witness? Is that who you got all of that information from earlier? Thanks, by the way...for earlier..."

Dev continues to ignore me.

"I was in a tight spot..."

"You're breaking my cover," says Dev from behind the paper.

"Maybe we should order at the bar so that it looks less conspicuous?"

"Double gin and tonic, please," says the broadsheet.

"Double?"

"Hendrick's if they've got it."

"I was thinking more along the lines of a shandy."

Dev lowers the paper an inch so that only his eyes are visible. "Cheapskate." Then he retreats behind it, tutting. "You'll never get me to come up to your room with *that* attitude."

I shake my head and go over to the bar to order.

"Double gin and tonic and a cup of tea, please."

The barman nods and goes about making the drinks at a leisurely pace.

There's a laugh from down the bar, like a pneumatic drill.

I shake my head. Déjà vu. I've heard that laugh before. The woman in the leopard-print miniskirt is sitting at the bar, except today she's wearing a denim skirt. She must have sealskin legs.

"I'll guess you're having what she's having?" says the barman, and I feel goose pimples prick the back of my neck.

I leave a five-pound note on the bar and return to the armchair. The broadsheet has been folded and put away.

"What's the matter with you?" he asks.

"Something really weird just happened." I search for a piece of paper, a napkin, anything I can find to make a mark on. I want to know if I've been here before.

"Although I'm a highly skilled professional, I try to avoid using my interrogation skills outside of working hours. It's good to compartmentalize, you know? So just tell me what happened." He taps his glass to my teapot.

I find a beer mat and make a mark with my pen. "Just now…at the bar. Something happened in the exact same way it happened last night."

Dev circles his wrist to chivvy me along.

"There's a woman. The one in the miniskirt."

He clocks her. "Mutton dressed as lamb. Yep."

I stifle the urge to reprimand Dev. "She has an unusual laugh. She laughed just now. Exactly as she did in the pub last night, and then someone said something when they heard her and when it happened just now. The barman said the exact same thing—a smart remark like he thought it was funny. I think it might be from a film or something. It was odd."

Dev considers me while swilling his double gin around the glass. He sniffs it, puts it delicately to his lips, and then gulps it down in one. Once it's drained, he places a fist to his chest while he burps. "It's like you said, isn't it? These fish-for-brains islanders aren't culturally refined specimens like you and I, what with our theaters and our wine bars. They'll just respond with stock answers."

"Don't include me in this."

"Hear me out. How many times have you heard someone say 'Thanking you' rather than just fucking 'Thank you,' or 'How's the weather up there?' when speaking to a tall person? People resort to stock phrases, don't they? No imagination."

"Maybe." I'm not convinced. It wasn't like that. It wasn't even a cliché; it was like the ghost of yesterday left its imprint and no one can scrub off the ectoplasm.

My mind wanders to the article in Dev's paper and the question I've been burning to ask him since I read it.

"Look, there's something I've been meaning to ask you about."

"Yes," he says, before I've asked the question.

"Yes, what?"

"That suit does make you look fat."

"That wasn't my question."

"You're welcome. Always willing to help a lady in need of a sartorial steer."

"Yeah," I say, taking in his crumpled clothes. "It was actually about your magazine… You said it was an anti-fascist magazine, but I noticed there were some other articles in there about, well…" I want to say "conspiracy theories" but no conspiracy theorist ever goes by that title.

"Anti-fascist *and* parapolitical," he says.

"Meaning?"

"We uncover the darker side of the security services."

"So that's why you're helping me… I thought being anti-fascist meant you were pretty left-wing?"

Dev chuckles at this, and his buttons strain against his stomach. "Being anti-fascist is just about not being a massive fan of your Hitlers or your Francos."

"But that's everyone," I say. "No one likes them."

"That's because it's not some extreme position. It's just not wanting to live in an authoritarian state."

"So…when you say you're anti-fascist, you're actually more concerned about the behavior of the security services than people like Eades who want to blow up innocent people and start a race war?"

"I thought we'd agreed that you're defending Eades so maybe you should let off the whole assuming-he's-a-racist-murderer thing for ten minutes."

"I'm just being realistic. Being a good lawyer is about being able to look at it from both sides."

"At the moment, you can't even look at it from your own side."

"We're going off topic," I say. "There was an article in your paper." I lower my voice to a whisper and look around.

"Very good," says Dev. "Very stealthy. Next you should hold a sign saying, 'Secret Conversation in Progress.'"

I can't stop myself from rolling my eyes. There's only so much you can take of the man. "I think what happened to the man in your article is happening to me."

CHAPTER TWENTY-FIVE

I'M EXPLAINING TO DEV everything that's happened since I received the first note. We're halfway through our second drink and I'm on the 999 call, the one where a disembodied voice told me that they're watching me—whoever "they" are.

I leave out the part where I tried to steal boats.

When I tell Dev about the arrest, he rubs his face with the palm of his hand. Not a delicate scratching of the temple or cradling of the nose, but a ruffling motion as though greeting a dog. His face emerges remarkably unperturbed, and he fixes me with his bloodshot eyes.

"This is Special Branch. No doubt about it. It's called 'psy-ops' because it's a form of psychological torture performed over an extended period of time, resulting in the victim losing all hope and ultimately committing suicide." Dev continues to fix me with that red-eyed stare, deadly serious. Then he breaks his solemnity to mime someone hanging themselves, eyes rolling for comic effect.

"Fucking hell," I say, leaning back in my seat to put some physical distance between us.

Dev chuckles and says, "They're trying to stop you from doing your job properly. If today's anything to go by, it's working."

"But this hasn't been 'over an extended period of time.' Let's just speak hypothetically and say the Met *did*—for whatever reason—want to ensure the deterioration of my mental state. They've got a couple of weeks at most while the trial is ongoing."

Dev wags a finger, "But it's different here. You're away from home, stranded, without support, with no one to turn to… All of that serves to send you loopy-loo faster." He drinks his second gin and tonic at that, not bothering to quell his slurping noises.

I shake my head and run my fingers through my hair. "None of that makes sense. The police can't target lawyers for doing their job. This is the UK. It's a democracy with checks and balances."

Dev rubs his face again. "You're hard work, do you know that? Democracy indeed…" He chuckles darkly. "They're hiding something. There's something out there"—he jabs at the window—"they don't want you to find."

Yes, my daughter, I think. For some reason, I don't tell Dev about my suspicion that she's here on the island. Just as I haven't told him about Delia Lewis, the barrister from the robing room, or the fact that I saw a little girl who seemed to disappear. I don't think DC Parks was lying earlier. Perhaps she really didn't see anything. Maybe they found a place to hide.

"You're trying to use one unproven fact to lend weight to another. What about the notes delivered to my hotel room? That's got nothing to do with Special Branch. Those notes had the Odal rune stenciled onto them. They say I need to 'get him (Eades) off.' That's the opposite of what the police want."

Dev waves his hand as though shooing away a cat. "Smoke and mirrors, smoke and mirrors. This is classic Branch."

I'm not so sure. It being the Met's Orwellian machinations certainly fits Dev's agenda, but that's too far-fetched for words.

I tell Dev about what I found earlier, the cave where the hollow earthers meet and draw Nazi symbols. "So, these people seem to be controlled or manipulated by this Smyth fellow. Maybe he's the one who's behind the threats. Perhaps he's a member of the Order of Eights and Sevens, has tried to set up a cell here, taking advantage of this group of men here so that they will help him while he evades the authorities."

"There's no way of knowing who's a member of O87 and who isn't. It's not like the masons; there's no funny handshake or unusual sock and trouser arrangement. But I can tell you that all of this intimidation—posting of threats and pictures of your daughter—is exactly the sort of thing DC Parks would do."

"She doesn't seem that subtle to me."

"You're just seeing the tip of the iceberg at the moment." Dev picks up his drink and takes a sip. The glass shakes in his hand.

I realize that it's not just hatred he feels toward her; it's fear.

"What did she do to you?" I ask.

He sighs and ruffles his face again. When he speaks, there's a defeatist undertone. "She has been the perpetrator of a personal vendetta against me for the last five years. She's ruthless and stupid. Not a good combination."

I consider this. Ruthless, yes, but DC Parks does not strike me as stupid.

"How did she pursue this vendetta?"

"Phone tapping, threatening my family in obscure ways, like sending me pictures of their house just to prove she knows where they live, leaving parcels of dog shit at the office, breaking into my flat...loads of stuff. I've seen the inside of a police cell more times than my mother's kitchen. And every time I make a complaint to the police, she lies and covers up evidence. That's what people like her *do*. She didn't go into the police to catch the bad guys; she's in it for the power."

"How did she get you locked up in a cell?"

"Planted evidence. Ensured the police found it."

"What evidence?"

Dev shifts uncomfortably. "Pictures of, well... Think of the worst pictures imaginable."

I don't know how, but it's as though Dev has opened one of the cubbyholes in my mind. It's dark inside, and it makes me feel sick even though I don't know what's in it. "I don't need to imagine," I say.

There are no memories I can draw on of cases I've done involving those images, but they've left a psychological scar no amount of memory loss can erase.

Dev nods, sobered. "She nearly ruined me. Luckily, I know people. People who know what they're looking for when it comes to planted evidence. One of the perks of being a reporter, I suppose."

He leans back, his ankle resting on his knee, and scratches the back of his head. I don't blame him; the thought of those pictures is making me itch. I can't stop thinking about them. Perhaps they *were* his and Dev is just altering the truth to suit his own version of events. But that's the harm all of this does, isn't it? It plants that seed of doubt and makes you question whether the person you thought you knew is the real them.

Is that what she's doing to me? Damaging my reputation, planting evidence so that the Assumption Island police suspect me of a murder? It's working. The way Trevor looked at me…

When I was arrested, I didn't want to believe I was capable of murder. But then I think back to the memory I had earlier, while I was in Stan's house. A memory of assaulting an old man. If those cigarettes belonged to the man from my memory, then I must have been remembering Pat, whose postcoital cigarettes I've been carrying around in my pocket. I feel sick. But if we did have a relationship and argued, that might be a compelling motive for murder.

Why can't I remember his face? How useless, how inefficient our memories are that they can only hold on to specific details. No wonder witnesses have such a hard time describing their attackers. Our minds aren't built to take photographs; we can only focus on distinct features, like Pat's blue eyes. But I do remember the anger I felt as I assaulted him.

I look through the window. The rolling green hills are like monsters crouching in the twilight. When we were leaving court, it still felt like daytime, even though everything had taken on a lilac hue. But from inside the dimly lit bar, the sky looks pitch-black.

"Am I going on my own, then?"

Dev's question breaks my reverie. "Going where?"

"To speak to the witness." Dev sticks his tongue in the space between his bottom gum and lip and rolls his eyes in a way that is both offensive and alarming.

"You're despicable."

Dev claps his hands. "Chop, chop, go up and get ready."

"I wanted to go back to the cave at six—to see if they're still there."

Dev shakes his head. "No time. This witness is pretty skittish, so we've got to tread carefully. Turning up late might mean he won't see us at all. Meet me in half an hour."

"What will you be doing?"

"Procuring transport."

<hr>

When I approach the hotel desk, the receptionist manages to reach behind her into the cabinet on the wall and select my key without tearing her eyes away from the pages of her paperback.

"Good book?"

"Mmm?" She looks around for who asked the question and seems surprised to find me standing there. "Oh, it's you."

I look down at the room key in my hand, a little worried that she gives out keys at random without confirming the guest's identity.

"Someone wants to speak to you," she says.

"Who?" I ask, quelling the rush of anxiety. I'm less than forty-eight hours into my new life, and I've already learned that nothing good can come from other people trying to contact me.

"A police officer, I think."

"Male or female?"

"Male."

DS Grant. The "good cop," as far as I can tell. "Did you get his name?"

"Kant or something."

"The philosopher?"

"If you say so," she says absent-mindedly, her eyes returning to the pages of the paperback as though magnetically attracted to them.

"Did you take a message?"

She addresses the book rather than me. "Only that he wants to speak to you and that he'll return at a more convenient time."

I leave the reception desk, feeling uneasy. How does he know when will be a convenient time?

———————

On entering my hotel room, I'm struck by the chill. Nothing about it feels like home. I check under the bed and in the wardrobe before I start removing my clothes. And even then, I do it quickly to reduce the time when my skin is exposed. Then I reach into my handbag and pull out the toy horse. I hug it into my chest until the plastic hurts my sternum. Stroking the mane of the horse, I fight the urge to imagine myself, at home—wherever home is—stroking my daughter's hair, then combing it before tucking her into bed.

Dabbing the corner of my eye with the heel of my hand, I replace the horse in my handbag and look around.

Half an hour. I should be reading the next witness statement, combing through the unused material, doing anything I can to get an edge and an early night. My fingers linger over the turned-down picture of my daughter. I owe it to her to do a good job.

Instead, I sit down at the desk and punch in the number for reception to test Dev's theory about phone interference. I get that same crackly noise coming down the line.

"Reception."

"There's something wrong with my phone. I'm getting loads of interference. Can you hear it?"

"Hear what?"

"The crackly quality of the line."

"We don't always get the best reception on the island."

"This is more than just a bad line. There's something seriously wrong. I want a new phone."

"I'm sorry, but unfortunately we won't be able to provide you with a new phone."

"Why? This one isn't working. Are you saying there are no spares?"

"I'm sorry that you feel that way, but unfortunately we won't be able to provide you with a new phone."

"Can I speak to your manager?"

"Give me your name and the details of your complaint." Everything she says is so placid, so monotone, it's even more infuriating than a bad attitude.

But I do as she says and make my complaint before slamming the phone back onto the receiver feeling no less agitated than before.

I walk to the bathroom to splash my face with water, but the cold tap is still too stiff to turn.

"And the bloody tap's broken!" I yell at the handset.

After splashing my face with warm water, I sit down on the bed and lie back.

My last memory is of the frosted ceiling lamp.

When I sit up, I'm no longer in my hotel room, but in a much more luxurious suite. The enormous bed I've been lying on is dressed in soft cream cotton sheets. The chiffon curtains that hang from the four posters ripple in the wind.

Laughter rises from the street below. I get off the bed and go over to the balcony to investigate.

The wind whips my half-dressed body. I'm wearing a silk slip. I lean over the balcony and spot a group of revelers below. This is a British city at Christmas. The Edwardian street is lined with buildings made of Bath stone, which are draped with gaudy decorations.

The door opens.

"What were you doing out on the balcony?"

I splutter, not sure what to say. All I know is that I'm in danger.

The man with the piercing blue eyes strides toward me and pins me to the wall.

I struggle to breathe.

"Don't, don't, I'll—"

Breathing smoke in my face, he whispers, "No one will believe you."

I knee him in the groin and throw him onto the bed.

Then there's a knocking sound.

I open my eyes. Someone is banging on the door to my hotel room.

"Half an hour, I said. It's been an hour! Stop doing your makeup and get out," says the voice: Dev's voice.

I'm back on Assumption Island. I check around me and there is no luxurious bed with cream sheets. Just the fusty old-fashioned one with the viscose headboard.

I open the door to find Dev standing outside.

"Ready?"

I turn to look at the room behind me, half expecting to see the luxurious suite.

"Look, if you've got someone in there, I admire your celerity and it provides some explanation as to why you're late, but don't try to kid a kidder."

I shake my head. "There's something…" I feel like I'm still in the memory, exposed and in danger.

"Yeah, well, this isn't the Ritz, sweetheart, so I think you'll have to slum it for a bit. Anyway, where was I? Oh, yeah: get a fucking move-on."

The Ritz. I think back to the luxurious hotel. The man I assume is Pat.

"Let me just grab a coat."

CHAPTER TWENTY-SIX

"YOU *ARE* TAKING THE piss."

We're looking at a motorbike, complete with sidecar. From the look of it, it could be from the 1950s, but nothing about its half-a-century lifespan fills me with confidence.

"Is this a joke?"

"It's got a cover. I'm not a total savage." Dev pats the sidecar before brandishing a pair of goggles and a helmet. "Say 'please.'"

"Why do I need these?"

"Ah, ah." He holds them out of reach. "Say '*please.*'"

"Fine—*please.*"

"The cover makes it less aerodynamic, so I'll be taking that off."

"You are despicable."

"You've said that already today, and repetition is a sign of poor vocabulary. Read some Dickens, will you? Then maybe you won't spend as much time firkytoodling."

I mutter under my breath, "What wouldn't I give to shove *Great Expectations...*" I'm reluctantly piling my limbs into the sidecar, and my train of thought strays away from shoving books into Dev's orifices and onto the extreme discomfort of my carriage.

Dev climbs astride the motorcycle and the beast revs into life as he turns the key, blasting me with exhaust fumes. I cough pointedly and wave my hand in front of my face but get little sympathy.

The sensation of being subjected to a slow form of carbon monoxide poisoning continues for the rest of the journey. The roaring of the engine—which is deafening inside the sidecar—is accompanied by the rattling of the metal cage I'm confined to. It feels as though at any minute, with one nasty jolt over a pothole, the sidecar will detach from the motorbike and continue its solo journey into the night.

The lights of the main town recede as we're swallowed by the gloom that settles in the middle of the island. I look around, hoping to get a better sense of the island's topography, but it's too dark. As far as I can make out, in the rounded bottom of the island is a vast expanse of green hills. We drive toward the pointed headland that forms the tip of the raindrop. The roads are winding, and before too long, they're fringed by trees. An opening in the trees gives me a view to the headland. A white light flashes in the gap before the motorbike's progress knits the trees, hiding the light once more.

I'm just about ready to pass out from the fumes when Dev stops the engine.

"If you think I'm giving you a hand, you've got another think coming."

"Perhaps you should read some Jane Austen and learn some chivalry," I grumble as I climb out of the sidecar, my knees protesting after being cramped for so long. A dull headache is clouding my vision, and it takes me a while to realize that we're at the edge of a wood.

Looming in front of us, at the forest's mouth, is an enormous concrete structure, its true size indecipherable in the dark. The pulsing white light from the headland is close by, but I still can't see its source. As we walk further into the trees, the light's potency fades until it disappears.

Dev swings his torch, until its beam finds a lichen-stained sign.

British Army Barracks
Assumption Island

I look around. Glinting in the wavering torchlight are the remnants of a wire fence. Cages of barbed wire lie rusted on the ground, scattered in clumps, like the husks of horse chestnuts peeking out from the undergrowth.

"Why are we here?" I murmur.

"You don't have to keep your voice down," he says, imitating me in a stage whisper. "And I already told you. To see a witness."

Dev walks off. I follow after him, tucking my fingers into my pockets and finding the little pieces of paper stashed in them. My line of vision is limited to the erratic movements of Dev's torch.

"Did you speak to this witness earlier?"

"We corresponded."

"Meaning?"

"No, I don't know what they look like."

"Then how do you know where they are? This place looks massive. Just crossing the car park is taking forever."

"Patience is a virtue. Seldom found in men, never found in wom—"

"Shut up."

Dev dismisses this with a grunt before sniffing and rubbing his nose with his index finger. The torchlight quivers.

"What's that?" I ask.

Looming on the other side of the car park is a large building, swallowing any trace of light.

"That was the barracks."

"Was?"

"Well, there's no one there anymore, is there?"

We approach the facility after a couple more minutes of walking.

The light from Dev's torch steadies and focuses on a large roller door. We reach it and wait, as though we're in a fairy tale and the bubbled, peeling metal door will melt away as soon as we say the magic words.

"Open sesame?" says Dev.

"Nice try."

Dev raises his fist and raps on the door. We wait for several seconds, but nothing stirs on the other side.

"He definitely said to meet here?"

Dev shoots a sideways look at me but remains silent.

I let out an exasperated sigh. My arms are folded to suppress the shivers, and my shoulders are bunched up around my ears. I look down and see something curious. A piece of paper pokes out from underneath the door. Without telling Dev what I've seen, I crouch down to pick it up.

Unlike everything else about the barracks, which reeks of neglect, the piece of paper is fresh, if a little dampened by the humidity.

Not here, look left.

By the time I've opened up the piece of paper, Dev is leaning close enough to read it over my shoulder. He backs off and heads left without discussion. I follow after him, stuffing the piece of paper in my coat pocket.

The torch beam swings from left to right, briefly highlighting the bark of the evenly spaced trees. Dev starts moving the light more slowly, searching the undergrowth, poking the beam into the shadows like a poker in a fire.

I've caught up with him, and I'm trying to scan the surroundings as well, but I can't see anything outside of the needle of torchlight piercing the darkness.

"Are you sure about this? Why are they playing games?"

Dev doesn't laugh at me for whispering now. When he speaks, it's out of the bottom corner of his mouth. "Has it occurred to you that they're as scared as we are?"

It hadn't. I don't like this at all, but I don't say as much. I follow him in silence until—

"Ah," says Dev, voice low.

His beam is pointing at one of the trees. Cut into the bark is an arrow. Dev sniffs the air like a dog catching a scent. For the first time, I see the journalist behind the mask of dry skin and bawdy jokes. I follow him as he walks along the path in the trees. The further into the wood we go, the louder the sound of the ocean becomes. We must be close to the coast, perhaps on the opposite side of the island from the main town.

Dev grunts. Another arrow. This time pointing off the path, into the dense trees and crowded ground.

Eventually, after countless bramble thorns and God knows how many minutes trying to work out whether we're walking in a straight line, we see something up ahead: a shed.

As twigs snap beneath our feet, a light flares inside.

———————

The light, as it turns out, was from a plastic lighter. From inside the shed it was a dull glow barely penetrating the dirt-caked windows, but in the pitch-black of the woods, it may as well have been a flaming brazier.

Now, that same lighter is illuminating the asymmetrical face of Dev's witness.

"Bell's palsy," he says. I feel immediately guilty for staring.

"I wasn't—"

"You were. They all do."

The flame makes it worse, I tell myself. Anyone whose face is lit from below looks ghoulish. But that doesn't quite cut it, and the bitter aftertaste of guilt lingers.

The witness moves the flame from underneath his chin and uses it to ignite a gas lamp hanging on the wall.

"Nice place you've got here," says Dev.

"Does for me."

Dev extends a hand. "Devin Hanlon, investigative journalist extraordinaire"— the hand goes unshaken—"and, well, she says she's a barrister, but you wouldn't know it from seeing her in court…"

I shake my head but don't bother to contradict him. I'm too interested in the witness's demeanor. He looks us up and down us as though expecting to find evidence of concealed weapons. He also peers out of the window at least once every thirty seconds.

"You already introduced yourself in correspondence," says the witness. "You can call me Dev."

"But *I'm* Dev."

"OK, then. Call me Kev."

"Kevin it is," says Dev.

I lean across and whisper, "This isn't going to work."

Dev turns to me, not with his head like a normal person, but twists his upper body—all of it.

"In court the witness has to identify themselves before they testify," I say.

Kevin lets out a low growl of a laugh. "I'm not testifying."

"This is a waste of time," I hiss at Dev, but he just waves his hand like he's wafting away a lethal fart.

"I protect my sources. So, Kevin, what's with all the cloak and dagger?" he asks.

Kevin glares back at him. "They'll get me." He jerks his head toward the window.

"Twitchy," says Dev.

"You would be too if you were me."

"Yet you live on this island, in the very cemetery of the secrets you're keeping. Don't you worry that it won't be long before you're the one who's six feet under?"

"Better out here than on the mainland. I can keep an eye on the gravestones. Make sure no one's changing the epitaphs."

"So that's what this is. You see yourself as a guardian."

"What the hell is going on?" I ask, finally too confused to stay quiet.

Dev cocks his head in my direction but speaks to Kevin. "Told you she wasn't very bright." Then he turns to me and speaks slowly and loudly. "We are on Assumption Island. For the last ten years, the Home Office—you know what the Home Office is?"

"Yes, of course I know what the Home Office is."

"Has been using it as their own personal shed. Think of it as a man drawer. A nice little dumping ground for all of the handy wires and tools you don't want to leave lying around the house."

"When you've stopped speaking in obscure metaphors—"

"Jesus Christ alive. Do you not read the news?"

"I'm usually a bit busy for that."

"Well, if you had decided to crawl out from under your rock and take a look around, you'd know that Assumption Island is dedicated to the trials and imprisonment of terrorists and foreign criminals. It's also the detention center for anyone making an application for asylum."

"Asylum? As in refugees fleeing war-torn countries?"

Dev flips his palms up. "I did tell you the government is out to get us."

"Right, so it's a prison, immigration detention center, court, fishing village, and...army barracks?"

Dev looks to Kevin and they both shrug. "That just about covers it. The latter being where our friend...*Kevin* fits in."

"I was in the army. Came out here for training."

"Why all the way out here?" I ask.

"At first, they made out that it was a new kind of survival training, but after a while it became clear that Assumption Island was sufficiently tucked away to avoid public scrutiny. So, the Ministry of Defense felt that we could be a bit more experimental with our techniques."

"Hang on—I thought this was the Home Office's...'man drawer'?"

"That's the problem with Cabinet reshuffles," says Dev. "The MoD were actually here first, and then the Home Office came along, and then they invited the MoJ to the party, so that they could carry out their plan of making Assumption Island a one-stop shop for keeping undesirables off the mainland."

"Including people fleeing persecution in their homeland?"

Dev holds up his meaty hands. "I didn't say I agreed with it."

"What does any of this have to do with the trial?"

"Patience," says Dev, "is a virtue, seldom found in men—"

"You've done that one already," I say before turning to Kevin. "What does this have to do with the bombing of Abbott House?"

"My expertise is in explosives. It wasn't long before the bombing back home became more important than carrying out little experiments out here, so I was sent back, where I began dismantling IRA bombs every other month."

"Are you the forensic explosives expert they're not calling?"

"There is life on Mars!" says Dev.

I shoot him a death stare.

"It's even weirder than that," says Kevin. "So, after coming back to the UK and spending time in Northern Ireland, I left the army and joined the Met's bomb disposal team. Same job, different badge. On the 23rd of May 1995, we received an anonymous call saying that we should go to Birmingham Crown Court. This was a classic IRA tactic. They gave warnings and later made out they never meant to kill anyone. So, we were expecting the worst. We got there, parked up, and were just unloading the equipment when we got a radio through from Scotland Yard telling us to get out of there."

"Was there another bomb scare?" I ask.

"No. We were just told to leave."

"Were you given a reason?"

"No. And when you're army, you follow orders."

"I'm not blaming you," I say.

"You should, because half an hour later Abbott House went off."

"But you weren't even sent there."

"It's about a five-minute walk away."

"You wouldn't have found the bombs."

"Might have been able to do something. Anyway, we were seen."

"Not that you'd know it from looking at the news," says Dev bitterly.

"No, it was hushed up," agrees Kevin. "Don't know what happened to the civilians who spotted us, but I was interrogated by Special Branch for months. Why did we go, where did we get our instructions…"

"But you said it was radioed in."

"No record of the call. They were making out like *we* were the ones who had prior knowledge."

"Smoke and mirrors, smoke and mirrors," says Dev. "Classic Branch. They were looking for scapegoats to try to hide the fact that they knew about the bombing before it happened."

"How did you come to that conclusion?" I ask.

"You can't have taken a closer look at the issues of *Beacon* I left for you, then."

"It's not like I had a glut of time."

"You saw the psy-ops one—"

"Ah, psy-ops. They developed the UK's program right here on AI," interrupts Kevin, a dark look somewhere between wistful and disgusted engulfing one half of his face.

Dev points a finger at him. "See. I'm not just some lone conspiracy loon."

"I never said—"

"You thought it, though. Poker face isn't one of your strengths. I'm still trying to find one of your strengths, come to think of it..."

"What was in the other article that I neglected to read?"

Dev holds up a finger and starts digging about in his messenger bag.

Kevin says, "He's right. They knew. Special Branch knew. When I went back to the office, I knew it was time to go Erskine."

"In English?"

Dev interrupts. "Seriously? Don't they teach you anything at law school? Erskine May's treatise on procedure in Westminster is the Bible of parliamentary procedure. Keep up, and no more stupid questions."

"Sure, very stupid. I'll remember that useless piece of info for the next pub quiz," I say. I turn to Kevin. "So you were saying. You 'went Erskine'?"

Kevin nods. "I played by Westminster rules and decided to get counterfoils. I used to be friendly with one of the telephone clerks. She showed me her notepad for the day. Written on the pad at 12:58, over two hours before the bomb went off, was a note."

"Have you still got it?"

"I was going Erskine; of course I kept it, but I'll never reveal where it is. On that notepad were the words *Anon caller. Birmingham. Tell Security Services. Possible bomb threat. Crown Court.*"

"Why cover it up? It wasn't your fault the tip was wrong."

"Search me. But I left the Met after that. Couldn't face another day propping up corruption. It was only then that I realized how deep this stuff was."

"Gotcha!" Dev pulls out a newspaper from the depths of the bag and tosses it at me.

I look down at what Dev threw me: *The Muslim Times.*

I read the front page, but it appears to be a story about the harsh punishment received by journalists in Saudi Arabia.

"What does this have to do with...?"

"Trust you to look at the front page." Dev grabs the paper from my hands and turns to the relevant article, which is on page 14.

MUSLIMS ON ALERT

The Muslim Times have been informed that Muslim communities in Birmingham should be on alert as there has been "chatter" in terrorist groups suggesting we might be their target. Although there is no evidence that what is often known as "the Balti Triangle"—perhaps the most famous if not the most accurately defined grouping of Asians in Birmingham—will be specifically targeted, we at *The Muslim Times* counsel extra caution and say that those attending the mosques in that area should be particularly alert to any unusual activity.

Anti-racist campaigners believe the motivation is Islamophobic and that the prospective perpetrators will be white supremacist neo-Nazis.

Jennifer Tattersall of the Ant-Nazi Alliance speaks to *The Muslim Times*: "Muslims aren't the Nazis' traditional victim of choice, but it is clear that since the Gulf War began, there has been an increase in anti-Muslim rhetoric, both in the media and in society more generally."

We have no more information but warn that everyone should be on their guard.

I look at Dev after reading.

"How could they possibly know that it would be a neo-Nazi attack?"

One corner of Dev's mouth pulls up in a satisfied smirk. "Interesting, isn't it, that the police were contacting Muslims and telling them to be on alert? They knew the prospective location, which you might think is particularly strange given that Eades is Welsh. They got the target half right and all."

I drum my fingers on the rotting windowsill.

"I still don't see how this helps. Their foreknowledge only proves negligence, not malice."

Dev turns to Kevin. "See what I have to put up with?"

CHAPTER TWENTY-SEVEN

IT'S GONE SEVEN AND the night is slipping away from me. All this time spent chasing shadows and I haven't gleaned any information that will help me with tomorrow's witnesses. A lump of guilt settles at the bottom of my stomach. I should be in my hotel room, trying to put together a case for my client. Tomorrow, either Dr. Sheridan, the occult expert, or Kwame Adebayo, the cleaner who removed two of Eades's bombs from the toilet, will give evidence. We might even get through both of them and on to the anonymous witness, A. N. Other.

My mind wanders to the face-down picture on the desk of my hotel room. I'm desperate to return, to turn it over, but I don't feel as though I can look her in the eye just yet. Not when I have so little to show for my efforts.

I need to get back to the hotel and start prepping my cross-examination, but Dev has other ideas.

We pull up outside the Pilot, a rickety pub on the outskirts of the main town.

"What now? I need to go back to the hotel and prep."

"Didn't you prepare before the trial?"

"Of course, but that's not enough. I need to put the finishing touches, go through my notes..."

Dev bats his hand. "That won't take long, and you need to hear this."

"None of this is helping, Dev. It's interesting but it's a distraction. None of this goes to the heart of the case."

"Patience…"

"If you say that one more time, I swear—"

"This is the last piece of the puzzle."

I've no other choice. I don't want to walk these streets alone after receiving the "you're dead" pager code. Reluctantly, I trundle after Dev into the Pilot. To get to the bar, we have to pass through a small corridor that smells of stale urine from the toilets. There's a public telephone on the wall with a big plastic cover like a translucent shell.

After we find a table, Dev unburdens his legs by collapsing onto a Windsor chair. He looks at me with wide eyes that alternate between me and the bar. "You don't think I'm getting the drinks, do you?"

"I got them at the hotel."

"Still a tight arse, then."

I pull out a menu in response and start poring over it. "You may as well order the food while you're there. Ploughman's for me."

He rolls his shoulders in a dramatic shiver. "Revolting. Leaves."

"It's just a sandwich."

"That's a salad by another name… Cold food." He shakes his head in disgust and approaches the bar.

I pull out the dog-eared piece of paper containing the batting order. Apart from Dr. Sheridan, the rest of the witnesses have been called in order, which means Dr. Sheridan could be coming at any moment. I expect Paxton to play him like a joker, pulling him out of the deck when he's most damaging to the defense.

Dev approaches the table holding two drinks.

"So, what are we doing here? I hope we're not just here for food."

Dev holds a pint in one hand and a glass of tap water in the other.

"Ran out of change; sorry," he offers by way of explanation, placing the tap water on the beer mat nearest me.

Taking a sip of the lukewarm water, I refuse to rise to the bait.

"Ah, here he is." Dev stands up and goes over to the man who's just walked in, putting a hand on his arm and steering him over to the table. "What's your poison, then?"

"Bitter," responds the newcomer. He has a pinched face framed by red hair, grown to below his ears.

Dev jerks his head at me. "Go and get this man a beer."

I go to protest, but I can see that Dev still has a hand on the man's shoulder to stop him from changing his mind and leaving. The man's eye twitches involuntarily, a trapped nerve spasming beneath his skin like a trapped insect.

I order a beer, parting with my sole remaining note, meaning I only have spare change left.

On my return to the table Dev says, "Meet Jason."

Jason regards me warily, the nerve in his tear trough glitching. I sympathize with him; my eyes have felt like that all day, dried out with tiredness.

"Jason has something he wants to tell you," says Dev.

"I'm not going on fucking record," says Jason.

"No one's asking you to. Just speak to the lawyer."

"Will this be confidential?" he asks me.

"If you want it to be, then yes." This is a lie. I have no obligation to him. Only client-lawyer relationships are protected by legal professional privilege.

"All right." I read mistrust in the look he gives me. "I'm a prison officer, working in the prison."

"And…" nudges Dev.

"I said something to the police at the time, but no one wanted to hear about it."

"Tell Miss Dalton about some of the undesirables you keep here on the island."

"The prison itself isn't that big. It's the Immigration and Asylum detention center that's massive. I work in the actual prison bit, where we have the most dangerous people."

"Most dangerous? Aren't most of them just normal criminals who happen to be foreign?" I ask.

"Exactly," he says. "There was one prisoner on death row—"

"But we don't have capital punishment in the UK," I say.

Dev shakes his head at Jason. "She's not the brightest bulb, this one." Then to me, he says, "Maybe not for murder, despite Maggie's best efforts, but we still have it for treason."

This fact jars with me. I don't know why, but I'm sure he's wrong. Capital punishment doesn't exist. How I can be so sure of this with no memories is a mystery to me, but something makes me feel uneasy. Everything I've been told about this place seems wrong. A place where the UK deposits asylum seekers and foreign criminals in the middle of the Atlantic, where Muslims are the first to be blamed for terrorist incidents… Everything about this place feels slightly off, as though it's been skewed by ten degrees.

"I apologize for my friend's idiocy, Jason," says Dev. "Please continue."

"We had this prisoner, Charles Smyth—"

"Smyth?" I ask.

"You know him?" asks Dev.

"I've heard of him," I say. "Haven't you seen the posters of him plastered about the place?"

They return blank looks.

"Sorry; carry on with your story." I lean forward now. Smyth indoctrinated those men down on the beach, made Stan believe the earth is hollow. He might be behind the threats I've been receiving. I need to know more about him.

Jason looks annoyed at the interruption. "Smyth was on death row awaiting his fate. One day, we were taking him his food and he said, 'The time for Assumption has arrived, May the 23rd will be a special day.'"

I frown. "So, you're saying a prisoner kept on death row hundreds of miles away from Birmingham knew of a terrorist plot before it happened?"

"He certainly knew about the date. Then he began holding his arm up and shouting, 'Eight eight, Heil Hitler!' Shouting it over and over again. We didn't know what to do with him. It was like he was possessed; he just wouldn't stop shouting."

Dev rolls his shoulders and says, "Creepy," before taking a sip of his drink.

"What does 'eight, eight' mean?"

"At first, we thought it was because it was his number. He would have been the eighth person to be executed on the island."

Where's the Eighth? Follow the Sevens.

Is this what DC Parks meant by the eighth? The eighth prisoner to be executed? If so, why does she think I would know where Smyth is?

I feel Dev's eyes on me. I return his gaze. It's clear that he's expecting me to make a connection. Then it hits me: Kevin's anonymous caller. Is this how they were tipped off?

"Did you tell the police that he was saying any of this stuff?" I ask.

"Not at the time. We thought he was raving mad, but I did tell them after I saw the bombing on the news in case they wanted to speak to Smyth and ask him how he knew about the date."

"Did they?"

Jason laughs, but not at me; it's a bitter chuckle. "No. They brought forward his execution date."

We sit in silence for several uncomfortable moments before I ask, "What did he do?"

"Escaped before they could execute him."

"I mean, what did he do to deserve execution?"

"Plotted with prominent Nazis who weren't tried at Nuremberg to usurp the queen."

"When was this?" I ask.

Jason shrugged. "Back in the seventies."

"Well, that was lovely," says Dev, clasping his hands together. "Bye, Jason." He stands up and tries to lift him out of his seat, but Jason stays put.

I'm frustrated with Dev. I was getting somewhere.

"Aren't you going to pay me?" asks Jason.

"Sources get paid for stories. No points, no prizes."

"Wait," I say, before Jason leaves. "Where's Smyth now?"

"His body's never been found, so he must be alive and hiding out on the island somewhere."

"Unless he drowned trying to escape," I say.

"You'd have to be a fool to try that."

I take the chance to ask one last question. "Do you know what 'follow the sevens' means? Or 777?"

Jason looks at me with wide, fearful eyes. When the nerve twitches, he pokes it as though it can be swatted away. "Those are the numbers Smyth used to scrawl on his cell wall." He recovers his composure and turns to Dev. "If you're not going to pay me, I'm off."

Dev escorts him out of the Pilot while I sit and mull over this new information.

Dev returns and drops down onto the chair next to me. "What was that all about?" he asks.

"All what?"

"Follow the sevens, 777?"

"I've got a theory," I say, before frowning and looking over at a group of men watching football.

"Well, sharing is caring, so any time now would be good." Dev makes a show of checking his watch.

"Can I ask you something about the O87?"

"Shoot."

"When was all of the literature published?"

He throws up his hands. "It's undated. Could be from any time. Why?"

"What if... I think I might have a candidate for the identity of Simon Cox."

"Go on."

"So, the Hollow Earth... That's something the Order of Eights and Sevens believes in, isn't it?"

Dev nods.

"Those people on the beach. They believe in the hollow earth because Charles Smyth taught them about it. They think that's what the Odal rune means. So, we've got this prominent Nazi imprisoned on the island, predicting the day of Assumption… What if he's more than some mad prisoner? What if he's Simon Cox? He's even got the same initials but swapped around. Maybe Simon Cox is Smyth's pseudonym. And what if he's here, on the island… threatening me?"

"Interesting theory," he says.

"But Jason has just proved my theory. Smyth knew about the bombing. Why would he know if he wasn't someone pretty high up in the Order?"

"You're missing the point of why I asked Jason to meet us here. His evidence proves that the police knew the bombing was part of a wider plot—how else would Smyth know about it?—but rather than disclose that information to anyone, they brought forward the prisoner's execution to cover it up! Can't you see it's all part of the same pattern?"

"It's not evidence, because Jason quite clearly said he wouldn't go on record, never mind give evidence in court."

I put my hand into my pocket to pull out the leaflet that Stan gave me. Instead, I come across the paradoxical note left by the owner of the coat, which says *I am not a number* on one side and *Yes, you are* on the other. After putting that in the other pocket, I find the leaflet. It has different logos that are supposed to prove that big corporations know the truth about the hollow earth. "Here. This is what Smyth is teaching this man I spoke to earlier."

He studies it. "Now this really is crackpot conspiracy-theory stuff. But everything I've told you about the police…"

He's like a dog with a bone. I realize that without placating him, he won't answer my questions about the O87. "Dev, I've no doubt you're right when you say the Met's hiding stuff. Of course, there's more to this case than meets the eye. But—"

Dev's face drops.

"Knowing something is one thing; proving it is something else."

"But now you know…"

"What I need to understand is why people are threatening me. Why they're sending me these notes with the Odal rune on them referring to my daughter."

"I told you, this is what Special Branch does! It's smoke and mirrors, all of it."

I sigh, rubbing my eyebrows. "OK, let's park my theory about who Simon Cox is. I need your help with something. Tomorrow, I need to cross-examine Dr. Brian Sheridan—"

A loud groan from Dev.

"What?"

"*He's* their expert? Jesus Christ, they've really done a number on this case getting him involved…"

"I need to find a way in, a way to undermine his credibility. Given this is your area of expertise, will you help me?"

"Say 'please.'"

I roll my eyes. "*Please.*"

"What do you need to know?"

"This is what I can make out so far. Sheridan says that Simon Cox is the Grand Master of the Order of Eights and Sevens. He doesn't posit Cox's identity and seems to be under the impression that the name might be the pseudonym used by multiple different people."

"Ah, the old multiple-author theory. I don't buy it, myself."

"Why not?"

"Most of the literature generated by Simon Cox has a trademark. Take this." He rummages around in his messenger bag and pulls out a piece titled "Major System Error: A Guide to Dismantling the System" and starts reading: "'Disruption of water supply would cause problems. Disrupt the supply of everyday commodities, basic public services…' It's just the way he writes; you can tell it's the same person. When you've read as much far-right material as I have, you know who you're listening to."

"That matches what Sheridan says," I say. "He says that the beauty of the order is that it doesn't follow the normal organized-crime-gang structure; it's more like an ideology or a religion. He says that the aim of the group is to destroy society and rebuild it from the ground up... Which explains why Eades would attack a Home Office building."

"He gets some stuff right, in the same way a broken clock tells the time twice a day."

"A broken clock..." I say.

"Are you all right?" asks Dev.

I look for a beer mat, something I can use to draw a tally mark, make sure I haven't been here before. The beer mat is blank.

"Hello?" Dev waves a hand in front of my face. "Earth to Lila."

"I keep getting déjà vu. Someone said that same thing earlier to me today."

"Don't start cracking up on me now," he says. "Are you sure you want me to go on?"

"Yes," I say, nodding fervently.

"Overall, Sheridunce is a moron. Any expert I rate on this stuff agrees with me: Simon Cox may be a pseudonym, but it's only one person behind the mask."

"So, do you agree it could be Smyth?"

"I'm not saying that Smyth is definitely not Simon Cox. I'm just saying you don't have enough evidence to back up your theory yet."

"Why aren't you convinced?"

"Because Smyth has been out of circulation for years, awaiting his death sentence. It's pretty impossible to develop a whole load of far-right literature, invent a quasi-religion, and convince a load of displaced, disillusioned National Socialists to adhere to it. You can't do that sort of thing from a prison cell in the middle of the Atlantic."

"So, who could Simon Cox be, if not Charles Smyth?"

"There are any number of far-right sociopaths who could do this sort of thing. Makes it difficult to narrow it down."

Dejected, I take a desultory sip of water.

"The difficulty with members of the order is that they're extremely secretive and also participate in something called 'inside roles,'" he says.

"What's that?"

"It's all part of the order's wider plan to infiltrate different organizations. They see it as their duty to live among the enemy, basically as sleeper agents, so that they're poised to bring about the destruction of the old world when the time comes. There are at least five cabinet ministers on my list who are potentials for Simon Cox."

"Come off it, Dev."

"I'm serious. Why do you think this place exists? Whose idea was it to start 'offshoring' asylum seekers?"

"Wouldn't you just get bored after a while and realize that the total destruction of society isn't coming anytime soon?"

"Do you know how many times the end of the world has been predicted? Beliefs sustain people, and if you're like Cox or Eades, you become like a parasite, only able to live if you're attached to an ideology."

"Right, so Sheridan is wrong on Cox's true identity, but he's right about the plan to destroy society?"

"Yes and no. Where he's really wrong is this idea that the order doesn't have a hierarchy. Of course it has a hierarchy. Who's printing the literature? Who's funding it? Even the individual cells have different ranks and roles: Grand Master, High Priestess, et cetera."

"They have roles for women?"

"Yes, there are women, but they're not the sort to read *The Female Eunuch* and burn their bras. This is the part of the order's philosophy that is taken wholesale from Aleister Crowley's *Thelema*. The order, as part of their devotion to the left-hand path, perform sex-magic rituals."

"You are taking the piss now."

"As well as extraction, mind control, and all of their bonkers plans to journey to the center of the earth, every now and then they all wander into the woods and get it on."

"How does anyone know about their rituals if they're so secret?"

"Because in the same way the O87 have infiltrated society, society has infiltrated them back."

"You mean Special Branch?"

"The very same."

"How?"

"They plant assets. My magazine reports regularly on the antics their undercover officers get up to."

"I'm starting to see why you and DC Parks are such bosom friends."

"Looks like you're going to be in the same club soon enough." He raises his drink in a mock toast.

"What sort of stuff do the undercover officers get up to?"

"They act as agents provocateurs, mostly. They've also been known to have sex with members of O87 under the guise of getting information."

I frown at this. "I mean, they are a far-right terrorist group. I know it's not pretty, but if it keeps us safe…"

"Special Branch doesn't just do this shit to the far right. They do the same thing to left-wing groups. They did it during the miners' strikes. They infiltrate environmentalist groups and spy on them. Personally, I don't give a shit whether you're trying to save the beagles or preserve the so-called purity of the Aryan race. If you live in a democracy, you have rights, and the moment we start using the ends to justify the means, we're fucked."

CHAPTER TWENTY-EIGHT

DEV LEAVES TO GO to the toilet. I take the time to think through everything I've learned about the order. So, it's either a hierarchical organization headed by the mysterious Simon Cox with defined roles within each cell, or it's a model of leaderless resistance, whereby individuals take responsibility for their own dedication to the cause. I'm still not sure why any of that's terribly relevant to the trial, but I suppose it impacts on Eades's culpability.

Perhaps if I can get Dr. Sheridan to agree with me that there's a hierarchy and that Eades was responding to a direct order, I might be able to reduce his tariff when it comes to sentencing. He'll get life, but it would be a small win to limit the amount of time he has to spend in prison before being considered for parole. In cases like this, anything less than thirty years would be a resounding success.

I turn to thinking about Dev's theory about "inside roles." The idea that the incumbent government's populist policies are the brainchildren of neo-Nazis on the inside is certainly more attractive than accepting that our elected representatives are simply cruel, but I just can't see it happening. Eades is too consumed by hate to even pretend to be a functioning member of society. He can just about manage going to work and returning to his parents' home, where he can stare at the atrocities on his wall. There are pictures of what the police found in his bedroom: a gallery of newspaper clippings about violent crimes, of which the Abbott House bombing was one of many, Nazi memorabilia, occult paraphernalia, and *The Turner Diaries*.

He even made atrocities from the Second World War into cartoons. As though those weren't real people, real lives. Nothing about him suggests he's capable of filing these thoughts away on a shelf in his mind and going about his business. My money is still on Charles Smyth as Simon Cox's true identity. Something strange is happening if fully grown men are being brainwashed into believing something so fantastical as the earth being hollow. Only a charismatic cult leader would be capable of something like that.

There's a beeping sound and I realize that the pager in my handbag is going off again. I rummage around, pull it out, and manage to silence it. A number flashes across the green LCD.

777

Dev returns from the bar with our food.

"What does 777 mean?" I ask him, taking a bite out of my ploughman's.

Dev also takes a bite and speaks to me through a mouthful of food. "Oh, yeah, you never told me what all of that was abou—"

I pull out the pager to show him.

"Er," says Dev, "it has lots of meanings. Lots of occultist and neo-Nazi meanings, for starters."

"He's here."

"Who?"

"Smyth. He must have been listening in on our conversation, or perhaps he saw that we were talking to Jason."

I look around the pub. Smyth must be in disguise to have hidden for so long in this place. I get up and start looking at the faces of the customers, seeing if anyone gives anything away.

"Lila, what's the matter?" asks Dev.

I ignore him and continue to scour their faces.

Movement near the entrance. A figure is standing in the telephone booth. They must have used the pub's pay phone to page me. The plastic shielding obscures their face, but I can tell that they're staring directly at me.

They turn and run.

I follow after them into the corridor, only to find the outer door swinging closed. I push through it and look outside. I can't see anything in the pitch-black.

Hurried footsteps echo around the car park. Only, I can't tell this time whether they're going away from me or toward me. I stay still, turning left to right, trying to work out where they're coming from. The footsteps stop, and all I can hear now is the rain pattering as it hits the pavement.

The blow to the back of my neck sends a spasm of fresh pain into my skull. A flash of white light and I'm on the ground, rainwater seeping into my clothes.

I sense that someone is nearby. In the edges of my blurred vision, there's a dark silhouette knelt down beside me. Cold hands stroke my cheek.

"Get off," I want to say, but I can barely moan.

Every time I try to open my eyes, rain droplets blind me.

The person at my side pulls up my right sleeve. In the dark car park, where I think I might take my last breath, I recognize that they're wearing a purple coat. Dexterous fingers crawl over the skin of my forearm like spider's legs. The last thing I feel before losing consciousness is a searing heat in my wrist, a hot needle of pain.

———

I open my eyes to the blinding glare of a handheld torch. Dev's face is inches from mine but could be miles away for all I can make out of his features. I know it's him because of what he's muttering under his breath.

"Fucking amateur, bringing a tail with us when we're interviewing sources!"

"Did you see..." I mumble.

"Shh, shh." Dev hushes me, his voice surprisingly gentle. He strokes my hair as though soothing a sick dog.

"Who…?" I try to raise my right arm, but the pain in my wrist stops me.

"What's that?" asks Dev.

I groan and grasp my wrist.

"Holy shit," says Dev.

"What?"

He pulls my sleeve down. "We need to get you out of here."

"Did you see who…?" I ask Dev.

He shushes me again, before holding up his ham-shaped fist and asking how many fingers he's holding up.

"This isn't funny," I say.

"I know it isn't. You've compromised our investigation."

"Knew I wouldn't get much sympathy out of you."

With Dev's assistance, I manage to stand. He removes his jacket and drapes it around my shoulders. His hand is on my waist as we hobble out of the car park, and he allows me to lean on him.

"I told you your suit makes you look fat. In reality you've got a lovely—"

"Don't."

He flags down a lift and bundles me inside the stranger's car.

"She's not going to die on me, is she?" asks the driver.

"And they say it's only Londoners who aren't friendly," quips Dev, before passing a banknote between the front seats.

"Where's my coat?" I ask, patting myself down.

"Shh, now. Let's wait until we get back," says Dev, and I notice the driver's eyes flicker in the rearview mirror.

In the dull light cast by the orange streetlamp, I investigate my wrist. I use my wet jacket sleeve to wipe away the blood, revealing a fresh tattoo.

777

———————

I don't know what time it is when we return to the Castle Hotel.

Dev helps me into my room and sits me down in the armchair in the corner.

"All of this, just to get me into your bedroom," he says, looking around at the mess.

I'm shivering from the cold. My clothes are wet, and my hair is plastered to my face.

"I'll wait outside while you change," he says and promptly leaves for the corridor.

"How chivalrous," I mutter when he's outside.

My head sings as I bend down to peel out of my sodden clothes. Once they're discarded, I leave them in a pile on the bathroom tiles and change into some dry clothes. Even after I've wrung out my hair over the bathroom sink, the damp seeps into my shoulders.

I approach the door and say, "Dev? Are you still there?"

Once he replies, I open the door to him.

"How are you feeling?"

"My head is killing me...and there's this." I hold up my wrist to show him the new tattoo.

"What's all this about?" asks Dev.

"The woman who hit me tattooed this on my wrist."

"It was a woman?"

"I'm sure it was. You must have seen her. You were right behind me."

"No, they were long gone by the time I got there." He gets up and walks around.

"How long does it take to tattoo a wrist? Where were you?"

"I'm telling you, it took me a while to find you. I didn't know where you'd gone."

I cradle my head in my hands. "Got any painkillers?"

He rummages around in his messenger bag and pulls out a couple of white tablets.

"You have them loose? What are they?"

He shrugs. "They'll do the trick."

I swallow them dry.

"What does the number mean?" I ask Dev.

He looks at my wrist, his face screwed up as though he's the one who had a needle pierce his skin. "This is…"

"Dev, just tell me."

"So, in occultist circles, it pertains to the law of Thelema. In neo-Nazi circles, 777 is used by AWB, a South African white supremacist group. The sevens are often arranged in a triskelion shape, which looks a bit like a swastika."

In a moment of shining clarity that only a severe knock to the head can procure, I realize that all of this is nonsense. A distraction. The ravings of racist lunatics who have nothing better to do with their time than give one another nerdy tattoos and circle-jerk hatred.

My hand finds the photo of my daughter. I reach into my handbag and find her pink horse.

"Thanks, Dev. I'm going to get to work on the case now."

"Are you sure you'll be all right?"

"I'm sure."

"OK, see you tomorrow."

Once he's gone, I close my eyes, grateful for the peace and quiet. There is no time for rest, however, as I need to prepare for tomorrow. I sit down at the desk, determined to get some work done before midnight. The clock on the bedside table still reads 07:05.

"A stopped clock…" I say to myself. Then I shake my head. I've been hanging around Dev for too long and have started to make connections in things that aren't even there.

I need to concentrate, but so many thoughts are firing off in my mind. To-do lists, things that I need to look for in the unused material, things to check, ideas for lines of questioning that float around in fragments.

I push those distractions away and focus on the new information I've discovered tonight.

I sit down at the desk and notice the face-down photograph. I touch the back, daring myself to turn it over. I can't. I can't bear to remind myself of a face I may never see again. Maybe there are mothers out there who would find strength in seeing a picture of their child, who would be revitalized, but it just makes me want to cry, and no one feels stronger after crying. I would just end up feeling sorry for myself.

My fingers leave the back of the photograph. I open up the folder of unused material. There are reams of it. With a pad of paper next to me, I start going through the pages, looking for anything to bolster this new theory that the security services had foreknowledge of the attack. Why would they have let it happen if they knew about it?

I pull the neo-Nazi zines from their sheet protectors and scan the pages. I get the same sick feeling reading it as I did when reading Dr. Sheridan's statement. Most of it is drivel, lunatic ravings, and I can't stand to read it line by line. Instead, I scan the headlines for anything that might explain how the order is connected to the bombing.

I move on to what I consider to be "proper" work, trawling through the reams of unused material. It occurs to me that police officers make this stuff boring on purpose to deter defense lawyers from reading it in detail.

I start with the occurrence logs: the police records detailing every incident logged in relation to a particular occurrence number. Every 999 call, details of the crime alleged, the names and addresses involved, fresh entries with each new development.

The occurrence logs for the Abbott House bombing tell their own story. As time progressed, the likelihood of survival for many of the victims dwindled. Lumps of concrete tumbled from the wreckage, ambulances were called, victims were taken to the hospital. I can hear the sirens as I'm reading these logs, can picture the dust and devastation. Picking survivors out of the wreckage took hours, because each rescue brought the risk of toppling slabs of concrete, plunging everyone else in the building to death.

There are also the first descriptions of "persons wanted," and here is where it gets interesting. Officers carry out house-to-house ("H2H") inquiries, although in this context, in the city center, it's probably just random passersby. Lots of people reported seeing a man acting suspiciously on that day. He is recollected with varying degrees of precision but mostly described as Middle Eastern in appearance.

Is this where the press got the initial lead on this being an Islamist attack? I take a closer look at the descriptions provided of eyewitnesses regarding the man hanging around Abbott House, considered to be acting suspiciously.

Not dark-skinned but dressed like one of them.

Had a beard and a white cap.

Other reports say that he had a tan and might have been Mediterranean but wore traditional Muslim dress.

I search the documents in front of me for more clues. The names of the witnesses have all been redacted. They should have been asked to make witness statements, and those statements should have been tendered to us. Perhaps they were tendered but we decided not to call them to give evidence. Was that Pat's decision or mine? To put my mind at rest, I go through the witness statements but can't find any who say that they saw a second person on the day of the bombing. So, witness statements were never taken. The prosecution made a conscious decision not to pursue that line of inquiry.

I go through all of the box files and find an entire file dedicated to agreed evidence, witnesses who don't have to come to court because their evidence is not disputed. A lot of it is irrelevant because none of them saw Eades, many of them on higher levels of the building when the bombs went off. I wish I'd known what I was getting myself into before I started reading them.

CHAPTER TWENTY-NINE

ON MAY THE 23RD 1995, Sarah Blythe had a lot to look forward to. In her bag was The Outfit, chosen by committee during a trip to the Bullring with her girlfriends.

Every morning she got on the train at Selly Oak and traveled into New Street. Every day she got on Carriage 2. She never used to get on that carriage, but one morning she was on the platform when a young man—her age—had appeared and she'd found herself staring at him. He turned around and smiled at her. She blushed. When he got on Carriage 2, so did she. She sat facing away from him and pulled out her paperback and began reading it. She couldn't focus on the words. The romance in the book was nothing in comparison to what was happening in real life—her life—on a grubby commuter train.

This had gone on for months now. Her work outfits were getting steadily more glamorous, and she woke up early to tend to her makeup and hair. Then, she spotted it in the Metro:

I'm in the navy suit. Every morning I see you reading those romance novels and I hope that we can make our own story together.

She'd shown all of her friends, and after more in-depth debate than many had in the Houses of Parliament, they'd all agreed that she should write to the paper and agree to a date with her mystery admirer.

Tonight was the night. Also in the bag was the special underwear she'd bought—just in case. Of course, she'd giggle and say she wasn't "that type of girl," but if he insisted then, well, who was she kidding? She'd been reading Jilly Cooper's *Rivals* on the train that morning and decided that she should be like one of those women—a go-getter type, unafraid of accusations of being a slut, because, hey, women are allowed carnal desires too. This is the nineties, for Christ's sake.

She'd been watching the clock all day. The Criminal Records Bureau checks in front of her were unable to keep her interest. There might be a few dodgy characters going into caring or teaching professions next week because her mind was elsewhere.

Dodgy characters… She suffered a moment's doubt. Was this date a good idea? What if the man was a weirdo? What if he drugged her? She'd heard about that in the news. Date rape. Perhaps if she just did a little check on him…

The building shook. Rumbling could be heard all over, and smoke began billowing up to them. It was like an earthquake. People screamed and were thrown out of their chairs or fell over.

They began evacuating the building. It was a crush. Except Sarah couldn't move. She was trapped. She always worked next to the filing cabinets, and when the bomb went off, the cabinets had fallen, penning her in. She wasn't the only one. There was someone next to her, someone she couldn't see. She screamed for help, but no one could hear her—or maybe they could, but they were so scared for their own lives that they didn't stop to help. She heaved against the filing cabinets, but they were so heavy, much too heavy for her to shift.

Minutes later, the building shook again. This blast was much bigger, and rubble fell all around her, blocking her in. A large piece of concrete fell on her outstretched arm. She screamed and screamed until she found that she was breathing in the dust, and she began hacking and coughing.

Fingers closed around hers—she'd just about retained feeling in her arm. After a while, she felt the other person's grip weaken.

Sometime later, her fingers went cold. And then she began to lose the sensation in her arm, and she knew that it was serious. What an idiot she was. She'd been reaching for her bag—the one with The Outfit and the fancy lingerie. Why? Why had she done that?

Down below at street level, firefighters and paramedics were wondering how they were going to enter the building, how they were going to begin to pick apart the rubble. Neelam was in her second week as a paramedic. This was her worst nightmare—hundreds of injured people yards away who couldn't be treated. Then the reality dawned on her. She might not get out of this alive, either.

She just began digging. No one had a plan. There seemed to be no logic for the search. No structural engineer was on-site to say how to avoid it all collapsing. One thing she couldn't do was let the people trapped inside die alone. She had to get to them. What she saw when she managed to get into the building was horrendous. She'd seen someone degloved. Seen someone's ankle break so badly that the foot was hanging off by an inch of skin. But this was something else. The worst devastation anyone can imagine.

———————

Sarah heard someone shouting, "Hello?"

"I'm here." Her voice was so quiet, she doubted it could be heard. She coughed weakly.

"Where are you?"

"Cabinet. My arm."

"We need a surgeon! We need a surgeon now. There's a woman trapped! We need an ortho!"

Sarah heard the woman shuffle over to her.

"I'm Neelam. I'm here to help," she said. "I'm holding your hand. Can you feel it?"

Tears welled up in Sarah's eyes. "No."

"We need to get you out of here."

"Will I lose my hand?"

Neelam didn't want to give an honest answer. "I'll wait to see what the surgeon says."

Sarah was fading fast. It was like being in water, floating on your back in a star shape. At any moment she could lose buoyancy.

Then it was like she was looking at the world from under an inch of water, consciousness above the surface.

"Stay with me!" shouted Neelam. "She's losing consciousness. We need to operate NOW."

"There's no one available. You'll have to do it," said another voice.

Neelam had a rudimentary kit. They sent you out with tourniquets, local anesthetic, a saw, and scalpels. She couldn't risk putting this woman under. She was only just hanging on, and the anesthetic could make her too weak. She'd have to do this without.

Neelam picked her way through the rubble. She tried heaving the concrete out of the way, but it was no good. There were massive filing cabinets that had fallen against the wall. She and a fireman managed to put one upright so that Neelam could squeeze into the tiny gap and get a clear shot at the arm. Neelam quickly realized that the hand she'd been holding hadn't been Sarah's. It must have belonged to someone else trapped in the rubble. Someone who wasn't able to call out.

"OK, I'm going to have to do this without any tranqs or anesthetic, OK? Hold on to my leg and squeeze when the pain comes."

"Please, give me something."

"I can't... It'll kill you."

"Evacuate the building, get out now! It's going to fall," came a yell from far away, perhaps through a speakerphone.

"No," moaned the woman. "Don't leave me."

"What's your name, sweetheart?"

"Sarah."

"I won't leave you, Sarah. We're getting out of here together."

A tear ran down Sarah's cheek, making a clear track in the dirt and dust.

Neelam put a tourniquet around Sarah's arm and pulled tight. It was uncomfortable in that space. Neelam was straddling her, face-to-face. She'd have to be quick. They didn't have long left before the building would go. So, she began sawing away at Sarah's arm; all the while Sarah's face was directly in front of her. Neelam chose not to look into her eyes and to focus on the arm instead, but her ears, her ears filled with the sounds of Sarah's screams as she sawed away at her arm while she was fully conscious.

"Grab my leg," said Neelam, knowing it wouldn't work. Sarah was too weak to grip anything with her free hand. "I've got to do this. The building will collapse."

"Just fucking kill me."

Neelam hacked and hacked with scalpels. They kept breaking. She was on her third, and she hadn't even got to the bone yet. She pulled out the saw and began sawing. Then the saw broke.

"Give me your ax," she said to the fireman.

Neelam slid the ax in between her and Sarah. Her mother was Bengali, you see, and in Bengal they cut vegetables with a boti—a long curved blade held down by foot. Women kneel at the boti and take the vegetables to the curved section of the blade, running from bottom to top. She couldn't move Sarah's arm, but she could use the same principle.

Placing the bit against Sarah's bicep, she knelt down on the butt, pushing the ax from heel to toe and sliced the arm off in one.

When Neelam goes to sleep at night, she can still hear Sarah's screams.

Her part over, she pulled Sarah out of the hole and left it to the fireman to lug her out of the building.

Sarah survived. Just. She didn't make it to her date that night. She lost all interest in dating after a while. She would feel conscious about her prosthetic, which would be compounded by men staring at it before making jokes about how they'd like to have one because it would be easier to masturbate.

Meanwhile, Eades was being detained at Moor Street Station, less than a mile away from Abbott House. He'd got on the train without paying for a ticket, and they were keeping him while they were considering whether to charge him with an offense or just give him a penalty fare notice.

Eades was sweating. He was supposed to be away by now, back in Wales with his mam and dad. They might even consider alerting the police that he was missing. That would ruin everything. He told the officer that his wallet had been stolen. He begged for the penalty fare, saying he would pay double if it meant they'd let him go. After a while, they agreed and let him be on his way.

All the time they were searching for the man responsible, he was right there beneath their noses. Something had clearly gone wrong for Eades. He wasn't expecting to pay a train fare. Someone else had hold of the money. Someone else was supposed to take him away from Abbott House. But something must have gone wrong for Eades, because they weren't there. He was on his own.

CHAPTER THIRTY

READING SARAH BLYTHE'S AND Neelam Siddique's witness statements is becoming more difficult because the words are glassy and unfocused when I look at them through tears.

I search through the rest of the statements, not stopping to read about the experiences of the survivors; too traumatic.

In the log I find that Eades had been detained on the day of the bombing at Moor Street Station, probably less than a five-minute walk away from Abbott House. He was being kept because he hadn't paid for a ticket.

There's something in that fact, but I have to search for it.

There are no witnesses to his movements *before* he got into Birmingham City Center, and Blackwood to Birmingham is quite a trip. Surely someone would have noticed a man with a large bag on the train? And wouldn't the train companies have CCTV showing who bought tickets on that day? So, he can't have traveled there by train. Someone must have driven him there, and he expected them to drive him back. But they didn't. I think again of the CCTV after the explosion. The moment's hesitation before he ran toward Snow Hill. In that moment, he realized he'd been abandoned.

By whom? Who wasn't there but should have been? I need to find out what's contained within that missing thirty seconds of footage. It must hold the answer. There's no other good reason for them to redact it.

Dev's right. This is bigger than one lone nutter. Why does the prosecution want to hide that?

"How did you know?" I ask of the folders. "How did you know this was going to happen? And why didn't you stop it?"

Special Branch must have had an asset inside the organization, someone who was closely connected to Eades.

I search the unused material. *There's someone here who shouldn't be.*

Even after rereading the documents, I can't put it all together. My eyes are drooping, and I can feel a nerve start to spasm in my eyelid.

After splashing my face with water from the only working tap, I return to the desk and try to put it all together. It feels like it's too big for my mind to keep it all in. Exhausted, I lean back and look at the ceiling, eyes burning. I let my lids close for a moment.

I'm back inside the luxurious hotel room. I'm lying on the bed. Draped across a chair is a red dress, like a drop of blood staining the cream upholstery.

Laughter. I go outside to look, just as I did when I revisited this memory last time. Wind on my skin. Shouting. An argument. Hand to my throat. My knee in his groin. The old man lands on the bed.

The image fades and I sit up, the headache back with renewed fervor. What do these memories mean? I don't understand why I'm in this bedroom remembering what happened. I wish I could remember the accident; then I would know for sure. How I came out unscathed, physically at least; how Pat...didn't. Was I the one who turned the wheel? Did I do something to the car?

I go to the drawer and pop the last of the aspirin, telling myself I'll buy more when I have some time. I run myself a cup of water before peeling out of my clothes and crawling into bed without showering.

I stare wide-eyed, unable to sleep. I can't stop thinking about Sarah Blythe. And Neelam Siddique, the paramedic who had to straddle Sarah, her face inches from the woman whose arm she was hacking off while there were calls for the building to be evacuated.

My eyes droop and I find myself overcome with drowsiness. When I close them, two beetle-black pupils stare back at me. The pupils are surrounded by light-blue irises. The eyes rest in the face of a man sitting across from me. I'm in a low-lit bar, sipping a long drink.

I look down. I'm wearing the jewel-red dress.

The man I'm with pulls a cigarette from a gold Benson & Hedges pack before lighting it. With his spare hand he reaches across and holds mine.

Then I wake up in a strange bed and panic sears through me—where am I?

It's OK, I'm in the hotel. I turn my head to make sure I'm looking at that tacky viscose headboard, but instead I see a man in a glass box. My fingers brush horsehair curls. At the front of the room, the judge is staring down at me, his eyes boring into mine. Blue irises.

The back of my neck is coated with sweat. I peel wet hair from salty skin and turn the pillow over, relishing its coolness.

The alarm goes off. I must still be dreaming. This alarm isn't real; it's another nightmare. My bleary eyes part enough to see that the time is just gone 7:00 a.m. According to this clock, I've had a full night's sleep, but I feel less rested than before. It's like someone has rubbed sand in my eyes while I slept. I remember the clock isn't working, so I have no idea what time it truly is.

I try to close my eyes and go to sleep, but I can't seem to doze off. My watch is on the bedside table but it's too dark to see the time. When I switch the light on, it takes my eyes a while to adjust. The actual time is just before 5:00 a.m. Low tide.

Given it's unlikely I'll be able to get back to sleep, I could go to the cave, maybe see the ritual being performed, maybe find out more about Smyth or the people who have my daughter.

After wriggling into my only nonwork outfit, I leave the hotel room and take the same route down to the harbor, find the path up onto the cape and then down the other side onto the black sand beach. The Odal rune is still scored into the sand like a brand, but none of the flags or candles remain. Inside the cave, there is a flickering light, a flame.

I brace myself before entering the mouth of the cave.

The wind is still audible down here, but I'm not being battered by it. The noise of it howls overhead, while the tall black sides of the cliff protect me. The cliffs glisten, as does the black sand beneath my feet. I begin to enter the cave, the echoing of my footsteps louder even than the sound of my ragged breath. The cave drips, and running water can be heard in the very walls. The deeper in I walk, the closer I get to the source of the fire.

A dancing silhouette is cast on the wall. Emerging from behind one of the stalagmites is a shadow. As I draw nearer, its form becomes clearer. It has eyes, a face, a shabby, ill-fitting gray suit.

It's DS Grant.

"What are you doing here?" I ask.

"I knew you'd want to come back here at low tide. I've been waiting. They're watching us up there, but it's safe here."

He sounds a little wired, but given everything I know about the island, I can't say I blame him.

"Here. I wanted to give you this." He pulls out a file of paperwork and hands it to me.

"What's is it?" I move closer to the file so I can read it.

"Pat's blood alcohol report."

"What? This came back quick."

"That's because we have our own blood alcohol testing kits. We'll be waiting weeks for the full toxicology report to come back from the mainland, but take a look at those. You might find them interesting."

I scan the report, trying to make sense of all the numbers. "What am I looking at here?"

DS Grant points to a figure on the page. "Pat's blood alcohol levels were over three times the legal limit. Why didn't you tell us she was an alcoholic?"

"Wait, what?"

I start to pace back and forth in little circles, trying to process this. So Pat was a woman? I check the name at the top of the report. Patricia Singh.

DS Grant probably thinks I'm dealing with the revelation that she's an alcoholic, but really, I'm trying to piece together how I concluded that Pat was an old white man. I suppose in the first instance, I assumed. Since I came round on Monday morning, all of the other lawyers in court have been male. And then there were the flashbacks and dreams I've been having of the man who smokes the same cigarettes as Pat. The man I assaulted, the man I was in a sexual relationship with. Who on earth is he, if not Pat?

"You must have noticed."

"It's hard to process it all..." I say truthfully. "I can't believe it."

"Why didn't you try to stop her from getting in the car?"

"I don't know."

"S'pose it comes with the territory. I've seen lots of barristers and judges traipse out of that court and straight to the pub. Drowns out the noise, doesn't it?"

"How do you know she was driving?"

"Fingerprints."

"So, I definitely didn't..."

"Doesn't look like it."

"Am I being NFA'd, then?"

"Not officially."

"Why? You don't have any evidence. In fact, that report tells you all you need to know. Surely no further action is the only option you have now?"

He waves a hand. "We've got to wait for the postmortem, and that won't be here for ages." He shifts.

"So, I'm still under investigation?"

"For now."

"What about the witness? The one who said she saw me leaving the scene."

"This is not the first time that witness has made that allegation, and you are not the first person she's made it about."

"Why was what she said given any credibility, then?"

"Look, this isn't the only reason I came to speak to you, Miss Dalton." He stands up and walks toward the mouth of the cave, staring at the rune carved into the sand. "They're watching you."

"It was you."

"Yes. I could hear the interference on the line. I knew I needed to warn you, but I was worried they'd hear it or recognize my voice."

"Who's 'they'?" I ask, realizing this is the same question I asked Stan the day before.

"Have you heard of something called 'psy-ops'?"

"Yes, but you don't believe in that, do you? It's just some crazy conspiracy theory. How can interference with phone calls cause a psychological breakdown?"

"It's more subtle than that. These techniques have been developed for years. They break down your defenses, interfere with your memories."

"Who are 'they'?"

"You know what I'm going on about, don't you?" he asks, ignoring my question. "I guessed the other day, when you didn't know who the prime minister is. Have you noticed anything like that, anything wrong with your memory?"

"Why?"

"That is their ultimate goal. They want to erase your memories and replace them with false memories."

"That's not possible. Brains aren't machines capable of being reprogrammed."

"Do you want to know something sad? I don't know why I moved to this island. I can't remember the reason I left the Met. All I know is that there's a crime here for me to solve, and I need to find the evidence for it. Have you experienced anything like that? Any gaps in your memory?"

"Erm, maybe." We share a look. He knows this is an understatement. "So, who are 'they'?"

"O87."

"What?"

"Do you know about 'inside roles'—their commitment to take on the appearance of being a normal, functioning member of society in order to infiltrate power structures and take over from within?"

"Yes, but I doubt they've been very successful at it. It's so far-fetched..."

"You're wrong. Since the 1970s, they have been incredibly successful at this. Every branch of democracy—from the courts, the media, the security services, right up to the Cabinet—has been infiltrated by O87 members performing inside roles."

"That's insane."

"I knew that would be your reaction, but look at this logically. The media toes the government line, editing out any ministerial faux pas from their newsreel, reporting on other inane nonsense so that government corruption slips to the bottom of the news agenda. The government has been becoming more authoritarian for years now. They've done it little by little, one freedom at a time. It started with populist policies like shipping asylum seekers out to Assumption Island and making channel crossings illegal."

"But everyone knows their agenda; they've been voting for this."

"The members of O87 with inside roles have brought this mind manipulation to members of the public on a mass scale."

"This is crazy."

"Tell me you have an explanation for your memory loss. Have you seen things that aren't there? Things no one else has seen? Have you forgotten important details about yourself? I've been investigating these phenomena for a while now, and I know the signs."

I don't answer because he's right; I don't have an explanation for what has happened to my autobiographical memories.

"I haven't worked out how they do it yet, but don't look any of them in the eyes."

"That's what the witness wouldn't do yesterday. Hewitt said he couldn't look my client in the eyes."

Grand nods vigorously. "Have you noticed the boats?"

"Well, I know they don't start. Or at least the ones I've tried don't."

"I'll pretend I didn't hear the bit about you trying to steal property. This is a fishing village, right? I've never seen anyone go out on those boats. I don't know anyone on the island who actually fishes."

"So, you're saying what?"

"I'm saying that something is amiss about this whole place. And the people on this island have had their minds messed with so that they accept this version of reality."

"And that this is the ultimate goal of O87?"

DS Grant nods. "I've got to go now, but meet me at lunchtime at this address." He hands me a card. "Don't let anyone know that I told you this. They'll kill us both."

CHAPTER THIRTY-ONE

AS I'M CROSSING THE lobby of the Castle Hotel, I notice that the woman who normally sits behind the desk isn't there. I look around. She's replacing the worn paperback on the shelf of secondhand books deposited by past guests. The book is Jilly Cooper's *Rivals*.

She comes back behind reception, tucking her left hand beneath her cardigan sleeve with her right. There's something strange about the way her arm moves.

"Sorry about that," she says.

"Did you enjoy it?" I ask.

"Pardon?"

"The book?"

"Oh, yes—I've read it before, but I love Jilly Cooper."

I nod. I don't ask her why she pretends to read, and simply take my key from her right hand before returning to my room.

Last night's dreams continue to play around a loop in my head. Who is that man? It still seems strange to think his name isn't "Pat." I was so sure.

I'm overcome with a deep sense of hopelessness. I'm no closer to finding where my daughter is, and any time I dedicate to that task detracts from my ability to perform in the courtroom.

I get ready quickly. While I'm getting dressed, I take the wristwatch from the desk and position it over the tattoo on my wrist and tighten the strap one hole tighter than normal to keep it fixed in place.

As I'm brushing my teeth, I look in the mirror at my wrist to check if I've been successful in covering the tattoo. I'm nervous about using my hands in court today in case my jacket falls to reveal the three sevens sitting there: a grubby little neo-Nazi calling card. I start moving my arm around to see if the wristwatch slips when something in the mirror catches my eye. The drawer by the side of my bed is open. I didn't leave it like that. After spitting out the toothpaste, I go over to the bed and look inside the drawer. The Bible is there. Yesterday morning, it had been removed and replaced with a toy horse. Who came into my room to return it, and when?

I open it up. Inside, the pages are covered with Odal runes. My breath is sharp—almost painful. They've been in my room again.

CHAPTER THIRTY-TWO

"CELLS, WHO'S THERE?"

"Counsel to see Eades."

The buzzing stops. I'm at the bottom of the cold staircase with Trevor, and we shuffle from side to side to do something—anything—that doesn't involve talking to each other.

"Cigarettes?" he asks.

I shake my head. Trevor shrugs as though to say, "*Up to you.*" I don't care. Today is about not catering to the needs of men. This is the mindset I carry with me into the conference room.

Eades refuses to look at me. When I sit down, he turns to Trevor and says, "Why did you bring her?"

"Because I'm the only person willing to stand between you and the angry mob who want you to hang," I say, my voice darker than I've ever heard it.

"Show your brief respect, John," says Trevor.

Eades swivels on the bench until we're greeted by the back of his head. From the corner of my eye, I see Trevor try to make eye contact, but I ignore him.

"Who was supposed to pick you up, John?" I ask.

Nothing.

"Why did they abandon you? Leaving you with no lift so that you had to get the train? They don't sound like very good friends to me."

Eades begins whistling.

"John, stop doing that," I say, but he ignores me. "Why don't you tell us—" I go quiet.

This is wrong. I shouldn't be coaching him like this; it's deeply unethical. But I'm so close to the truth, I can feel it. If he would just open his stupid mouth and tell us what happened…

Eades pretends to be oblivious. I let him carry on whistling, let him feel like he's in control. Trevor seems quietly embarrassed. After another five minutes, I slap my thighs and turn to Trevor.

"Dearie, dearie me. This won't do. Goodbye, John." We get up to go, and just before I'm about to leave through the door, I say, "Simon Cox won't be happy with you."

The whistling stops.

"I do wish he'd stop sending me letters, but then I suppose you can't contact him from inside here, can you?"

Eades is looking at me for the first time. It's not a comfortable experience; he still regards me like meat on a spit. I hold my hand up to indicate to the guard that we'll need some more time and then pull out the Gideon Bible. I open it and show all of the runes inside.

"This was left in my room. What do you know about this?" I ask Eades.

Trevor goes where I don't feel able to. "Do you understand what your barrister is saying, John? If there were other people involved, you need to tell us, yeah?"

I hold my breath, waiting for the response. He turns his back on us and begins whistling again.

Both Trevor and I sigh in frustration. He spreads his hands and I shrug my shoulders.

"John, they're calling either the expert or Kwame Adebayo next. Is there anything you want to tell us, anything you want me to ask either of them?"

He stops whistling. Trevor and I look at each other. Then he starts howl-ing with laughter. It's almost mechanical, and I'm reminded of the woman at the bar.

I stand up and go and look him straight in the eye, inches from his face. He recoils from me, the disgusting coward.

"Where is my daughter?" I ask him. "They've got her. Where is she?"

Eades's laughter increases. He opens his mouth wide and laughs in my face.

Trevor and I leave the conference room, the sound of Eades's laughter echoing down the corridor and in our minds long after we leave the cells.

"What was that about?" asks Trevor.

I show him the notes I've received saying "*Get him off or you'll never see her again*" and he frowns at me.

"Well?" I ask.

"I don't know what to say. Have you told the police?"

I give him a look that says "*Really?*"

"Oh, speaking of the police…" I pull out the blood alcohol tests.

"Where did you get these?"

"Our friend DS Grant."

We stop in the red-carpeted corridor, and I wait for Trevor to finish reading the report. When he looks up, his eyes are bloodshot and watery. He shakes his head and looks away from me.

"I'm sorry," I say, lost for words.

"Fucking idiot," he says, and somehow, I know he's referring to himself. "She was the best fucking barrister I ever used to instruct. Too good for that twat down there." He points toward the door that leads down to the cells.

"I know," I say. "She was."

I don't know this of course, but this is like a wake for Trevor. He needs to tell me this.

"But she started with a gin here or there after a heavy day. And I never said anything. Even when she used to turn up smelling of it, I didn't say any-thing because it was her business, and you wouldn't have known from her performance." He hands the blood alcohol tests back to me. His voice cracks. "And I failed her. I should have done something."

"We all should," I say.

Trevor shakes his head. "No. I played my part. I was a fucking coward and I failed her."

He walks off for a cigarette, and I look after him.

His guilt stays with me long after he's gone.

———————

I make my way to the library and take the same seat next to the radiator, pulling out the documents, spreading them out on the table, trying to suppress the overwhelming sensation I get every time I look at the sheer mass of information there is to assimilate.

After fifteen minutes of quiet, solitary work, Dev arrives, holding a thick, black, sugary coffee.

"Peace offering."

"Thank you," I say, taking it from him, hoping he'll leave now. I need this time. I've carved it out for myself especially. The problem with Dev is that he's a constant source of auditory and olfactory distraction, with his farts and coughs and burps.

"What are we working on this morning?" he asks, draping his coat over the back of a chair before taking a seat.

"I'm working on Dr. Sheridan's witness statement. Then I've got Kwame Adebayo, A.N. Other, and then, finally, DC Parks. She's the officer in the case."

"Well, you know what questions you need to ask of her."

"Don't tell me how to do my job, Dev."

"Did you wake up on the wrong side of the bed or something?"

"No, I'm in the middle of a murder trial and I just want to work on it. I know this is all a game to you, but this is serious to me. This is my life. This case could make or break my career."

Not to mention determine whether or not I see my daughter again.

"So that's it, then? You're happy for me to give you all my information but now you've bled me dry, you want to be left alone?"

"I'm grateful, I really am, but I need to do some proper work. Not focus on all of this conspiracy bollocks."

"It's not bollocks. You think they'd have pursued you and assaulted you and *tagged* you if you weren't looking where they didn't want you to?"

"You sound just like DS Grant."

"Who's that?"

"Never mind."

Dev leans across, resting a hand over the document I'm reading. "Tell me."

"It's nothing to worry about. He's on your side if anything. He's the most senior officer on the island, and he was the one who interviewed me about Pat's death. But now he's giving me information. He wants to help, but he believes in all of this crazy stuff, inside roles, all of that."

"Why the fuck would you speak to the police?"

"Why not?" I shout back at him. "This isn't *1984.*"

"Orwell couldn't conceive of what this lot are up to."

"Because it's not real! You're right about some things, but the people who are threatening me are obviously connected to O87, not the police."

"It's like talking to a wall. I have more intelligent conversations with my bichon frise... Don't ask." He looks at me, expecting me to laugh. "Come on; let's go over the facts again. We'll find our way through."

I slump my head into my hands. I can't take any more of this.

He carries on regardless. "The police knew the bombing was going to happen. They must have had an asset in the order. That person might have even persuaded Eades to do it. We need to find out who they were."

"No, we don't. I need to read these papers." I remove his hand from the document I'm reading.

"Lila! Think it through. The police knew the bombing was going to happen. Isn't it obvious that your client is a patsy?"

"We don't even know that the police had foreknowledge of the attack; it's just speculation."

"What about all of the evidence? The tip-off to the bomb squad, the attempt to kill off Smyth to cover their tracks. They knew, Lila, they knew the bombing was going to happen, and—"

"So what if they did? It's not unusual for intelligence communities to pretend as though they don't know something is going to happen to protect their sources."

"There you go. They cared more about their own than the twenty-seven—"

"What does any of this have to do with the case, Dev? Please stop using me and my client to pursue your own personal vendetta against DC Parks and Special Branch."

"I thought you were interested in the truth," he says.

"Trials aren't about the truth. They're about what you can and can't prove. No jury is going to care or be the slightest bit interested in these theories. And, might I add, without evidence, that's all they are. The judge would go mad if I even tried…"

"Why don't you care about any of this? What about all of the stuff they've been doing to you? The phone calls, the harassment, the threats… You know where all of this leads and it's not good."

I look at the door to the library, hoping Dev gets the message. "I've made up my mind."

"You can't trust any of them. What about that copper who fabricated your chap's confession?"

"There's probably a sensible explanation…"

"Wake up! Smell the corruption! If you're speaking to the police, I'm not helping you anymore." He gets up from his chair to underline the seriousness of his threat.

"Good, because I don't need wacky theories and verbal abuse!" I scream back at him, picking up his coat and throwing it at him.

He catches it, looking shocked and more than a little frightened. I take a breath to calm myself down, embarrassed by my outburst.

I try again, a little calmer. "I need solid evidence and a strategy, and more than anything, I just need time. Please, Dev. Just leave it. I'm really grateful for everything you've helped with so far, but this is getting inappropriate now."

"Inappropriate?" He looks disgusted in me. "As if you're playing that card. I was just helping you."

"I didn't mean it like that…"

He turns away, pulling on his coat as he leaves, slamming the door behind him.

I stare at the closed door for a while until my breathing returns to normal. Have I just made a terrible mistake? Dev was the only person who actually tried to help. But then I feel a rush of anger toward him, for the way he outstays his welcome and intrudes on things that are none of his business.

I sit back down to the paperwork and try to go over the unused material again, finish the task I started last night, which was to fit together the pieces of evidence that don't add up. I pull out a scrap of notepaper and write down my thoughts.

Fact 1: Special Branch appears to have known that something was going to happen on 23rd May 1995.

I draw an arrow from "something" and write *"but it's not clear what— intelligence faulty? Source of intelligence?"*

Fact 2: No evidence that Eades caught train to Birmingham. When caught train from Snow Hill, didn't have money for a ticket.

I draw a second column with "inferences" to be drawn from these facts. The inferences I draw from Fact 2 are *"must have had a lift to Birmingham, was expecting someone to pick him up, they abandoned him, he was left to improvise, he is bad at improvising, someone planned the attack with him and left him to take the fall."* This may well be true, of course. But there's nothing to say that means there's a conspiracy. An analogy would be that he's the drug mule who gets prosecuted while the higher-ups get off scot-free because the prosecution can't prove their case against them.

Is Eades a patsy? Your common garden racist groomed to take the fall?

That still wouldn't provide him with a defense. If he knew he was killing people, then what does it matter that someone else was pulling the strings? Unless he was acting under duress, or being framed…

The zines in the house—planted? The missing footage… What about this second person? The drop-car driver?

What happens if I put the inferences from facts 1 and 2 together?

There's no time. My thoughts are interrupted by a knock at the door.

Malcolm enters the library. "The court is ready when you are, Miss Dalton."

"Thank you, Malcolm," I say, for once not being rude to him. "Does his lordship wish to have an early start today?"

"He doesn't want to waste any time… Life is allowed to waste like a tap left running."

"Who's that?" I ask.

"Virginia Woolf."

"You're better read than me."

CHAPTER THIRTY-THREE

"PLEASE GIVE YOUR FULL name for the court."

"Dr. Brian Leonard Sheridan."

"And your occupation?"

"I'm a research fellow at Bridewater University."

"And your area of expertise?"

"Political philosophy and its interaction with theosophical ideologies."

"In plain English?" asks Paxton, not bothering to keep a note of derision from his voice.

"It's an area of history and sociology that focuses on far-right groups and the influence of the occult upon them."

"Still a lot of 'ologies' in there, but I think we get the picture."

"My PhD focused on Helena Blavatsky and the Third Reich, but more recently, I've been focusing on the National Socialist Movement and its occult outcrops."

"Including the Order of Eights and Sevens?"

"Yes, including that."

Paxton frowns and looks down at the folders on his desk. He holds one up. "You should have a bundle in front of you. Please turn to the first polypocket and pull out the exhibit."

Sheridan opens the box file and does as he's told.

"Can that be Exhibit No. 1, my lord?" asks Paxton.

His lordship nods and Paxton holds up the zine, showing it to the jury. There's a lot of shuffling while the jurors retrieve the same magazine from their bundle and look at the front, with its amateurish red and black writing.

"Talk us through this—"

"Zine," finishes Sheridan. "So, this is a publication produced by the Order of Eights and Sevens, or O87 as we call it in the academic community."

"How do you know it's one of theirs?"

"It's called *The Extraction Bulletin.*" Sheridan points to the "u" on the masthead. It's been made to look like a bullet. "'Extraction' is a term used by O87, which means the removal of undesirable people from society until only the elite remain. In other words, O87 members feel that they need to assist evolution for the good of humanity by killing people they consider to be weaker specimens."

"And who do they consider weaker?"

"Anyone who doesn't conform to their white supremacist ideals."

Paxton leaves that to hang in the air like a bad smell. There was an intake of breath from the jury, just perceptible. Something about it rankles me. So, people are happy to lump foreign criminals in with terrorists, but put a KKK or Nazi label on it, and it's suddenly abhorrent?

I chance another look at the jurors. Half of them have their arms crossed, indicating there's something about the evidence they're hearing that makes them need to protect themselves.

"What else do the O87 want to achieve?"

"They want to destroy society as we know it. Rebuild it from the ground up. Create a new world order."

"In which?"

"In which they—the supers, as they call the elite members—are rulers of the galaxy. They call it 'ascension.'"

"So, these people want to leave their earthly lives? And become rulers of the Milky Way?" Paxton does a good job of sounding disdainful, as though this really isn't for him.

Dr. Sheridan lets out a dry laugh. "The O87 is different from other groups because their white supremacist and neo-Nazi leanings are entwined with occult beliefs."

"Meaning?"

"They're Satan worshippers."

A definite gasp at that. I try to take a sideways look at the jury without letting on that I'm doing so. A woman in the front row is fiddling with the pendant on the end of her necklace. When I look closer, I see that it's a cross with a red flame.

This is by far the worst part of the evidence for my client.

"And how does this Satan worship manifest itself?"

"In all sorts of ways."

"Specifically in relation to the principle of extraction?"

"Oh, well, in the O87's theology—and theology is the right word for it—to kill those who are seen as lesser is the purest example of true devotion to satanism. They're actually pretty derisive about traditional satanists who aren't willing to go to such extremes. O87 members are entirely devoted to their cause."

"The cause of ensuring that whites reign supreme and that the current system collapses?"

"Correct."

"So, if you were a member of the O87, and you wanted to bring about this collapse, what targets would you choose?"

"That depends on a number of factors: the organizational capabilities of any particular cell, the ambitions of the individual, their intelligence…"

"What about a Home Office building?"

"Well, yes, that would absolutely fit. It serves the dual purpose of killing the immigrants who rely on the building to attend to their civic needs and of destroying the Home Office. What is the Home Office but an encapsulation of the democratically elected government's control over their citizens?"

"And the date of 23rd of May 1995. What significance does that hold?"

"This one stumped me at first, but then it was obvious. It's the fifty-year anniversary of Himmler's suicide."

"And why is that significant?"

"Among neo-Nazi communities, Himmler is perhaps revered more than Hitler. He was the architect of the Holocaust, Reichsführer of the SS and, above all, an occultist. He had his own priest."

"And in terms of this symbol." Paxton points at the Odal rune. "Can you help us with that?"

"The Odal rune was one of the many symbols appropriated by the Nazis. It translates as 'nobility,' 'superior race,' or 'aristocracy.' It's distinct from its runic ancestor in that it has additional 'feet' or 'wings.' It was used as the emblem of ethnic German military forces such as the 7th SS Volunteer Mountain Division Prinz Eugen."

I rub at the line of 7s below my wrist strap.

"And the eights?"

"H is the eighth letter of the alphabet. So, 88 equates to HH, Heil Hitler. It could also refer to Heinrich Himmler."

"Thank you very much, Dr. Sheridan." Paxton takes his seat.

I take a few moments to assemble my thoughts before standing. I pick up my notebook containing the cross-examination I have planned. All of the questions are inspired by the conversation I had with Dev last night in the pub. I feel a pang of guilt after our argument.

"In your statement, Dr. Sheridan, you talk about an individual called Simon Cox. Who is that?"

It's dangerous to ask open questions in cross-examination. The rule is to ask closed questions, pinning the witness down to your narrative. But the benefit of asking an open question is that any answer is given freely and is therefore more powerful. It comes back to the first rule of cross-examination: don't ask a question unless you know how they're going to answer. That's true to an extent, but you can ask and hedge your bets on how they answer. It's all about weighing the risks. Is there an answer they can give that will decimate their case? Or is it one of those questions where there's only one sensible answer, and anything else the witness says will only make them look like liars? That might sound very complicated. That's because it is, but done well, cross-examination should look effortless.

"He is often thought of as the ideologue-in-chief of the O87."

"He's the author of the seminal materials, isn't he?"

"That's the name used by the author or authors, yes."

"I'll come back to that point in a moment," I say. "Cox, whoever they may be, were they influenced by Louis Beam's essay 'Leaderless Resistance' in *The Seditionist*?"

"Yes."

"What do you say the organizational setup of O87 is?"

Another open question. I know what his answer will be because he's written about it in his statement. The art of cross-examination is making facts the witness has already overtly accepted seem controversial, like I'm uncovering some secret. Sheridan answers just as I wanted him to.

"Just that. There's no central body that administrates—"

"Who produces the magazine?" I hold it up for effect. The expression on my face says "genuinely interested" when really I'm happy he's fallen into my trap.

"It could be any number of disciples."

"Isn't O87 a much more structured group than you've let on?"

"No, it's leaderless resistance."

"Where are you getting that from?"

"The literature."

"*Their* literature?"

"Of course."

"Why do you trust it?"

"Well, it's not a case of trusting…"

"You've just given me an answer that you've taken straight from their literature."

Sheridan's mouth is open; then he closes it as though he's just realized. He casts around for an answer before blurting out, "Is that a question?"

I smile good-naturedly. "OK, I'll phrase it as a question if that helps. Why do you trust it?"

"It's not a case of trust—"

"Why do you rely upon it when coming to conclusions?"

"It makes sense for them to follow this model of leaderless resistance. If you put these ideas out there, all people have to do is copy them. It makes it difficult for law enforcement to track them down."

"Could the literature you're relying on be decoy propaganda designed to put law enforcement off the scent?"

"No."

"Is that a possibility you've ever considered?"

"Well, er, not exactly."

"So, you're eliminating a possibility that you've not fully explored?"

"No, look, there's no reason to suspect that O87 is anything other than a nonhierarchical organization."

"Who pays the printing costs? Who organizes the distribution list? Who ensures that the literature generated conforms to the O87 philosophy? This is an organized group, isn't it?"

Paxton gets to his feet. "Compound questions, my lord."

The judge nods and sneers at me. "One point per question, Miss Dalton."

I bow my head and go to ask the questions one at a time, but Sheridan answers anyway.

"All Cox had to do was leave a repository of literature and for others to take it seriously. You only need a few people to act on it."

"This Simon Cox," I say, cutting him off from that line of reasoning. "Who is he?"

"I think he's several people."

"A bit like the theory about Shakespeare?"

"I suppose."

"Do you have any training in linguistics? Can you distinguish one person's style from another's?"

"No, I'm a sociologist."

"So, what exactly is that opinion based on?"

"The sheer volume of material."

"Do you know how much spare time Simon Cox has? How long he's been producing?"

"No."

"Isn't Simon Cox one of many pseudonyms for one individual?"

"Some academics ascribe to that view."

"But not you?"

"No."

"Can you give me some percentages, some idea of how many experts think Simon Cox is one person?"

"It's hard to put a percentage on it…"

"Just give the jury a ball-park number. How many experts to your one opinion will say it's one man?"

Sheridan's eyes dart from me to the jury and then to Paxton, hoping he'll be given a lifeline. "Nine?"

Bingo. A little surge of adrenaline keeps me going. "Nine out of ten occult experts think that?"

Sheridan nods.

"You need to give an answer for the tape!" shouts the judge. "Is that a yes?"

"Er-er, yes, your honor," says Sheridan. His brow now has an unpleasant sheen.

His lordship mutters under his breath, "It's 'my lord,' but carry on."

I look back at Sheridan, who fixes me with an expression of deep dislike.

"Do you agree that having multiple names is something of a far-right trope?"

"Yes."

"The opinions in your report are all based on what's written in the O87's literature?"

A smug smile. "Straight from the horse's mouth."

"Let me get this straight. Everything in your report is based on the writing of this unidentified idealogue-in-chief, Simon Cox?"

"Who knows who they are?"

After a long run of quick questions, I stop there, let that sink in.

"Who knows who they are," I repeat slowly. "You're basing your professional opinion on the literature of people whose identities you have no knowledge of, and whose veracity you can't speak to. Is that why you're one in nine?"

"The literature speaks for itself. It's only intended to be read by disciples, not others."

"And, if we look at some members of O87, known members who have been prosecuted. Some of them have joint memberships in far-left groups, anti-fascist groups, Islamist groups... Is that right?"

"Yes, but that falls in line with what I say in my report; members of O87 are trained to perform inside roles."

I ignore his answer and carry on with my planned line of questioning. "Are you aware of members of various different far-right groups having fallouts, including known members of O87?"

"Yes, they're a volatile group of individuals brought together by hate. It makes for a fractious environment."

"Some of the arguments are about whether some in their ranks are state assets. Is that correct?"

Dr. Sheridan spreads his hands to placate me, but his cheeks are reddening. "These are paranoid people. You've got to understand, their entire mythology is built on this idea that the government is out to get them and that they, the far right, are the marginalized and persecuted group."

"All of these whistle-stop tours around different parts of the political spectrum... Isn't that something you would expect an intelligence asset to do?"

"Well, you could make that case, but I think it's unlikely. It falls more in line with the idea of performing an inside role while remaining true to the O87."

"Just to recap: we've got individuals who seem to change political direction

according to the wind, right-wing groups being brought to their knees by suspicion of infiltration… Have you ever considered that the O87 might be infiltrated by Special Branch?"

"No, definitely not. It happens the other way around."

I pause. "How do you know that?"

"It's in the literature. They tell followers to become something other than
yourself. A priest, a police officer, someone in a system of some sort, so that
they can become that person while staying true to the core beliefs of the O87,
which are chaos, violence, and murder."

"But John Eades wasn't performing any inside roles. He was very overt
about his right-wing opinions."

Sheridan ponders this for a moment. "Not all members of the order are
capable of that sort of thing. It requires a great deal of intelligence. There are
lots of O87 members who are just thugs."

Best to cut off this line of rationale. I don't want the jury to get used to
seeing Eades as a "violent thug." "Earlier in your evidence, you said that the
target would depend upon the organizational and financial power of a particular cell. Would you have expected more than one person to be responsible for
this attack?"

"I can't say."

"In your professional opinion, after studying the far right and their cell structure for"—I check his CV—"twenty-five years, is this the attack of one man?"

"It could be."

"But in your opinion?"

"On the balance of probabilities, it's unlikely."

———

"What the hell was all that about?" asks Paxton as we're walking away from
court for a ten-minute midmorning break.

"You didn't stand up to interrupt."

"None of this is in your defense case statement," he bites back.

"Then cross-examine my client about it."

Paxton scowls, knowing I'll never call Eades to give evidence and walks away. Andrew falls into step with me.

"What *was* that all about? Was it on instructions?"

"That's privileged," I say.

"Come on, Lila, scout's honor and all that."

"We're barristers, not little boys with kerchiefs." I don't look him in the eye while I say this. Then I stop and turn to him. "Who's A.N. Other?"

"Your guy knows who he is."

"Then why protect his identity?"

"You know why."

"Who is he?"

"That information is covered by public interest immunity."

"He's an asset, isn't he?" I ask. "He's an informant and that's why you're dancing around it. I couldn't work out why there'd be an anonymized witness in this case but then it all fell into place. You've got someone on the inside."

"No comment."

"That's what I'd advise someone in your situation to say."

"It doesn't have to be like this, you know," Andrew says, leaning closer and placing his hand on my lower back.

Dev rounds the corner and sees us in this intimate pose. The look of disgust on his face makes me feel ashamed. We spend an unnaturally long time looking at each other, our faces blank. After a moment I recover and walk away from Dev.

Andrew catches up with me. "What was that all about? He looked like he was annoyed with you."

"He's a journalist for an anti-fascist magazine. Have you forgotten who I'm representing?"

He shrugs. "S'pose."

"Anyway," I say, changing the subject, "who's next?"

"Kwame Adebayo."

I nod and keep my face straight in front of Andrew. I'm not looking forward to cross-examining this witness. There are some witnesses who are unimpeachable, no matter how hard barristers might try, and it comes from nothing more and nothing less than being someone who is so obviously telling the truth.

Only once everyone is in position does Paxton call his next witness.

Kwame Adebayo can be heard before he's seen; the syncopated rhythm of crutch and foot signals his approach. As he turns the corner and emerges from behind the dock, there's an audible gasp. Adebayo only has one complete leg. The other is a stump. Perhaps it's too early in the healing process for him to have a prosthetic. Perhaps he finds it uncomfortable. I push away more cynical thoughts about why he chose to come to court without one.

I study the jurors' faces as Adebayo limps past them. Each pale face looks upon him as though he's a war hero.

The witness box—a feature barely noticed until now—really is a box. The closest thing I can compare it to is a pulpit, with a wooden roof and dusky-pink curtains drawn to one side. To get up into the box, you have to ascend a few short steps that turn ninety degrees. With each step, everyone watches Adebayo struggle. Crutches abandoned, he's using his upper-body strength to climb inside.

Once seated, he's a little out of breath, so he's given a minute to regain his composure.

"You don't need to stand, Mr. Adebayo," said the judge.

After an extended period of hearing Adebayo's breath gradually lengthen and slow, Malcolm reads out the words of the oath, and Adebayo repeats after him.

I take a deep breath and read over Adebayo's witness statement. This witness could ruin everything.

CHAPTER THIRTY-FOUR

AS KWAME'S MOP HIT the toilet floor for what must have been the hundredth time that day—how many times would it have been that week?—he couldn't help thinking about the piece he heard on the radio as he buttered his toast that morning. A sports scientist had been on talking about repetitive strain injury, or RSI as he began calling it once the interview was in full flow. Tennis elbow is another name for it because no one would call it mop elbow or binman's elbow or brickie's elbow. The swirling of his mop reminded him of that interview, made him take notice of the repetitive motions he made with it day after day. Same shit, different floor. Literally. Because that afternoon he was cleaning the toilets.

In an attempt to fool his mop elbow, he tried going in zigzags and then straight lines. Anything to avoid the circular motion that served as a depressing metaphor for his life in the UK. He found that altering his movement caused more pain in his elbow than the familiar circles and concluded that staying the same was altogether less risky than branching out into something new.

The tiles he was mopping seemed to have been chosen by the Home Office in an open attempt to mock his efforts. They were gray and mottled and matte, making it impossible to get that gleaming look. There were only three differences between the before and after shots of Kwame's work. First, there were no longer toilet paper and various other bits of detritus on the floor. Second was the disinfectant smell left behind by the wet streaks. Third, he propped up a yellow sign warning of the hazards of recently mopped floors.

Resigned to the fact that his toil and increased risk of RSI were barely noticeable, he picked up the mop and bucket so that he could move onto his next task.

As he emerged from the toilets, he saw an angry figure coming toward him. Hunched over, burdened by a large sports bag slung across one skinny shoulder, the man walked with purpose and a look of detached hatred on his face. Kwame was no expert in body language, but hostility radiated from this man.

Kwame's fingers tingled as the first signs of adrenaline kicked in. His life before he came to the UK was anything but boring, and Kwame had learned to smell danger. He'd had to. It was the only reason he was still alive. At three o'clock in the morning, Kwame had woken because he'd smelled danger. He was right. Minutes after he'd managed to collect all of his worldly belongings and flee, the shooting began. He watched the column of smoke from his burning village rise behind him. Now, his sense of smell dulled by disinfectant, he could still recognize a dangerous man when he came across one.

"What's in the bag?" asked Kwame.

The man paused for half a second too long. Much too long for what he said next to sound natural.

"I homeless," said the man in a fake Eastern European accent.

It was Kwame's turn to stand still for too long, a hesitation he'd live to regret for the rest of his life. It took him much too long to process everything: the man's pause, his poor attempt at the accent, the heavy sports bag...

"OK."

That was all he could think of for the moment.

He stayed where he was for a little while after the man disappeared into the toilets, weighing up his options.

He pressed on, going over to the den in the corner where the security guards watched the CCTV covering the front door.

"I've seen someone acting suspiciously."

"Fuck's sake, Kwame, this isn't Uganda."

"I'm from—" He never got to say where he was from because the two guards fell about laughing. He waited for them to stop before carrying on. "Have you been watching the camera?" He waved at the screen.

Kwame didn't like stereotypes and generalizations—perhaps anyone who's been on the wrong end of them comes to have a singular wariness of them—but when it came to the security guards, he found the cliché to be startlingly accurate. He remembered the advent of CCTV, when they could stop walking around and observing on foot and could begin watching from their secluded room in the corner. Their first instinct of course was to look at women, and they couldn't wait for the technology to improve so that they could zoom in.

"What do you think we've been doing? Are you saying we're not doing our jobs?"

Kwame looked around at the discarded food packets, playing cards, and overflowing ashtrays, trying to keep accusation from his expression. Security and cleaning were all part of the same team, grouped together under the vague header of "facilities," but cleaners were at the bottom of the squat pyramid and security was at the top.

"Did you see a man walk through carrying a big sports bag?"

"What did he look like?"

"He was about this tall…" Kwame held his hand at the same height as his shoulder. "Thin in build and with… What do you call them?" He gestured toward the tips of his nonexistent hair.

"Black or white?"

Kwame sighed. "White."

"Wouldn't worry about it, mate. Not some raghead with a suicide wish, is he?"

It wasn't worth it. They'd never get it. He turned and left them to their unhealthy attitude toward women and people of color and even more horrifying approach to personal hygiene. If no one was going to listen to him, he'd have to do it on his own. Ditching the mop and bucket, he strolled back toward the men's toilets and waited outside, listening. He could hear the sound of a lid banging against the toilet seat. He opened the door just a crack and looked through. Waiting on the floor, inches away from him, were two brown-paper bags that definitely weren't there when Kwame left the toilets. Not wanting to confront the angry man, Kwame reached through and grabbed the bags.

There wasn't enough time to look inside. He wanted to be away before the angry man came looking for him. So, Kwame hurried off and stepped into a corridor marked PRIVATE: STAFF ONLY, before opening the brown-paper bags. What he found inside changed everything.

CHAPTER THIRTY-FIVE

SO FAR, ADEBAYO HAS done a good job of sticking to the script. He's by far the best witness the prosecution has had. Often Paxton has struggled to keep his witnesses under control and ensure their answers are in time with his lordship's pen, and more than once they've veered off course. All of that witness management without being able to ask a leading question. You've got to hand it to Paxton—he's bloody good.

But Adebayo's economy with words has made the prosecutor's job so much easier. The cleaner doesn't elaborate too much. He answers the exact question that Paxton asks, meaning that the jury is getting each bit of evidence in bite-size chunks. More than that, it's clear that he's not in love with the sound of his own voice, desperate to have his day in court. He's the perfect witness.

But there's something strange about his witness statement. There's a gaping hole in it, a hole I'm going to dig around in. The anticipation of it is making me jittery, and I have to stop myself from bouncing my knee, which would send tremors down the fold-down bench to where Andrew is sitting.

I look up at the ceiling to take my mind out of the well of the court. It is at least three times as high as any normal room. At the center is a large cupola.

"The jury has seen today that you're without a leg," says Paxton. *Without a leg.* Only someone like Paxton can get away with putting it like that.

"Yes," answers Adebayo.

"Tell the jury how that happened."

They've reached the part where the gaping hole opens up in Adebayo's evidence. His reaction is promising. He hesitates. His eyes flicker toward DC Parks.

"In the explosion."

Paxton is wise to ask no further questions.

I get to my feet, still jittery, and take a slow breath in a feeble attempt to control my nerves. Sometimes there are witnesses who will only make the case worse for the defendant. You're duty-bound to ask them questions because you have to put your case to them, but every answer they give digs a deeper hole for the defendant. Adebayo has everything that could make him one of those witnesses. My intention, therefore, is to be quick. Get in, get out.

"I'll pick up where you left off. The explosion." I wait, take another deep breath. Adebayo is polite and considered. I haven't asked a question yet, so he waits patiently for me. "In which explosion did you lose your leg?"

"The first one."

"Where did it come from?"

"The walls."

"Of which room?"

"The security guards' room."

"Why were you in there?"

"That's where I took the fast-food bags after I found them in the toilet."

"So, you weren't anywhere near the waiting room?"

"No."

"Yet the explosion came from 'the walls.'"

Adebayo looks me straight in the eye, unwavering. "Yes."

"Not from the waiting room?"

"Definitely not."

"Thank you, Mr. Adebayo."

Paxton turns to share a quick look with Andrew, and the judge's eyebrows twitch up toward his wig.

"Er, my lord," says Paxton. "I wasn't anticipating finishing today's witnesses so quickly. There is one more lay witness for the prosecution before we hear from the officer in the case. Perhaps your lordship wouldn't mind adjourning until tomorrow so that the witness can be ready to give evidence?"

"Isn't he ready now?"

This must be A.N. Other. The witness I suspect is flaky. Paxton's doing everything he can to avoid ditching them.

"My lord, I'm afraid not. Unfortunately, special arrangements need to be made for this witness, and those will be in place by tomorrow."

The judge rolls his eyes.

"Please accept my deepest apologies, my lord."

"Early day, then, I suppose," the judge says, before turning to the jury and thanking them for their patience.

Once the last juror is out of the courtroom and the door is closed, the judge stands and gives us the start time for tomorrow. There's a flurry of movement as members of the prosecution turn in their seats and have whispered conversations, heads together.

I've stopped turning to Trevor for reassurance, and I've definitely stopped turning to look at Eades. One thing I can't stop myself from doing, however, is looking over at the press bench. I don't know why I seek Dev's approval. After all, he's the ethical equivalent of a waste pipe. But I know he was only trying to help, even in his ignorant, bumbling, getting-his-greasy-fingerprints-everywhere kind of way. It was coming from a place that's perhaps the only good part of him. The part that wants to seek the truth, and doggedly.

But he's not there.

I put my hand in my pocket and feel the edges of the paper that DS Grant left at the bottom of the hollowed-out Bible. It's not safe to open it in the corridor, so I dip into the toilets.

At the sink, I splash my face with water, forcing myself to stay alert. I look up and into the eyes of a stranger. Every time I see the woman staring back at me, it makes me do a double take. I'm not sure what I was expecting to see. Maybe it's just that the dark-green circles under my eyes are so pronounced that I no longer look human, never mind like myself. When I get into the cubicle, I lock the door behind me, put the toilet lid down, and sit, pulling the note out of my pocket.

So exhausted from the night before, I feel my eyes droop, and in the space between my eyelids closing and opening again, I have a micro sleep. It makes me feel groggy, like I've just been forced awake by an alarm. I look down at my watch, working out how much longer I have until the meeting with DS Grant. I look again.

It's an hour later than I'm expecting it to be. What happened in that split second? I can't have been sitting in this toilet a whole hour. But then I look down at the piece of paper lying on the floor, as though it fell from my limp fingers.

Perhaps I did go to sleep for an hour, but it felt like a fraction of a second because I was so tired. Or maybe my watch is wrong. I shake my head, pick up the card, and commit the address to memory.

If my watch is correct, I'm already late to see DS Grant, so I totter back to the robing room—a staccato jog in my heels. It's empty, which confirms my suspicion that it really is an hour later. I check the wall clock and my panic surges. I'm late to meet DS Grant by over half an hour.

I tear off my wig and gown, stuffing them into my bag, grab my handbag, and run for the exit in the court building, freezing and empty now everyone has left. All the while, I'm repeating one phrase over and over in my mind. The address. 4 Parish Row. I remember it from my early morning wanderings. It's just off the high street.

Feeling exposed in the square outside the court building, I take a quick look left and right to make sure no one is following me. The Castle Hotel in all its shabby glory is only across the way. I could go upstairs to change my clothes, as I cut a conspicuous figure on the island, but time is ticking away, and I know that DS Grant has something interesting to show me. The strangest thing about this island is that the madder the conspiracy theorist, the more they seem to make sense. Perhaps I'm losing *my* grip on reality. I shake my head and resolve to get to the meeting place as quickly as I can.

I tug the lapels of my jacket in tight, a feeble attempt to keep the wind from going straight through me. I wish I still had that purple coat… My stockinged legs already feel whipped by cold. The only thing I can do to distract myself from the frostbitten sensation is repeat the place-name over and over in my mind while visualizing its position on the map.

4 Parish Row, 4 Parish Row, 4 Parish…

Past the Castle Hotel, I head down the hill that leads toward the high street.

Once I'm on the high street, my heels stick in the stones, and I feel more precarious than ever on the uneven pavement. I stop repeating the address for a moment so that I may curse my impractical shoes. The pain in my ankles intensifies, and I dare not imagine what they look like underneath the tights. Exposed skin? Blood? They feel rubbed to the bone.

It's full of run-down shops, but what I like about the high street is that it's a proper one. Everything is a one-off. Totally unique. The butcher's and the greengrocer's and the florist's are all named after the owners, rather than some franchise. It's quaint. I feel a sense of nostalgia for those simpler times.

As I approach the end of the high street, I peer down every alleyway because Parish Row should be somewhere nearby. It feels like the hustle and bustle of the main drag is thinning out. Shopfronts are replaced by terraced houses, the street quieter. Then I see it. Parish Row is just off the main drag, a little hangnail of a street jutting off at forty-five degrees.

Parish Row is lined with terraced houses, giving it the feeling of a Victorian slum. At the very bottom of the street is a chapel. It doesn't look as though it's been in use for decades. The garden is so overgrown there might be wild things growing in it. On closer inspection, lumps of rock are sprouting from the ground, gravestones.

Were I not in such a hurry, I'd go over and take a closer look. What sort of place lets a graveyard go to seed? Whose ancestors languish here?

Instead of answering those questions, I look at the houses for any clue as to which is number 4. The houses are so dilapidated. Windows are boarded up, vegetation creeping up the walls.

I pause.

Why would DS Grant want to meet here? Is this where he lives? Aren't police officers paid well enough to live somewhere nicer?

I peer closer at a front door. So rusted that it has started to blend into the rest of the door is a brass number 4. I try the handle and it yields with ease.

The door opens, a vortex into the past.

I'm exaggerating, of course.

But of everything that I expected—mold-infested walls, rats, maybe even a stray dog—this wasn't it. The place is a time warp. Assumption Island *is* pretty dated. It's like time knocked but no one could be bothered to get up and answer the door, so they were just stuck with whatever was lying around at the time. But in here, it could easily be the 1950s. A concerted effort to preserve an era. The hallway is pastel pink. Not the color I would have chosen for DS Grant, but, hey, who am I to judge?

Everything inside is pristine, not a speck of dust anywhere. I close the door quietly behind me.

"DS Grant?"

Nothing.

I look at the carpet runner beneath my feet. There are frills surrounding the edges. When I look at the wall to my right, I see a row of picture frames. The portraits inside (complete with yet more doily edges) are all of dolls. Their eyes stare out at me.

Written below the row of pictures is the phrase "We Live Inside," accompanied by an Odal rune.

"O-*K*," I say to myself. "DS Grant?"

I get to the end of the hallway and open the door into a mint-green 1950s kitchenette. There is just one thing wrong. Lying face down on the floor is DS Grant.

CHAPTER THIRTY-SIX

I DON'T KNOW THAT he's dead. I mean, he looks pretty dead, but there's no blood. I get closer and roll him over, ready to try CPR. All the time I'm thinking about forensics. If he is dead and the police know that I'm the one who found him, and all I have is this story about him asking me to meet him here and a handwritten note, I'm screwed. Instant arrest and maybe even a charge.

I won't let that happen. I'll be back in the UK by then. It takes weeks to process forensic evidence, and I can only imagine how long it would take to send the evidence to the UK and have it delivered back to Assumption Island.

This is ridiculous. I'm thinking like a guilty person. Thinking about how long I have to change my name, get a fake passport, and disappear into a different jurisdiction before the forensic evidence catches up with me.

There are angry red marks around his throat and there's a stench of urine, complete with a yellow puddle slowly making its way across the linoleum toward my feet. I go around to the other side of the body, pull back my hair to stop it from falling in his face, and hold my ear an inch away from his mouth. No breathing. *Shit.* How long has he been like this?

This is my fault. He was waiting here for me. Perhaps if I'd been here on time, hadn't fallen asleep…

I lace my fingers, ready to put the heel of my palm on his sternum and start pumping.

The heel of my hand pushes down on something hard. A crunching sound. There's something inside his jacket. I open up the buttons and slip my hand inside an inner pocket, pulling out a manila gusset envelope bulging with what looks like a VHS tape. I take a look inside. As well as a tape, there are some papers. I leave the envelope to one side.

I start pumping his chest again. I know this is the right thing to do, but I'm not sure on the specifics. Did I ever do first aid? I can't remember the ratio between the compressions and the breaths. I decide to keep going with the compressions. In any event, if he is dead, I don't want to leave my saliva on his lips. I know what someone like Paxton would make of that evidence in front of the jury.

The Kiss of Death, ladies and gentlemen.

He'd smile, knowing a phrase like that will stick with the jurors long into retirement.

I've been pumping for about two minutes and nothing. The blue in his lips is getting worse if anything, and the paleness of his skin only serves to highlight the petechiae blossoming around his eyes.

This isn't right. Someone knew he would be here.

I gasp.

How could I have been so stupid? If they knew he was here, they'll know I was supposed to be here. I've been set up. Or maybe the murderer is still somewhere in the house.

I look down at him, feeling guiltier than ever. If I were lying there, I'd want someone to at least try. Ring the emergency services and get some fucking help.

I get up, stashing the envelope in my handbag, and stagger out of this time capsule of a house and into Parish Row, leaning back against the grimy stone wall. I find that I'm panting, my chest struggling to take in the cold air.

I'm shaking. I can feel the tremors as I crouch down onto my haunches, feeling safer closer to the ground.

What do I do? Call for help? Then I'd have to tell the police what's happened.

Nothing about my experience so far on Assumption Island fills me with confidence that I'll be treated fairly. Perhaps it's best just to leave. Say nothing about it and get the first plane out of here. I can't believe it. I'm an officer of the court and I'm thinking of perverting the course of justice by failing to report a fucking dead body.

It feels too soon to leave him. I'm not sure where I get that sense from. There are no rules about how long you should stick around before leaving a dead body.

Instead, I just stay here, prevaricating. When will they find him? What state of decay will he be in? Does he have a family? Will his poor wife have to try to identify him? It's unspeakably cruel. Yet if I ring the police...

They're watching you.

That was the warning that DS Grant gave me. If he were here, if he were alive, would he be telling me to run? Would he be saying I should forget about him and save myself? I mean, how much can he really be helped at this stage? I stand up and go to leave the cul-de-sac, then turn back again.

What if they're waiting for me in the street?

I look up at the perennially overcast sky and ask God-knows-what-God I pray to for some guidance.

"What the fuck?"

I turn around and see Dev, a piece of paper in his hand, looking like a tourist with a guidebook.

"What are you doing here?"

I wave at the door helplessly before breaking down into sobs. It's all so hopeless.

Dev opens the door and disappears down the corridor. I wait outside, shivering and sniffing.

He returns after ten seconds. "Lila, who sent you here?" He's gripping the tops of my arms a bit too tightly.

I wince and he relinquishes.

"He told me to meet him here." I pull out the manila envelope. Dev's eyes light up.

"We've got to get you away from here. This is serious."

"But…I should tell someone."

"No," he growls. He composes himself before continuing, "Are you mad? You? Finding a dead body? No way. We need to get away, find somewhere safe."

"Where? Where on this island is *safe*?"

Dev's eyes are darting around. They land on the chapel. "In there—come on."

"What?"

He's pushing his way through the waist-high weeds and treading on the bramble. I follow reluctantly after him. I don't want to have to make my own decisions anymore. I'm happy to be led. As we're climbing through the brambles, I catch sight of one gravestone. I look again. That can't be right. It says 1997.

There's a creak up ahead and I know that Dev has managed to open the door.

When I finally get to the chapel, my shoes are ruined, and my tights have gashes on them where they snagged on the brambles, revealing fresh cuts.

Dev pulls the door closed once I'm in. The darkness inside the chapel is complete. If anything, it's colder in here because the air is so still.

A light flickers into life: Dev is holding his lighter. He carries it aloft and squints into the darkness before trudging over to what looks like a mini-altar. After blowing away clouds of dust, he lights an altar candle, and its shuddering flame pierces the otherwise complete gloom. Dev leans in toward the candle, cigarette in his mouth to light it.

"For fuck's sake."

"Finding bodies is stressful." His words are muffled by the cigarette between his lips.

I shake my head. Suit already ruined, I lean against a dusty pew, taking the weight off my feet.

"What were you doing looking for that house?" I ask.

"Same question could be asked of you."

"I told you, that was where he told me to meet him. I think it was so that he could give me this." I hold out the envelope, minus the VHS. I can't say why, but I don't want to show Dev the tape. That piece of evidence is just for me.

Dev reaches out his hand to take it from me, but I don't hand it over.

"Suit yourself," he says, a cloud of smoke billowing from the corner of his mouth as he says it.

"You next."

"One of my sources told me to go to that house. Bit creepy, wasn't it? How it was all pink and green. Looked like a pervert's house. Someone who has a thing for fucking old shit."

I pace a groove in the dusty floor. "It's my fault he's dead."

Dev doesn't respond, just continues puffing on his cigarette.

I challenge him. "Come on, then; where's your quick retort?"

"I'm doing that thing we talked about, you know, thinking? It's a bit easier when you're quiet."

I hold up my hands in surrender, turning away from him. As I walk down the aisle, the dust underneath my feet muffles the sound of my footsteps. It's hard to work out what denomination this chapel is. The guttering light only allows brief glimpses of its sparse furnishings. At the back of the room, things get a little more informal, with some plastic chairs placed around in a circle. The candlelight licks at some rudimentary drawings. It looks like they were done by children, and I feel a tug of longing for my daughter.

From behind the wall at the back of the chapel, I hear footsteps.

"There's someone here," I breathe.

Chairs scraping, paper rustling.

"Dev, there's someone behind that wall." I strain to listen again. One person? More than one person? "Bring the candle." When I hear my voice, it's a panicked whisper.

Soon, the cigarette smoke is closer and the candlelight stronger, and I know he's behind me.

"Can you hear that?"

"Not if you don't shut up."

We both stop walking to listen.

Footsteps on the other side of the wall. A door closes.

I look to Dev. "Do you think they left?" I ask.

"Why would I know?"

"Shall we go and see?"

"After you."

CHAPTER THIRTY-SEVEN

I CREEP FORWARD. DEV sighs impatiently so I go a little faster. There's a door in the back wall. When I turn the handle, the door creaks and I hold my breath. Instinctively, I feel the side of the wall for a switch. Finding one, I palm it down and a fluorescent strip light flickers, blinding us after the pitch-black of the chapel.

I turn away and shield my eyes. When I try to look closer, it's through a squint.

The room is empty. It's clear that this is the community hall part of the chapel. Lining the walls are stacks of chairs, leaving free space in the middle. On noticeboards, children's drawings of biblical passages are pinned to felt. One noticeboard catches my eye. The sunlight has faded everything apart from letter-sized squares.

I heard rustling before. Were they taking down posters? Why?

"Looks like a bit of a kumbaya fest in here," says Dev.

"Why would there have been someone back here? It looks disused from the outside."

"Perhaps the killer came in here to chill out after the murder."

My blood runs cold.

"Could they be waiting for us outside?"

Dev shrugs. "Could be."

"You're a bit too nonchalant for someone who's just seen a dead body and stumbled across the murderer's potential hiding place."

"I'm not as into the heart-on-my-sleeve crap as you."

"Can you be serious for one minute?"

"Who cares if they're outside? We're in here. Anyway, you still haven't explained why that police officer wanted to meet you in that house." Dev says.

"Are you seriously suggesting I had anything to do with that?"

"I've never seen you this manic. Normally you're catatonic with stupidity, like your mind is swimming in Valium."

"Always so rude."

"Yeah, well, manners maketh minions, so I'll fucking carry on as I am, thanks. What did he want to tell you?"

I recount this morning's conversation with DS Grant to Dev. As he listens, his eyes widen.

When I finish, he shouts, "FUCK!" and goes as if to push over one of the stacks of chairs.

"Psy-ops, mind control, the government. Infiltration by the far right. Control of the media. This is it! It all fits. It's everything I've been working toward. Exposing the fascism at the heart of the government, the secret services' dodgy techniques... Fuck! Psy-ops was just an experiment. It was all part of a bigger plan: the use of mind-control techniques to gaslight the population so that when the masks come off, everyone is compliant." He's pacing now. "*Inside roles.* Fuck. They did it."

I hold my hands up. "Dev, come on."

He rounds on me. "Do you know what this is? *Do you know what this is?* This is the ability to blow open the biggest story of my career, and the source is just *lying* over there in some weird time warp of a house, and if I report his death, I'll be arrested. And I'm living in an authoritarian state ruled in secret by the far right, so the justice system is rigged." He shoots a glance at me and adds, "No offense," as an afterthought.

I hold my hands up as though to say *"None taken."* He goes as if to knock something over, like a stroppy tennis player, but instead stops himself at the last moment and U-turns in my direction. "Give it up; show me."

I clutch the manila envelope closer to my chest, not ready to divulge its secrets.

"I need to see what's inside," he says. "What it contains. This guy. *This* guy." He starts laughing now, and it's manic.

"Dev, take a breath. Jeez." I hand him the envelope.

He gives me the palm. "Don't tell me to calm down right now. I've just lost the best source, the biggest... Anyway, let's see what he's got in here." He drops the documents from the envelope into his hand and starts flicking through them. His eyes dilate as he reads.

He continues riffling through the pages, until he gets to one page that makes him stop.

I look over his shoulder. "What's that?"

"What does it look like?"

"I don't know, some sort of cage."

"Yep, it's something like that."

"Are you going to shed some light?"

"You know the one thing we've said is wrong with this case? From the beginning. This is a bombing case with no munitions evidence." He holds the paper out to me, held together by paper clips.

I take it from him, turning my back. It's a forensic explosives report. It would take me a long time to get through the jargon, so I turn to the conclusions. There is no evidence to suggest that the large sports bag was the source of the explosion. There are only two minor explosions reported, and they are said to have come from two much smaller bombs that detonated in the security room.

However, those small explosions were not the primary cause of the explosion. In fact, they were most likely triggered by the main explosion, which literally came from the walls. In the basement and ground floor of the building, a cage of wires and trip points had been inserted. That was what had caused the big explosion in Abbott House. Those people had been working in a ticking time bomb for as long as the cage had been installed.

"But…but it's a 1960s building. The O87 didn't even form until the seventies."

"The report doesn't say *when* it was built into the walls, but it could have been inserted after. They'd have had people go in to do the wiring."

"Who? Who would have had people to go in and do the wiring?"

"The government."

"What?"

"The government is responsible for the bombing of Abbott House."

"That's crazy."

"Crazier than you being tailed by nutters who believe the world is hollow?"

"Yes! You're talking about the government killing its people for no reason."

"There's always a reason."

"You're saying that the O87 have such a handle on the government that they can order the mass murder of civilians and civil servants?"

"The murder wasn't the end goal. It was this." He opens his arms wide to imply the enormity of the conspiracy.

"What's 'this'?" I mimic his gesture.

"I've got it. I've worked it out." Dev paces around like a caged animal.

I lean back on one of the stacks of chairs. "When you're ready."

"You know what, you were the one who gave me the idea."

"Me?"

"I was listening to your cross-examination of Sheridan earlier, about what you were saying about Simon Cox. I think you're right. *He's* the asset. It all makes sense now."

"Wait, so if Simon Cox isn't the Grand Master, who is?"

"Fuck knows—"

"Maybe I'm right about that as well. It's Smyth."

"Don't get ahead of yourself, darling. Beginner's luck. Some of us have been playing this game a lot longer than you. Anyway, that's not the point. I believe that the asset, whether Simon Cox or someone else, knew about the bombing and decided to let it happen anyway. In fact, that's my best-case scenario."

"What's your worst?"

"That the plant was actually an agent provocateur. I think they planned the bombing and encouraged Eades to go through with it."

"Dev..."

"Don't give me that. I'm telling you, it's the sort of thing they do."

"You're not making any sense. Special Branch's job is to prevent loss of life and to stop disasters like this. Why would they let it happen?"

"Because it's all part of their bigger plan. They want to demonize extremism—"

"Not the worst thing—"

"And their endgame is to bring in tough new anti-terrorism legislation that will curb the right to protest, the right to form organizations. It will allow powers of arrest without reasonable suspicion."

"That's ludicrous."

"That's what this trial is all about. Do you know that Eades is the first non-Irish white domestic terrorist to be tried on Assumption Island? They are going to make a public example of him and use it to bring in tougher legislation."

"You can't know that."

"I do. They're going to start bringing in more authoritarian legislation. Anti-terrorism legislation on its face, but really, it'll be a Trojan horse clamping down on the right to protest, have public demonstrations, and generally make a nuisance of oneself."

"Who's your source for that?"

"It was in the government's manifesto."

I shake my head. This is all so implausible. My head is aching from the exertion of having to process it all.

"We need to speak to Kevin again," I say.

"I agree. He needs to explain what we're looking at here." He shakes the bundle containing the forensic explosives report before walking over to the back of the room. "Right. Ready to test whether there's an ax murderer waiting outside this door?"

———————————

Dev opens the door to what looks like another overgrown bit of land, too wild to see if there are any gravestones. The light is fading now that we're past the afternoon's apex. Dev lifts his knees to stamp down on the brambles, and I follow after, wincing as the thorns slice fresh cuts and reopen others. After twenty feet, we reach a stone wall with a rotten wooden door.

He opens it and looks left and right. When he steps out, he waves for me to follow through. We're in an alleyway that runs down the back of terraced houses.

"Why didn't we go out the other way?"

"Don't want anyone to see us near that body."

"How are we going to get to the woods?"

"Taxi."

"Why didn't we just do that the other day?"

"Taxis don't run after seven p.m."

"It's practically medieval here."

"Come on, before it gets dark."

CHAPTER THIRTY-EIGHT

AT THE OUTSKIRTS OF the wood, which I can't help but think of as Kevin's wood, I can see the headland rising up beyond the trees. With the black loom of the trees around us, the flashing light is visible at the end of the point. In the reddish half light of twilight, I can see at last where it comes from: a lighthouse.

Though the sun is moments from sinking over the horizon, the dregs of daylight make all the difference, and it doesn't take as long for us to find "Kevin's" hut as it did when we were searching in the pitch-black.

As soon as we get to the shed, it's clear that something is wrong.

"What's this?" I ask, pointing at the ground. In the dirt someone has carved an Odal rune. I look up at the shack. No light pushes through the mildew-caked window.

Silence.

"Do you have anything on you?" I ask.

"Such as?"

"A weapon?"

"Who carries weapons?"

"Like a set of keys or something?"

Dev's eyebrows reach new heights as he shakes his head and carries on walking. I crouch down and pick up a hefty stick from the forest floor. Dev tuts.

Our approach to the door is slow. The forest sounds have been turned up to maximum volume. There's something in the woods nearby. I look around.

It was only a bird rustling in a tree.

Dev puts his hand to the door and pulls it open.

Kevin's body must have been leaning against it because it falls at Dev's feet. His eyes are bloodshot. He has red marks around his throat and his lips are blue.

I scream.

Dev looks furious. "What the fuck did you do that for?"

The second dead body in as many hours. I realize what this means. What's happening. Someone is covering their tracks, and if they know about DS Grant and Kevin, they know about us.

"We need to get out of here." Dev turns to leave.

I can't stop looking at Kevin.

"Come on." Dev tugs at my arm, a little rougher than expected.

I allow myself to be pulled.

I find that I've been walking for a long time when I finally come round. So long, we're nearly at the edge of the woods. It's like driving for ages but not remembering the miles you've covered.

Dev reaches over and gently pries the stick from my grasp, laying it back down on the ground. I didn't realize I'd been holding it like a saber.

I see a large concrete building up ahead. The building is enormous and square, an industrial complex. The path runs directly alongside the wall. It's as though the forest has claimed it for its own. Moss, weeds, and creeping plants have dug their claws into the concrete. The barbed wire that tops the wall is rusted and hanging off in parts.

We walk along the side of the building until we come to a large asphalt space. It's sunken and potholed, revealing the hard core underneath. Vegetation pokes out of the tarmac. We're back at the barracks. We walk toward the opening on the other side, where I can only see the back of the sign.

It's another couple of minutes until we find the road.

The taxi is idling when we reach the place where dirt track becomes tarmac. Dev and I climb in the back.

"Where to?"

I look to Dev, who pauses, drumming his fingers on the rear door.

There's nowhere that's safe for us to go now. Nowhere on the island we can't be found. If Kevin in his secret shed in the woods isn't safe, what hope do we have?

"To the Castle Hotel."

I go to interrupt, but Dev flexes his wrist at me. A small motion, but I get the hint and go quiet.

The sun disappears behind the gray horizon as we start the drive back to the other side of the island. Where is safe? Where can we go?

What's scarier: that an underground terrorist cell is murdering people and we're next on their list, or that the British government is seeking to cover up evidence and is complicit in a miscarriage of justice?

We pull up outside the hotel.

As soon as we approach the glass entrance door, I see that something is wrong. There are two police officers at the reception desk. Behind them is a familiar profile. DC Parks.

I lean in to Dev and whisper, "What are we supposed to do now?"

"Act normal," he breathes back, barely opening his lips.

"Meaning?"

"Turn around and walk away. Meet you at the staff entrance, behind the bins."

I do as he suggests. He goes straight into the foyer, while I circle around the side of the building. At the rear are two cleaners smoking by the back door. I wait with my back pressed to the brick. As soon as I hear the door close, I approach slowly and hide behind the bins.

Five minutes later, the door opens.

I jump in fright but it's only Dev. He gestures inside, one hand on my shoulder as he steers me into a cleaning closet. He perches on an upturned bucket, while I lean against a bulk order of bleach.

"What now?" I whisper.

"We need to work out what to do with this information," he says. "We need to act normal for now, or they'll know that we're spooked. If they know we know, they'll kill us more quickly to shut us up."

"What do you mean 'act normal'? Kevin is dead because we spoke to him. DS Grant is dead, and they think I've got something to do with it. Why else would they be at the hotel? They're looking for me. I know it. They think I'm responsible."

My hands are shaking so I ball them into fists.

"Correlation doesn't equal causation."

"Come on. There's a pattern. Bodies turn up and I'm connected to them. Don't you feel guilty at all?"

"No. I'm not responsible. DC Parks is behind all of this."

I clench and flex my fingers in frustration. "You don't know it's her. It could be anyone."

Dev considers this. "Let's err on the side of caution and act as though it is DC Parks who's behind these murders and focus on getting you on the first plane off this shit heap."

I nod, surrendering to Dev's vehemence, and then rest my head back against a box of bleach bottles. The trial is over for me. If I go to the courtroom tomorrow, they'll arrest me. I'll never see her again. I would do anything to be able to go up to my room, turn over that photograph, and clutch it close to my chest.

"Don't you have somewhere to be tonight?" asks Dev.

"Somewhere..."

"Lover boy?"

I slap my forehead. "Andrew. I'll have to stand him up."

"What a shame for him. That'll keep him on his toes."

I nod but I'm not really listening. I feel suffocated, like the trap is closing in and my escape routes are disappearing.

"We need to get out of this broom closet," I say. "It's claustrophobic."

"What do you suggest? The hotel is out of the question now that the police are looking for you."

I think hard. "How about the chapel?"

"The one next to the dead body? There'll be a perimeter around it."

I slump back. "I don't know. Are there any abandoned houses?"

"Not that I know of. I've only been here as long as you, remember?"

I fight the urge to scoff. *Remember.* If only I could.

"The courthouse," I say, struck by inspiration. "The windows are old, so they'll be easy to pry open. We can take refuge there."

"What about tomorrow morning?"

I think it over. As enticing as the idea of running away is, Eades's acquittal is my only chance to see my daughter again. I can't hide forever.

"I've got to finish the trial."

"They'll arrest you."

"They don't have any evidence," I say.

"That won't matter to them. And you've lost your only friendly police officer."

"I have to carry on. I have to. Let's just get through until tomorrow morning and hope they wait until after the trial to arrest me."

"You need to get off the island."

"How am I going to do that?"

"Tomorrow morning, a plane will land—"

"I thought there weren't any flights until Friday?"

"There aren't. The plane lands on Thursday, stays overnight, and leaves again on Friday. The last witness, A.N. Other, is coming on tomorrow's plane. That's why they wanted to delay calling him."

"Are you saying I should jack the plane and fly it single-handed?"

"If you could do that, good luck to you, but I was suggesting something a little more pedestrian: stowing away."

I take a deep breath.

"Your call," he says. "How are we going to get into these windows, then?"

"We'll need a ladder."

Dev looks to his left. There are stepladders in the corner.

———————

After many whispered arguments, Dev and I agree on how we're to smuggle the stepladders across the square, which is overlooked by the hotel, the police station, and any number of side passages or alleys DC Parks and her team might want to stand in.

We steal uniforms from the store cupboard and put them over our clothes. I'm wearing a blue tabard, while Dev's white overalls are comically tight. We decide that I'll go first.

If the disguise fails, I'll be arrested, and Dev can hang back.

If it works, I'll wait in one of the stone recesses for him to come with the stepladder.

———————

I step out into the square. The most direct route is straight across the expanse of tarmac. But that also feels the most exposed. A safer but more circuitous route means sticking to the outskirts and hiding in the darkness of the buildings. I take that option.

The wind from the ocean howls in my ears, making it impossible to tell whether I'm being followed. I reach the corner of the court building and wait in an alcove.

Each passing minute feels like an eternity. I hear Dev before I see him, huffing and puffing with the effort of carrying the stepladder. Then the figure dressed in white overalls comes into view. He sets up the ladder and I climb up.

Once on top of the ladder, I pull the screwdriver that we also stole from the closet out of my handbag and start to force open a casement window. Every scratch or bang feels like I'm setting off an alarm. Eventually, the metal gives and

I'm able to lever the screwdriver to open the window. I slide my arm through the gap and release the peg stays. The window swings wide open.

I climb in first, followed by Dev. We pull the stepladder into the room and close the window, not daring to turn on a light in case someone sees a light flickering inside what is supposed to be an empty and secure building.

Dev leads me out of the robing room and into the corridor. The stone floors and columns of the main hall stand like sentries in the gloom. Dev takes my hand and I let him. We turn right and go through a door. I can just make out the words PRESS ROOM on a brass nameplate.

Inside, Dev starts rearranging the furniture and crouches down on the floor, rummaging around.

"Ah," he says and then flicks a switch.

The faint red glow of an electric fire turns the air amber.

"Thanks," I say.

Even with the fire it's cold.

"Come here," Dev says. "Sit by the fire. You might catch your death, and I don't need that kind of bad publicity."

I find myself relenting, wanting to feel the warmth of another human being. I sit down on a plastic chair next to Dev. He puts an arm around me, and I rest my head on his shoulder, feeling safe. Both the heat from his body and the electric fire warm me, and I feel myself sinking into his embrace. He kisses my head. It could be mistaken for platonic, but I can tell from the way he squeezes my arm that it isn't. I nuzzle into his khaki overcoat, which smells surprisingly clean. Perhaps the crumples speak of a man who washes his clothes religiously but never irons them.

A hand on my head strokes my hair. I feel him squeeze my shoulder. His hand slides down my arm and to my waist. I don't want him to stop.

This revelation is both exciting and terrifying. He must be ten years older at least. I don't care about that right now. I just relax while our bodies meld together. For the first time since I've been on this island, I descend into a deep sleep.

————————

I wake up just as dawn is breaking, my mouth dry and my head pounding. My cheek is on Dev's lap. When I sit up, he doesn't seem to notice. Our little room is so hot from the electric fire that all of the moisture in my body seems wicked dry. I turn it off.

Dev is slumped over the chair. His messenger bag is on the table next to my handbag. I pull out the VHS and go over to the television set in the corner. I crouch down in front of it, checking over my shoulder to make sure that Dev is still asleep. He is.

I feed the tape into the player and press the sideways triangle on the video recorder. The CCTV crackles into life. The picture is in color. The camera is pointed toward a revolving door. I check the time stamp and realize what this is.

The missing thirty seconds of footage.

Eades approaches Abbott House from the right side of the screen and walks through the revolving doors into the building, weighed down by the bomb.

As the footage draws nearer to 15:25:19, I feel my heart starting to pump a little faster. I'm waiting for the time stamp to jump to 15:25:49 like on the old footage. It doesn't. The time ticks over to 15:25:20 and I let out a quick breath.

Eades disappears inside the revolving doors. Then, from stage left, we get something that I wasn't expecting.

A woman in a trench coat follows after Eades. She looks identical to me. Or the person I see in the mirror, because I still haven't accepted we're one and the same. The coat she's wearing looks identical to the purple coat I bought from the secondhand shop.

I scratch the tattoo on my arm.

She pauses, turns away from the revolving doors, and lifts the material covering her chest to her mouth and lowers her chin as though she's speaking into something.

Then, there's movement in the right-hand corner of the screen.

Standing in the negative space between two office blocks is a man wearing a taqiyah and a thobe. He's got a long, white, unkempt beard. The footage is too grainy to tell what ethnicity he is. But I remember the reports from the unused. He was in there, easy for us to find. The woman—me—wasn't mentioned.

In the half second after the woman speaks into her lapel, the man in the takiyah puts a hand to his ear. The woman turns away from Abbott House and walks over to him.

I realize what this is. This is the moment the O87 accomplices who were supposed to be the drop-car drivers decided to abandon Eades to his fate.

The screen goes black.

"You bitch."

Dev is awake. He's standing behind me.

"I–I have no—" I stammer.

"Explanation?"

"No, no *idea*. Listen to me, Dev. *Listen*."

"I trusted you, introduced you to my sources. You bitch, you've been pulling the wool over my eyes the whole time."

"I haven't, I promise. I didn't know. I'm not…" I gesture at the television screen. "I don't know who that is."

"It's fucking you, isn't it?"

"There's something else. There's something I haven't been telling you. I've been… Ever since… I've lost all of my memories."

"Oh, yeah, pull the other one."

"When I first stood up to address the jury. On the first day. That's the first thing I remember. I have no memories of anything before that moment. I don't know who I am."

"If that's true, you'd have said something earlier."

"No one would have believed me. And what would they have done if they did?"

He's silent for a long time. My ears are ringing, and all I can hear is this piercing sound, like it's ripping through the fabric of my flimsy identity. I'm a terrorist? A white supremacist?

"Get out," he says.

"Dev, please. We've got to work together; we've got to help each other."

"Get out of here, or I'll hand you over to the police myself."

I cry, a pathetic whimper. He turns away, not wanting to see my crocodile tears.

"You know," he says, before I leave, "the purple coat? The one you said was stolen the other night? I've never seen you wear it until I saw that video."

CHAPTER THIRTY-NINE

THE CORRIDORS OF THE court building are tunnels of darkness. What am I supposed to do? Keep running? Hand myself in? Perhaps this is why DC Parks has been on my back since day one. I'm the person we've been looking for. The missing piece.

A figure moves across the main hall like a shadow that has lost its owner. I recognize a familiar profile.

"Malcolm!" I call, unsure what my next move will be.

"Lila, you're in early. How did you get in? It's not opening hours yet."

"I don't have time to explain now. I'm on the run."

"Oh?" Malcolm looks amused, like this is a welcome complication in an otherwise boring morning routine.

"Yes, the police think I'm guilty of murder and I'm being followed, and I don't know what's going on and I need to represent my client. I just don't know what to do and I don't know why I'm telling you all of this either because I know you can't help, and given your job in court, I suspect you're duty-bound to hand me in now, but I just need someone to talk to…" It all comes out in a rush until a lump in my throat stops me from talking. "I'm never going to see her again."

"Who?" asks Malcolm.

"My daughter."

A shocked expression passes briefly over his face before he rearranges his features into a sympathetic expression.

"I'm sorry to hear that," he says. "Well, if you want my advice, I think you should hand yourself in. Otherwise you'll just look more guilty in the long run."

I nod slowly. "But my daughter..."

Malcolm holds me by the arms. "Lila, look at me. Things will be OK, I promise."

Like a child, I believe him because I want to, because the alternative is so much worse.

I wipe my tears with my sleeve and nod. "Will you tell the judge why I'm not there?"

He laughs good-naturedly. "Of course, but I think that's the least of your worries."

The truth of his words washes over me in another wave of hopelessness.

"Come on." He takes me by the hand. "We'll go together."

———————————

The fact that I've handed myself in does nothing to curb the officers' enthusiasm. They cuff me and put me in a cell with barely contained glee. DC Parks comes and looks through the letter box on a few occasions.

My fingerprints are taken, my fingernails swabbed, and my clothes removed. Every inch of my body is photographed, including the fresh tattoo on my wrist.

After a while, I'm back in the interview room, sitting across from one uniformed police officer and one plainclothes one. I realize one of them probably got a promotion this morning on the back of DS Grant's murder.

"Lila Dalton, you have been arrested on suspicion of three murders. Patricia Singh. DS Jack Grant. And an as-yet-unidentified body that was found in the woods last night."

Kevin, I think to myself.

"You do not have to say anything..."

I have the right to legal representation, as the plainclothes officer explains to me, but I decide not to take it. To our left is a large mirror. I know without understanding how that it's double-sided and on the other side is probably DC Parks, leering at me with her lopsided smile and lipstick-smudged teeth.

I wait for them to lay out the evidence, and they do, bit by bit. The entry in DS Grant's diary that said he was going to meet me. That makes no sense. It was a secret meeting that involved DS Grant passing me sensitive information. He'd have never put it in his diary. But there it is, my name, penciled in next to the numbers 777.

Next are the pictures of his body. I wonder if I should try to feign surprise; surely it's suspicious that I'm not at all shocked by the images of a dead man, but it all seems so futile, so hopeless. I was there. There are more images of the scene, including a trail of footprints that look like mine, because they are. There's an anonymous witness who saw me enter and leave 4 Parish Row shortly before the body was discovered. Again, I wonder who that could be. Apart from Dev, there was no one around.

Then there are pictures of Kevin, poor, paranoid, not-even-his-real-name Kevin. They lay down a photo taken of the Odal rune scored into the earth next to his hut, followed by a picture of me in the woods, holding a stick like a saber.

I don't remember a photo being taken. There was no flash, no shutter. All I remember is wandering through the woods in a trancelike state, holding a stick.

"I know how this looks—"

"We found dirt under your fingernails," says one of the officers.

"But that was just from picking up the piece of wood from the ground."

They share a glance, unimpressed.

"We haven't gotten to the murder of Patricia Singh yet."

"She was drunk. I've seen the report. It was nothing to do with me."

"We still haven't finalized that case. It's not looking good, is it?"

I don't answer but stay quiet, bouncing my knee up and down. A cold sense of dread has settled over me like a wet coat. I start shivering.

One of the officers reaches over and touches my wrist gently. He pulls up my shirt to reveal the fresh 777 tattoo that sits where a bracelet would.

"We've looked into this number, and we're told it has connections to extremist groups."

"This was done to me," I say, pleading with them. "You've got to understand. Someone's been following me. They hit me over the head and did *that* while I was passed out."

"When?"

"Two nights ago."

"Can anyone verify that?"

An image of Dev, disgusted in me and calling me a bitch, flashes in my mind's eye. "No."

The plainclothes officer scribbles something down.

"Listen," I say, "you've got to understand. I'm not well." At last, the insanity defense. The only thing I have left.

The officers don't speak for another twenty minutes while I tell them everything that happened since I came around in a courtroom to find myself staring at twelve strangers. They fidget and write things down but let me tell the tale. As I'm speaking, the different symbols and clues seem to come to life around me, weaving together, taunting me, hinting at solutions but never letting me see the whole picture.

I punctuate the story with sips of water that the officers are only too happy to ply me with. I tell them about my daughter and how I'm scared for her and want to return her little pink and purple horse to where it belongs.

They nod and take notes. After a while, I stop speaking.

The only part I leave out is what I just saw on the video with Dev. I still haven't worked that out yet.

They rub their eyes and cradle their foreheads when I finish. "Can you give us a minute?" one of them asks before turning off the tape.

I nod and let them leave. When they're outside, I turn and face the mirror, imagining that I'm meeting DC Parks's eyes, and stare defiantly out at her.

Rather than waste time engaging in a pointless battle of wills against her, I turn my attention to the evidence on the desk. I pore over the photographs, the angles they were taken from. It feels like there's a big hole in the middle of all this, the eye of the storm. I sit back, thinking about everything that has happened, trying to piece it all together.

DC Parks comes to visit me. After making sure the tape is switched off, she sits on the table, leg dangling over the side.

"Not going to tell me where the eighth is?"

I stare back at her, not saying a word.

"OK." She gets up and walks around. "You know it's empty in there?" She points at the two-way mirror. "I told them all to clear out. No one else can hear what you're saying. So, tell me, come on."

I don't say anything, I need time to consider. Is this the right decision? Am I putting my trust in the right person?

"Whatever. You know what? When I saw that you were defending Eades, I nearly fell off my chair in the office. No matter how many times you change your name, or fake your own death, I will always know who you really are."

Still, I say nothing, though I'm dying to ask her who I am. Who was that woman in the video?

"It reminds me of when serial killers ring up to give the police false tips. It's like you sickos get off on being close to it."

"You've been in my room," I say. "I could smell your perfume."

She smiles at me. "Perks of the job. Guess what?"

"What?"

"I was listening carefully to the story you told those officers."

"And?"

"I decided to check out what you said. Here's what I found in your room when I checked earlier this morning." She slaps an evidence bag on the table, inside it a thin rope. "A ligature we're sure matches the one used to strangle DS Grant."

Another evidence bag goes down on the table. *The Extraction Bulletin.*

"You don't understand. You've got to see what's going on here. The real murderers are framing me."

"I'll tell you what we didn't find," she says. "No threats, no horse, no picture of a little girl."

"No," I say, sobbing freely now. To take the only totems of the life I once had is surely the cruelest thing that's been done to me so far. "No, they've hidden it all. They've stolen the evidence."

"You said that those things would be in your handbag, which was seized on your arrival. The horse. Various threats. A hollow earth leaflet. None of them are there. Who do you suppose took them?"

"I don't know, but you've got to believe me."

I don't even believe myself.

"There was one thing, though," she says. "I have no explanation for this, so I hope you will." She holds up the pager.

"That's not mine. It was delivered to me, in the horse…"

"This is a very interesting piece of evidence."

"Why's that?"

"We've been able to track where the messages were sent from and to on each occasion you were paged."

"And?"

"The first, when the number 187 appeared, was sent from a phone in the Castle Hotel."

"No," I say.

"The second, which is the second 187, is from the court building."

"No, no, you've got this…"

"The third one was sent from the Pilot."

"Yes, I knew that. I knew they could see me when they sent it to me…"

"Have you been sending these messages to yourself?"

"No, you don't understand."

"You were in all of these places at the time the messages were sent."

I look at all of the pictures, all of the evidence, the new and dangerous knowledge that seeps out of them. The void in the middle of the evidence solidifies and takes shape.

"We can help each other," I say.

"I don't think so."

"I know who's behind all of this. I know who Simon Cox is."

"So, tell me."

"No, because you already know who it is, and you haven't been able to get them."

She leans back in her chair. "Go on."

"I'm the only one who can."

"How did you work that one out?"

"It's my job, isn't it? I've been suspicious about this A.N. Other from the start. I can get a confession from him with the right questioning. I know I can. Once I've done this last piece of cross-examination, the truth will be clear."

"How do I know you won't run away after you've performed this magic trick?"

"I'll be in the court the whole time."

She gets up and paces around. I can see the internal tug-of-war being played out across her features. "OK, but you'll need to take this with you." She palms me a Dictaphone. I hesitate before taking it. Then I stash it in my handbag.

CHAPTER FORTY

MY HEAD IS CHURNING with information as I walk into the courtroom. Everyone is watching me. The rumor that I've just been released from police custody must surely have spread to all corners of the prosecution team by now.

I look at Paxton with a question on my face. "Is he here?"

"He's here," he says, inclining his head toward the witness box, which has its curtains drawn to protect A.N. Other's identity.

I nod and turn back to the front of the room, waiting for the judge.

Once seated at the bench, he looks to Paxton. "Ready for the jury?"

"Yes, my lord."

"Let's get them in then."

Once the jury has filed in and taken their seats, Paxton rises to his feet.

"My lord, if I could call the next witness. His name has been anonymized and his identity protected so that he is known by the name 'A.N. Other.'"

"Very well."

Paxton and I have to switch seats so that the curtains can be drawn back slightly, but so that only he and I can see the witness.

As soon as I see his face, I recognize him. I can't stop staring as he rises to take the oath.

I've still got the articles and issues of *Beacon* that Dev gave to me. I dive into my handbag to pull them out. I riffle through them and turn down the relevant pages. Then I pull out the issue of *The Muslim Times* and the photocopied note that Kevin gave to me and Dev.

I lean across to Paxton. "Are you going to be making any applications to withhold disclosure?"

"What?"

"Public interest immunity? Your chap is a spook."

Paxton's eyes widen and he turns to converse with Andrew, who in turn speaks with the four people behind him. DC Parks looks at me, holds my gaze. A smile plays at the corner of her mouth, and I know I'm right.

A moment later, Paxton leans across. "No idea what you're talking about."

"Can we have silence when the oath is being taken?" The judge's cheeks redden.

A.N. Other begins his evidence. He trots out the same story as in his witness statement. He was part of Eades's cell until he was scared by Eades's plans to bomb a government building. But, yes, he knew that Eades wanted to bomb something even when they were part of the same cell. No, he knows nothing more than that because he left the order, feeling it was a bit too hard-core. He decided to join the BNP instead, which seemed a bit more his sort of thing.

Once the examination in chief is complete, I stand up.

"My lord, I want to put the CCTV to this witness."

"Very well, make the arrangements, will you?" He waves at Malcolm, who nods and disappears to find the television set.

In the meantime, I turn to A.N. Other. "I just want to confirm, your evidence is that you knew the accused, Mr. Eades?"

"Yes."

"You and he were part of a cell together, you said?"

"Yes."

"You both grew up in South Wales, is that right?"

"Yes."

"But you told the jury that you backed out as soon as bombs were mentioned."

"That's what happened. I wasn't into any of that."

"Did you go to Birmingham with him on the day of the bombings?"

"No."

"Have you ever been to Birmingham?"

"No."

I pause. "I'm going to ask you again. I just want you to think about your answer. Have you ever been to Birmingham?"

"No, I've never left Wales."

I leave another silence, allow that answer to sink in. By this point, the new usher has arranged the CCTV. I pick up the black-and-white tape; the one that had no missing parts. Once it's slid into the slot below the monitor, I wait for it to play out.

"Did you see that?"

"Er, yeah."

"That's some closed-circuit television footage from the day of the Abbott House bombings."

"Right."

"My lord, permission to leave counsel's row?"

"If you must."

I stand next to the television as the clip plays again. I point to a figure on the footage. While everyone else is running away from the bomb, there's one figure who's running toward it. When I first watched it, I thought it must have been a family member of one of the people in the building. Only love could make someone that crazy. Now, I know it was something else entirely.

"Is that you?" I ask.

He frowns at the monitor. "No, and you can't prove it's me. It's just someone who looks like me."

"Are you sure about that?"

"Yes."

"Because earlier you told us that you'd never been to Birmingham."

"I haven't."

"So, you wouldn't have been to London, either?"

"Definitely not."

"I'm going to hand you up a copy of *Beacon*, which is an anti-fascist and parapolitical magazine that reports on the far right. I want you to look at page twelve."

"Are copies of this to be given to the jury?" asks the judge.

"My lord, I will ask for copies to be made as soon as this witness has given his evidence. As his identity was hidden from the defense, it wasn't clear until now that these questions would have to be put forward."

The judge nods, placated.

I return to questioning the witness. "Page twelve shows a picture of a National Front rally. Is that you?"

"Er..."

"Also in that picture is Mr. Eades, is that right?"

"Yes."

"So, could it be you?"

"Could be."

"When you said you'd never left South Wales, was that a lie you told to the jury?"

"Yes."

"It's not just a coincidence that there's someone who looks like you in this picture in London and someone who looks like you on this CCTV in Birmingham, is it?"

"No comment."

I stop questioning and embrace the silence.

I open another copy of the magazine. This time, there's a picture of a climate change protest with officers showing an excitable attitude to policing the march. Holding a placard is someone who looks a lot like the witness.

"This looks like you as well."

"My face isn't all that... I've just got one of those... You know?"

"And finally. A picture here."

This time the picture is of a man wearing a thobe and sitting cross-legged.

"Is that you with a grown beard?"

"Erm..."

"So, in the last two years you've flirted with neo-Nazism and climate activism, and you purported to have converted to Islam?"

"No comment."

"Are there any other causes that have taken your fancy recently?"

"No comment."

"You weren't just a member of the cell, were you? You're an undercover officer with Special Branch, aren't you?"

"No comment."

"This isn't an interview under caution," says the judge. "You've come here to answer questions. You can't pick and choose which ones to answer."

A.N. Other turns to the judge and speaks through gritted teeth. "I *can't*."

"Speak up so the jury can hear you."

"I can't." Then he mumbles something incoherent about the Official Secrets Act.

"What was that?" I say. "The Official Secrets Act? So, you are in the employ of Special Branch?"

"No comment."

The judge raises his hands in exasperation.

"Is that why, when everyone was running away from an explosion, you decided to run toward it?"

"No comment."

"Because the bombing was called in, wasn't it?"

"No comment."

I ask for the note to be handed up.

"You should have in front of you a note. This was taken on the notepaper of a phone handler. It reads: '*Anon caller. Birmingham. Tell Security Services. Possible bomb threat. Crown Court.*'"

"Now, the target is wrong. But who told them about the bomb threat?"

"No comment."

"Was it you? Did you get the location wrong? Were you fed false information?"

"No comment."

"Is that why lives were lost, because you made a mistake?"

"Miss Dalton, this is a trial, not an inquest," interrupts the judge.

"I apologize, your lordship. One more question." I hand up *The Muslim Times*. "Here is an article in *The Muslim Times* saying that members of the community needed to be on alert. Did the police know about the bombing before it happened?"

His eyes drop. Defeated. "No comment."

"Really? No comments to make at all?" says the judge. "I have to say, I allowed Miss Dalton her questions, but I'm not really sure how they help her client."

"My lord, that will have to be something that will be dealt with in my speech."

The judge harrumphs before turning to Paxton, "No re-examination, I suppose?"

"Wait—" It's A.N. Other.

"You've had your turn," says the judge. "I thought the Official Secrets Act prevented you."

"I–I want to answer her questions."

The judge looks at us all as though to say "*Very well.*"

A.N. Other takes a big breath as though about to take a jump into cold water before launching into his speech. His words flow quickly, as though he needs to get this over and done with before he loses his nerve. "Yes, my role was to infiltrate the O87. And yes, I thought that there would be a bomb threat. Yes, Special Branch did have foreknowledge that Eades was being instructed by the higher-ups in the organization to plant a bomb. We didn't know where. I called it in. The bomb squad went to the Crown Court...mistakenly. It was

Abbott House, instead. We had a tip from an anti-fascist newspaper who had an undercover reporter on the inside in O87. They were killed in the explosion. They and another member of the public had taken the bombs from the toilet to try to dismantle them…"

The explosion came from the walls.

"By that time, it was too late. You see, the far right have all of these manuals and handbooks on how to build bombs, so they would have had some knowledge of how they're put together. That's why we don't have forensics explosive evidence or anything else because it would have revealed that the bombs were tampered with before explosion; the explosives guys said it looked as though someone had tried to deactivate them and that would have blown her cover. The work she did would have been lost… But the bomb was planted by Eades. It was my fault all those people died. I gave the newsroom the wrong information. I believed what Eades told me. He must have suspected me and given me the wrong target on purpose."

He looks down at his lap, perhaps at his wrists, wondering what cuffs will feel like. Tears leak down his face, but I can tell that a weight has been lifted.

"There's no conspiracy," he says, his voice wobbling. "The police weren't trying to get Eades to plant a bomb so that we could bring in harsher legislation. God, we wouldn't have the resources to do something that elaborate. It was just a mistake. Just ineptitude. Everything else is just…a cover-up of the ineptitude. Because who can sleep in their beds at night knowing that the police were too shit to save them from one idiot with a bag of ANFO?"

By the end of his monologue, he's broken down in tears. I sit back, stunned. At the same time, I'm panicking. All of my best points, all of the hidden evidence. There's little I can say in my speech now. Eades will be convicted on the back of that, and O87 will never let me or my daughter leave the island. This knowledge is accompanied by a perverse sense of pleasure. The answers I've been chasing have, at long last, been given to me. There was no conspiracy. Everything that Dev said was total fantasy. This was just a failing police service trying to patch up its own ineptitude.

Paxton rises to his feet. "Some re-examination, my lord."

"I should imagine so, after that."

"Why have you told us all of this? You must know you might be convicted for a breach of the Official Secrets Act?"

"Because I lived with these people. I know what they do, how they manipulate the narrative. And I am not going to stand by and let people like *her*"—he points at me, the venom in his voice palpable—"paint this picture of some big conspiracy against the far right. They'll use it to peddle more conspiracy theories, attract more people to their cause. That's what they do; it's how they operate, by distorting the truth. I'm not going to let it happen."

"Thank you," says Paxton.

A.N. Other shrugs. Gets up, leaves the witness box, looking like a man leaving for the gallows.

CHAPTER FORTY-ONE

I WATCH AS EVERYONE filters out of the courtroom.

"Are you coming down to see him?" asks Trevor.

"No," I say.

DC Parks regards me with a knowing look that says "I'll be waiting outside, so don't try anything."

One by one, I watch Paxton, Andrew, the suits who sit behind them, the clerk, and the ushers leave the room. I sit, looking down at my prepared notes, and realize that the case has fallen down around me, and I'll never see her again.

There's one person left in the courtroom who's just as depressed as I am, perhaps even more so. Dev. He looks like he's been deflated. Casting around in his vast swathes of far-right material, he tries to piece together his broken career, rummaging around in the rubble of a life dedicated to information-gathering, exposing the powers that be. I feel a pang of sympathy.

"What are you going to do with the tape?" I ask.

He holds it in his hand, considering it. "Haven't decided yet. Decisions like these take time."

I nod.

"Gloat away," he says.

"I'm not gloating."

"You were the one who said it was nonsense, that I was a conspiracy theorist."

"Oh, Dev. I couldn't have done it without you."

"Done what?"

"Ruined the most important case of my life."

He looks down at the floor. "I'm sorry."

I wave a hand.

"Never mind," he says. "We'll be OK. I'll make sure of it."

"How are you going to do that?"

"I can help you win your case. There are still holes in the evidence. We can do it, Lila."

"I thought I was a bitch?"

"No." He shakes his head. "I was wrong. *They*'ve got it all wrong."

I shake my head. "I think A.N. Other rode a coach and horses through all of your theories."

"I know there's a way out of this, Lila. We can find it, together."

"I've got a plan anyway," I say.

"What's that?"

"I'm going to find out who Simon Cox is. Then I'm going to do a deal with DC Parks. If I get a confession out of Cox, I think they'll drop the prosecution against Eades."

"You think she'll keep her word?"

"What choice do I have?"

"Are you saying that Cox is on the island?"

"Oh, yes. He's here."

"And you know who it is?"

"Yes. And you do too, Dev. I just don't know why you've been hiding it from me until now."

"Me?"

"Come off it, Dev. You can take me to Smyth. Tell me where he is."

As we're speaking, I write in my notepad.

"What's that?"

"I'm just leaving my instructing solicitor a message."

Dev nods. "Why won't you let me help you escape?"

"I think my daughter is being kept here on the island. I'm not leaving until I know she's safe."

"OK," he says, resigned. "I'll take you to him, but I can't guarantee your daughter's safety."

"I wouldn't have expected you to." I make a little origami figure out of the notepaper and leave it on the writing desk in front of me. "How are we going to get out of here without DC Parks following us?"

Dev holds up a pass, the type that Malcolm wears on a lanyard around his neck.

"Where did you get that?"

Dev taps his nose in the manner I've become accustomed to when he talks about his morally questionable journalistic techniques. We use the pass to get through the corridors at the back of the court. From there, we find the staff car park.

"What now?" I ask, looking around at the twenty or so cars.

Dev pulls out a long piece of wire that he feeds into the gap between the door and the chassis of a car. He manages to loop the wire around the door lock pin. There's a click and he opens the door. After he jump-starts the car, we drive away in the stolen vehicle.

"Can't trust taxis. Can't trust anything anymore," he explains as he drives away.

"Why?" I ask.

"They'll be onto us. They'll know you've escaped by now."

We find our way to the road that cuts through the middle of the island, past the prison, and to the woods.

The main town gets smaller as we zoom away. Eventually we find the edge of the woods, but instead of stopping and walking through, Dev takes a right-hand turn and starts driving over a grassy field. The car bumps and jolts as we go.

After five minutes of circling the outside of the trees, I see the lighthouse. Dev stops the car at the edge of the cliff.

"Is this where Smyth has been hiding?"

"Come with me."

"Dev, are you sure about this?"

"I'm sure. Now, do you want to meet the Grand Master of the Order of Eights and Sevens?"

"Yes."

"Say 'please.'"

"For fuck's sake, stop playing games."

"Say '*please*.'"

The word tumbles out of my mouth. "Please."

I follow after him toward the cliff path, no longer protesting.

There's a large plateau of black rock surrounding the lighthouse. To get to it, we have to climb down the steep coastal path. It's slippery and coated with loose stones. When we reach the bottom, we climb over the black rocks.

"What's here?" I ask Dev.

"I'll *enlighten* you shortly."

The lighthouse sits atop a small hill at the edge of the plateau. We climb the rock steps up to the door. The noise it makes when Dev opens it is ominous. The rust is baked in, and the squeal of the hinges cuts through the gray afternoon.

Dev takes a hurricane lamp off the wall and lights it, casting uneasy shadows in the small circular space. Beyond its reach, I can make out a spiral staircase.

The latticed metal steps—also rusted—creak as we climb. The ocean's whisper fades the higher we get, making me feel like I'm going deaf. I don't know where we're headed, but the air gets colder and the force of the wind pelting the walls increases the longer we climb. Occasionally, Dev's lamp highlights pictures of old lighthouse keepers or medals.

I count the steps as we go. We're on forty now. I've been counting in tens, keeping a tally on my right hand, which is stuffed into my pocket.

We pass two landings before reaching a ladder leading to the loft.

"Ladies first," says Dev.

I sigh but put up little resistance. The anticipation has been building with each step.

My head and shoulders breach the trapdoor. Unsure if the room is deserted or simply dark, I climb out of the hatch and into the room, looking around. Above us is the lamp swinging around 360 degrees. The strobing light illuminates the room in flashes.

"You said you were going to enlighten me," I say. "I didn't think you meant literally."

"Did I say that?" He puts his hands in his pockets and starts strolling around, looking at the walls as though in an art gallery.

"Where's Smyth?"

"Who?"

"*Smyth.* Dev, come on; don't do this. I'm here to see him."

"Hmm?"

"Where is he?"

Dev doesn't answer, just stares back at me. I look around again at the empty room.

"I'm leaving," I say.

He steps in front of me and holds his palm out.

"Get out of my way." I put my hand in my pocket and feel the Dictaphone.

"Don't even bother," he says.

"Get the hell out of my way. I'm done with this." I go to push past him again.

"Just say '*please.*'"

I stop. I make no more attempt to push past. My mouth opens to protest, but the word that escapes my lips is detached from me. "Please."

"Very good. Now go and sit down on that bench over there. And take your hand out of your pocket."

I do as I'm told, going over to sit on the bench he pointed out. Once there, I remove my hand from my pocket.

"Don't get up until I say so."

My chest tightens with panic. "What's happening?"

A stupid question. I know exactly what's happening.

Dev doesn't answer, so I try a different tack. "You were at the scene of DS Grant's murder minutes after I found the body," I say. "Why?"

Dev stares down at me. There's a strange expression on his face. For the first time, he's serious. All of that jocularity gone.

"It is so obvious when I think about it," I say. "You know so much about the far right, and you were very keen to impose yourself on this case, leading me down certain pathways, gaining my trust with helpful evidence. All along, you've been pushing me to different conclusions, teasing me when I didn't get there myself."

Dev doesn't say a word. He doesn't stop me either; it's like he gets off on having his accomplishments recited back to him. For now, he's letting me speak so I use it to buy time, hoping that I can keep a conversation going while my subconscious works a way out of this mess.

"And DS Grant was right," I continue. "The O87 can perform inside roles. You've been infiltrating the criminal justice system from the start. And where was the weak link? Who let you in? I did. I turned to you with ever-increasing desperation. All the while my mistrust of the factions of government that are supposed to keep me safe, that I'm supposed to be a part of, deepened."

I want to get up, to run far away from here. I can't. I'm stuck on this bench, unable to move until Dev gives his command.

"And it also explains why you didn't see whoever tattooed my wrist. You were the one who tagged me, weren't you?"

Still, he says nothing.

"Dev?" I say. "Aren't you going to fess up? Or should I call you Simon Cox?"

"If you want." Dev isn't concentrating on me, too busy fiddling with something large and bulky. A radio.

"What's that? Who's coming?"

He rolls his eyes.

"Come on; you must want to talk, or else you'd have told me to be quiet and I wouldn't have been able to say anything, would I? Tell me how it works. How long does it take until you can control someone's mind?"

Dev ruffles his face in the manner I've become accustomed to him doing when he's frustrated or confused. "OK, you want to talk? Let's talk. It'll be something to do to pass the time until they're here."

"They? Who are they?"

Dev's face cracks into that familiar smile, although nothing is right about it. The broken, yellowing teeth are the same, as is the lopsided jaunt of it. But the eyes. The eyes are hollowed out.

"You'll see shortly," he says.

"Who am I?" I ask. "Who was the woman on the video?"

"Who...are...you?" asks Dev. "Good question. I've been wondering about that for a while now."

"So, I *was* in the order?"

"You're a traitor," he says, his voice laced with malice.

"I was in the order but had a change of heart?"

"You pretended you were one of us, that you cared about the cause. But all that time, you were undercover. You traitorous bitch."

"But... No. That's not... I'm a barrister. How could *I* have been undercover?"

Dev shrugs. "This"—he gestures at me—"this barrister act is probably just another cover. You never exactly struck me as being up to the job."

My head is spinning, trying to pin down just one version of the facts. "None of what you're saying makes sense."

"Stop lying. I know your real name. It's not Lila Dalton. It's Delia Lewis."

"What?"

"Stop pretending!" he bellows at me.

I go quiet and feel myself shrinking into the wall behind me.

"Move your left foot," he says. He's enjoying showing off, demonstrating his power over me.

I look down; my foot wiggles.

"Now your right foot," he says.

"No, no," I say. "Please, don't do this." But my foot is already wiggling. Now both are.

"Get up," he says.

My feet stop wiggling and I get to my feet.

He passes me a knife. "Cut your finger."

I take the knife and make a nick in my skin. A little bubble of blood blossoms from the tip.

"Give me back the knife."

I hesitate, wanting to fight back, turn the knife on him, but instead I hand it over.

"Walk over to the window."

"Wait," I say as I'm walking over, "I haven't finished asking my questions."

"Well, I've finished answering them, you traitorous bitch."

"Who have I betrayed?"

"*Your race!*" he shouts. "Now, go over to the window. I'll show you how we punish race traitors."

I do as he says and look out of the window. Several stories below, the waves crash into the black rocks.

"Please," I say, disgusted by how scared I sound. "Please, I have a daughter, a child. Think about her."

"If her mother's a race traitor, so is she. Bad blood flows downhill."

"What do I have to do? I'll help you, I'll do anything. Just tell me what this is all about. Come on, tell me. What came first, being the editor of *Beacon* or Grand Master of the Order of Eights and Sevens?"

Dev sticks his tongue in his cheek as though searching for something stuck in his molars.

"Was it you who tried to pin it on radical Islamists? Were those your guys posing as Muslims? The one who everyone thought was the second man?"

"I've got nothing against jihadists," says Dev. "We've got more in common than most people realize. I'll let them do their thing in their country, and I'll do my thing in mine."

It's not your country, I want to spit at him.

Dev leans against the wall and crosses his legs. "Do you know what's really funny about all of that stuff with the Muslim bloke people thought was working with Eades? That was a pure coincidence. That's what inner cities are like, you see. Full of 'em. Fucking swarming."

I feel sick. No time for that. No time for outrage.

"Get ready for the war," he says.

"Did you write all of the literature? Are you the Grand Master? Did you invent extraction?"

"No. Himmler developed the final solution decades ago. I simply continued his noble work. Now, step out onto the ledge."

My legs seem to move of their own accord. If I think about it, I'll faint. I step out on to the ledge of the window. The wind buffets against my body. All I can hear is the roar of the sea as it smashes into the rocks below. I try not to imagine how it will feel when my body is pummeled by the waves.

"Last year," Dev continues in his sermon, "something happened that will change the fabric of society in ways you won't even be able to conceive. The internet became fully commercialized across America. The way information can travel and be disseminated will mutate in ways that will become both dangerous and exciting." He has to shout above the roar of the wind and sea.

"What does that have to do with a race war?"

"Until now," Dev resumes, and I realize this is something he has rehearsed, "the world has lived under the guise of an absolute reality. There are known truths. From this point onward, that will break down so rapidly that the singularity of truth and reality will disappear."

I blink. The wind is wicking the water from my eyes.

"Soon countries and nationalities will no longer matter. The World Wide Web won't discriminate by currency or language. Those borders are going to break down. And what do you think is going to happen when the things we hold dear, that give us a sense of identity, what it means to be British, disappear? People will mix. The white genotype will disappear. Globalization is genocide. We will become extinct."

I hate the way he uses the word *we*. I am *not* like him. It takes every ounce of my strength not to look down.

"This is going to be warfare like we've never seen before. Forget guerrilla tactics. This is going to be an information war. And the casualties will be logic and truth. The bombs will be lies and rhetoric. I'm not the only one who's figured this out. Right now, there are plenty of rich people gearing up for what's coming. They know they need to secure their wealth to ride the storm. They know the truth."

"What truth is that?"

"That *we* are the superior race. We are going to have to fight back if we want to preserve whiteness. The country will soon split into two factions. Those who accept that fact, and those who don't."

"You're mad. You've actually lost the plot."

"I am going to build an ark for whites, for when the apocalypse comes."

"And mind control?" I shout back at him.

"People will be controlled by the internet. Even weirder, they'll think *they're* in control."

"Tell me about DS Grant."

"What about him?"

"How did you know I'd be there? It was you who gave the anonymous tip to the police, wasn't it?"

"Perhaps."

My mind is spinning, unable to think fast enough. I run through the three techniques of cross-examination, trying to trip him up, get him riled, but time is running out, Dev is becoming more impatient.

"Perhaps? Who else would it have been? And how did you take those photographs of me in the woods?"

"I have a special camera. It's a good gadget for undercover journalists. As you should know, since you are one, you traitorous bitch. Lift your foot."

My foot moves from the safety of the ledge. It doesn't take long before the muscles in my other leg scream in protest.

"Did you kill DS Grant because he was getting too close to the truth?"

"I didn't kill him because of that."

"But you did kill him?"

Silence. My hair is being whipped around my face, stinging my eyes. I don't know how much longer I can stand on this ledge. Please let it be over soon.

"Enough," says Dev. "Soon, I'm going to ask you to jump. Any last words?"

"What about Kevin?"

"Why are you so interested?"

"I need to know, Dev. If I'm going to die, I need to know. Just tell me." My leg is shaking with the effort of it. Tears well up in my eyes again, I'm not sure how long I can stay on this ledge, muscles screaming at me to let go, to fall.

"Did you kill Pat?"

"Why are you so interested?"

"Because I know you set me up, Dev. It's a simple question. The answer is yes or no." This is a classic cross-examination technique; force them into a yes or no, make it clear that it's an answer that requires no further explanation. Sweat beads trickle down my back. I hope it works; I hope he tells me.

He moves over to me, covering the distance at a speed that I wouldn't have thought possible for a man of his size. I flinch against my will. He reaches into my pocket but doesn't find the Dictaphone because it's in the other one.

"Tell me," I say, my voice wobbling as much as my leg. "Did you kill Pat so that I would have to represent Eades?"

"I didn't kill it. I extracted it," he says.

"Trevor told me she was the best barrister he ever instructed."

"Thank you," says Dev, cracking that awful smile again. "He'll be next on my list of race traitors."

He reaches into my other pocket, the one with the Dictaphone inside.

I put both feet on the ledge, relieved to be able to plant my weight properly. Any relief is quickly replaced by fear. The act might finally be over. I've got the confession, but now Dev has the proof in his hand. He could throw it over the ledge.

Luckily, he's distracted. He looks down at my feet.

"Lift your foot," he says.

My foot stays where it is.

"There is no such thing as mind control," I say. I turn to face him. "That is just some weird fantasy you and your friends dreamed up."

"But manners…" Dev looks confused and then angry. He looks down at the Dictaphone, furious.

The rusty stairs creak.

"Here they come," I say.

The clanging of foot on metal echoes up through the spiral staircase. The hatch door opens and from it a dark shape emerges. There's a flash of gold. The glint from a pair of spectacles. Standing up to his full height, wearing an alpaca jumper and jeans, is Malcolm, holding the origami note I left for him. I'm disappointed to see him. I was expecting DC Parks and the cavalry, not a strange man with a penchant for riddles.

Dev goes to throw the Dictaphone out of the window, but I snatch it off him. In the process, I lose my balance. The pull of gravity is instant. My stomach plummets with the sensation of free fall.

I scrabble for the ledge. Time is behaving differently. It's as though I'm experiencing it at a slower speed, but my reactions still aren't quick enough. My fingers grasp for the parapet.

A hand reaches through the window and grabs my suit jacket. I look up. Malcolm is reaching through the window, only just able to keep hold of me. He's the only thing stopping me from crashing into the rocks below. I slip.

More footsteps, more people coming up the stairs.

"Get off her," shouts Dev, and I can hear him and Malcolm struggling.

"No," I wail.

Then I hear DC Parks's voice. "Oi!"

More scuffling. Malcolm's grip is waning, and I can tell he's still having to fight off Dev. He tries to get hold of my arm. A tearing sound. The suit is ripping. My sweaty fingers grasp the Dictaphone in one hand, while the other tries to stay holding on to Malcolm.

Two more pairs of hands grab my arm. It feels like my arms might come out of my sockets. They pull me through the window, and I land on the floor in a heap. I'm flooded with relief.

My shoulder is sore; it feels like it's been dislocated in the struggle.

Somewhere at the edge of my understanding, I hear DC Parks speaking to Dev.

"Devin Hanlon, I'm detaining you…"

The two police officers who interviewed me earlier were the ones who pulled me through the window. They now wrestle Dev to the floor. It takes me a long time to stop panting. I stare down at the Dictaphone, slowly digesting the fact that I almost died, still not quite believing I'm out of danger.

Strong fingers enclose mine. DC Parks is trying to pry the Dictaphone from my grip.

I look around in time to see Dev being manhandled through the hatch.

"Do we still have a deal?" I ask.

"We'll see," she says, tugging the Dictaphone out of my grasp.

I sit on the floor, my head in my hands for a long time. At some point, a foil blanket is draped around my shoulders. People leave, I'm not sure in which order.

After a long time of the world moving around me while I stay still, I realize it's just me and Malcolm.

"Thank you, for everything," I say.

"You're welcome."

"She's not going to be able to do anything with that evidence," I say.

"Why's that?"

"It's entrapment, isn't it?"

Malcolm laughs. "A lawyer to the end. Come on. My place isn't too far from here. Let me make you a cup of tea."

I accede as Malcolm places an arm around my shoulders to coax me up and toward the spiral staircase.

CHAPTER FORTY-TWO

I'M SWADDLED IN A blanket and drinking hot cocoa spiked with rum. The cup is warming my fingers but it's agonizing—like my bones have splintered and are pushing into my nerves.

Malcolm potters around me. His cottage has a rustic feel. Everything is built for survival, including the dead carcasses of animals drying out in the pantry. Something delicious-smelling bubbles away in the Dutch pot on the stove. On the wall hangs a small wooden plaque bearing a kitchen prayer. It really isn't too far away from the lighthouse. When we pulled up outside, my first thought was of a long-forgotten fairy tale that had left its imprint: Don't go into the cottage in the woods. Its roof is covered in grass, the wooden slats are black, while the windows are white crosses.

I eye Malcolm's precise, orchestrated movements. It's strange to see him in a knit jumper and jeans rather than his more formal court attire. I remember the first time I saw Malcolm, his usher's uniform all but removing any traces of the man beneath, his hidden intellect, which he drip-feeds in snippets of quotations to those willing to listen. I never did ask him anything about himself.

"It's nearly eleven o'clock," he says.

I nod. I really should get back to the hotel. The case is still ongoing, though I'll try everything to get it kicked out on the basis of Dev's arrest.

"Another late one for you?" asks Malcolm as though he read my mind. "I suspect on such a big case you'll have a lot of preparation to do."

"I've got so much to do." My voice sounds weak and reedy, like a child's.

"I'll give you a lift back to your hotel once you're warm."

"Thanks." I scan the living space. "Why do you live all the way out here? Where it's cold and…lonely?"

Malcolm stops pottering and stands still, his lips tight with thought. "I needed to get away from things. Money, luxury, technology…"

"Why?"

"Excess generally causes reaction and produces a change in the opposite direction, whether it be in the seasons, or in individuals, or in governments."

"Who's that?"

"Plato."

"And you lived with an excess of money, luxury, and…"

"Technology. Yes. Definitely."

"What did you do?"

"I was a self-made billionaire."

I almost choke on the liquid chocolate. "You're kidding."

"I'm not."

"Why on earth aren't you living on a luxury yacht somewhere warm and sunny?"

"There's no such thing as an ethical billionaire."

I ponder this for a few moments. "How did you make money?"

"I made an app, short for 'application.'"

Suspecting this is one of those just-out-of-reach facts I'll remember later, I don't ask any questions. Instead, I say, "That doesn't sound particularly unethical."

"If you knew what it did, you might not say that."

"What did it do?"

"Its primary function was to allow people to connect, converse, and interact for free. As long as they have an internet connection. Sadly, there were many unintended consequences."

I finish the last of the cocoa.

"Are you ready to get in the car?" asks Malcolm. I sense he's reached the end of what he's willing to tell me about his past life.

"The car" is an old Land Rover that looks like it could be taken apart and put back together with a spanner. We climb in and I'm greeted by the musty aroma of dirt and stale water.

Malcolm pulls away and the car throws me about as it navigates the potholes.

"Aren't you going to ask me what happened at the lighthouse?"

"That's not my business, miss."

"You don't need to call me 'miss.'"

Malcolm stays silent.

As we drive toward the town side of the island, I look out of the window. The only movement comes from the lighthouse's strobing light reflecting on the black ocean. Funny, how I almost expected it to stop, as though something as constant as a lighthouse should stop working just because something dramatic happened to me inside it.

I ponder this in silence until we arrive outside the Castle Hotel.

"Thank you. You didn't have to do that."

I get out and watch Malcolm pull away. He doesn't go back toward the main road that cuts through the island but pulls up outside the court building. I wonder what he has to do in there at this time of night.

Once I'm in my room, I shake off the dirty clothes and stuff them in the corner of the bathroom.

The hot shower is at once glorious and the most painful experience of my life. The chilblains in my hands and feet scream in protest until all I'm left with are pins and needles.

I watch the dirt run in ribbons along the white acrylic. Though it's not white anymore. It's the same gone-off cream as the rest of the hotel.

Toweling my hair, I reach for the cold tap to pour myself some water. Frustratingly, I always forget that it doesn't work. Unwilling to accept this, I battle with the handle of the tap. There's a metallic scraping sound inside. I push a finger into the spout and feel something with my fingertip. My fingers aren't thin enough to get any purchase, so I go and grab a pencil. I slide it up into the spout and waggle it around for several minutes until finally, something gives. Reaching up again with my finger, I feel something small and metal, like a hook. I manage to get some purchase on it, working it out until it drops from the tap into the basin.

It's a pearl earring matching the one linking me to the car crash. Pat's other earring.

I think over all the weird stuff that Malcolm has said to me. *Life is allowed to waste like a tap left running, Science should be on tap, not on top?* And the first day: *Water, water, everywhere.* These were clues. Is it him, the person who's been leaving me all of these cryptic messages?

I run from my hotel room and quickly make up the distance between the Castle Hotel and the court building. I bang on the front doors, shouting Malcolm's name.

The door swings open, but the inside is too gloomy to see who opened it. I step inside. The glint from Malcolm's golden glasses gives him away.

I hold up the pearl earring for him to see, a charge laid, a piece of evidence exhibited.

"Hmm, that's interesting," he says.

"Is it? Why is it?"

"Well, if I'm not mistaken, Patricia Singh's pearl earring was missing. There it is. That's interesting, isn't it?"

"Why? What do you mean? I spoke to DS Grant. He showed me Pat's blood alcohol test. He told me the witness couldn't be trusted…"

"Poor Cathy."

"Who's Cathy?"

"The witness. I'm afraid she does this."

"So, she didn't see the car crash?"

"She saw *a* car crash, but not the one that killed Pat. Pat has never stepped foot on this island."

"What?"

"Those blood alcohol tests you saw are real, but they relate to a crash that happened back in the UK."

"But DS Grant said..."

"DS Grant was working from false information. Information given to him by Cathy. She sees the same traumatic incident from her life before she came to the island, and she's brought it with her. She sees the same crime over and over again."

"Why?"

"Because she never gave evidence about it. Because of her cowardice, a murderer walked free. It eats away at her."

"You know so much," I say. "Why do you know so much?"

"This is one of the benefits of being an usher," he says. "We see everything. We meet the jury, we're on first name terms with the judge, and we speak to the barristers. There's no part of the court building we can't go into. Everyone else is restricted to their section."

"Not about the case or the court," I say. "About the island, about me."

I step into the court properly and make my way up the imperial staircase to the main hall. "You've been leaving me messages, clues. It's you."

He returns my critical glare, unflinching.

"Where is she?" I stride up to him, grab him by the jumper he's still wearing. It annoys me, that he's dressed so casually. "Where is my daughter? You must know where she is."

"That's not quite right, I'm afraid," he says. That familiar perturbed expression clouds his features. Such a polite form of sadness. It makes me want to scream.

"I want to see my daughter again."

His face darkens and his voice drops a level. "I was worried about this."

"Where is she? Is she on the island?"

"I'm afraid that you don't have a daughter."

"No, you're wrong. I've seen her."

"You didn't. You don't have a daughter."

I can't speak for a long time. Finally, I croak, "You're lying."

"I'm not. I wouldn't lie about something like that. Now, I know that doesn't sound very convincing from someone who's told you quite a lot of lies, but I promise you I'm telling the truth. I'm sorry."

"Then why is her note in my wallet? Why do I have a picture of her?"

"Because that note was written by *you* to *your* mother. When you were a child. I suspect you kept it in there for sentimental reasons. Your mother died when you were very young. That might be the last thing you wrote to her. The picture... That's a picture of you."

"I saw her. I saw her on the island."

"You didn't. I'm sorry. I know you think you did, but you didn't." He's so sure. It's the same level of certainty as when he told me the woman in the purple coat doesn't exist. I don't believe him.

"I miss her. I have a daughter and I *need* her." I hate how pleading my voice is, but I have nothing else to bargain with.

"I'm sorry, Lila. What you're missing is a figment of your imagination." He does sound genuinely sorry. His voice is strained with vicarious pain.

My throat is sore. I can feel hot tears leaking out of my eyes. There's nothing I can do to stop them. "You're lying." My voice trembles under the weight of the sobs.

"You've mistaken something that was meant for your mother and assumed it was meant for you. Your mother, whose name was Delia Lewis, died in the nineties when you were eight years old."

"But this is 1996 and I'm in my thirties so that can't be right."

"It is right."

"You're insane."

"You're not the first person to say that to me."

I launch myself at him. It's an animal reaction. I begin to start tearing him apart when I feel a sharp stabbing pain in my neck.

The world goes black.

CHAPTER FORTY-THREE

I OPEN MY EYES but can barely see, so I stare at the floor, waiting for my vision to adjust. Once used to the darkness, I realize that I'm looking at my reflection in black glass.

I sit upright. My head fills with pins and needles, and a wave of nausea washes over me.

After three slow breaths, I look at my surroundings.

Dull light comes from caged lamps. Otherwise, it's dark in here. Water drips somewhere nearby. Each droplet echoes until replaced by the splash of the next. The place must be vast. Squinting, I look for more detail.

I'm sitting on a wooden chair. It's the only piece of furniture in the middle of the stone floor. The black glass I saw earlier was actually just a puddle. Perhaps I'm back in the lighthouse. No, the space is too large. I seem to be in the atrium of a vast industrial complex. Metal-grate staircases rise up from ground level, creating an impossible labyrinth of galvanized steel.

Lining the walls of the ground floor are cells. Figures stir behind the bars, but I can't see them clearly. The levels above also seem to house prisoners. Looking up makes me feel sick, so I stop trying.

Next to me is a little table with a register book. It looks like the list that the prison guards use to book visitors in and out. I pick it up and scan it.

1. Alasdair Paxton QC

Why is his name on here?

2. Mr. Justice Milton Bing QC
3. Devin Hanlon
4. Andrew Serkiss

Why is there a list with everyone's name on it? I scan down the list, not recognizing names five through seven. Then I get to the eighth name.

8. Sarah Blythe

Where's the Eighth. Is this it? Have I finally found the eighth?

As well as the list of names, there are columns of dates. The date in column three next to Sarah Blythe is 5.7.1969. By reference to the column header, I discover that this is the "born" column. The date in the fourth column is 25.12.2001. That is the "transferred" column. But that makes no sense. This is the 1990s. How can there be a date in the future on this list?

On instinct, I feel my wrist, where the 777 tattoo still stings. That was the arm Malcolm used to save me at the top of the lighthouse.

I flick through the pages, scanning the names. Most of them are foreign to me, but every now and then I see one I recognize, like "Stan Lynch" or "DC Stephanie Parks," and, more sadly, "DS Jack Grant." Finally, I come across my own name.

777. Lila Dalton

Follow the Sevens… This is the other half of the puzzle. I'm number 777 on this list. The list tells me that I was born in 1987 and transferred in 2025.

"Ah, good, you're awake."

Malcolm leans against one of the metal staircases.

"Get away from me," I say. I turn and go as though to run away. Where to, I don't know.

"There's no need, Lila."

I turn and run, looking for something, anything that will give me leverage. I keep coming up against prison bars. This place is a maze of metal and wet brick. I can't find a way out. I see it. A fire extinguisher. I rip it off the walls and hold it aloft.

"Let me go."

Malcolm smiles placidly.

"Please put it down, Lila."

I carry on holding it, feeling increasingly stupid. I look around, but there's no exit. The room is lined with cells. Perhaps I have to go up to get out. I move toward the staircase, but Malcolm steps in front of me.

"Why did you drug me? Why am I here?"

"Please put down the fire extinguisher and I promise I'll explain everything."

I look around. There's nowhere to run. I place it on the floor but keep my eyes fixed on Malcolm the whole time.

"Lovely."

"Why did you drug me?"

"Because I wanted to move you without using force."

"Drugging someone without their knowledge is force."

"You did attack me."

"Because you've got my daughter! I know you have. You know who the woman in the purple coat is and you're working together. Where is she?"

"Lila, I've already told you. You don't have a daughter. The girl in the picture is you. As for the woman… You're the one who's been wearing a purple coat."

"Yes, but I bought it in the secondhand shop because it was hers."

"Will you let me explain now?"

I scoff, but it turns into a violent shiver. I'm so cold. The water keeps dripping, torturously repetitive. I look into the nearest cell, trying to see who lurks inside. A shadow paces around the few square feet. I can't hear their footsteps.

I walk over and pick up the list. "Why are these people on your list? Tell me why my name is on it."

"You're here because society has a problem and I have created a solution. Let me ask you this: How do we decide whether someone is guilty or not, Lila?"

"Don't play games with me. Tell me what this means. Why I'm number 777 on this list." I hold it out toward him.

"I'm not playing games. It's a genuine question."

I huff and say, "Well, you gather evidence, present it before twelve of the accused's peers, and they decide if they're sure."

"Yes, exactly. However, in the outside world, everything is different. It's changed. You heard Dev speak about the internet and the changes it will bring to society. Well, he was right. The internet dismantled our concept of singular truth. People became increasingly nationalistic and tribalistic. The free press, democracy, everything else crumbled with it. Especially justice."

"Why is my name on your list?"

He ignores me and carries on with his sermon. "In the outside world, every misdemeanor, every perceived slight, results in social banishment. Every crime, act, and omission is debated on the internet and the person is sentenced, without anyone hearing any evidence or weighing up alternative versions of events. There's no more innocent until proven guilty. The mob is now judge, jury, and executioner."

I sit down on the chair where I first came round. My head is in my hands as I try to wrap my mind around this new information.

"It's normal that you're reacting like this. I wouldn't expect anything else."

I scowl at him. "Where is my family?"

"You'll see them again soon."

"When?"

"When the trial is over."

"Why did you bring me here? Why was I…transferred?"

"You're here because you chose to be here."

"I would never have chosen this."

"I promise you; you did."

"Then you can't have given me all of the information."

"I, like Dev, saw the way things were going. The rise in populism, the onslaught of fake news and post-truth politics—"

"Is this about your…"—I try to remember the word—"'application'?"

"I'm afraid so. I started planning for this experiment very early on, once I could see the tide turning. I approached you, and I told you my plans to save the justice system. I offered you a choice: carry on battling a broken justice system, living in a world where everything was crumbling, or come with me and help me to save the world. I recruited hundreds of people—mostly barristers and judges and victims and criminals—so that I could house them here on the island where they would help me try important crimes."

It takes me a long time to mull this over. I'm reminded of Cathy, the woman who sees the same traumatic incident from her past and has brought it to the island with her.

I also think about DS Grant. Determined to find the answer to a riddle he can't remember, which left him looking for questions where there weren't any, seeing conspiracies around every corner… Except he was right, wasn't he? Someone was controlling us, wiping our memories, putting us on an island where the boats don't work but no one notices because no one fishes…

"Did you tell me when I took up the offer that you'd wipe my memories?"

"For the benefit of the experiment, I couldn't tell you too much, no. But I promise you, you wanted this. You wanted to be part of the solution."

I think about everything I know about myself. About my ambition, my need to win. It was more than just my desire to see my daughter again. There's a swell of pain as I remember she doesn't exist. A figment of my imagination, Malcolm said.

It was also about my need to prove myself, and to prove that there is always another side to the story. I can see myself being susceptible to the sort of thing Malcolm offered me, in the same way I was susceptible to Dev's conspiracy theories.

"You said that some of the people on the island are victims and criminals…" I pick up the list again. "Sarah Blythe was a victim of this offense, and you made her a receptionist on the island where the person who nearly killed her was being tried. Why?"

"There's a limit to the human resources available to me in this experiment."

"Did you alter her memories too?"

"Most people on the island have had some form of memory alteration, some more drastic than others. It depends on what we don't want them to remember. Dev, for example, has had very little in the way of modification. He only needed to accept that the case takes place on Assumption Island—a place designed to ignite his most feverish fantasies of conspiracy and corruption. Otherwise he is as he was in 1996."

"I can't believe Dev would sign up to this."

"Anything to stick it to 'the man,' prove a conspiracy theory."

"Why this case?"

"I wanted to choose a case that split public opinion, where the verdict and even the decision to prosecute were enormously controversial. This case was perfect because one side thought that Eades was a patsy who had been set up by an increasingly autocratic government that wanted to restrict freedom of speech, and the other side thought he was evil and represented everything that was wrong in the world. It was a case that generated an inordinate number of conspiracy theories, especially among the far right, who saw his conviction as confirmation of the system's victimization of conservatives."

"They would think like that."

"But of course, the way the case was tried at the time didn't help. A lot of evidence was covered up. Much more has come out in this trial than in the original. So, I hope that both sides will feel that these proceedings have been a proper exploration of the evidence. You have helped us to find the truth."

"But trials aren't about truth."

"Exactly."

"What do you mean? How are you supposed to restore a singular reality by using a system that has no interest in it?"

"Because the adversarial system, the challenging of evidence, the procedure, the decisions about hearsay and admissibility of evidence, all of that is about analytical thinking. Looking at a set of facts and listening to evidence and coming to common-sense conclusions. Trying to find the truth is impossible. We never truly *know* something; all we can do is be satisfied to the relevant standard of proof."

"But…this case has so many examples of a broken system. Missing CCTV, hidden evidence, disclosure failures…"

"And haven't you done a good job of using the rules of evidence and procedure to reveal all of that?"

"Not really."

"Trust me, you have. You've shown that it's not just black and white. Good and evil. There are gray areas."

"The bombing of Abbott House was not a gray area."

"And that's a perfectly reasonable view. But the evilness of the act hasn't changed the scrutiny you've applied to the evidence, has it? You haven't let the fact it's a right-wing attack on innocent people cloud your ability to find and identify the facts that contradict the prosecution's case and employ them to your client's benefit."

"But even after I've been round the houses looking for clues, we still don't know what really happened."

"Why does that matter?"

"How are you going to restore humanity's faith in an archaic justice system when it can't find all of the answers?"

"Why does it have to be a perfect system? Why *all* of the answers?"

"Because people's lives depend on it."

"That's true. But nothing is perfect. All we can do is make a system that is just. Justice and fairness are not the same things, after all."

My head is hurting from all of this abstract thinking. "OK, I understand why you've chosen this case, but why me?"

"I told you that your mother died when you were very small. On the 25th of May 1995, in fact. She was one of the victims of the bombing."

I'm knocked sideways by the revelation.

"She is the woman you saw on the missing piece of footage. You *thought* you were looking at a video of yourself, when really it was her. Which is why, of course, I tampered with it."

"*You* tampered with it?"

"There was nothing of evidential significance in those thirty seconds—"

"You weren't to know that."

"I did my research. It was paramount we didn't remind you of your mother, because it would ruin the whole system."

"Was she a terrorist?"

"No, not at all." Malcolm removes his glasses and polishes them. "She was a left-wing reporter who went deep into the far right to expose them. She was the one who originally tipped off the security services about the real attack, but they ignored it and went with their own information, which turned out to be faulty."

"So, she died…"

"Trying to save the lives of people she'd never met."

Tears prick my eyes against my will. He hands me a tissue. I say, "But I've seen her here on the island. Wearing that purple coat." I touch the tattoo on my wrist. "She was so real."

"She wasn't there, Lila."

"What does that mean?"

"Time is an illusion created by human memories. Everything that has ever been and ever will be is happening right now, in this moment."

"Is that another one of your quotes? Do you have a book or something?"

Malcolm smiles genially. "No, it's just quantum mechanics. Even if we were to accept that time is linear, the way we experience it isn't. Every time we revisit a memory, the memory becomes part of the present. We touch the new memory, handle it, leave our fingerprints over it. Time is less like a straight line and more like a word written in pencil that's been erased and rewritten time and time again, so that we see the ghost of our previous attempts beneath the new word. Your memory of your mother is like one of those ghosts. No matter how hard you try, you're haunted by your memory of her, and she's ingrained into the fabric of your conscience."

"Why did you erase my memories?"

"Would you have represented the man who murdered your mother if I didn't?"

Why have I only just put two and two together? If she was killed in the bombing, Eades murdered my mother. A rage like I've never felt before wells up inside of me and I want to do something, hurt someone, break something.

I go for Malcolm but can't get to him. Every time I try, he's just one inch out of reach.

"I'm sorry," he says.

"No, you're not. Do you know how twisted that is? Getting me to defend the man who killed my mother?"

"Aren't you happier knowing that, although Eades might be convicted, he's had a fair trial? No more conspiracy theories, no more doubts?"

"I couldn't give a shit about whether he has a fair trial."

"But now there can be no arguments. He was given the best possible chance of being found not guilty, but the jury might still find him guilty."

"So what? He's evil."

Malcolm grimaces and scratches his head. "I'm truly sorry, Lila. It was the only way."

"To do what?"

"The only way I could prove to everyone that the trial would be fair."

"Everyone?"

"The trial has been broadcast to the outside world, to show them what a proper justice system looks like."

I feel suddenly exposed and start looking around for cameras.

"They can't see you. They can only watch what happens in the courtroom."

"But if the point was to show impartiality, why would you have one of the victim's relatives defend the perpetrator? Surely, they'd think the opposite?"

"They might. Except I put a right-wing white supremacist on the prosecution. Just to prove that both of you had had your memories altered so that you were both totally impartial. You see, no one believes in impartiality anymore. No one believes it's possible to represent someone whose views contradict your own."

I mull this over, wondering who the right winger on the prosecution could be. "Paxton?"

"Yes. From a long line of inbred nobles." The corner of his mouth twitches.

I'm not really in the mood for smiling or finding anything ironic. It doesn't feel like there's a funny side to anything anymore.

"How do I know all of the legal concepts?"

"There are four types of long-term memory. Only your episodic memory, which relates to events you have experienced, has been altered. Your semantic, procedural, and emotional conditioning are all still intact."

"I've still got so many questions."

"Go ahead." He laces his fingers and looks at me. No, he looks through me.

"So, if my mother died when I was young, who brought me up? Who looked after me?"

His face darkens. "From what I could gather of your life history, your father was never involved in your childhood. Your mother raised you alone, so after she died, you were raised in the care system." His expression sobers. "Any more questions?"

"Yes. So, who was threatening me? Interfering with my phone?"

"Dev was monitoring you and threatening you." He gives me a strained smile.

"If he was sending the threats, who—" I stop myself, thinking back to what was in the visitors' book.

Malcolm smiles at me, expecting me to go on. I touch the tattoo on my wrist without thinking. He notices and a question mark passes across his features. Making a quick decision, I decide not to ask who left me the cryptic clues. It seems that Malcolm doesn't know the answer to that mystery, and any information that I have and he doesn't is to be cherished. I bury the question deep inside me, hoping I can pull it out and examine it when I'm alone.

"So…if he was sending the threats, did you think he was just the editor of *Beacon*, or did you know who he really was?"

"Part of the preparation for this project involved years and years of research. I would choose my cases and then delve deep into the evidence. Dev was just a reporter at the original trial. Yes, he was the editor of *Beacon*, but he took an unusual interest in the case. He wrote one of the key articles that sparked the conspiracy theories. When I brought him here, I had no idea what a handful he would turn out to be. I just wanted him to steer you in the right direction, but he turned out to be a lot more…involved."

I rub my forehead as though it will help the thoughts swimming around up there to settle.

"And DC Parks's interest in me?"

"Well, Delia Lewis, your mother, was supposed to have been killed in the explosion. When Steph Parks saw you and thought you were the same person, it made her wonder whether you were really an undercover reporter or whether you'd been turned."

"She thought I was her. My mum." The last words are strained because I'm forcing them through the lump in my throat.

Malcolm doesn't answer but looks in his pockets. "That reminds me, I've been meaning to return these to you." He hands me the horse and the picture of the girl I thought was my daughter but I realize now was me.

Malcolm backs off, leaving me to stroll around the prison. I don't want to get too close to the cells, but I'm intrigued.

"So, each of these…"

"Represents the crimes that will be tried here on my island."

"There will be more?"

"This is only the beginning. I've got loads of cases I want to try. The next one is the trial of a man who was never prosecuted. He raped hundreds of women and got away with it."

"And there have been people watching the trial? On the outside? The whole time…"

Malcolm beams at me. "They've been so impressed with you, Lila."

I know he's trying to save the world, undo the mess he's created, show society what a functioning justice system can look like…but I'm not sure I like what he's done with it. He's turned it into a weird reality TV show. And I could have done without knowing that millions of people are watching me as I'm performing. Seeing every mistake.

I feel so violated. At the same time, I'm too exhausted to argue. I simply nod.

"I can see that you're tired. It's nearly morning, and I understand that this has been a hell of a lot to take in. I'll take you back to the hotel. Then you can finish what you've started."

"One more question before I go."

"I owe you that much."

"Is Eades guilty?"

"Only the jury gets to decide that."

EPILOGUE

SHE CAME OUT OF the cells feeling dirty. Then began the ascent to the upper levels of the court building. Speaking to her client always left her feeling like that. It was her second week on this trial now.

She hadn't seen him or spoken to him before the trial. She couldn't remember being involved in the preliminary hearings. Well, she couldn't remember much. Couldn't remember anything before that first day when she'd been standing up in court about to address the jury and her mind had gone blank.

Would her memories ever come back? Sometimes at night she dreamed about being in a bar. Lazy jazz music and a pair of blue eyes. Then she would wake up in a strange bed in an unfamiliar room. It unnerved her, how the testimony of the victims started to seep into her subconscious, become at one with her memories.

She had reached the main hall now. Her patent brogues squeaked as she made her way across the black-and-white stone floor. Once in the robing room, she threw off her wig and went to look in the mirror at the bags under her eyes. Nothing to be done about those, so she ruffled her gray hair and tried to do something with her eyebrows instead. She plucked a stray black hair that had grown halfway up her forehead. What did it think it was doing up there? And what business did it have being anything other than steely gray like the rest of her hair? She licked a finger and tried to smooth the rest of her wiry brows.

Giving it up as a bad job, she left the mirror and walked over to the oxblood-leather table in the middle of the room and swung her feet up onto it.

God, her client made her feel sick.

"They wanted to," he'd said to her. "They consented. I think they wanted favors out of me, you know. They were using me because of my connections."

Her client had been a high court judge. The thought of it... *Him* presiding over trials. Well, he didn't look quite as grand sitting in that cell, his bald pate shining in the artificial light, his white tufts of hair unkempt and sticking out at odd angles.

He was pathetic.

"Some of them just wanted a pupillage or a leg up. And now they're embarrassed about having sex in return for favors. They're making out like something else happened. Making out it was me who forced it on them. It wasn't like that at all..."

She'd wanted to slap him until he shut up. But that was part of the job. Putting on a simpering expression and letting them witter on until they ran out of steam, and then maybe they'd be able to give actual instructions.

She scanned the batting order. They still had another eight complainants. She didn't know when this trial would finish. It could go on for weeks...

In that moment, she was overcome by a strange sense of déjà vu. From somewhere at the back of her mind, a thought sprouted and took form. Make a mark in a book and you'll know if you've been here before. So, she reached for her copy of *Archbold* and turned to the pastedown at the back of the book. Before she could put pen to paper, she found herself staring at a sea of blue ink.

Fountain-pen tally charts littered the back of the book. She flicked through; there were thousands of tiny marks. She drew a line next to an uncompleted chart of three.

"I've been here before," she said.

Walking over to the bay windows that looked out over the rolling green hills of the island, she felt as though the ground was moving beneath her.

There's something I know, a truth, that's buried deep inside me.

Touching the furniture around her, she realized what it was.

"The world is hollow," she said aloud. "This isn't my world."

She touched the scar on her wrist, the three sevens. The next revelation came to her in a violent crash of knowledge. *I am just a number.*

At that moment, a young woman burst into the robing room. She looked like she'd just been given a piece of terrible news. Barely looking at the woman already there as she walked past the table, she ripped off her collarette and threw her wig at one of the wing-backed armchairs. There was something in the way she did it, as if the robes were on fire or infested or something. Every movement was panicked.

Then she looked in the mirror. "Bastard."

"Don't hold it against him, dear. Almost all men are."

After their conversation, the elder of the two women got to work. She needed to pass this message on, this truth. Why couldn't she quite remember it? Without really knowing what she was doing, she scribbled down a note and slid it into the woman's wig tin.

Where's the Eighth?

Follow the Sevens

READING GROUP GUIDE

1. If your life depended on defending someone who'd committed an atrocity, how do you think you'd handle the situation? Is there a line you wouldn't be willing to cross, and how would you determine what that line is?

2. Imagine yourself in a situation where you woke up not knowing who or where you were. How would you respond? Would you play along or raise an alarm?

3. One of the themes of the novel is the question of whether knowledge is power. Do you think that the characters in the novel with the most knowledge have the most power? How does Lila's quest for knowledge change over the course of the novel?

4. A question posed by the novel is whether the justice system is a means of finding the truth. Do you think *R. v. Eades* was a court case where the jury would be able to work out the truth of what happened? Why or why not?

5. Do you think that Jonathan Eades is guilty or not guilty? What evidence would you need to be convinced of his guilt? What evidence would cause you to doubt his guilt?

6. Did the novel challenge your views of the justice system? Do you think the traditional system of jury trials works? Have you served on a jury that made you question the traditional system?

7. One of the key characters in the novel is a journalist. What role does journalism play in the criminal justice system? Has that changed since the advent of the internet?

A CONVERSATION WITH THE AUTHOR

This is a legal thriller with a speculative twist. What made you want to write this kind of story? What was your favorite twist to create and why?

My first inspiration was the type of book I wanted to write: one with a high-concept plot that explored complex themes. This is because many of my favorite books, TV programs, and films have a speculative element to them, such as Dennis Kelly's *Utopia*, The Wachowski sisters' *Sense8*, and Blake Crouch's *Recursion*. I wanted readers to feel the same excitement and wonder I felt when consuming those stories. The decision to combine speculative fiction with the legal thriller genre was much more prosaic. I am a practicing barrister and have lots of experience in courtrooms doing jury trials. As such, I thought it would be great to set the novel in the legal world because then I wouldn't have to do so much research! My favorite twist to create was the one at the very end of the novel. The question of what the *"Where's the Eighth? Follow the Sevens"* riddle means and the question of who the woman in the purple coat is are probably the two most intriguing mysteries in the novel, so their resolution had to wait until the very end.

How did the novel evolve over the course of writing? Were there any major changes?

The novel didn't evolve a great deal during the first draft as I am a fairly meticulous planner, so the draft I produced was very close to the story I imagined. However, once I was taken on by my agent and secured a publishing deal, there were lots of changes. The manuscript grew from around 80,000 words to around 100,000 words. My agent asked that I include more twists and subplots as well as a few other changes to the characters, which were fairly major. The publisher wanted me to give the ending more space as there are at least three twists in quick succession, so more chapters were added at the end to give the reader space to process the reveals.

What does your writing process look like? Are there any ways you like to find creative inspiration?

Once I have the nub of an idea, I'm often very impatient and want to start writing immediately; however, I really benefit from planning and inspiration-gathering time because ideas always come half formed or in fragments. With *The Trials of Lila Dalton*, I figured out the big twist at the end very soon after having the idea for the opening, but I had no idea what the case was about or how she would go about investigating it or what clues she might find along the way. So, I had a beginning and an ending with no middle. For the themes explored in the finale to resonate with the crime the defendant is accused of, I decided to do some research into trials that have acquired lots of conspiracy theories over the years. This involved listening to a lot of podcast episodes that gave brief overviews of conspiracy theories. Once I found out about the Oklahoma City bombing and the London nail bombings, both of which took place in the 1990s, I then purchased books, newspapers, and magazines relating to those terrorist attacks so that I could research them in more detail. This gave me lots of inspiration for what the twists and turns in the trial could be.

What chapter or part of the book did you have the hardest time writing? What part was the easiest for you?

I struggled initially with the opening scene as that really had to land for the reader to be intrigued enough to carry on. I reworked that chapter over and over again. After that, I would say that each of the courtroom scenes caused me a lot of headaches because I had to think very hard about how the cross-examination would work and what each witness would reveal about the case that wasn't known before. Finally, the scene in the lighthouse was one that I struggled with and had to rewrite several times. This is when the threat to Lila finally becomes realized, so it was important that the reader felt the fear and anxiety that is imperative in the finale of a thriller.

If you were writing a spin-off of this novel, which character would it follow and why?

I probably would not do this, but if I had to write a spin-off novel, then it would be a direct sequel and would follow two characters: "old" Lila (the woman in the purple coat) and Malcolm. It would be a cat-and-mouse chase as Lila seeks to escape from Assumption Island once and for all.

ACKNOWLEDGMENTS

Firstly, to my agent, Jenny Savill, thank you for plucking *Trials* from the slush pile and helping me turn it into something worth reading. I'd also like to thank my U.S. agent, Robin Straus, who fought tirelessly to get a U.S. publishing deal. I'm further indebted to all those at Andrew Nurnberg Associates whose patience and warmth were much appreciated. Special thanks go to Silé Edwards for her sage advice. I mustn't forget Jenny's trusted reader, Delena McConnell, who encouraged me to include more "emotional trickery." For anyone who felt tricked by this novel, you have Delena to thank.

For their bright ideas and enthusiasm, I'd like to thank (in no particular order): Laura Macaulay, Kirsten Chapman, Harriet Wade, Lindeth Vasey, Steven Cooper, Rima Rashid, and Tom Martland. All of those at Pushkin Press have been a dream to work with. Thanks also to Mark Swan for his beautiful cover design.

The team at Sourcebooks were delightful, and I can't thank Anna Michels and Rachel Gilmer enough for taking a chance on this book.

Special mention must go to my first readers, Jamie Phillips, Alan Killip, and Sarah Wakefield, who looked at this when it was a rough first draft. Special thanks go to Jamie, who has read this at least twice. All those on my Curtis

Brown Creative Online Course also get thanks, especially Julie, Andrew, Celia, James, Kate, Kirsty, and Gary, all of whom were kind enough to point out some fairly major plot holes in the first few chapters with kindness and grace. Thanks also go to my fellow pensmiths at Cardiff Writers' Circle whose enthusiasm spurred me on during the more challenging chapters. Last but not least, thank you to all those at the BXP Team, especially Angela Nurse, for listening to my writing woes. We all owe gratitude to the two Marks for creating such a welcoming community.

And, finally, to my parents, who encouraged my creative endeavors from a young age. If I wasn't announcing that I was going to be the next Britney Spears, it was only because I'd decided on Audrey Hepburn instead. Never once did they tell me that such dreams were not for the likes of me. I owe them everything.

ABOUT THE AUTHOR

L. J. Shepherd lives in Cardiff with her cat, Coral. She studied English literature at Christ Church, Oxford. After graduating, she decided to pursue a career in law. Laura began practicing as a barrister in 2017. Since then, she has prosecuted and defended in many jury trials in the Crown Court. She is now a human rights barrister instructed in high-profile public inquiries. *The Trials of Lila Dalton* is her first novel.